STANDING FAST ON FOREIGN SHORES
STORIES IN THE LAST BRIGADE UNIVERSE

Stories by
Antoine Guillaud, Nic Plume, David Appleby, John Babb, Kevin W. Steverson, Larry Hoy, William Alan Webb, Gustavo Bondoni, Jason Cordova, Christo Louis Nel, Jamie Ibson, H. David Blalock, Tim C. Taylor, and Mark Stallings

Edited by
J. Gunnar Grey and William Alan Webb

δ
Dingbat Publishing
Humble, Texas

STANDING FAST

Copyright © 2022 by Antoine Guillaud, Nic Plume, David Appleby, John Babb, Kevin W. Steverson, Christo Louis Nel, Jason Cordova, Jamie Ibson, H. David Blalock, Tim C. Taylor, Mark Stallings, Larry Hoy, Gustavo Bondoni, and William Alan Webb

Primary Print ISBN 9-798-8-19672525

Published by Dingbat Publishing
Humble, Texas

All rights reserved. No part of this book may be reproduced in any form or by any means without written consent, excepting brief quotes used in reviews.

This book is licensed to the original purchaser only. Duplication or distribution via any means is illegal and a violation of International Copyright Law, subject to criminal prosecution and upon conviction, fines and/or imprisonment. No part of this book can be reproduced or sold by any person or business without the express permission of the publisher.

Thank you for respecting the hard work of these authors.

This is a work of fiction. Names, places, characters, and events are entirely the produce of the author's imagination or are used fictitiously, and any resemblance to persons living or dead, actual locations, events, or organizations is coincidental

Preface

From the moment that *Standing The Final Watch* first introduced the Last Brigade Universe, I have been asked about what happened to the rest of the world as America was collapsing. There have been hints of it here and there, references to certain events, particularly in The Collapse books, but nothing more. Until now, that is.

In the past I have said that the Last Brigade Universe came to me gradually, that I discovered its revelations in the same way that you did. I'm no longer sure that's entirely true. Bits and pieces of it seem familiar to me from way back, like old friends I'd forgotten about until I saw them again. I'm now pretty certain that my mind has been writing this subconsciously for decades. Sure, some of the details may be new, but not the overall framework of the alternate history itself.

I have always been a writer for whom characters drive the narrative, instead of the other way around. For example, a recurring theme of my writing is the pivot of history around one person, the ability of individuals with a strong enough will to change the course of great events. Whether for good or bad, this has been a hallmark of human history throughout recorded history, and the LBU is no different. Nick Angriff, Green Ghost, Tom Steeple, without any of them having outsized influence over their contemporaries, this alternate history could not exist.

But for those who hadn't noticed, I'm an American, and great people are not limited to those living in the United States. Indeed, most examples I can think of come from other places and times. So the LBU would be a barren landscape without the stories of people living elsewhere during the collapse of the world economy. Hopefully you, the reader, will enjoy this enough for us to expand the concept moving forward.

I say 'us' because I'm only the curator of these stories, although it was me who sweet-talked, cajoled, ~~lied to,~~ and otherwise convinced a lineup of amazing writers to contribute to this anthology. There is an honor to asking such busy and successful people to take time from their lives to help you build your universe, and having them say 'yes.' I am deeply gratified that they did.

At the end of the day, though, this book is for *you*. If I did not have the most loyal and awesome readers any author could ask for, I'm not sure that I could pour the sweat and effort into this that it requires. Fortunately for me, I do.

Bill
May 4, 2022

Table of Contents

Preface
William Alan Webb

More Majorum 7
Antoine Guillaud

Rebels' Cause 32
Nic Plume

**Virtute et opera: By Virtue and Energy
The Motto of the ancient Kingdom of Fife** 55
David Appleby

Maximizing the Value of North Koreans 90
John Babb

They Call Me The Breeze 115
Kevin W. Steverson

The Hare and the Hunter 133
Larry Hoy

Pine Gap 155
William Alan Webb

Triple Frontera 188
Gustavo Bondoni

Los Banditos 226
Jason Cordova

To Kill a Brother 250
Christo Louis Nel

Do Unto Others 283
Jamie Ibson

Green Leaf: Civil War 310
H David Blalock

The Sussex Job 349
Tim C. Taylor

The Rising Sun 384
Mark Stallings

More Majorum

Antoine Guillaud

Late summer 2026

The news was dire, very dire. It isn't that I hadn't seen it coming, but I hadn't expected it to come that fast... and I hadn't been able to implement all my plans.

Let me introduce myself. I am Michel, I am about to hit the wrong side of 50 and the world is going into a hell basket quite fast. I am a vet, an *ancien combattant* as we say in France. I have traded on that status to reach my current position: mayor of the small yet charming Ile d'Aix.

I grew up not far from here, in the mainland, near the swamps of the Charente, in a small village called Saint-Hippolyte... So even though I am not an aixois, I am still looked upon as a local... What my people don't know can't hurt them, but I did some obfuscation about my military career. It was common knowledge and a well-appreciated fact that I had served in the Legion Etrangère, but it had been merely a stepping board towards a more discreet military career. After the legion I joined the COS (Commandement des opérations spéciales, the French SOCOM) and spent the latter part of my career at the DRM (Direction du Renseignement Militaire, i.e. military Intelligence). Hence I had a fairly accurate global picture of the state of the world. That advanced knowledge led me to the island... I already owned a house here, courtesy of a late uncle, and I began to actively plan for the worst. Which is why I threw myself in local politics and managed to get elected mayor. The island looks wonderful on postcards, true enough, but the tourists don't have voting rights, only the permanent residents, and I managed to win them over.

Through my contacts I had managed to acquire enough hardware to repel a not too serious invasion, our food stockpiles were solid, and I had managed to attract quite a few like-minded people on and around the island, some of them personal friends, some of them military people who shared my analysis of the situation. If you wonder why the nice ice seller has biceps on a par with those of Arnold Schwarzenegger as well as an eastern European accent... well, there is a reason.

It was the end of the summer 2026 and France, well, the world actually, was heading towards hell faster than I would have believed possible, thanks to the stupidity of its politicians and to Russian cunning.

As the world was reeling from many crises caused by North Korean hubris, Antikap goons, and a general collapse of the global economy, the Russians saw no other way out of the crises than good old-fashioned military invasion. Of all the countries in the EU, not many had the will or the means to fight. And if nobody faulted the courage of German Gefreiter or Polish cavalry, the only army really in fighting trim in the EU was the French army and it was already engaged on many fronts, securing the EU southern frontier in North Africa and stemming the tide of jihadists, or ensuring Turkey didn't reenact a push to the Balkans like the Ottoman empire did in the 16th century. The Russians had managed to neutralize an early French response to their crushing invasion of eastern Europe thanks to sympathetic (and bought) politicians, one of whom they even managed to put in the Elysée palace, confident in her promises that she could think about her decision long enough to not have to make it. A—quite convenient—brain stroke later and her successor offered the full commitment of the French army in the defense of its NATO allies. Alas! As the Rand Corporation had written a few years back, the quality of the French Army wasn't supported by strong logistics, and it hindered her fighting capability during a protracted conflict. Even though the US managed to initiate Reforger support flights, it wasn't enough to overcome the logistics shortcomings. In the end, the Russian army was able to take Paris and to put yet another Quisling in charge, but it had been bled quite badly and was only able to occupy a few strongholds and to hold them, lacking both the numbers and the popular support to occupy the land. Their underhanded tactics calling for the activation of jihadist cells and of right-wing activists to spread chaos all but ensured the spawning of resistance cells all over France. As a result, chaos invited itself as organization and the rule of law dissolved.

Which leads me to the dire news I had just mentioned. Among the measures our Russian friends had managed to implement was one particularly sneaky one: they opened the gates of the prisons and disarmed the police, in a bid to force the population to turn to the Red Army as a protector. And a returning jihadist had just proclaimed himself emir of Rochefort, the nearby town, and was already making noises about expanding. Due to my former function, I was quite aware of who the guy was and of where he had been formed. Nice back-up plan from our Russian friends to further paralyze us...

I closed my eyes briefly and thought about my options! It wasn't as though we weren't prepared or that I hadn't seen it coming! I just hadn't anticipated the accelerated tempo nor the Russian meddling. And to boot, I had my very own Rubicon, stepping outside the law and the orders of a state I had sworn to serve faithfully, so many years ago! We had seen the decay of society and planned accordingly and yet, we had tried to cling to a semblance of normality, which explained why our island, small as it was, still had youth camps going on over summer, for example.

"Any news, Michel?"

"No, Suzanne, no news. Should be good news, heh?"

Suzanne was my assistant, secretary of the townhall, and a friend of 20 years. Quite tiny, unflinchingly courteous with a thick, long mane of black, luxurious, shiny hair and a ready smile. This smile was very brittle today, as she inquired about the fate of my son. He had followed in my footsteps and joined the army, straight from high school into prep school, then military officer school, then infantry school, and his ranking high enough that he got to choose his regiment. Like me, he opted for the 13th Demi-Brigade of the French Legion. You wanted to call a unit a band of brothers in the army, that was it. Created from civilian volunteers at the eve of WWII in 1940, it distinguished itself in the service of the France Libre, stopping Rommel cold at Bir-Hakeim for sixteen long days, managing a fighting retreat which didn't turn into a rout, and went from fight to fight till the end of the war. And now, like the rest of the army, it had been confronting the Russians. We knew there had been many battles, we knew the casualties were high, but with mobile service and internet down, information was quite hard to get. Even my backchannels were unusually quiet. And so here I was, an old man worried about his people but also a father worried about his children, particularly his son.

"Mr. Mayor, the ferry just docked at the harbor..."

"Quite early today."

"Perhaps they will have some news about Rochefort..."

Law and order had been going down quite fast in Rochefort, thanks to the emir. The old preacher was a decent guy, but his successor was something else entirely. A drug dealer who saw the light in prison, so to speak, spent some time training in Africa, courtesy of Chechen brothers in arms, before being sent back to Europe to sow chaos. Never mind that the first language his trainers heard in their life was Russian and that they were all very, very well-trained, as far as jihadists went. Our boy Yusuf had potential; hence he got the best training there was. The Russians wanted to soften Europe up in every possible way, and jihadists were a cheap way to achieve that goal! Dear Yusuf al-Faransi was well known to me as well as to the cops in Rochefort, but the oh so sensitive mayor didn't want to do anything to offend the sensibilities of the minorities, or of our new Russian masters of course... and he was hedging his bets, just in case the Russians managed to really implement their version of law and order. To add insult to injury, I had had confirmation that the jail on the Île de Ré had just really released every convict, as the guards followed orders and left their station. Right now, we had between 600 and 1,000 criminals back on the streets and the island of Ré wasn't far from us, so we could expect dear Yusuf getting reinforcements fast, a bit too fast for my taste. Rochefort was still roughly okay by daylight but getting dangerous at night, as self-defense groups were popping up everywhere, reminding me more of thugs than of organized citizens militia. Which is why we had always a close watch on the pier, just in case someone got ideas.

I quickly donned a lightweight bulletproof jacket and put my shirt back on, making the jacket not so obvious. I also clipped a holster on my belt, small of my back, underneath the shirt. I quickly checked my piece: I chambered a round, and ensured the safety was on before putting it back into the holster. This shirt was a bit special, just a size too big for me, as I very much wanted my Sig-Sauer ready to access and quite invisible. I took a quick look in the mirror of my office: working out regularly and only walking or biking had kept me reasonably fit for a 55-year-old guy. Short grey hair, green eyes, broad shoulders, 180 cm tall, still good for one last fight or two, I guess.

I then put on my sunglasses and earpiece and told Suzanne to hold the fort in my absence.

I got my first surprise coming out of the ferry in the person of a nurse still in uniform. She was young and pretty, a brunette with blue eyes and a slender body, and I got the impression I knew her.

"Mr. Mayor?"

"Yes, miss...?"

"Chotard, Amélie Chotard. I am a friend of Marie."

Now it came back. My daughter had indeed had a couple of friends in the area, whom she met during summer vacations. "Nice of you to visit, but why did you ask our pilot to hurry?"

"You know what is going on in Rochefort now?"

"Yes, the situation is chaotic and law enforcement has more or less abdicated, which is understandable, as they have families too."

"I would like to resettle to the island with my family." She said it so fast, she almost made it sound like one word.

"Miss Chotard, we have limited resources and even a small family..."

"I was asked to deliver a message." She interrupted me.

At those words, my face froze. "A message?" I asked.

"Yes, it comes from your son." She whispered the words.

My face hardened all at once, fear over the fate of my son battling with anger in my soul that she chose to barter with me on such an issue. "My son is with the army!"

She took her phone out of her pocket and unlocked it. Then she showed me the screen.

It was him, wounded, with an unhealthy pallor on his skin, but he was awake.

"Where and how?" I growled.

"He is at the hospital in Rochefort. A military chopper landed last night at the air force base in Échillais and then a small ambulance convoy brought some military wounded to the hospital. Apparently, the high command ordered to split them between civilian hospitals, as they were worried the Russians would take over military ones. They wanted to avoid prisoners of war as much as possible. And the boss of orthopedics at the Rochefort hospital is a vet and a reservist."

"How many wounded?"

"Twelve. Eight grievously, four lightly, and they had four medics with them."

"Doctors, you mean."

"No, army medics. One of them made a joke about it as I called him doctor. Saying his doctorate was in German literature, not in medicine, and he said it with a German accent."

I mused a second over this. "Show me the pictures again!" I ordered her.

This time, I took a closer look at each picture. All the guys had the same uniform and shoulder patch...

"Okay, Miss Chotard, I shall honor the promise of my son. Your family and you are welcome to our island!"

She had a small smile and I saw a tear roll on her face.

"Why the tear?"

"It's my kids. I have them confined at home since the troubles began in town and they usually behave. But they grew restless and two evenings ago they went out and were caught by one of the gangs before I managed to find them."

"And?" I asked gently.

"They are small, you know. My boy is eight and his sister is six... So, they didn't do anything violent to them, but they made them smoke some stuff, as a joke, and..." Her voice broke down. "The leader, he invited me to follow him into a dark alley and told me all would be good for my kids if I was nice to him... So I had to service him before gathering the little ones and going home. But yesterday, he saw me on the street and behaved as if I were his plaything, to use as he wants. Thank God, neighbors were around, and he didn't become too pushy or violent, yet I am not sure how long I can keep saying no. I went to the cops, but they won't help; they are afraid, too. And then I saw the soldiers arrive and I recognized your son, and he recognized me. All communications are down, and he needed to contact you, and so he used me as his messenger."

"I will take care of your family and of you! But for that I will need your help, too."

"Anything!"

With a clear goal, it was time to get to the nuts and bolts. Time to get my son and his comrades in arms in Rochefort out of the hospital before the Russians caught wind of their presence.

"Your usual station is at the floor where they put the soldiers?"

"Yes, I am the head nurse for the orthopedic surgery ward!"

"The area they are in, is it isolated from the rest of the hospital?"

"It is a separate ward on the second floor. We don't have other patients at the time. The boss explained they were dispatched from another hospital with no free beds, as victims of a big car accident on the highway. As there are no newspapers running and no internet any more, nobody questioned his claim. Their data so far is only on paper files, nothing on the computers, and they came in the dead of night. Not many know they are there yet."

"Do you have access to their medical files?"

"Yes, why?"

"Two reasons: I want to make sure we get enough drugs, bandages, and so on to ensure a full recovery if possible, and I also need to plan transportation…"

"How long do you think it will take?" she asked in a trembling voice.

"Couple of days, tops! I have an idea to ensure your kids are safe, but it could be dangerous for you."

"I want them safe, even if I have to do it again with that guy. If it keeps them safe, I will cope, somehow. "

"Tell him that you plan to send them to your sister next weekend. That way you could have quality time for him and not rush it."

"He won't let me go with them," she objected.

"Of course not, but I will send someone to pick them up. And she will look like a plausible sister or sister-in-law."

"I don't have contact with my in-laws since the divorce. I live alone with the kids. It doesn't make the situation easier. As soon as the kids are gone, he will want to come visit me, and I will have to…"

"Yes, but you will be at the hospital for the day! And you shall be very convincing in that you are looking forward to some relaxation after your shift." I was talking softly, soothingly.

"It isn't you who will be raped if he doesn't want to wait." She hissed.

"I know! Alternative: we pick the kids up just before we go to the hospital. I don't expect trouble, but it will be less discreet and hence more dangerous."

"And where would you move the kids?"

"To the rally point where we would all meet at the end of the operation, before going back to the island."

"I think it would be better for the kids to move first," she whispered in a soft voice.

"Yes," I agreed gently. The strength and devotion of a mother for her kids never failed to move me, even after having witnessed it time and again during my service years.

"My next shift is tomorrow, the night shift, for three days, then I get some vacation."

"Okay, tomorrow, you gather the information I need, and you prepare your kids for the move. Clothes, shoes, favorite toys. As though they would go on vacation for a week or two... The people I will send will be aware of our true purpose, so give them the data. And now, next question: would you know if some colleagues of yours would be ready, willing, or happy to come to the island?"

"Yes. A couple of nurses for sure, and at least one M.D. There is a lot of talk at the coffee machine when we change shifts and only our sense of duty makes us stay, but we are all afraid."

"Okay, don't tell them anything, but we will try to work something out. And one area we are short of is healthcare professionals. We can use a couple of specialists in case we have to live off the grid for a time."

"But Marie..."

"Marie is not there yet, but last news I got from her says she was on the move." My tone was a bit harsher than I wanted, but I was worried about her. She knew how to take care of herself, but I wasn't sure if she would be in the right mindset from the start. Ruthlessness was what was called for right now and it was hard on her, as she took her Hippocratic oath very seriously. "Mademoiselle, one last question, if you please! Did my son give you a specific message, besides sending you here with the news?"

"No. He was wounded and drops in and out of consciousness, and there is always a medic in the room hovering over him and another wounded, a somewhat older guy."

"Okay. Next time you see him awake, tell him *Order 66*. And then tell him everything you told me. I won't give you a radio as it would be too dangerous if you were caught with one, but when my people come get your children, give them the answer my son gave you."

"I will do it! Can your boat bring me back right away?"

"The ferry, no, but we have other means of transportation to bring you back to Rochefort. And in case I didn't mention it, thank you for taking this risk, thank you a lot. Ah, and just in case, give me your number. Not that I have big hopes in life returning to normal, but you never know."

"Of course, just in case."

I took her personally to Rochefort with one of our boats. She had played it smart and parked her car at the Fontaine aux Lupins. It was a regular boat spot on the way to the island but out of the way. Going by daylight, there seemed to be no roadblocks to hinder her passage.

It gave me time to think before moving assets in position and more time with Miss Chotard, to try and figure her out.

The drop at the Fontaine aux Lupins went like a charm and I had enough time with her to realize she wasn't playing me. She was just a mom trying to survive in hell. I now knew where she lived, and it gave me the keys to begin the planning of the first part of the ops: get the kids out. For the second part, I already had an idea; finalizing it would depend upon the physical fitness level of the wounded. It was time to gather my people for the ops.

At the beginning of my planning, a long time ago, I had envisioned different scenarios, but at the end of the day, they all had the same core issues: bodies and kit. In both cases, my military past helped me find solutions: legionnaires wanting to retire on the island were welcome to do so and were offered jobs in the area. Not necessarily on the island itself, as it wouldn't have been sustainable, but near enough that we could get them to safety fast enough. To put it simply, I had a network of shooters near at hand and they were all armed. To ensure they kept their skills sharp, I had managed to get them shooting licenses, be it for sport shooting or skeet or hunting. It gave their personal arsenal the fig leaf of legality and it gave us the opportunity to regularly organize training sessions, in collaboration with the nearby air force base. To that, I had been able to add quite a sizable arsenal of small and not-so-small arms. When you know the right persons, having a confiscated shipment of weapons marked for destruction isn't the same as having said weapons really destroyed. Some of our specialist items were stored in caches on the island as well as enough food to keep 1,000 people fed for about a year.

Considering the operation, I went for the easy part first: exfiltrating the kids. Two of my people were of the right age and could pass for relatives. As always when it was about to get serious, I only sent meeting orders electronically, nothing operational. Corporal Ikewicz had been a good legionnaire but not NCO material till he met Denissa during an operation in the Balkans. I hadn't known such a mountain could melt so easily but pretty, petite Denissa had her Adam wrapped around her little finger, which led her to follow him to France clandestinely after the operation ended. I was still at the 13 at that time and I had had to pull some strings to ensure they could marry fast enough to have her first child carry the Ikewicz name. Ten years later, adjudant-chef Ikewicz retired, the proud father of four, and became the tenant / bartender of a small brasserie in Rochefort. The kids of Amélie would be safe with the Ikewicz family and we would be able to get the whole family out before the real ops began, if all went well.

I needed Mouse. Mouse was one of my former legionnaires, a really nice guy, small and wiry, who had had some difficulties with the law in his youth, mainly for his ability to disable security systems of cars and to speed off with them, and that at an age where he couldn't legally have a driving license. Long story short, an old-school judge encouraged him to change his ways and recommended the army, as their next meeting wouldn't necessarily be that friendly. Mouse wasn't stupid and knew that his juvenile status would soon vanish, due to him hitting majority, and so he joined the legion and discovered a family. He was now our top mechanic, but still the go-to guy if you had lost your car keys.

"Garage de l'Océan!"

"Hi, Mouse. Since when do you answer the phone yourself?"

"Since I don't want my secretary getting home after dark!"

"Care to drop by for a beer? You should be in time for the

fountain."

A poor code, but it indicated the pick-up place would be the small stop at the Fontaine aux Lupins.

"Sure thing, mon colonel."

Two hours later, Mouse was in my office, sipping a Kronenbourg, like in the good old days. "Okay, boss, what's up! Not that I don't like free beer but…"

"Yohann has reappeared."

Mouse's eyes lit up with joy. "Where?"

"Orthopedic ward at Rochefort's hospital."

"And what are we waiting for?"

"Mouse, he isn't alone."

And then I told him everything I knew. Once I was done, he kept silent for a moment.

"Okay, so you want to bring them out to the island, and you don't want our Russian friends to know where they were brought to."

"Yes, I have a bad feeling about the situation in the whole region. We don't have many Russians in the area, they didn't even occupy the air force base full time, but if they get wind of the presence of the guys there, they will want to arrest them as prisoners of war, if only to avoid them joining resistance cells and bringing their expertise in murder and mayhem. And soon voices will begin to blame the military for all the problems, the defeat, the capitulation, which will lead to denunciations, like in the good old days. I don't want a trail leading back to the island; even without the Russians around, I wouldn't want it. And I definitely don't want good soldiers taking the blame for the fuck-ups of politicians."

"Good soldiers?"

"From what I saw and heard, all people of the 13th. Not sure where the helicopter pilots came from, though."

"Wondering where they are right now as well!"

"Yes, that too! But to make a long story short, I need you to borrow a truck."

"Borrow? Should I then infer that you are looking for a specific truck?"

"Yes Mouse. I am looking for a very specific truck, as far as the markings go. I want a big laundry truck with the logo of the Blanchisserie hospitalière de La Rochelle."

"Okay, that's our way in, but how many pax do we plan to evacuate?"

"By my count, ought to be between twelve and twenty, perhaps more. But those more would be locals, and we can probably bring them in one or two at a time and not right away. It's just the soldiers I want out of the hospital and on the island ASAP."

"She played you, you know."

"No way, man. She was really, really going for it, believe me. If it hadn't been for her kids, we would have gone at it the whole night. And once she is done with her next shift... I am going to really ravage her. She was begging for it, man."

"Right, and now the kids are on vacation, and she is working. And you? Just taking care of this small borough for the emir."

"Just? Come on, Abdul. It's in the middle of town, lots of rich people to squeeze, and some real lookers. As soon as the emir has asserted control, our main problem won't be getting any; it will be keeping our strength up."

"Omar, what makes you think she will be back after her shift is done? Well, for that matter, what makes you so sure she is at the hospital?"

"I know her name and she has shown me her work planning for the next week."

"And you really think she will be back to her flat and not run to her sister and stay there?"

"There is one way to be sure. Her shift ends tonight. Let's drop by and escort her home," Omar said.

"It's not our area, man," said Abdul.

"You're right, but the emir rewards initiative. And getting our hands on the stock of drugs at the hospital would help me secure my position."

"Okay, so we gather the guys?"

"Yes, Abdul, gather the guys. We will hit the hospital tonight and escort my girl home."

"Your girl, how sweet," chuckled Abdul.

"You will be first in line once I tire of her, old friend."

"Then begin soon. I wouldn't mind sampling her."

We were set and ready to go. Adam and Denissa had the kids safely tucked aboard their small sailing boat and on their way to the island for a daily cruise. I had the information I needed, and Mouse got the car. The only weird thing was the answer of my son to my cryptic message. Sure, he got the confirmation code, but added one tidbit of information I didn't really care for. It looked like we would need to have a serious conversation soon.

The laundry truck was roomy enough but sitting on the floor made the men bitch, as usual. I had chosen to go with minimal firepower; we wanted to exfiltrate people from a hospital, not start a shooting war. The only extra security for our exfil was Karel. He was a bit long in the tooth to be part of an assault column, but he was safely tucked away in a sniper's nest half a klick away from the hospital, ready to give us cover, if need be.

I was sitting at the passenger side in the truck as we entered the hospital compound. Security was nil. We approached the service entrance, looking like a regular delivery truck on its way to bring the fresh laundry. Once inside the docking bay, we would have a short hop to the elevators, and once in control of the elevators, we would be gold, as Mouse was confident in his ability to jam all doors save the ones we wanted to use to ensure a swift exfil.

Only... there was a bus parked on our spot with a Russian BTR-T in front of it, unloading troops who were entering the hospital.

"Mouse?" I growled.

"There must have been a leak, mon colonel."

"Okay, let's check them out. We play it by ear."

"Like the good old days."

Thirty seconds after the troops vanished inside the building, I checked my piece. My suppressed SIG-Sauer P226 was now locked and loaded, its safety off. I exited the truck, a fake smile plastered on my face, and moved swiftly to the bus's driver door. I was wearing civilian clothes.

"Good evening, sir, can you tell us where we can make our laundry delivery?"

The Russian gave me a cold, flat look. "Nyet. Papers, please!" The driver of the BTR was also outside, enjoying a smoke and looking at the altercation with a smirk. I slowly moved my right hand towards my hip pocket, reaching for my wallet. The Russian soldier was still looking intently at my right hand when my left came up and I double-tapped him in the face. The BTR driver had time to open his mouth but not to close it, as Mouse's first bullet hit him in the throat.

Two Russkies down, with three rounds—not too shabby. I quickly checked the bus whilst Mouse did the same for the BTR. Luck was with us as there were no more bad guys around. The dead guys were well equipped: body armor, AK-74, tactical radio (and didn't I let a long breath out as I realized the radios were off), grenade.

Mouse called to me. "Nobody else, but those guys aren't regulars. The truck and the BTR are too clean."

"Guys, we need to move fast. Somehow the Russians got word of the presence of our guys at the hospital. Given the presence of the BTR and the size of the truck, I think we are outnumbered."

"We need to hurry, boss. Seems clear to me where they are heading to."

"Boss, we don't have phone signal, but I was a patient here last year and the Wi-Fi seems active."

I snapped my phone from my pocket and checked the icon out. Indeed, Wi-Fi connection as a guest, which meant I could use the phone as a phone as well. Praying for a miracle, I speed-dialed the mobile number of Miss Chotard.

It rang, and on the third ring, I got an answer. "Michel?"

"On the premises and on my way. Be aware, there are hostile elements in the building, probably heading your way. Can you get me my son on the line?"

I heard some quiet words spoken into the room then I heard the voice of my son. "Okay, Dad, Amélie gave us the warning and we are kitting up as we speak."

"Son, you need to get out. There are too many."

"No, Dad, we will hold the fort till the cavalry gets here."

"Well, technically, you are speaking to the cavalry and the bad guys outnumber us badly," I added in a frustrated tone.

His laughter warmed my heart. "You have a tactical radio?"

"Yes, just in case. Why?"

"Go to the emergency frequency and go to scramble three."

"And then?"

"And then you tell the pilot of the chopper to haul ass. Call sign is Rapace 1. Tell them you're 13 Actual."

"Son, I am not sure of the size of the opposition. It can be they have enough to take the chopper down. The unit sent isn't that small, they even brought a BTR-T, and I wouldn't rule out reinforcements."

I could hear the impatience in his voice as he answered. "Dad, the chopper comes from the special forces regiment, and it has its full crew... two minimi machine guns as well as a manned sniper berth."

"From the 4th RHFS?"

"Yup. And I am prepping a reception for our party crashers."

"You plan to transform a hospital into a war zone?"

"Yes and no. I happen to know that the floor we are in is empty, except for us and the medics taking care of us. The head of orthopedics moved everybody away from the second floor, except us and his team, in preparation for a thorough disinfection procedure scheduled to happen soon."

"Okay, I got the picture. Let's prepare a thorough party crashing then."

Mouse had followed my half of the call and at that point he wordlessly handed me a tactical radio set. One of the good things of the Felin (Fantassin à Équipements et Liaisons INtégrés, Future Infantry Soldier System) program was that its communication suite accepted the use of older systems, including the old PCR-4 radio systems, which my guys and I were using.

"13 Actual to Rapace 1."

A short pause, then a soprano voice answered. "Rapace 1 to 13 Actual. Confirmation code needed."

"*More Majorum.*"

In memory of our predecessors, indeed.

"What can we do for you on this fine night, 13 Actual?"

"Scramble for pick-up at the hospital. Same pax as on the way in, with at least six more. On the bright side, only a short hop needed. How good are you for fuel?"

"Tanks are topped, and we are starting the warm-up as we speak. The crew is good to go."

"Assume a hot LZ. Hostiles in the neighborhood. Also, avoid the habitations on approach. Come from river then from the north. We need to plan the egress carefully and to stay away from the radars."

"Not our first rodeo, 13 Actual. ETA 5 mikes. Stay alive, the cavalry is on the way."

At the same time as I was speaking to the pilot, I was considering the tactical picture, which didn't fill me up with joy. There was too much uncertainty about the numbers of the opposition for my taste and having to egress with wounded people, in the middle of a hospital, was going to be iffy and casualty prone.

"Okay, Mouse, you disable the transportation of the bad guys first, quick and dirty."

"We don't want to use the BTR, boss?"

"No, the only armament is the cannon, and it would make too much ruckus. We want to be discreet once we are out of those precincts."

He nodded, accepting the decision without further ado.

"Then you and I take the elevator to the second floor with Mike and Paul as back-up. Frank and Ernst, you guys ensure the way out stays clear of hostiles."

"RoE?"

"CQC house... we try to avoid hitting civilians, but in doubt, your safety comes first. Make no mistake, people, this is war, and I will be damned if I let a bunch of godless Communists stand between me and my son, and on French soil to boot. *More Majorum!*"

"*More Majorum!*"

Then the fun began.

There is a world of difference between infiltrating a hospital to bring some patients back with us and infiltrating the same hospital right on the heels of a hostile military force. With every nook and cranny a potential ambush spot, we needed to be careful, following the old motto "slow is smooth and smooth is fast." At least, I had made sure our weapons were suppressed, not wanting to rouse the alarm and to create a panic if I could help it. But I hadn't planned on the Russians crashing the party and we weren't really kitted to deal with them toe to toe. On the other hand, it would be mostly close quarters combat and long weapons aren't as much of a help as on an open field.

Our Russian friends had behaved in a professional manner and had posted two guys to block the elevators and keep an eye on the main entrance. Our luck was that we were coming from the back, the loading area where the Russians had left their vehicles. As such, we surprised the two guys, who were busier watching the nurses than checking their surroundings. Mouse and I engaged them, moving in with the smoothness of long practice, and came within five meters before they became aware of our presence. As we registered in their consciousness, it was too late: a double-tap and an Indian beauty mark later, the two sentinels were down and the way to the elevators clear. As the girl at the reception was about to scream, Mouse saved the day by rushing to her.

"We are the Résistance; you have nothing to fear from us! Where did the other Russians go?"

"Orthopedics. They claimed they needed to verify the identity of some of our patients in the ward."

"How many of them?" asked Mouse.

"Twenty, plus the two you just killed," she answered in a trembling voice.

"Thank you. Two of us will stay with you till we are done. Really sorry about the intrusion," said Mouse courteously. Then, as he turned away, he said, "So, boss, how do we do it? Rush the stairs or elevator?"

"Stairs! If I were them, I would block the elevators on my destination floor anyway."

And up we went, in a classical formation, two teams of two moving slowly but smoothly from the ground floor to the second one. We hadn't even reached the first floor before the familiar noise of automatic weapons fire caught our attention.

"On the double, people!" I told my guys.

We moved faster towards the sound of battle, knowing that we needed to overwhelm the enemy quickly before they had time to realize their transport and the communication node going with it were gone. Reaching the doors, we began communicating only by sign. Mouse got ready to open the door and I had my suppressed SIG in a shooting position. As Mouse gently opened the door, I began to inch my head to get an angle of vision. We had good and bad luck both. Good: the enemy was in front of us. Bad: he was between us and my son.

I entered the corridor leading to orthopedics and began servicing targets. Mouse, Mike, and Paul followed in a quiet dance of death. We managed to deal with six guys before the first scream betrayed our presence. We then had to take cover as the return fire was both heavy and accurate. We had managed to hit their rear echelon hard and fast but now they had us pinned down, as the four of us had to defend from two directions. On the other hand, they also had to defend from two directions and had the numbers to make our lives difficult. As discretion wasn't any longer an issue, I contacted Karel, our sniper.

"Eagle, do you have eyes on bad guys?"

"Affirmative, boss. Ready to engage at your call."

"Mouse, throw a grenade! Eagle, service targets as soon as the grenade explodes."

That way, I was hoping to augment Karel's survivability. Confusion was always high on the battlefield and the grenades would nicely add to it. Karel's first shot came right as the ringing of the first grenade diminished in my ears. As luck had it, the legionaries at the orthopedic center followed our lead and added a couple of grenades, giving Karel a few seconds of tranquility.

As usual in combat, my brains were analyzing the tactical situation and I was leaving Mouse in charge of my security. Which means I wasn't really looking in the right direction as I got showered in blood. The Russians had also stationed two guys at the elevator on the second floor. They had been out of sight at first, but their boss had managed to order them to engage us. I was pinned down with my friend bleeding freely right beside me.

I returned fire with my SIG, but the suppressor didn't work in my favor this time: it's hard to feel cowed by weapons fire you don't hear. I gambled big and threw a grenade in their direction. And as they ducked, I rushed them, shooting as I went. The first guy went down, and I immediately switched my aim to the second, who was realizing fast that my grenade hadn't exploded. The gun misfired and I threw it at the Russian, going for a body tackle. I threw him off his feet, but he managed to throw me over him, using the momentum of my charge against me.

We then went to business right away, fists and feet flying. I landed a solid kick on his sternum, but his body armor absorbed the hit and he answered with a solid blow on my right shoulder, hitting my brachial plexus and immobilizing one limb through pain for a couple of seconds. As I went on the defensive, I realized one second too late that he had used the small respite to draw his secondary gun and he was aiming it at me. The sound of his gun was deafening, but he had missed, somehow, and then he toppled over, revealing Mike right behind him, his Glock still aimed at the guy.

"Thanks!"

"Any time, boss. Now you cover me whilst I stabilize Mouse."

Mike happened to be a combat medic and he began a quick check on Mouse. I made eye contact with him, and he smiled and gave me a thumbs-up. I let out a breath I knew I had been holding: barring complications, Mouse would live.

I continued covering my sector. Paul was at the opposite side, blocking any rush by the enemy. The enemy had realized the presence of the sniper, but by then it was too late, particularly as the Special Forces Caracal entered the fray, its sniper completing Karel's work. And just like that, for the first time in more than a year, I laid eyes on my son.

"Thanks for the timely arrival, Dad. They had us pinned down with time on their side, as they had called for reinforcements."

"No reinforcements, son. We had luck and got to their BTR before the communication went out and their tactical radio has a very limited range, particularly in an urban setting. Sitrep?"

"We got two dead and three wounded. One of the dead guys is a civilian who rushed towards the Russians at the beginning of the fight. Besides us, there are five civilians in one of the rooms, ready to come with us, one of them being Miss Chotard, the other four being two nurses, one doctor, and a surgeon."

"Good, very good indeed. And now, would you care to explain your presence here, as well as this cluster-fuck? Not that I am not happy to see you, but the keyword of our whole operation was discretion, not destruction."

"I am just following orders, Dad. The CEMA *(Chef d'État-Major des armées, French equivalent of the Chairman of the Joint Chiefs of Staff)* had us move out when it became clear that we wouldn't be able to hold the Russians at bay, whatever we did. The helicopter got hit during a skirmish in the east and its electronics are fried, hence our transport mode. As for the battles, the ammo shortage did us in."

"And what were your orders from the CEMA?"

"To evacuate wounded of the 13th to the coast and then try to contact you."

"The CEMA asked you to contact me?"

"Yes, Dad. He knows about your project and thought you could use the manpower."

"And?"

"And one of the guys with me isn't of the 13th, but the CEMA insisted he comes along."

I was beginning to have a very, very bad feeling about that one. That feeling became a certainty as I saw my former boss come towards us, looking every bit the officer, even considering his unhealthy pallor, the heavy bandage on the right side of his torso, and his arm in a sling.

"Mes respects, mon général."

"Well met, Michel, nice to meet you again."

"Indeed, albeit the circumstances aren't optimal."

"I know. On the other hand, did you really think I wasn't aware of your preparations?"

Give it to him, he went straight to the jugular. But you didn't become head of military intelligence by pussy-footing around critical issues when time was of the essence.

"No, of course not. Some problems solved themselves too easily for me not to believe there was a helping hand or two in the background. And of course, now you come to collect."

"Not exactly. I come to give you some more information so that we can plan a bit for the future. I will have to stay off the radar of our Russian friends, as I am officially dead, but I need to set some stuff in motion."

"In motion?"

"Yes, it is very important that we keep control of as many islands as possible. More I can't say. But... there are plans. We aren't dead yet and I will be damned if some Russkies or Antikap or haji have the last word in France. But as it is, we need to play a long game and there will be a lot of darkness before the light shines again on our colors."

"Is it that time again in our history, then?" I mused.

"Yes, Colonel, pretty much. Not exactly the same circumstances as in 1940 but... remember why and how the 13th was created and remember what it is famous for."

I parsed the last sentence over and over. And then it hit me and I gave him a very, very flat stare.

"Let me guess. We should only focus on the islands around next but not towards Brittany?"

His tight smile gave me the answer. There was a deep, deep game in play right now and I, and my island, were only tiny cogs.

"To put it simply, we also had Antikap on our radar for

quite some time and it led us to some interesting discoveries, which also led us to the implementation of different sets of contingency plans."

"Didn't help against the Russians, sir," I snarked.

"I know, it came too early. The CEMA saw the light and set things in motion as soon as he was in the driving seat, but it was a hard political sell, and it is never very popular to ask for more ammunition and more troops to be able to take the losses we saw coming and keep fighting. The old president understood the problem and had pledged to upgrade the military budget, but him dying of a heart attack just before the last round of budget discussions, then the new all-too pro-Russian follower, it threw some wrenches in the whole process."

"A heart attack, for a young, fit guy in his 40s, with the best available medical care?" I snorted.

"Well, his head of security suffered a fatal accident a couple of days later. And as luck had it, his successor suffered a stroke, too. A curse, perhaps?"

His bitter smile spoke volumes about the events which had happened in the last months. It wasn't his job at military intelligence to watch over the security of the president, and yet he took it personally.

"No proof?" I asked.

"Nothing conclusive enough to convince the boss of the necessity of a first strike. And once the fighting began, all players agreed to keep the nukes out of action. We don't want to live under the Russians, they don't want to live under us, or the Chinese, but we don't want to kill the planet either. Well, there are some exceptions, but those have been discreetly taken care of and the people in charge of nukes are the most level-headed anyway."

"And so we bide our time?" I asked bitterly.

"Yes, stupid as it is, for a nation to function as a nation, it needs people ready to sacrifice everything. You should brush up on your historical texts, Michel. Reread Ernest Renan, he summed up the idea of nation perfectly: 'A nation is a great solidarity, built upon the sacrifices offered and upon the sacrifices one is disposed to do again.' Right now, not many are ready to make sacrifices, to work for the common good. For that will to come again, our people must realize how good their life was, and be ready to fight to get it back."

I took a deep breath. His words cut deep, and it was the

shame of our generation that we didn't do enough, somehow. "Ask not what your country can do for you—ask what you can do for your country."

"Yes, exactly. JFK got it right. And now we do what we can and we endure, in the hope that someday, the lights of civilization will shine again upon our corner of the Earth, but first, we have to walk through the shadows."

"That bad, sir?"

"Yes, Michel. In some ways, it would have been better had we not bled the Russians so white. It would have, perhaps, given them a chance to impose some sort of order. Right now, they can't hold onto much. They can just sow chaos and hope that our citizens support them on a platform made to restore order. At last reports, they have about twenty thousand effective, in a country of sixty million inhabitants, without any local support base, except the usual politicians who would do anything to feel important and justify it through any means. It's not even ten percent of the German occupation troops in WWII, they don't have secure supply lines with the motherland, and there is no real cohesion among their units."

"Actual 13, we have got company incoming," the voice of Rapace 1 interrupted the history lecture.

"What kind?"

"Gang-bangers, I would say. Not well armed, but about ten guys in three cars."

"Any of them look wounded?" I asked.

"Nope, doesn't look like it."

"Frank, Ernst, fall back to us. Get the civilians up with you, on the double," I ordered.

"What do you think they want, Michel?" asked the general.

"Prescription drugs would be my bet. I would let them come to us and neutralize them rather than play cat and mouse. They don't have the firepower or the training to face us, not on those odds, and that's not even counting the snipers."

Karel was checking their progression through his scope. "13 actual, they are heading your way. They took the stairs near the entrance, not the elevators, and exited on the second floor."

We could already hear their voices, loud and arrogant. And then, from behind me, I heard a sob.

"It's him. It's him!"

I turned my head and looked at Amélie, pale as a bedsheet and shaking.

I began to give a series of rapid orders but was interrupted by the general, using his command voice.

"Michel, we use the weapons of the Russians for this, quick."

I relayed the orders, and we were in time, barely, just as the gang-bangers got their eyes on the first dead Russian.

"What the fuck, man!"
"We got to go, Omar."
"No, wait, Abdul."

In that moment of indecision, we struck. A couple of the thugs had been savvy enough to have their guns out but hadn't counted with an enemy getting so close to them. It was over in moments.

The last thing a guy called Omar saw was Amélie spitting on his face.

The general calmly ordered the guys to bring the weapons back to their Russian owners and to leave them there, then to move some of the bodies. After dropping two of our Sig-Sauers in the hands of the thugs, we had hopefully left enough traces to convince the Russians that there had been a shoot-out involving drugs, and vice-versa. As luck had it, there was a big reserve of drugs on that floor, and we emptied it of anything useful before making good our escape.

As we boarded the helicopter, I ordered Karel to egress following the primary plan, as it was obvious our actions hadn't been detected. Paul and Mike left with our truck, also according to the plan. I was pretty sure the Russians wouldn't get much help from the local cops, and with a bit of luck, there would soon be difficult times for dear Yusuf, provided the Russians bought our little charade.

Fifteen minutes after the first gunshot, we were gone from the precinct, and five minutes later, aboard the helicopter.

"Tell the pilot to come to the island from the seaside, please. Discretion is of the essence."

"Rapace, we move nap of the earth. I am transmitting GPS coordinates; we need to reach the coordinates coming from the sea to avoid attracting unwanted attention."

"Copy, 13 Actual. We have some heavy cloud cover, light conditions are four, heavy winds, expect a bumpy ride."

One hour later, after a scenic sea tour, we were landing inside the old Fort Liédot, an old Napoleonic area fortification, long mothballed, then reactivated as a museum. As the mayor, I had been able to restrict access to quite a few areas and the fort was once more functioning as a military installation, at least, the parts closed to the public. In no time, we had Mouse and the civilians on their way to our infirmary, followed by the walking wounded. Some of my guys began securing the helicopter, before camouflaging it under nets. I was unsure whether to ditch it or not, as parts and fuel would be a bitch to get, but the added mobility made me consider it, at least for now.

As the pilot came to greet me, I had another surprise coming. "Hi, Dad, Colonel, sir."

"Clara, how?"

"The copilot of this helicopter was killed in the action which took out our combat electronics, and I got his job. Two years out of flight school and flying a COS helicopter, would you believe that?"

"In this crazy world we're living in, my daughter, I will believe that, yes." I embraced her fiercely and felt her sob in my arms.

"Any news of Marie?" she asked.

"No, but of you three, somehow she is the one I am the least worried about. Your big sister is a strong soul."

"I can't help being a worrier, Dad."

"I know, pumpkin, I know. Now go take care of your crew. We will have time for talking later."

As my daughter walked away, the general came to me. "Michel, I am calling a marker now."

"As I don't believe in coincidences, like having my youngest daughter moved to a COS helicopter so early in her career, forget about the marker. What can I do for you, mon general?"

"Bring me to Fort Boyard with a small boat, please, and that before the sun rises."

Fort Boyard was an old fortification which was supposed to protect the channel leading to the great maritime arsenal of Rochefort in the 19th century. It was famous, not as a fortification, but due to a TV game in the 1990s...

"I shall take you there personally, mon general."

"Merci, Michel."

Two hours later, I was back, with a lot to ponder.

Two days later, I went back to the fort but was only met by silence and emptiness. The same couldn't be said of Rochefort. My local contacts reported an interesting story, with the Russians having raided safe houses of the emir, killing quite a few of his followers. Our decoy plan seemed to have functioned.

A couple of weeks later, life came to a halt, quite literally, as the remaining stockpiles of fuel dwindled. We had our stockpiles on the island and kept a low profile, watching and hearing in despair, as a civilization was dying around us.

And I kept pondering the last words of the general.

"Your job is to keep your island secure for the time being. At some point, you will probably be able to expand. I would suggest going for the other islands first, Oléron and Ré, but ultimately, it's your call."

"And you, sir?"

"Don't ask, Michel, don't ask! My task is another, and hopefully, we will someday be able to restart civilization. Yes, there are plans! But then, there always are plans and I can't promise they will all succeed. I can only say that, in the end, all plans depend on the hearts of men. Don't let evil win. *More Majorum!*"

Rebels' Cause

Nic Plume

Fall 2026, Viernheim, Germany

Mike had just settled at the kitchen table when the front door thumped shut with a muffled thud.

Ah, there goes the neighborhood, he thought with a smile as colorful curses sounded through the closed kitchen door. Moments later, his cousin entered.

"One of these days I'm going to break my neck coming through that damn rug curtain thing or whatever it is," Sven complained.

Mike didn't bother looking up from his bowl of soup. "It's a heavy wool blanket and it helps keep the heat in," he pointed out as he scooped another spoon toward his mouth. "In case you haven't noticed, it has an opening in its center through which you can walk right in."

"And yet, I can never find it." Sven eyeballed the contents in Mike's bowl as he deposited a bulging paper bag from the local bakery onto the table. "Oma's potato soup?"

Mike nodded, but Sven was already making a beeline to the pot on the stove.

"What did you get?" Mike reached for the bag. The round bulges looked promising.

"Seven Brötchen and two Laugenstangen. They didn't have any loaves of bread but Mom said she got extra at her baker in Lorsch. She'll drop it off later." Sven grabbed one of the bowls their grandmother had set out and filled it with the steaming creamy soup.

Mike opened the paper bag and inspected the fist-sized rolls it contained. "They look smaller than normal."

"They are," Sven replied. "But the price is still the same."

Mike pulled out the two Laugenstangen and put one by Sven's place at the table. The brown, elongated pretzel rolls were their favorites, though Mike preferred to eat them with a sweet topping like honey, jam, or the ever-excellent Nutella. The latter was much harder to get nowadays, though. Unlike jam and honey, the former of which Oma made herself and the latter a beekeeper friend supplied her with.

"Oma and Opa went to Schriesheim?" Sven asked as he sat down.

"Yeah." Mike nodded. "They'll be back in three or four days."

Sven frowned. "You know pretty soon they'll stop coming back at all."

Mike glanced at his cousin. It was true that their grandparents had been expanding their weekly overnighters in their cabin lately, but who could blame them with what was currently going on in the world. From up there the Rhein-Neckar valley still looked like its old, pre-Russian-invasion self. Plus, they were both retired and with Mike and his mom having moved back in, they didn't need to worry about leaving their house unattended. Mike shook his head. "No, they won't."

"Why not?" Sven looked at him. "I mean, it's perfect up there. They're within walking distance of the town but far enough up the mountain to not be easily found or noticed, and fully off the grid. Solar panels for the little power they need, a rain collection system for water, and heating and cooking that can be done through oil, propane, or wood."

"Which all still need to be bought or collected." Mike laughed. "Plus, having to walk thirty meters downhill to the outhouse in the cold is not my idea of idyllic living conditions. Never mind the outside shower."

Sven shrugged. "I could deal with sponge baths until the temps are warmer if it meant not having to deal with the Russkies."

"And digging a hole every few days to empty the poopbucket into?" Mike studied his cousin. It sounded as if he was starting to think that going off grid would be a good idea. The question was, was that his idea or someone else's?

Sven grimaced at the thought of having to handle a bucket full of feces.

Got ya, cuz. Mike smiled. "Sven, going off grid is not going to change the fact that the Russians invaded. That's a fact we have to live with, and I prefer to do that here, in a house with running water and electricity." He looked around the kitchen, amazed how quickly it had felt like home again.

After he and his mom had first moved here, it had been the familiar in a world that had turned upside down. A refuge where he had felt safe to grieve not only the loss of his dad but the loss of the only life he had known up until then. Viernheim, and Germany in general, had always been the place he visited to see his grandparents, cousin, and aunt; the place where his mom was from and where she and Dad had met. But his life had been in the States, in Brandenburg, Kentucky to be precise, right outside Ft. Knox, where his dad had been stationed. But that had changed one sunny afternoon when he was fourteen. When the white Dodge Charger with military plates had pulled into their driveway and three soldiers had come to their door to inform them that there had been a training accident and that his dad would never come home again. The next few years had been rough, on all of them. Packing up their lives and moving in with Oma and Opa had been just the first step. But they had gotten through it, together. He had finished school and become an engineer, and moved into his own apartment three years ago. And then some terrorists had turned his and the whole world's lives upside down again. And now Germany and all of western Europe was part of the New Soviet Union.

"Is your mom still joining them?" Sven asked, pulling Mike back into the present.

"Yes, she left a little while ago. She'll help them with the walnuts and chestnuts and wants to learn more about picking mushrooms."

Sven grimaced. "Mom does, too. I just hope they learn it well enough to not feed us toadstools."

Mike laughed. "I think toadstool is the one mushroom we won't have to worry about them wrongly picking."

"Yeah, I guess." Sven grinned. "Let's just hope they'll be as well versed with all the others they learn to pick."

Mike nodded in agreement and then turned serious. "Sounds like you've been hanging out with your friends again."

Sven studied him between bites. "What makes you say that?"

At least he didn't deny it this time. "You're not the outdoorsy type who willingly gives up his games and electronics,"

Mike said. "Not too long ago, you shuddered at the thought of having to use Oma and Opa's outhouse. Now, you're considering their cabin the best place to be."

"Not too long ago, we didn't have Russkies telling us how to live."

"The whole world is a dumpster fire right now. Having the EU in charge wouldn't be that much different."

"Yeah, it would."

"That's your friends talking."

Sven nodded. "But those friends are also why Mom was able to get extra bread. And they can also get us other things we need."

"And they can get you killed. Just this morning the news radio reported about another raid on a suspected rebel hideout."

Sven studied him. "Remember that year when we did the school swap? First you came over here for a month and went to school with me and then I came to stay with you. You were two grades above me, so we didn't have any classes together, but that's actually not what stuck with me about the whole experience. You know what did? The raising and lowering of the flag and the reciting of the pledge of allegiance each day. That pride, that patriotism I saw and felt from everyone, even the youngest student, was something I had never experienced before." He paused. "But I see it now, in my friends. We're German. Not Russian or Soviet, but German. And that's worth fighting for."

"Yeah, but that fight is not going to end well if you can't keep your activity hidden well enough to not be caught."

Mike had just hung up the last piece of laundry when the doorbell suddenly rang up a storm. By the time he came up from the basement, the front door had opened and his aunt was pushing through the dark curtain. Her jeans and jacket were mud spattered and her forehead streaked as if she had rubbed a muddy hand across her face.

"Tante Silvia," he said. "Are you okay? What happened?"

Sven appeared on the stairs from above. "Mom. What's going on?"

Tears welled up in her eyes as she started to speak "The cabin," she stammered. "They raided the cabin and arrested

Mutti, Papa, and Elke." She reached for her forehead then paused and stared at her dirt-encrusted palms.

Now that she stood in the hallway light, Mike could see that her jeans were not only spattered but caked in mud from the knees down. Sven grabbed her hands to inspect them. She pulled them out of his grasp.

"It's just dirt." She mumbled. "I slipped and fell when I cut through the woods to get back to the car." She inhaled shakily. "I just haven't had a chance to wash it off." She looked around as if having to orient herself, then turned to the halfbath next to the front door.

Sven grabbed her by the shoulders. "Mom." His voice had changed from concerned son to professional paramedic. "Let's go into the kitchen. We'll clean you up there."

She stared at him momentarily, then nodded and allowed him to guide her into the kitchen. As her eyes met Mike's in passing, they filled with tears again.

Mike's chest tightened. He had never seen his aunt like this, but bombarding her with questions out here in the hall would not help. He stepped back to allow Sven room to maneuver her into the kitchen. Sven pushed her into a chair and then went to the sink. Mike expected him to get towels or rags to help his mom clean up. Instead, he opened the cabinet door and pulled out a glass and filled it with water.

Mike knelt in front of his aunt. "Silvia, what happened? Who raided the cabin?"

She took a few gulps of the water and took a few steadying breaths. She looked back at Mike, then Sven, who had crouched beside her. "I didn't go close enough to see their identifications, but they spoke Russian and from the way they acted, I think they were from Security Services."

Sven frowned. "What are the SS doing at the cabin?"

His mother flinched. Most people, and especially the older generations, avoided using the acronym. Younger people had no such qualm. Some even used it specifically to draw out the historical comparison. In the past, Silvia had always reprimanded Sven for using it—but not so this time.

"The cabin is illegal," she said. "Zoning regulations don't allow any kind of permanent buildings on that part of the mountain. Never have. But as long as the buildings weren't obvious, the city of Schriesheim or the county never sent anyone to enforce those laws. I think the Russians have a different opinion."

"But that's not a reason to arrest everyone," Sven said.

"No," Mike agreed. "But it's an excuse to check everyone's papers and background."

"So?"

"That would've shown that Dad was an American soldier," Mike said in realization.

Sven frowned at him. "But you've lived here for twelve years now."

"Doesn't matter," Mike said. "A lot of the Americans that got arrested right after the invasion had also been living here for years. They and their families were still rounded up and carted off."

Sven's eyes widened. "You think they'll come here next?"

Mike nodded. "I'm the American in the family. If they went after Mom, they'll definitely come after me. And if they arrested Oma and Opa, they'll arrest you two, too."

Silvia nodded. "We need to hide."

"Yes, but where?" Mike asked. "They know where we live and probably also who our friends are."

"I could ask—" Sven started.

"No, you can't," Silvia interrupted him. "You're only going to draw attention to them."

"But they probably know someone who could help us."

"Which is why we can't lead the Russians to them."

"Okay." Sven nodded. "Where are we gonna go then? We can't stay here or at your place, and we can't go to any of our friends. If it was summer, I'd say we could just go hide in the woods for a while, but the nights are getting too cold to sleep outside." He considered for a moment. "Unless we go to some of the old bunkers the Ammies left behind."

The bunkers were old weapons depots the US Army had built in the Viernheimer Heide, a forest located between Viernheim, Lampertheim, and Käfertal. For decades during the Cold War, large sections of the forest had been fenced off and off limits to Germans. Other parts of the forest, especially between Viernheim and Käfertal, had been used for training. Mike's mom had told him many stories of roaming the woods when she was young and running into GIs hiding in the woods or being forced off the trail by an Army vehicle or convoy. She'd also told him stories of roaming the woods with his dad and other GI friends. Of going to Karlstern to play mini golf billiards or to watch the bison in the big wildlife enclosure over there. Of sneaking into Sullivan Barracks where his dad was stationed at the time and visiting him while he was on CQ (Charge of Quarters) duty or on guard duty at the barrack's back gate, which lead right into the forest. And of exploring old tunnels and structures that weren't supposed to be there.

"Maybe not the bunkers. Everyone knows about them," Mike said as an idea started to form in his mind. "But I might have a place that is out of the weather and not marked on any maps. We just need to find it."

Mike dug through the attic cabinet that held their hiking and skiing gear. He had already pulled out three backpacks and stuffed the bottom of each with a sleeping bag and a rainsuit and was digging through the collection of winter gear when the shrill trill of his grandparents' landline phone suddenly reverberated up and down the three flights of their home's stairway. Heart thumping in his chest, he stepped through the attic door and looked over the railing to the second floor. Silvia came out of his bedroom with an armful of clothing she had retrieved for him. Her eyes were wide as saucers. In front of her on the floor lay two more piles of clothes she had retrieved for herself and Sven, who was in the basement packing food.

Mike grabbed the backpacks and bolted down the stairs. He was crossing the second floor landing when he heard Sven answer the phone below him.

"Michaelis residence." His voice sounded calm and collected. After a moment of silence, he said, "Thanks."

The receiver clicked back onto its base. Sven looked up the stairs to Mike and Silvia. "We got to go. The SS will be here in about ten minutes."

Mike frowned at him. "How do you—?"

"Friends," Sven cut him off. "Grab whatever you got packed, we're leaving now."

Mike looked at his aunt, then both dropped to their knees to stuff the clothing she had collected into the backpacks. They ran down the stairs to find the front door open and Sven by the open trunk of his car in the short driveway.

"We're taking your car?" Silvia asked.

"No," Sven replied as he pulled out the medical backpack

he always carried with him. "They've already put an alert out on our cars. We're going on foot."

Mike looked at the shopping bag of food Sven had brought up from the basement. It wasn't much.

"We're going to need cash for food," he said.

"Papa has a stash in his office." Silvia started up the stairs.

"No time." Mike stopped her. "We'll grab Oma's grocery wallet." He went into the kitchen and retrieved the small wallet where his grandmother kept the money she used for groceries. He had never understood why Opa gave Oma what seemed like a cash allowance specifically designated to buy groceries at the beginning of each month, but now he was glad it was there. As he pocketed the wallet with one hand, he opened the next drawer with the other. As usual it was filled with candy and cereal bars. He unshouldered his backpack and emptied the drawer into its open top, then grabbed the two bottles of water he had put into the fridge that morning and the packages of cheese Oma had bought the day before. The former he put into the bottle-sized netting pouches on the sides of his backpack and the latter he added to the candy. He pulled the pack's drawstring tight and closed its flap and then went back into the entryhall to retrieve his jacket from the coatrack before slipping into his backpack's shoulder straps.

Silvia had joined Sven in the driveway. Her backpack was now full while the smallest of the three backpacks Mike had pulled out of the attic was empty and lying in Sven's trunk. Sven was carrying his medical pack on his back, the shopping bag over his shoulder, and a sleeping bag in his arm. He closed his trunk and headed to the sidewalk. Mike took a last look around the entryway, then stepped outside and locked the door behind him. He hoped he would be back, and soon.

He pocketed the keys and grabbed the sleeping bag from Sven. They hurried to the end of their cul-de-sac and the greenspace trail that ran along the eastern edge of East Town, as their neighborhood was called. It would keep them out of sight of the main road and bring them close to the tramway that would take them to the north end of town. They could walk there if they had to, the forest they were heading to was not that far, but the train would by much faster.

Moments after they turned the corner of the last house of their cul-de-sac's row of townhouses, they heard revving engines and squealing tires behind them. Mike turned to look around the corner, but Silvia held him back with a shake of her head.

"If they see you peeking, they might want to know who you are."

They were approaching the small street that ran behind their house when banging car doors froze their steps again. The street was only about half as wide as their cul-de-sac, but it dead-ended onto the paved greenspace trail and offered a clear view of anyone walking along it.

Sven carefully peeked around the corner of the privacy fencing that kept them out of sight, and immediately hugged the fence again.

"SS," he whispered. "Probably making sure nobody escapes through the backyard."

"Are they coming this way?" Mike asked.

Sven shook his head. "They're standing around the cars and a couple are huddled by the fence, probably breaking the lock to get through the gate."

"We can wait until they're through and then cross," Silvia suggested.

"Only if they don't leave anyone with the cars." Mike said as he studied the overgrown dirt berm that made up the far half of the twenty-meter-wide greenspace. It served as a soundbarrier for the highway that separated East Town and Bannholzgraben, the next subdivision, which also had a train stop. If they could cross the berm... He shook his head. The brambles were just too thick to get through with any kind of speed.

Sven followed his gaze, and his train of thought. "We can't go through that."

Mike nodded. "Then we wait until they're in the backyard."

"And if they do leave someone by the cars?" Silvia asked.

"We walk and act normal," Sven replied.

"And hope that they won't consider it odd that we're carrying all this stuff," Mike added.

Two SS did indeed stay with the cars, but their attention was on the house and yard. Mike had just passed out of their sight behind the next row of houses when the crash of breaking glass echoed from behind them.

As if the sound had been the start signal to a race, the three broke into a dead run, but soon switched to a fast walk.

Mike wondered how soldiers were able to do this as he struggled to get his ragged breath under control. His dad had regularly gone on day-long marches in his battle rattle, as he had called it, and carrying a set of packs that weighted much more than what Mike's pack did. But then, soldiers' fitness training was much more intense than the biking, hiking, and daily jogs Mike did.

They arrived at the train stop soon after and frantically checked the posted timetable for the arrival time of the next train. The next five minutes were the longest Mike had ever experienced, and his heart skipped a beat each time a car crossed the tracks at the end of the platform. The train finally arrived and none of the other passengers gave them more than a cursory glance. He still couldn't keep himself from shrinking into his seat and trying to hide from them.

Four stops later, they got off at Benjamin Franklin Village, the old U.S. Army base where Mike's dad had been stationed when he and Mom had met. But it wasn't until they entered Käfertaler Wald, the section of forest that separated Viernheim from the Mannheim suburbs, that his stomach finally started to unknot.

"So, how do we find your tunnels?" Sven asked as they walked along the forest trail.

"They're not my tunnels," Mike replied. "Mom said that beside the locked doors in the basement of the barracks, there were two small landing strips in the woods. Since my dad's barracks where she had seen the doors was one of the buildings that was razed, I figure we start with the landing strips."

It was mid-afternoon, giving them about four more hours of daylight. The high canopied pines of this forest would darken the forest floor sooner, but they should still have at least three hours to find a place to spend the night. Hopefully it was not just a spot on the forest floor. They didn't bring any tents or even tarps to protect them from the cold dampness of the ground.

"One of those old barracks buildings is still standing," Sven pointed out. "We could check it."

"And how are we going to get into it? Ring the doorbell and ask to see if there are doors in the basement that lead into tunnels that aren't supposed to exist?"

"I'm sure we could come up with some kind of a cover story."

Mike raised his eyebrows. "Like in a spy movie?"

Sven chuckled. "Yeah, we're definitely not undercover agent material."

"You can say that again." Mike smiled ruefully. "We almost got caught leaving the house, and that was with a ten-minute warning."

"I still say that they arrived quicker than ten minutes. There's no way we took that long."

"The important part is that we did get away," Silvia said. "But I agree with Mike, the less contact we have with people, the better right now." She looked at him. "Tell us more about these landing strips. I don't remember anything like that in these woods."

"Elke never told you about them?" Sven asked.

Silvia shook her head. "We didn't hang out with the same crowd, and I wasn't into exploring old ruins like she was."

Mike thought back to the old picture he found when he was eleven. "When we moved into our house in Brandenburg, an old picture fell out of a box of photos I was carrying. It showed a sandy clearing with two concrete structures. The larger of the structures reminded me of a clamshell-shaped amphitheater we had seen when we went to Disney World the summer before. But in the picture, there was no stage. Instead, sand was piled into the arched opening. It also wasn't as colorful as the one in Orlando, but to me it still looked so similar that I asked Mom about it.

"That's when she told me the stories about the old Nazi tunnels. They used them to keep soldiers, vehicles, and even planes out of sight from the Allies during World War Two. There were entrances in the basements of the local barracks. Mom saw the locked doors in the basement of Dad's building in Sullivan Barracks that were said to give direct access to the tunnels."

"The barracks were that old?" Sven asked.

Mike nodded. "Mom said you could still see the Nazi swastika stamped into the bottom of the stairway railings. Instead of replacing the railing when they took over the barracks after the war, the US Army just painted over the imprints, leaving the depression of the hooked cross in the black paint.

"The doors in the basement were always sealed with padlocked steel bars when Mom saw them, but she said one of Dad's friends found one unlocked one day. He went inside and ended up in a tunnel with stairs leading down to a flooded tunnel that was large enough to hold vehicles. The story goes that when the U.S. Army tried to explore and clear the tunnels, multiple GIs were killed by boobytraps the Nazis left behind. So, instead of risking more lives, they flooded the tunnels, sealed the entrances, and destroyed the records of them."

"And the clamshell stage?" Silvia asked.

"It wasn't a stage but a hardened hangar entrance that led underground into a large tunnel that connected to the airfield at Coleman Barracks in Sandhofen. The clearing in front of it was a skinny landing strip with dirt berms on each side. Mom said there was another one next to the one in the picture, but it was in much worse shape with the building next to the hangar completely collapsed. On the picture, you could see dark rectangular shapes right above the sand on the building's side facing the arch. Mom said that the lower of the dark shapes was the top half of a doorway that allowed them to enter the building. On the inside, the sand drift was angled down, giving them access into the basement of the building."

"Hold on," Sven said. "The Americans wiped the tunnels off the history books because they deemed them too dangerous to clear?"

Mike looked at his cousin. The idea to hide in the tunnels did seem much crazier now that they were in the forest than it had when he had first thought of it at the house. He shrugged. "We'll just have to be careful."

"Right."

"First, we have to find an entrance." Silvia said. "Considering that they were sealed eighty years ago, it's questionable that we can even do that. So let's take this one step at a time and not worry about things we might not even have to deal with."

Mike nodded. "Okay. So, Mom said that the landing strip had trees growing on it, but it definitely stood out as too even and straight to be a natural feature. And, of course, the berms marked it clearly. So that's what we're looking for. A long strip of forest that seems unnaturally even with small, perfectly straight rises along its long sides. That shouldn't be that hard." He grinned at Sven's raised eyebrows.

Mike was sure that the hangars had been within a short walk to the back gate of the old Sullivan Barracks, but after two hours of searching they were still coming up empty. Maybe they should try their luck with the old barracks building, as Sven had suggested, or maybe they should just give up and go somewhere else. If the tunnels had entrances from the barracks, then those would surely have been found by the new tenents after the U.S. Army relinquished the buildings to the Germans. And that would've been big news.

"Maybe we should just go to the bunkers, like Sven suggested," he said. "There's nothing here."

"Maybe looking for the landing strip is the wrong way to go about this," Silvia said thoughtfully. "It's been thirty years since your parents saw it, so weathering and wind could've completely changed the look of it. Maybe we should be searching for signs of the concrete buildings."

Mike frowned at her. "They were pretty big. We would've seen them if they were still here."

"Not if they were buried." Silvia shook her head. "The sand dunes of the Tante Anna Nature Preserve aren't that far from here and you said that the picture showed sand around the buildings."

"And how are we going to find buried buildings?"

"The corner of a concrete slab sticking out of the sand," Sven said thoughtfully. When he noticed Mike and Silvia's gazes had zeroed in on him, he explained. "One time, when I was picking blackberries this summer, I was following this trail through some brambles. Going up a small hill, there was that piece of concrete sticking out that reminded me of a stair step, but I didn't look at it closer and the thorns had caught my bare legs a few times already, so I just moved on."

"Where?" Mike asked in excitement.

Sven puffed out his cheeks as he slowly exhaled, in thought. "The trail came off the fitness trail that's over by the old water works. But I don't remember exactly where." The corners of his mouth turned up as he looked at the others. "But I'll recognize it when I see it."

Twenty minutes later they stood in front of a thicket of bushes and brambles that was almost as tall as they. The small trail Sven indicated looked more like something rabbits or maybe foxes traversed than a path people walked on, and Mike would've easily missed it had Sven not pointed it out.

The trail led them over a small rise that the thick undergrowth had completely obfuscated. Past the apex of the rise, the trail went downhill for a good two meters into a fifteen-meter-wide depression in the forest floor. From the inside of the depression, they could clearly see its rectangular layout and the berms bordering its long sides. The underbrush was much thinner here and the tree canopy above them much thicker, giving the depression a feel of a protected shelter hidden from the world.

Mike turned in a slow circle. This could definitely be the landing strip his mom had told him about, but he couldn't see any signs of the concrete structures the picture had shown. An overgrown hill that was a good six meters at its tallest took up the near end of the depression. It was covered in blackberry brambles as thick as the bushes that hid the depression from view. Trails snaked through the brambles; two going up and one going around the hill's side.

Sven pointed to the left-hand trail leading up where the berm seemed to meet the hill. "I'm pretty sure it was on that trail."

Mike shrugged out of his backpack and went to investigate. It was hard to identify the exact shape of the ground because the brambles were so thick here, and the trail was barely wide enough to walk and often crossed by blackberry stalks that caught his pants. Halfway up the hill, he was just unsnagging himself from the latest stalk of thorns when he stepped on a linear edge crossing the trail. He looked down. Nothing but sand and leaves. But he definitely felt a hard edge. He moved his foot from side to side to uncover what lay below. The grey color of a concrete slab came into view. He took a closer look below the brambles around him and found more telltale signs of concrete peeking out.

"I found something," he called to the others, who had deposited their packs next to his and were investigating the other trails.

Silvia, who had been on the trail next to his, came over to help him search. After a few minutes, hidden behind some tall brambles, they found a horizontal slab of concrete with a stairway leading down next to it. The stairway was filled with large tires held in place by iron rods. In order to access the stairs, the tires would have to be removed, but from the size of the tires and the way they were wedged in, that would be hard to do by hand. Someone had definitely tried to make this inaccessible.

Sven called for their attention from the far side of the hill. When they reached him, he was standing on a large slab of concrete with jagged edges lying against the side of the hill. He pointed out others and on closer inspection it became clear that they were standing on the backside of the concrete clamshell in the old picture. Either on purpose or by nature, the large tunnel entrance had been covered by the sand-rich soil of this forest, which had given the local flora a foothold to grow. As the trees grew, roots had found their way into the buried concrete and caused the concrete slabs to crack and shift, which in turn brought some sections of the buried structure back to the surface.

While their latest find showed that at least one of the hangars, or what was left of it, still existed, it was clear that it would not be the access point into the tunnels they were looking for. But the old picture had shown that. Thirty years ago, when the picture was taken, the hangar had already been filled with sand, leaving only the very tip of the arch uncovered, so it was very unlikely that they would find an opening to the tunnels through it. Their chances for finding that access lay much better with the blocked stairway Mike and Silvia had found.

As they had suspected, they were unable to remove the tires or iron rods, but time and weathering had worked in their favor and they were able to enlarge a hole and squeeze through.

The room below was partially filled with sand, forcing Mike and the others to crouch as they explored the rectangular space. Its center, by the stairway, was semi even, clear of debris, and dry. A cut-out in the wall to the left was filled with debris, making it hard to see if it was an alcove with a collapsed wall or a hallway that had been filled in. To the right, the ceiling angled downward as if there might have been a ramp or stairway under the sand. The sand in that direction had also a downhill slant to it, but nowhere near as steep as the ceiling. Five meters in, the two were just barely half a meter apart. Sven illuminated the opening with his flashlight but it was hard to see how far it went.

"Let's get our bags in here," Silvia suggested. "Even if it's a dead end, this will be a good place to spend the night. We can even build a fire without having its light give us away."

Sven and Mike agreed and went to collect their bags and wood while Silvia dug a pit for the fire. By the time they had brought everything in, it was getting dark outside, turning the below-ground room nearly pitch black. They built a fire and made a meal of some of the rolls and cheese. They hardly spoke, each lost in their own thoughts. Within minutes of finishing their meal, Mike was back on his feet. He grabbed his flashlight and started for the angled ceiling.

"You don't want to wait until morning?" Silvia asked.

"Daylight is not going to change the amount of lighting down here, so we might as well keep going." He didn't add that keeping busy kept his thoughts from dissecting what had happened. The last thing he wanted to do right now was let his thoughts wander, because his imagination would run rampant with what was happing to his mom and grandparents, and what the future might look like for all of them.

Silvia nodded. "They'll be all right."

Mike paused to look back at her. "I hope so." This was exactly what he did not want to do; discuss the possibilities. "I can't lose her, too."

"Tante Elke is the toughest woman I know." Sven looked at his mom apologetically. "If anyone can deal with this, it's her."

Silvia nodded. She looked as if she wanted to add more but then, instead, gestured past Mike. "Can you see anything?"

Mike swallowed the knot that had formed in his throat and smiled thankfully at her. He turned back and studied the small gap at the back of the room. It looked like it continued on but in a downward angle, which the beam of his flashlight could not fully illuminate. He went to his knees, then his stomach as the space tightened. The sides of the opening closed in as he crawled forward, forming a sandy pipe-shaped tunnel of sorts that continued to go downhill at an ever sharper angle. About two meters down, it seemed to open up again, but getting there would be a pain.

"Well?" Silvia asked.

"It gets tight for a bit but I can see it open up again further down."

"You're still on sand, aren't you?" Sven asked. "Maybe we can dig out some of it to widen the opening."

Mike agreed; even moving the sand by hand would be better than snaking himself downhill face-first without knowing what to expect on the far side. He held the flashlight in his mouth and placed both hands onto the sand in front of him to push himself back out.

The sand under his hands suddenly gave way, starting an avalanche of sorts that took the sand below his chest with it. He tried to catch himself to keep from going over the edge, but wherever he grabbed, the sand gave way. He slid forward with a yelp and quickly became engulfed in the sliding sand. Sven and Silvia yelled behind him. Something hit Mike's foot. Maybe Sven trying to grab him or Mike was kicking the concrete ceiling as he fought to halt his momentum. Sand filled his nostrils and the flashlight ripped from his mouth.

An eternity later, he finally came to a stop. He sat up and wiped the sand from his face. It was pitch black around him, but he could move and breathe, so he was not buried under sand. He looked around.

"Mike. Mike!" Sven yelled from behind him.

"Sven. No, you can't go in there," Silvia said.

"Mom, I gotta go after him. If he's buried under sand, he only has a few minutes."

"I'm fine," Mike called out. "Not buried."

"Are you hurt?" Sven asked.

"No, don't think so. But I lost my flashlight. I can't see anything."

"Can you see our light?" Silvia asked.

"Hold on." Mike looked around.

"Be careful moving," Sven said. "Don't know what's around you."

Mike nodded. Then, remembering that they couldn't see him, he said, "Yeah, just give me a minute."

He explored his immediate surroundings with his hands. The sand felt harder here, as if it wasn't as deep as it had been up top, but he couldn't find the incline he had slid down. He rolled onto his knees to turn around. Light shone from up ahead. Feeling his way with his hands, he moved toward it. A few moments later, he finally found the sandhill he had rolled down, and he could see the beams from Sven and Silvia's flashlights better.

"I see your light. But it doesn't go very far. You'll have to come closer for me to see better."

"Okay," Sven replied. "I'm going to come toward you. Mom, hold my legs."

The light brightened and dimmed as Sven moved, before shining down the sandy hill right into Mike's eyes.

"Got you," Sven said. "Oh, sorry, didn't mean to blind you." He shone the light at different angles to illuminate the area around Mike. "That doesn't look too bad. Mom, I'm backing out to turn around. I'm not going down there head first."

The light disappeared, then returned as Sven made his way down to Mike, dragging his backpack behind him.

"I said, I'm fine," Mike said.

Sven nodded. "Then my exam won't take long, will it?"

As soon as he could sit up, Sven paused to look around. The sandpile formed the beginning of a small tunnel that curved to the right fifteen meters from where Mike sat. The air smelled musty but not too stale and the arched walls and ceiling were uncracked and solid. Ancient-looking lamps hung from a conduit that ran along the arch's apex, but otherwise the tunnel was unmarked. Sven slid the rest of the way to Mike and handed him his spare flashlight before evaluating him for injuries.

"Talk to me, boys," Silvia called from above.

"Mike's got a few cuts and scrapes that I need to clean up, but it looks like he found what we're looking for." Sven grinned. "Though I would've prefered he do it in a less dramatic way." He opened his backpack and pulled out alcohol pads and a butterfly closure.

Mike hissed as Sven cleaned the small cut on his forehead but didn't argue the point of needing to make sure it didn't get infected.

"How safe is it down there?" Silvia asked.

Sven looked at Mike expectantly. "You're the engineer."

Mike frowned. He was a civil engineer, but he had no experience with underground structures. The tunnel looked solid, however. He said as much. A few minutes later, Silvia appeared at the top of the sandpile with Mike's backpack. She tossed it downhill then went back up to retrieve her own pack and the bag with the food, which they had not been able to fit into their backpacks when they had repacked them.

Mike's pack stopped tumbling three meters from the bottom, so he climbed up to grab it. As he did, he felt around the sand for his missing flashlight. It took a concerted five-minute effort before they finally found it.

A few minutes later they moved on. The small tunnel led to a huge tunnel that could easily fit three semi trucks next to each other. To the right, it was blocked off with sand and dirt. To the left, it led off into darkness.

Fifty meters down this tunnel, they came to a Y-intersection where the tunnel they had been following and another, parallel-running tunnel of the same size, joined into one. Ten meters past the intersection were two doors across from each other. They tried the one on the left and after some effort got the old hinges to move.

The door opened into a two-meter-wide tunnel with straight walls and an arched ceiling that led to another door twenty meters away. A centimeter of water covered its floor, but it wasn't deep enough to get their feet wet.

"I don't think that's a good idea," Sven said when Mike started down the tunnel.

"I just want to see what's beyond that door."

"Yeah, but this tunnel is dry, so that water is not coming from this side."

"These doors are not water tight," Mike pointed out. "So if there's water over there, it should be at or below the waterline in here."

"Should is the imperative word here, and the word that has ended many a silly venture," Sven said with a grin, but he followed his cousin nonetheless.

They walked to the next door and looked through the small rectangular window in its upper half. But without light on the other side of the door, they couldn't see anything. This door took a bit longer to open and squealed loudly as it did.

The first thing they saw beyond it was water, and the submerged steps past the doorjamb. The tunnel itself was as wide as the one they had left behind but not as tall, and it was filled with vehicles and equipment that sat partially or completely submerged in water. The rusting hulks of halftracks, trucks, and what might have been a tank or two sat bumper to bumper with vehicles and machines that were not as easily identifiable.

Sven whistled quietly beside him. "Man, this would be a nice arsenal to have."

"After eighty years in water, I doubt any of it is recoverable."

"I don't know, I've heard of old tanks being pulled out of bogs and lakes and restored."

"Yeah, with heavy use of specialty equipment and reproduction of parts. Plus, the expertise and time needed to complete the work."

"I see multiple hatches and cargo beds above the waterline. Maybe there's stuff that never got wet."

Mike doubted that the humidity and passage of time had left anything unscathed, but his mind still puzzled through the challenge of how to check.

"So, here is proof that the Americans did indeed flood tunnels with vehicles in them," Silvia said from behind the guys' shoulders. "And they did that because the Nazis boobytrapped them."

Mike and Sven looked at each other, then turned to watch Silvia walk back to the other tunnel. Once she stepped through the far door, she looked back at them.

"We're going this way."

The second door, across the large tunnel, was just as hard and loud to open, but it lead into a stairway that could've been in any old building. At the bottom of the stairs was another, much heavier, door.

Its locking mechanism and hinges moved much easier and opened into what Mike could only describe as a dormitory of sorts. It had two large rooms, two small rooms, and a latrine with rusted showerheads, toilets, and a long trough-like sink.

A few metal frames remained of what could've been bunkbeds, chairs, and tables, but any parts that were not made of metal had long since disintegrated. Otherwise the complex was devoid of furniture and equipment. What was also missing was a mechanical room and a kitchen or similar space.

He said as much.

"An outpost, then, or a guard station or barracks for the landing strip," Sven suggested.

Mike nodded in agreement.

"So, there must be a larger complex further down the tunnel," Sven ventured.

Mike shrugged. "Unless they were supplied by the aboveground barracks."

"Let's go and see what else we can find," Sven said and turned toward the exit.

"Why don't we just stay here?" Silvia asked. "This place is dry, secure, and out of sight, exactly what we were looking for."

"Because there might be something better further in," Sven replied.

"There also might be booby traps."

"We'll be careful."

"Says the guy who has never had to deal with traps, explosives, or any other kind of life-threatening device."

"We're too close to the entrance, way too easy to find."

Mike ignored their continuing argument. He was much more interested in studying the structure around him. Until they fell silent, at least. He turned to look at them and found both looking at him expectantly. He tried to remember what they had said last, but couldn't even recall who had spoken last.

"Well?" Silvia asked.

They definitely had addressed him, then. "Well, what?"

"What do *you* want to do?"

"Oh. Well. I'd like to go further in, too. To see if there are other accessible exits and where they take us."

He didn't mention that he also wanted to know how the infrastructure of the complex was set up. Where did the electricity and water come from, and were those sources still viable and accessible?

Silvia didn't like his choice, but agreed to move deeper— with the caveat that they would be more careful.

The next doorway they found led into a warren of tunnels that reminded Mike of a hamster maze. Multiple branches dead-ended in cave-ins or brick walls but they finally found another complex of rooms, this one much larger than the last one. It had rooms in a variety of shapes and sizes connected by hallways or other rooms. Many were empty, but some had skeletal remains of furniture, giving at least a hint at their original purpose. The latrines were the easiest to identify, of which there were multiple, in different sizes. They also found a large kitchen with the remains of an industrial-sized cast iron stove. And finally a collection of smaller rooms that Mike easily identified as a command or control room. Unlike the other rooms in the complex, which had the standard wiring for lighting and a power outlet here and there, these rooms were brimming with cables. Multiple power outlets and clipped wires hinted at missing consoles, and one of the rooms boasted a wall plate with multiple connections that were marked as telephone and telegraph lines. A large board on one wall held the faded remains of a map. Mike could make out the name Darmstadt, but a large chunk of the map was missing and the rest was faded to near unreadability.

Mike sighed in frustration and disappointment. A map to help them find their way around this maze of tunnels would've been nice. They continued to search, looking for any hints of where they might look for exits to the surface or where they were in relation to the above-ground topography. If the tunnels had been marked with any kind of signage, it had faded or been removed. Of course, they could remap this warren, but that would take a long time and without having any indication of what sat above them, it would be a pain to do accurately.

Mike was considering how best to go about that when he spotted a door that seemed different than the others. It appeared bulkier and more industrial, with two heavy-duty lever-action handles. The room beyond it was ominous and filled with hulking dark shapes and old piping, other debris scattered throughout the floor.

He had found the mechanical room, or at least one of them, and it was filled to the brim with the machines and equipment that had supplied this complex with the utilities it needed.

But the best part was that attached to the far wall, and covering most of it, was a metal plate with lines and symbols engraved into it.

And he was able to read it—mostly, anyway.

"Sven," he called over his shoulder.

Sven, who had been studying a large boiler in the far corner, turned to him. "What?"

"I think we need to contact your friends. I might have a solution to their problem of being too easily found out."

"How so?"

"You see this schematic? It's the blueprint of the power and water lines running through this complex. And since the ceiling of every tunnel we've come through has been lined with the conduits that hold these lines, it's a pretty safe bet that we now have a decent map of the tunnel system. And from what I'm seeing here, it's huge."

"How huge?"

"As in covering the whole Rhine valley between Karlsruhe and Frankfurt huge. If even half of what is shown here is in as good a shape as the tunnels we have been in, it would be the perfect place to build a resistance movement that is completely off the digital grid." Mike traced his finger over the schematic, following one water line along a series of tunnels and rooms. "Call our friends."

VIRTUTE ET OPERA: BY VIRTUE AND ENERGY

The Motto of the ancient Kingdom of Fife

David Appleby

Introduction

The world stood in silence, over eight billion people figuratively holding their breath, the shockwave still reverberating round a damaged planet. Everyone alive at the time remembered where they were on 9/11; everyone alive now remembered where they were during the Washington Inauguration massacre and the devastating aftermath. Scribes would later attribute that as the first leaf in autumn to fall, then, like ripples spreading across a pond, the leaves fell faster and further from the tree, scattered and blown by the wind of chaos. Eventually, autumn passed into winter and America was dead.

America was dead, and the rest of the world followed just as they always had. China imploded; Russia, as so many times in the past, overreached. A newly isolationist Japan turned inward, its historical distrust of gaijan again fueling mistrust of the few trading vessels that managed to avoid the piracy now rife in the surrounding seas. Africa, the Indian Sub-Continent, and Indochina descended into violent tribalism, racism, and brutality, although some enclaves survived better than others. Thus, Thomas Hobbes' warning from history manifested itself worldwide—life indeed became nasty, brutish, and short.

Yet amid the chaos, in America, in a dozen or so hidden places, hope slumbered.

Hope slumbered, oblivious to The Collapse, to the fear and terror of the billions, to the plight of the normal man.

Throughout the world thousands of micro-battles were fought, daily struggles between the haves and have-nots. Yet in some places the fight became more than survival; it became one of knowledge and eventually its preservation.

Part One

Fife, Scotland, November 2027
St Andrews University
23 November 2027, 15:00 UTC

Alan Christie had been many things during his lifetime. Student, teacher, researcher, writer, speaker, accountant, and then unfortunately a manager. Now as he trudged slowly down the stone corridors of St Andrews University, he prepared to take a new role, one that he had never once in his life envisaged, that of a politician, and maybe soldier. If, and only if, he could get the University Senate and administrative Council to agree with the plan.

Beneath the heavy grey sky, the walk to Parliament Hall in St Mary's College seemed to take an eternity although it was less than five minutes from his own office. Now as he approached the meeting hall, he went through everything again, straining to find any objection he had not already considered and had a defense ready. Ready for anything, he hoped.

Over the previous six weeks, since the late-night conversation over a bottle of Talisker with his friend and deputy Phillip MacAllister, alongside Head of the School of Physics Trevor Minto, they had mapped, brown-papered, and finalised what they had taken to calling The Plan. Multiple permutations, backup, and contingency routes had been discussed then rejected, only to be brought back in. Hours, indeed, days had been spent on equipment and materials, then the sometime fractious but good-natured bickering over The List. After various quiet conversations with other senior senate members, Alan was ready. The question was, would the University and the city be?

Two hours later he had his answer

"Alan, Alan, stop. Just wait a minute." Trevor chased the chancellor down the hall. "Just bloody wait a minute before you go and do something stupid, again. You'll do that, and you know you will. So, before some poor wall, or, Heaven forbid, a student gets in the way, and you get another broken knuckle, just wait up!"

Alan turned; "Why Trevor, why?" Leaning back on the wall, he looked at his friend. "Why... they shot us down."

"NO, they didn't, and you know it. They merely, and I stress this, merely suggested that some parts were unworkable. You even said we may have to address at least one of their issues. For pity's sake, did you actually think they would just roll over and go woof?" Trevor said, then looking back toward the senate hall, he shrugged. "Just means we've more work to do, and I propose your office with that new malt from Crail. Is Phil back yet?"

"Not sure. He did say he'd be back before dark. If not, he's smart enough to stay out overnight and head back in the morning. I would," Alan said.

"Well, we'll see shortly, I suppose. Just remember, he's cycling and..." Trevor desperately tried to hide the grin forming.

"And... anyone else on the road has no idea how much danger they are in. Forget raiders..." The thought of Phil on his old three-speed had taken a little of the sting out of the meeting result and he too was beginning to raise a smile. "You're right, of course. We, or rather I, didn't think this through properly. Malt it is, although Heaven knows it's getting harder to source these days. Still needs to be opened sometime and Phil's going to need it, not to mention the two from your department playing sheepdog and looking after him. They're both UOTC and know protection, although I fear road safety may not have been in their training."

As both men wandered back out toward the street, it was rapidly approaching sunset and both men knew energy rationing meant streetlights were now a luxury St Andrews couldn't afford any more. Besides, most of the lampposts themselves had already been removed for the metal to be recycled.

Interlude One:

The Collapse had come hard to the UK, swift and devastating. Fife and particularly St Andrews had been lucky, and everyone there knew it. Isolation meant the ravages of the rest of the UK had largely although not completely passed them by. The trigger, the shot heard around the world, had been the

New Madrid disaster, and, although the seismic social waves had taken longer to propagate, they had washed up on the shores of every country in the world with the same economic impact the 2004 tsunami had on the Indian Ocean rim.

Hyperinflation and the collapse of trade routes led to international trade virtually ceasing overnight; then, for the UK, came the ultimate economy killer. Russia invaded Western Europe in a massive resource raid. A sudden need to be self-sufficient brought down the government, a series of weak coalition parliaments collapsed, the longest lasting a mere twelve months. In a desperate attempt to do something, the last standing authorities pulled out and dusted off the old Cold War continuity of government plans and devolved power to the regions. Some areas fared better than others.

OP Breakfast, overlooking the River Forth.
Call sign O21A
23 November 2027, 19:30 UTC

Major Derek Palmer lifted his head and looked over the lip of the OP toward the river south of him. New model NVGs from Leuchars gave him a clear if predominantly green view of the river below. Scanning right to left and moving slowly so he could pick up any movement, he saw the sight that still saddened him. The tangled wrecks of the Forth Bridge and Queensferry Crossing now sat in the water, starting the slow process of decay. The rail bridge was the only one of the three not destroyed. Not because they didn't want to, but rather that they couldn't afford to waste the explosives blowing the solid monument to Victorian over-engineering.

Derek and his oppo Walter were about half a mile back from the bridge and overwatch to the CP on the rail bridge. Since they were unable to blow the bridge, two trains had been deliberately derailed to block the up-and-down lines. A narrow corridor through the two necessitated the checkpoint and now constituted the sole access north on this side of Fife. The Kinkardine bridges had also been blown at the same time and limited access to Fife from the west, limited but not totally stopped.

"Sunray, Sunray, this is Oscar two one alpha, message over," Derek said.

"Sunray, send, over." A crackled response was barely audible, as Derek had the volume cranked right down.

"Longview across, I can see a small group attempting crossing. Over."

"Sunray, confirm numbers and intent. Over"

"Numbers approximately thirty, three zero, persons, small arms only visible at this point. Intention unknown. Over."

"All stations south, Sunray. Standby. Out."

"Oscar two one alpha, Oscar two one bravo. Message over."

"Oscar two one alpha, send, over."

"Sunray says tactical fire decision is yours; however, protection of two one bravo is paramount. Don't let them get jumped again, Derek."

"Roger. Out."

Derek nudged Walter in the ribs. "Stand to, mate. Here we go again."

Derek and Walter, apart from being ex-Forces, had several other commonalities. Both had served in the Cold War, based with the Berlin Brigade charged to resist a Soviet takeover of West Berlin, both knowing their life expectation in that case was minutes rather than hours. The second was they were both well over sixty, both slightly larger than they used to be, and both members of the local veterans Saturday Breakfast Club at Loch Ore. The club having volunteered en masse when St Andrews put out a call for help from anyone with military training, they were immediately snapped up and commissioned. Both men had seen action; both knew that the blocking force Derek currently commanded was the line that had to be held. That was why they were there—they were veterans and in place as a steady hand to calm and encourage the youngsters.

"Walter, power up your goggles and have a squint at this." Derek was back with his head over the lip, safe knowing that the scrim made him virtually invisible.

"Okay, I see two groups left and right of the tracks. Concur?"

"Walter, look at the old lifeboat station." Derek laid a gentle touch on Walter's shoulder, prompting him to look down to the right of the bridge.

"Oh, fuck. Where did that come from?"

"I've no idea, but I think we need to make it go away."

Derek was getting distant memories of battle training; he

knew it reminded him of something, but he couldn't quite place it, then it hit him. Remagen, the Ludendorff bridge. Although this time the roles were reversed, and he was defending. Yet he knew as local OIC he would apply those bloody lessons from the past and hopefully not lose any more kids tonight.

"Charlie," he said to a smaller figure behind him, "I can't risk an open radio net call with company over there. I need you as a runner to Sunray. Okay, facts. The people crossing have got their hands on a Stormer. It's Starstreak enabled, and we're well within its range gate. That gives them potentially twenty rounds of nasty to throw at us. It's also Morpheus equipped so it may be able to DF on us. As of now the AAC boys and girls at Glenrothes are officially grounded on my authority. If the crew down there are smart, they've rebuilt the IR and Pulse to manage ground targets and we're lovely elevated and exposed here, happy happy joy joy."

"Derek," Walter jumped in, "they're almost to the end of the first span and into Choke One. I think we need to discourage them a bit."

"Wait one, Walter." Derek turned back to Charlie. "Go..." He turned back around. "Okay, Walter, let Bravo know they are free to engage at their discretion. Tell them not to expose themselves, and probably best to Noddy up in case they get as far as Choke Two."

Walter lifted the field phone, a hard-wired link to the CP, and relayed Derek's orders.

Derek turned to the fourth member of the OP squad. "Ready, Steve? Same as before. You run the bridge; I'll take the Stormer if necessary. Walter's got nothing to do, so he's paying for the Banjos later."

"Ha, bloody ha... I'll go as far as making a wet but after that you're on your own. You are senior, Rupert," Walter said.

"Okay, time. Walter, keep the CP line open. Steve, you know the drill, one warning. I've got the Milan. Tac control is with Bravo for engagement call. Standby. Standby."

Forth Rail Bridge
23 November 2027, 19:45 UTC

Giles Hamilton was scared. A lifelong follower, he moved as necessity dictated to power, to protection. Now he found himself stuck in a dark place both physically and mentally. The darkened bridge loomed above him and the track bed made for uneven footing. Fine icy rain was soaking into his clothes, but the chill didn't come only from that. Still, since The Collapse his refuge amongst the Neo-Comms had represented stability, semi-regular food and safety. Tonight, that was changing. He still wasn't sure how he had ended up in an assault team; he was still a civil servant carrying an SA80, not a soldier.

Slowly, he and the rest of his team advanced. The lead scout checked ten meters ahead for traps and IEDs. Ten was too close, Giles thought, twenty meters would be better, and twenty kilometers ideal. Despite the cold chill in the air, and in his belly, he continued forward into the darkness as they approached the brick arch at the end of the first span.

Suddenly his world changed, the safety of the darkness violently stolen by the sudden glare from a bank of floodlights that had been appropriated from a football ground. He felt pain in his retinas and skull as his optic nerve overloaded. This was Choke One, put in place as the sole non-lethal deterrent.

"Walkers on the bridge, walkers on the bridge. This will be your only warning. Step to the middle of the tracks and turn back. Repeat, this will be your only warning." The voice boomed from hidden speakers.

As suddenly as they lit, the lights extinguished. Left behind was an old motorway warning sign, salvaged from the Queensferry crossing, at the exit from the arch, itself big enough to almost fill the gap. The message scrolling across was unequivocal. In glowing orange words, it read LETHAL FORCE WILL BE USED BEYOND THIS POINT. NO FURTHER WARNINGS WILL BE GIVEN.

Suddenly that too extinguished, leaving Giles and the team knowing they had been spotted, and with their night vision destroyed they had no choice but to retreat. However, the team boss had other ideas and as Giles knew this wasn't a democracy.

"Right, forward. Keep going. Anyone straggling, I'll put a fucking bullet in you myself. We're doing this for the people, and that demands sacrifice. Tonight, that means us, if necessary, but we go across."

OP Breakfast, overlooking the River Forth
Call sign O21A
23 November 2027, 20:00 UTC

"Boss, they're not buying it." Steve looked through the spotter scope, then moved slightly to his right and slid the butt plate of the L115A3 rifle gently against his shoulder. "Permission to engage at Choke Two?"

Derek thought. Tactical control was with Bravo, but this had happened before, and they'd lost five people. He wasn't prepared to have that responsibility and guilt on him again.

"Walter, tell Bravo we're taking back tac control and will initiate. Steve's up for the first shot, so he goes then Bravo. Steve, see if you can spot the boss, and if so, that's target one." Derek thought. "Also tell Bravo, on Steve's shot it's Disco time for ten seconds."

Walter relayed the orders and then gave a thumbs-up.

Derek took one more view of the overall picture, knowing that as soon as shots were fired, he'd lose that big picture rapidly. "Steve, the show's all yours. Fire when ready."

Steve snugged the big rifle in tight, and took in the sight picture and the built-in windage indicator. He had been regularly shooting distances with the STIC and knew the range to virtually every sleeper on the bridge. From previous engagements, many bore signs of damage from the huge 8.59mm rounds and were stained with dried blood. Drawing a breath then letting it half out, he gently and smoothly applied three and a half pounds of pressure on the trigger.

Forth Rail Bridge
23 November 2027, 20:05 UTC

Giles heard the shot a second after it hit, and panicked, looking anywhere for some form of cover. However, his night vision was still impaired, the green blob still sitting behind his aching eyes. He felt a thump as the body of the team leader bounced off him as it fell, an eight-inch hole blown in the back where Steve's massive Lapua Magnum had hit the exact center of the target's body mass. Derek's Disco order now took effect. Three banks of football floodlights now started strobing at 15 cycles per second, triggering acute discomfort and in one case an epilepsy attack. Added to the visual bombardment, high- and low-pitched aural triggers via the loudspeakers caused further disruption. Then Bravo added a deadly element to the mix. Two belt-fed Minimi Light machine guns opened up from the CP, cutting into the would-be raiding party as two burning CS gas canisters dropped from overhead into the middle of the mob. Amidst all this chaos, Steve continued slow regular accurate shots and Derek's MILAN launch went almost unnoticed.

Whilst being a considerably older weapon than the Javelin that replaced it, the MILAN was still as potent as ever. Travelling at two hundred meters per second, it covered the launch to target in just under six seconds, striking the Stormer just below the Starstreak mount and exploding. The impact sheared the mount, dislodging the whole section, cracking a missile body leading to a catastrophic fire as the double-based propellant ignited. Then the whole south bank of the river lit up like daylight as the remaining missiles cooked off, shrapnel tearing into a reserve force yet unseen by Derek's squad.

On the bridge, Giles was sobbing in fear. Unable to see or breathe properly, he staggered, looking for something solid to rest against, then was mercifully relieved of this burden by a Minimi round that took the top of his head off. No feeling, no pain, just instant blackness.

With the massacre on the bridge and the loss of the Stormer, the short battle was over.

Leuchars Station
24 November 2027, 07:00 UTC

Colonel Angus MacDonald finally had his command in Leuchars Station. Not the way he wanted, it was by attrition rather than appointment, but it was his.

He had come through the ranks after joining the REME in the early nineties, a career built on the principle 'We're all in this together.' Unfortunately, the latter had led, on occasion, to some disappointment from the higher ranks and more than a few chats without coffee. However, twelve years after enlisting he had reached staff sergeant with the prospect of getting his warrant in a year or two. Then one bloody day in Afghanistan his career, literally, exploded in a different direction.

He had been NCOIC of a small FOB acting as a bellringer for Kandahar when a special forces CH47 went down under fire seven miles away. Sporadic radio communication said everyone was injured, and although they had perimeter out, the area was too hot for a Medevac by chopper. Ground support was over an hour away, so MacDonald decided to deal with it.

Selective hearing loss prevented him hearing his boss shouting over the net to stand down whilst he rounded up volunteers. His REME team was joined by a few from the Engineers who had been reinforcing the FOB and two medics. So against orders he led a convoy of three Warriors, three armored Land Rovers, and an unarmored ambulance to the crash site. Bulldozing through the insurgent lines, he applied the shock and awe approach. Given the speed of his arrival, the surprise was almost total, and he recovered back to the FOB with the survivors and at a cost of three wounded amongst his people, one of them being him.

This led the brass to a conundrum. He had defied orders and deserved charging. However, the French Foreign Legion detachment he had rescued and their team commander Captain Nevard insisted on his recognition. So a field promotion to first lieutenant followed the Military Medal from both Britain and France, and off to Sandhurst for a crash course in being a gentleman. They already knew he could command.

"Okay, stand at ease, everyone." MacDonald again managed to preempt the ten-hut call. "Whose go is it first to ruin the morning?" He strode forward to look at the Chinagraphed map. Markings showing current activity and that of the previous 24 hours was always kept on paper. Electronics, as they knew, could fail.

"I will, sir," said Major Duggie Sinclair, the current watch commander. "And I'll keep it brief. As usual, any questions, please feel free to interject. OP Breakfast had a brief engagement with assumed Neo-Comms yesterday evening. Nothing unusual, nothing we haven't seen before, except..." Sinclair paused.

"Except what, Major? Do enlighten me." MacDonald sipped the black coffee he had brought into Leuchars command bunker.

"Except, sir, they had a bloody Stormer, sir. Full load outside so at least eight Starstreaks attached."

"I notice the past tense. Is there bad news attached?"

"Not really, sir. Thirty people tried and failed to cross. I can't even say they tried to force a crossing, and an unknown number retreated under sniper fire. Sniper had a rather lovely view of the area due to the remains of the Stormer burning away. Current estimate is forty enemy KIA on the bridge and shore, unknown number WIA. Total expenditure: one MILAN HE round, roughly five hundred Minimi 5.56 rounds and a dozen L11 rounds. From the after-action report, it seems Disco worked rather well."

"Thanks, Duggie. Anything else overnight? Perimeter or internal? I've been worried about the southwest quadrant for a few days now. Also the Stormer worries me, a bit like the Warrior at Kinkardine Bridge last May. I assume someone has checked round the back to see we're not missing one. I know we only have three and would hate to think none of you could count!" MacDonald raised an eyebrow and stood with a wry smile,

"No, we still have three, although only partial loadouts for them." Duggie checked his notes again. "One raid on a farm at Dollar, nothing stolen. QRF from Saline was there in ten minutes. We might want to think about strengthening the flank there."

"Ok, thanks, Duggie. Start an OPLAN and let me have something within forty-eight hours." MacDonald knew there was a very good chance it was already in Duggie's stack of paperwork. "Avril, your turn. Anything national or international we didn't know yesterday?"

Captain Avril Carter, MacDonald's intelligence chief, looked down to her notes. "Nothing really new. Inchcomb and May OP's reporting lights in the area around Leith area and possibly something around the Castle area. That's new, we've really seen nothing there since St Giles burned last year, we're monitoring. That's local in a nutshell, nothing from Northwood HQ since the hold-fast order in June. Some comms from the NATO deep bunker at Mons although the burst data links are getting shorter. Seems the Russians are running round like headless chickens; most units seem to be uncoordinated and may be pulling back."

"Thoughts? Be honest," MacDonald said.

"It's Afghanistan all over again for them. They're fucked, they know they're fucked, and they don't know how to get unfucked. They've overstretched; supply lines would never have fully supported the op in the first place, plus they severely underestimated the opposition. 1st and 10th Panzer's Leopards are still rumored to be running around behind lines using old

Reforger caches. The Panzer-grenadier units have gone insurgent. Mountaingruppe are making the whole Alps very unhealthy for anything with a red star. The French, Dutch, and Belgians have gone full Maquis and together with general civil resistance it's giving the whole op one big bloody nose."

"Sounds like some good news. Prognosis?"

"Chinese fire drill, full pullout in less than nine months. Although we have no idea how long unit cohesion will last with the surviving NATO units after. Nothing to fight means desertion, troops go AWOL back to their families same as is happening here. Some modelling with the School of Economics at St Andrews may help us understand the aftermath, but frankly we've never been in this much shit before, and the models probably can't handle it."

"Okay. So essentially, same as yesterday. Russians will retreat and everything will collapse further. Ironic, isn't it? The Russians invade and it's the only thing holding Western Europe together." MacDonald finished the last of his coffee. "Right, listen in. Here's what I need done. Duggie, threat analysis on the western flank, Kinkardine upwards to the Tay. Head over and have a proper look yourself. Also assign someone to speak to Clayton Lively. I'd like to know if his bunch of lunatics can come up with anything else like Disco. Avril and I are heading over to St Andrews. Alan Christie has been after a chat for a week now and it gives Avril a chance to skull sweat with the Economics people. Dismissed."

The room cleared rapidly.

Part Two

St Andrews University
24 November 2027, 12:00 UTC

Three slightly nervous men—Phil, Trevor, and Alan—awaited MacDonald when he arrived at Christie's office, escorted by the two students from the UOTC, both in belt order carrying SA80s, the same two that had accompanied MacAllister the day before. The two students turned to leave but Christie stopped them.

"Please stay both of you, take a weight off and relax, kettle's on and we've opened a new jar of coffee. You've both had an awful night."

Both students looked surprised but complied, dropping their webbing and taking the two chairs furthest from the chancellor.

Alan turned to MacDonald, who couldn't quite hide his surprise at seeing armed students. "Colonel, please park where you like. Coffee's instant and the T-Bags are second use but guaranteed hot."

"Thank you, Chancellor."

"Alan, please."

"Righty ho, in that case I'm Angus unless we're with the troops when we have to be a bit more formal." He turned to the two students. "I'm assuming Alan has a reason for having you here that I'm not privy to; however, given you are technically still civilians even if officers in training, we'll work out something."

Slightly intimidated, the student nearest the door answered first. "Thank you, I think sticking to sir would probably be best. We don't want to pick up any bad habits." She shrugged. "I'm Kelly; this is Neil."

"Okay," said Alan. "That's nicely de-formalised the room. Trevor is playing Mum with the drinks and I'm about to ask a big big question of all of you." He took a mug from Minto and continued. "Angus, I gather one of your staff is over at Economics right now? I can save you a bit of time as I know their preliminary results. In short, we can sustain this standard of living for a while, up to three years. However, after that we'll all need to cut back. The only model that works and maintains any kind of cohesive society is much more agrarian. We cannot afford to support the towns and city as they are now. We can come back to that later."

Alan waited a moment. Instead of the shock he expected all he saw was resignation on their faces. Even from MacDonald.

"So, how do we maintain society? How do we avoid a Manchester or Liverpool?"

Blank faces stared back.

"Phil, Trevor, and I have some ideas and the beginnings of a plan but we need the help of everyone in this room, including you two," Alan said, nodding to the two students. "Yesterday, Phil, Kelly, and Neil went down to the Troywood bunker. You know, the old ROTOR and Regional Government one near Crail? They got back early today and confirmed the condition along with answering a long list of questions Trevor had. Trevor would have gone himself except I needed him for the Senate meeting yesterday afternoon." Alan cleaned and adjusted his glasses.

"We've been talking amongst the three of us for a while now and and... err... We've come up with an idea, well, two actually. The first I just mentioned, moving Fife to a sustainable basis. This is what Trevor and I spoke to the Senate about yesterday. The second needs to be much more close-hold. Ideally, just everyone here. If not, as few others as possible. Phil, would you like to take it from here?"

"Thanks, Alan," Phil MacAllister said, rubbing the rather large graze and rapidly forming bruise on the left side of his face. "Does anyone here read science fiction?" He looked around;

MacDonald nodded slowly, as did Kelly and Neil.

"Okay, our second idea is based on an idea from *Lucifer's Hammer* by Larry Niven and Jerry Pournelle. Yes?"

Neil had raised a finger. "Don't tell me on top of the world falling apart we're about to get hit by a bloody comet?!"

"No." MacAllister said, smiling. "Although that would really be the final nail in the coffin, wouldn't it? We've an idea that we've borrowed from the book. After the impact, one scientist sacrifices his life to preserve books, specifically those with the knowledge to help a civilization survive and rebuild." He paused as if gathering his thoughts.

"That's where I was yesterday, along with Kelly and Neil to look after me. What we're proposing is to go one better. To store as much cultural and technical media in the bunker as possible. Some original items such as the First Folios, the Gutenberg Bible, and the like. The rest we take some top-end servers and load as much data onboard as we can."

MacDonald managed, just, to hide his surprise. Kelly and Neil failed totally. Alan gave a carry-on gesture.

"In deference to another great book, we've called it Plan Hari. Basically, we're going to try and preserve the entire knowledge base of both St Andrews and Dundee Universities."

Now MacDonald looked surprised, although he only said one word. "Ambitious."

"Ambitious, yes; impossible, no." Alan walked across to the large map of Fife pinned to the wall. "What we plan is this. The bunker is going to be our repository. It has two floors and a total of 27,000 square feet of area available. Some of that is already allocated to Trevor and his team, although I'll let him explain his side in a minute. We chose the bunker as it met three requirements. One, it's close; two, it's got an independent water supply; and three, it's easily concealable and secure." Alan looked around and seeing no immediate questions continued. "The only question remaining is security down the line. This is one we still need to answer. However, for the moment I'll let Trevor explain his side."

Trevor smiled and took over. "My side, or rather my team's side, is technical and power management. Obviously, we cannot depend on the grid even if we are relatively certain of maintaining the current partial service locally. So, we had to be inventive, and my team is very good at that! In fact, all I did was point them in the right direction. First a little history. In 2018 Rolls Royce started working on what's called SNRs or Small Nuclear Reactors. By 2021 they had it down to the size of a house. Then other breakthroughs had it down to the size of a standard shipping container by late 2022. My team took this, and we scaled down further. We now have a powerplant capable of generating twenty megawatts for a hundred years. It's the size of a small van, but modular and uses passive cooling. We propose using two of these in the bunker with the cooling supplemented by the artesian well water. This gives us secure power."

MacDonald indicated he had a question. "Not wishing to rain on the parade, but wouldn't these be better used in the general community?"

"Not at all, that's what the others coming off our new production line are for." He smiled, slightly smugly, and continued. "That's part of our main plan to make us self-sufficient. One in each village or community, along with a push to get as much land into cultivation as quickly as possible. So, with the SNRs and the wind farms, we are aiming for being more than self-sufficient; we're also looking toward a regular surplus that can be used for trade. Things are going to get a lot worse out there before they get better. We can use power in the barter economy we're seeing emerging, and we'll be able to barter from a position of power." Trevor smiled at his own pun; Alan winced, obviously having heard it before. "Your assistant should be getting the full brief from the Economics team."

"Okay. I see the main part, but I'm not sure exactly what I'm doing here," Angus MacDonald said.

"That's easy. "Alan said. "We need to borrow your brains, your best intelligence people, and if you have any, we'll take a psychic, too. We need to plan and predict when and more importantly how we're going to open the bunker."

Phil leaned forward in his chair. "The problem is one of logistics combined with security. How do we seal the bunker but safely make sure the secret isn't lost? Who do we tell? Who can we trust? This is where we're stuck, so we're open to suggestions. Obviously we can't ask anyone to hide for fifty or so years underground even if we could provide the provisions. We also need some help with transport logistics and local security."

"Okay, thanks," MacDonald said. "All makes sense, and, for what it's worth, I along with my command will do everything we can do to help, with the exception of anything that weakens the Fife perimeter."

"Thank you, Angus, I don't think we can ask for more than that," Alan said, looking relieved. "Although we weren't entirely joking about the psychic!"

Interlude Two

Following the devolution of governance to the regions, there were some successes, however, also many spectacular failures. In some areas frightened people remained in the cities. These rapidly devolved into vicious urban hellscapes. Gang warfare split along political, sectarian, and racial lines. In savage communities, gangs fought for dominance and territory. The larger cities, Liverpool, London, Manchester, and similar, became disease-ridden visions of hell as first healthcare, supplies, and then utilities failed. Hundreds of thousands died of simple, curable infections, millions more from starvation, and those that fled found a countryside population unwilling to support hungry mouths with, suddenly, no transferrable skills. Many took shelter with the strong and communities allied en masse with an emerging despotic faction.

The Neo-Comms emerged in the early 2020s in northern England, a local copy of the American agitators Antikap and funded the same way. With the fall of central government, their influence spread rapidly, and, in some areas, they became the default government. Drawing their ideology more from the latter half of *Animal Farm* than anything written by Marx or Engels, the two-class system began anew—although no longer two classes, it rapidly became two castes, with a serfdom kept in place by strict rules, capital punishment, and fear.

As with any dictatorship they rapidly became expansionist and looked outward. Lothian was stripped bare, and Edinburgh was in ruins; however, across the water lay an even more valuable target. Fife.

Three months later
St Andrews University
14 February 2028, 10:00 UTC

"Good morning, everyone. Welcome to the fortnightly update meeting," Alan said, looking round the room at the now familiar faces. "This is really a strategy and progress meeting, but first, I'd like Angus to have a chat, as the last two weeks haven't been fun for his people."

Angus stood, as usual sipping from Alan's strong-brewed coffee he had come to love. "Right, if I could sum it up in one word, it would be, err... challenging. We're seeing more and more attempts by the Neo-Comms to either infiltrate or influence Fife. They've set themselves up as a Fifth International although underneath it's corrupt to the core. Avril has worked a miracle and managed to get a few ex-14 Int Company people deep undercover and we're getting semi-regular intelligence. By the way, it's Major Carter now; she's taken charge of Intelligence and Logistics. Major Sinclair has been bumped to lieutenant colonel and my 2IC. Field promotions, but I've no one above me to say no, so my word stands." He paused and looked at the empty mug.

Trevor, knowing it was coming, had the next one ready.

Angus continued. "We've seen several attempts to force the bridge, but with the setup now it's going to be almost impossible. We're concerned about water crossings; however, there's been nothing at all since the exodus during the sacking of Edinburgh. The problem is mainly the west. Multiple raids in the last weeks. The QRF is working well and just hearing an Apache out of Glenrothes seems to get them to bug out. We've reenforced the flank there but if we're going to have major trouble, that's where it's coming from. Duggie has contingency plans and has started a program to rip down every road sign in Fife and parts of Kinross. He then wants to set up, so we deny the main roads and force anyone onto the back roads. He has trees set already to drop and set up abatis at key points. To be blunt he's setting killing zones which could be any tree-lined road. Questions? No? Over to you, Alan."

Alan shifted in his chair. "Okay, we have news both good and bad. Project Hari and good first, I think. Data collection is going well; we estimate seventy-five percent collected, collated, and loaded so far. That will be complete in ten days. We've decided to go cold with the data farm so that's going to stay powered down after testing. The bunker itself now has SNR capability and is fully powered. Monitoring systems go in this week, and we've done it with a team of only five. I have to say thank you to Trevor, Kelly, and Neil for making this happen so quickly. Bad news—we've still no idea how to lock and time it. That goes right back to our first meeting. On the economic front, we're seeing some resistance from the town population to moving. No one disagrees with the plan, but no one wants to move. SNR capability is being rolled out at the rate of one per week, and we've requisitioned every electric vehicle we could for common use. Obviously, owners are not happy and there's some serious grumbling but it's working; we have core transport. In short, it looks like that side will work, may take a while yet, but will."

Like with Angus, Trevor had Alan's tea refill ready and handed it over.

"Okay, that's the main briefing. Anyone have anything to add?" He looked round as everyone shook their heads. "Okay, let's keep hammering on and anything urgent, shout. You all know I will!" He grinned and made a grand 'out' gesture to everyone in the room.

Outside in the corridor, Kelly and Neil dashed after Trevor, attempting to corral him before he got to his lab, catching up to him on North Street as he headed west toward the School of Physics.

"Dr Minto, Dr Minto, can we have a word please before you get buried in paperwork again?" Kelly said. "Neil and I would like your permission to go outside the group with the lock and time issue."

"We've a very vague indication we may possibly have something to work with. It's a longshot now but think it's worth a go," Neil said. "Oh, and can we borrow a car? We need to go to Anstruther."

"Can I ask what your 'vague indication' is?" Trevor said, although he looked more amused at their obvious discomfort than actually expecting an answer.

Kelly spoke up again. "Actually, sir, we'd rather wait until we know if it pans out. Even by our terms it's a bit out there."

"Okay, I'll trust you for now. Take one of the electrics. Any idea how long you'll be?"

"At least overnight." Kelly looked at Neil, smiling. "We're going to the pub for the evening."

"Ah, do you need expenses?" Trevor dragged his wallet out and opened it. "Here's fifty pund, and you'd better not be financing a piss-up at my expense."

"Would we, would we really?" Kelly cocked her head and smiled. "Besides, Neil falls over after two pints!"

"That's a lie," came the protest. Neil too grinned. "I can drink at least three."

Anstruther, East Neuk of Fife
14 February 2028, 19:00 UTC

Neil pushed the door of the Boathouse Bar open, feeling the wave of warm fug roll over him, a nice change from the belting rain outside. He and Kelly shouldered toward the bar, busy at this time as most tried to be home before the power rationing kicked in; SNR capability was new and not fully rolled out. Besides, many here were fishermen, an early start the next day guaranteed by the tides.

"She's over there," Neil said, pointing to the far corner and waving. "Head over; I'll grab drinks. Usual?"

"Yes, although a dash of water in the malt. You always forget."

Neil turned to the ancient bar as Kelly headed toward the lady sitting in the corner, who rose as she approached.

"Hi, I'm Kelly. Neil's on bar duty and will be over in a minute." She held out her hand and got a warm handshake in return. "Neil's told me a lot about you, Professor Brixham, but not why we're here and not your office."

"Firstly, it's Natalie, please, not professor. I get enough of that in the office. Besides, I'm not up to St Andrews much these days. Renaissance Art history isn't actually wildly in demand now." She sat back down. "Neil was a bit vague as to why here as well. He knows I prefer the Dreel Tavern. Still, as a son he's always been vague bordering on obscure. The whole physics thing becomes gibberish when he opens his mouth, well, physics from anyone's mouth, actually." She grinned just as Neil arrived, bearing the drinks.

"Hi Mum, how's Dad?"

"Same as usual, moaning, although expanding to a smallholding is keeping him occupied." She turned back to Kelly. "He's another historian, although military, in his case."

"So why here rather than the Dreel, and why so urgently?" Natalie said, eyes glaring at Neil as only a mother interrogating a child could.

"Err... Mum. Err... Well..."

"Spit it out," Natalie said. "Assuming it's not a sex scandal."

Neil turned bright red, but Natalie's joke did its job.

"Okay, do you remember the other Christmas talking about someone called Basil in here? You just said at the time he'd mentioned working for NASA in the past."

"Basil? Oh. Bernie Sampson, you mean. Yes, but that was a long long time ago. He said he worked there but left in the late nineties. Some kind of security officer, I think."

"Just to poke the braincells, do you remember anything else? You mentioned he said something about working on long-term spaceflight."

"Okay, you are now buying my drinks for the rest of the evening for the braincell crack." She reached over and swatted him round the ear. "Yes, he did mention the Mars and Beyond Program but never gave much away. Think he was worried someone might hear him; for years he jumped every time a tourist walked in."

Kelly looked up. "Sorry, Neil said Basil and you said Bernard. Am I missing something?"

Natalie stifled a chuckle. "His name is Bernard, Bernard Sampson, but when he moved to the village, oh, I think in 2002, he worked his way through the pubs until after a couple of years he'd drunk the town dry of Basil Hayden's bourbon. When that became unavailable after the economic disasters, he was forced to imbibe the water of life instead. So, we all call him Basil now and he goes along with it. He's gone native and actually works at the Kingsbarns distillery now along with, like today, the occasional fishing trip helping Alf. I saw them get back as I arrived, so they should be here in an hour or so. Now, Kelly, since my son is buying, would you like another drink? I assume you'll stay tonight. Spare room is aways made up." She looked pointedly at Neil. "Aren't you meant to be at the bar by now?"

Three quarters of an hour later, two older men walked into the bar to a raised chorus of hellos. Natalie nudged Neil on the elbow and pointed. "Basil is the one on the left. Do you want an introduction or are you happy to stammer your way through it yourself?"

"Introduction, please, Mum."

The trio stood and, led by Natalie, walked across the now quieter bar. On first impressions, Basil was typical for the local workers, roughly six feet tall, hard muscle from the boat and shoveling grain at the distillery, although tending to fat around the waist with late middle-age spread. However, there was an edge, something darker Kelly couldn't quite place. As they approached, he looked suspiciously at Kelly and Neil then behind them toward the door, although that quickly faded as he recognised Natalie.

"Professor, good evening. Forgive me, bit scruffy at the moment and probably smell of fish as well. Join me? Alf's talking about the trip and he's ecstatic that the herring are back. Good news for everyone, we think." Basil gestured with a join-me wave. "So, Professor Brixham, to what do I owe the honour?"

Natalie leaned forward. "Good evening, too, Basil. I can't quite place it. Is the aftershave cod or mackerel?" The snort behind revealed she had caught Kelly just taking a swallow of her drink. "Actually, I'm just playing matchmaker. These are my son Neil and Kelly from the University. They've got a couple of questions. I can't help them but said maybe you might?"

"Can't think how." Basil's voice was mainly local, but something underlying hinted at a more distant origin. "So, how can I be of assistance?"

Neil spoke first. "Firstly, not to be rude, but is it Basil or Bernard? I don't want to offend."

"Either. Gave up worrying what people called me years ago."

"Okay, then, some background. Kelly and I are working on something, and we'd like your help. Mum said you might have some background that could possibly assist. It's just an idea now but we're looking at a long-term project that needs some management. Mum said you'd worked with NASA on long-term spaceflight. Anything you can give us on that would be useful. Stress management, enhanced sleep, boosting alpha waves, anything like that." Neil paused.

Basil's face had gone as white as his white fisherman's gansey and the hand holding his pint had developed a tremor. As the colour continued to drain out of his face, his eyes darted, as if in panic, round the room.

"Are you okay, Basil? Is something wrong? Have we said something to upset you?" Neil stopped again, putting an arm out and gently touching the older man's wrist.

"No, no," said Basil. "I just didn't expect to have that come back to me, especially not here. What do you really want to know, because I can't give you a lot? I do have to say your mother knows that I didn't leave my previous employer on exactly good terms, but then she knows the basic story." He paused and looked at Natalie. "She knows most of my stories by now."

"It's okay," said Neil. "I was just worried by your reaction. For all the world just for a moment you actually looked like you'd seen a ghost."

Basil looked up with watery eyes. "That's because I did, lad. It's just ancient history catching up with me. Can you give me a few minutes? I need a bit of time to think. I may not be able to help you directly, but I may have something that can."

Kelly spoke quietly from the other side of the table. "Can we spend the few minutes buying you a pint or a dram, then? You look like you need one." She walked up to the bar and nudged into a space next to where Alf and another fisherman were deep in conversation.

Basil sat for a few minutes, his face unreadable apart from the odd twitch under his right eye. Eventually he looked up. "I'll be back in a few minutes. Just need to head home quickly." He stood and grabbed his heavy jacket and swung it on, with that leaving without another word.

"Is he always like that, Mum? He looked terrified for a minute." Neil raised his pint and finished the last drops.

"Neil, Kelly. There're things you need to understand about Bernie. He has, as you may have gathered, not had an easy life. From what I know, and you do not repeat this—" She tapped a finger on the table. "—he left America under a cloud and is very frightened. From what I suspect he's not Bernard Sampson, but I have no idea who he really is. It took years for him to stop jumping at shadows. There's something there but I don't know all of it. He spent years travelling round the far East but eventually ended up here and settled into the village well. He does take a long time to get to know and trust people. If I hadn't been here, you wouldn't have got the time of day from him. But... If he trusts you, you can rely on him."

A cold draft wafted across the room, announcing Basil's return. As he headed to the table with a small bag tucked under his arm, Neil took the empty glasses and headed to the bar.

When Neil returned, Basil looked around again. "You have to know this is my baby, my insurance policy, although none of that matters now." He took a long swig of his beer. "Have any of you heard of CHILLY? It was part of the long-term space exploration projects. NASA wasn't just looking at Mars, they were looking much further. When I, err... resigned if you will, I brought this with me. I honestly don't know if you can use it, but it's yours now. For me Anstruther is all the insurance I need now." Basil said with a quick glance at Natalie as he slid an old disk drive across to Neil. "As for tonight, you'll buy me one more beer then that's it for me, otherwise I'll be more hungover than Alf when we take the boat out. Just remember, I'm here and always open to a free pint." He smiled and tapped his now empty glass. "Neil, Kelly, just remember everything is different now; the world we knew is gone, you have to change your mindset. Trust no one. Except me, of course!"

"Thanks, Bernie, this will mean a lot to many people," Kelly said. "I'm speaking for both of us. If you ever need a friend, we're here."

"And me as well," said Natalie.

Dundee University
School of Biosciences
27 February 2028, 19:00 UTC

Professor Evelyn Moore was short, sixtyish, with a confidence that no obstacle put in her way would survive contact. Working up to head the Biosciences school had been her ultimate goal. No ambition for higher office—she just wanted to lead and direct research. Bureaucracy and paperwork were there to have petrol and then a match thrown on. However, today the obstacle had been intellectual and at the moment may as well have been solid diamond, but she'd crushed diamond before...

"Trevor, I get the idea. In fact, I love the idea. We have a couple of post-docs working on something similar. But I do have to say this is a completely different way of looking at it. Some of it borders on pseudoscience. The approach to decrystallising tissue is novel, to say the least."

"Eve, by novel can I assume you mean unworkable?" Trevor dropped his head slightly and smiled.

"That's not what I meant, as you full well know. Some of the chemicals here I've never heard of. Hell, some of them shouldn't actually be possible to compound. But we're supposed to push boundaries, aren't we? You and I have before." She looked directly into Trevor's eyes, and he could feel the blush starting at neck level and moving upwards, heat in his face increasing as he slowly turned scarlet.

"Okay, okay... You still haven't answered the question. You've just restated the problem." Trevor frantically tried to steer the discussion. "Can you do it, though?"

"Of course, given enough time."

"How long is enough time? Are we talking days, weeks, months, or some post-pension date?"

"Days no, weeks maybe, months probably."

"Months we don't have. Try for weeks?"

"We'll try, you know we will. I've some ideas where to start; nothing definite but a start."

"Right, the hardware is under Neil's management. He and Kelly have the whole department at St Andrews and a good chunk of design engineering here, too. Luckily it's not original research, just duplication."

"Yeah, luckily. Right." Eve rolled her eyes. "Trevor, you do know how dangerous this is?"

"Unfortunately, yes. It's still the best option, though."

"Okay, away with you. I have work to do." She dismissed him with a smile. "If you ever want to push the boundaries again, you know where I am."

Trevor fled.

Interlude Three

The Collapse left a failed world. Hopes and dreams of billions died in six short months. The death of international trade was followed by the almost complete loss of international communication following the Kessler Syndrome event in early 2026. The loss led to isolation, not only internationally but also within national borders. Phone and internet connectivity died as submarine cables were swamped by traffic. Governments, or what was left of them, prioritised these routes and again the common man suffered.

Throughout the collapse and follow-on, Fife took swift action, becoming isolationist and protective of its borders. Access routes were blocked or destroyed, aggressive patrolling led to one of the safest areas in Britain, and local economic changes created a home-grown currency named after the old Scottish coinage. Rationing was enforced then lifted in part as the Council worked to make the local economy self-sufficient. Power needs were taken care of by the universities at St Andrews and Dundee. The population was deployed to ensure utilitarian principles held and that the Council would do its best to provide the best outcome for the most people.

The military remaining put itself under the control of the Council as the Fife militia and assumed a business-as-usual posture, just with a smaller area to protect.

Part Three

Outside his office, Alan could hear a church bell summoning people to the Good Friday service. Church attendance had grown rapidly following The Collapse and this almost guaranteed that any stragglers would be pushed to find a pew. Alan however had other problems. In the scheme of things they were good problems to have, but problems nonetheless. His reverie was disturbed by a sharp tap.

"Come in, Angus." He'd known at once who it was; everyone else knocked softly as to almost not disturb him. Angus had become a close friend and enjoyed making the chancellor jump. As Alan looked up, the colonel plonked himself in the chair and deflated.

"Coffee, I assume? You look shattered."

"Long night, I'm afraid. The Neo-Comms are trying something new since Duggie sewed the western flank up. We've had over a dozen small boat raids, normally targeting a high value resource. The fish warehouse at St Monans, flour plant in Kirkaldy, places like that. It's hard doing a full coastal watch as well as landside. Anyway, I believe you summoned me."

"It's really I need your guidance. I phoned the base and asked Avril down, too. "Alan stood and walked over to switch the kettle on. "We're almost there, almost. However, between us we have to make the hardest decision of all."

Another rap on the door indicated the arrival of Major Carter. Alan got out a third mug.

Once tea had been served, he continued. "We are currently five weeks away from being able to activate Operation Hari. Name's changed as we're well beyond planning now. The vault is full, system tests have completed, it's consumables now, then good to go. The hardest part is now the staffing. We have three operational CHILSS units based on the American design, although I have no idea why they didn't do anything with technology like that. Anyway, we need to staff it and we need trained people. I have two volunteers, you can probably guess who, and now a third space. I'm open to suggestions."

Avril shifted in her chair. "I assume you are meaning Kelly and Neil? Are they up to it? Do they understand the full ramifications? Essentially, they are both going to die for sixty or seventy years. No one they know will be alive, and we can't even begin to predict the world they will wake up in."

Surprisingly it was Angus who replied. "Avril, they're both UOTC trained, and I think with some help from the boys from 23 Reserve in Dundee we can get them right up to speed. I think though they'll need a steady hand as the third place. Give me twenty-four hours. I'll get Derek up from the bridge. They're back in the hole this week and I'm sure a week in turf lodge being cut short will not upset them in the slightest."

"Avril, can you do one piece of work for us?" Alan asked. "It's way out of your usual field, but I can't think of anyone who could it better, and you do have a knack with obscure data."

Avril's expression was cautious. "Okay... what do you need me to do?"

"Simple. I want you to live up to the name of the operation. I just need you to predict the next hundred years."

Leuchars Station
1 May 2028, 09:00 UTC

It was the first time they had all been together, but Angus and Alan now had all the key players in place. From the University came Alan, Phil, Evelyn, and Trevor. From the military was Angus, Duggie, Avril, Derek, Walter, Steve, and Charlie. Kelly and Neil stood slightly to one side, already feeling distanced from the main group. Only here in this room and now had it become real. Still enthusiastic but now tempered with caution. No longer theoretical—they were going to have a longer nap than anyone since Ichabod Crane.

"Right, listen in." Angus started the briefing. "This is the final planning meeting and go/no-go point. Major Palmer and his team are here in two capacities. Firstly, they have been overseeing Kelly and Neil's training at the gentle hands of the 23rd SAS in Dundee."

"Gentle, my arse," a voice muttered sotto voce.

"May I continue with your permission, Mr. Brixham?" Angus said with a stern glance. "As I said, 23rd have put them through their paces. Full basic CBRN training. Weapons familiarisation, Hearts and mMinds philosophy and wilderness survival suitable for Fife year-round plus of course fitness."

"How could we forget?" It was Kelly this time.

"Enough! Secondly, Alan, Phil, Trevor, and I have, with consultation, added a third person to the hibernation team. Steve has volunteered to defect from Derek's band of rogues and go with them. Steve is an ex-para reg sergeant with broad experience including being the sniper on Major Palmer's team. I for one would like to thank him for his volunteering. I was going to say sacrifice, but we hope it's not that." He turned to Neil and Kelly. "Once you wake, the sergeant is in charge. No ifs, buts, or maybes. His word is law. Plus given he's a sergeant, he'll probably scare you more than I would!"

Steve did nothing but give a thumbs-up with a smile.

"Okay, last thing. Major Palmer is going to brief how the 5th is going to work, as Lieutenant Colonel Sinclair has some serious concerns about the recent raids by the Neo-Comms, so he and the major have had a skull session, so we actually have a plan. Major Palmer, over to you." Angus sat back.

"Right all, listen in," Derek said, rolling out a map on the table. "Colonel Sinclair has been looking at patterns of coastal raids recently. Most have been by RIB in and out to warehouses, but we've also had two with larger boats. Leven got hit two nights ago and the community warehouse hit for over a ton in supplies. This means despite the nature of the operation, we treat it as a live operation. Whilst low risk, we treat it as a real operation, no fucking about. Anyone pissing me off gets a size nine enema. The two platoons coming with us know what they are doing. Trust them, listen to them, and do as you are bloody told." He turned to MacDonald. "I heard about Afghanistan so, with respect, that includes you, sir." Palmer waved them into the map. "Okay, so here's how we're going to work it…"

Troywood near Crail Fife
5 May 2028, 21:00 UTC

The sun had only just dipped below the horizon, and it was deep twilight as a convoy of four trucks and a Landrover turned left off the B9171 onto the back road that led between Kingsmuir and Crail. Having gone ahead by an hour, Derek and Walter both winced as they heard the loud diesel engines, much louder than they expected given how little was powered by diesel any more. Precious supplies from Aberdeen were normally rationed for farm machinery.

"Okay, Walter, as soon as they're off the trucks, get them out in a wide perimeter then put out the listening posts as per the op-plan, everyone fully loaded, ready to go. I want trip flares further out, too, although no L109s. I don't want to ruin the venison round here."

"Yes, sir." Walter gave a mock salute as he slammed to attention.

"Fuck off, Walter. You call me sir again and the whole scran tab is on you next time we're at the Orebank." Derek smiled as the trucks turned right and up the short lane to the bunker proper. They came to a halt line abreast, and Derek reverted to Major Palmer. Two platoons jumped from the trucks and quickly formed a rough block, waiting for the off.

"Right, section leaders to Captain Michelson for last minute brief then deploy as planned. Remember, there's no conclusive information either way on raider activity, but do not take chances. Rule round here is you split before challenge so you can't both get hit by one burst, L shape if possible, challenge once, if no response, you are free to fire. Bodycam will catch everything so stick to those rules and I will back you to the hilt. If I find any of you huddling together, the CSM and I will be having words with you tomorrow."

The troops from the newly reconstituted Black Watch fanned in a widening semicircle across the open field toward the coast as two sections vanished into the woodland behind to set up listening posts at the rear on the inland side. Derek waited fifteen minutes then waved to the Landrover and gave a thumbs-up. Kelly, Neil, Trevor, and Steve emerged from the back and Alan with Dr Moore from the front.

Colonel MacDonald wandered over with Dr MacAllister.

"All secure, Major?" MacDonald checked, looking round in the now almost total darkness as Major Palmer nodded. "All right, then. Last chance to back out, people."

"No, sir. Good to go," Neil said, then turned to the others. Kelly nodded and Steve just gave the usual laconic thumbs-up.

"Okay, so Dr Minto, Dr Moore, and I are taking you down for a nice little doze."

Unused to military protocol, Moore interrupted. "Have you all taken the medication we gave you and nothing to eat for twelve hours?" Nods all round. "Good, in that case I think we're ready to start. Make sure you have more water before settling down."

Then in the background the pop-whoomph of a Schmoolie being launched was suddenly drowned by the sound of automatic weapons fire. The sky lit up as the parachute flare detonated

---

OP1 NE of Troywood
5 May 2028, 21:35 UTC

Corporal Amanda Hunter had her section spread in a broad line along a hedgerow to the eastern side of a farmhouse just over two kilometers from the bunker with a listening post slightly further out. Two Section was five hundred meters away on her right flank and she was acutely aware there was no one to her left.

A slight crackle in her right ear was replaced by the voice of Private Webb. "Got rustling ahead, Corp, nothing definite but doesn't sound like deer."

"Okay, Tony, Adam, keep it calm, report anything else."

"Got it. Although... Ahh... Shit..."

The trip flare Tony had set 30 minutes before fired and the field in front of him suddenly became a battlefield in the harsh white light of the parachute flare as he saw thirty or forty people, all armed, charging toward him. As they, obviously surprised, started to raise weapons, he did the only thing he could. Opened fire.

The first 5.56mm rounds chopped down the nearest man and Tony changed target to another, successfully dropping him as well.

"Adam, leapfrog back to the section, you go first." He continued to put weight of fire on the incoming hostiles. "Wait one, magazine." He dropped flat to reload as Adam took his place firing. "Okay, go go go."

Tony rose up and continued firing as Adam sprinted for five seconds then dropped and turned. "Ready, go go go," Adam shouted, hoping Tony could hear.

Most of Adam's shout was drowned by the volume of the gunfire; however, Tony faintly heard one go. He lowered his weapon and ran.

Hunter changed frequencies and shouted across the radio net. "First section 2nd platoon. Contact, contact left northeast. Taking incoming fire."

Troywood near Crail Fife
5 May 2028, 21:37 UTC

"Get moving right now." Derek turned to the bunker and pointed. He then tapped his radio. "Okay, Amanda, what have you got?"

"Sir, about forty hostiles heading south toward us. They tripped a flare, then the listening post opened fire. I've ordered cover fire to retrieve them but we're hanging out here."

"Okay, get your section together and hold the road and farm side. I'm going to get two sections from 1st Platoon up to you. Now listen carefully. They cannot know we're here; they must think it's just a patrol they have run into. When relief gets there, fall back south and bend it easterly away from us. I'm going to move the rest of 2nd Platoon in a north-facing line, so you'll be rejoining through our fire. IR beacons on for everyone."

"Got it, sir."

Derek turned and started barking orders as the scientific team disappeared into the farmhouse that acted as cover for the entrance. "Get your arses moving, people... NOW!"

OP1 NE of Troywood
5 May 2028, 21:37 UTC

Tony started his run back to Adam when he felt something pull at his left leg. Then he heard the *whipp* of the bullet that had just missed, but the second didn't, catching Tony in the right thigh, nicking the femur but thankfully not the artery. The leg suddenly burned then went cold and numb as the shock set in. Tony hit the ground and tried to crawl.

Adam saw his oppo hit the ground hard and immediately shouted back to the section line. "Cover, cover."

Two figures broke from the hedgerow and flanked him, slamming into the dirt of the potato field. Two more followed, bounding forward as the LSW fire team opened up to provide cover.

Adam didn't hesitate. He leapt to his feet and rushed forward, grabbing Tony by his webbing and starting to pull him toward the section. All Tony could do was grunt in pain as he tried to push with his left leg.

From the overwatch position, Hunter looked across the field. The SAW had acted as the great leveler and decimated the oncoming troops.

"Pour it on," she ordered. "Hammer the fuckers."

The LSW fire team bounded backwards, two of them running across to lift Adam's burden as both sections poured fire onto the field. Then the firing intensified over their heads as 1st Platoon joined the firefight.

With the increased fire, Adam and the LSW fire team dragged Tony back behind the hedge. As soon as they hit the road, Adam yelled, "Medic, medic..." as he rapidly opened his battlefield first aid kit, strewing the contents everywhere as he grabbed an Israeli bandage.

Troywood near Crail Fife
5 May 2028, 21:40 UTC

Derek set the deployments, then took a moment to look at the 1:100000 map of the area. The sudden realisation of what was happening was like a bucket of cold water down his back. He grabbed his radio and hoped he was in time.

"OP 4 and 5, new possible threat. Threat axis is east, repeat east. They're not after us; they're after the distillery. We've just got in the way."

OP4 SE of Troywood
5 May 2028, 21:42 UTC

Sergeant Martin Higgins redeployed rapidly to form a north-south line facing east along the A917. Derek's warning was just in time.

The Neo-Comms had landed north and south of the distillery, aiming to pincer and seize it from the land side then exfiltrate via the beach behind Cambo House. Higgins didn't plan on letting them complete the last part.

"Righty ho," he said to his section. "Wait till they get into the fire-sac then hit them. However, once we open fire, I want thirty seconds of hell then we're going to attack, not just hold, so be ready to move."

Troywood near Crail Fife
5 May 2028, 22:00 UTC

Passing through the farmhouse, the team headed down the tunnel, dropping 100 feet in the process then, passing through the double set of blast doors, entered the complex proper. It had previously been a museum before being abandoned in 2025 and left. Salvage teams had already stripped the exhibits outside for anything useful and all that remained was the farmhouse and complex below.

Trevor led the team past the powered-down data farm and the newly built climate-controlled vault for the solid art and books. Their path then took them a level lower, past the armoury, to the CHILSS room, where the three pods waited. Kelly, Neil, and Steve had already changed into plain grey jumpsuits and knew the drill, and quickly prepared themselves.

"So, goodbye then. Godspeed and sweet dreams," said MacDonald, shaking their hands one by one. "We'll not forget you, and we'll keep a light on."

Dr Moore stepped forward. "Okay, one at a time, left

wrists, please." As they held them out, she used a pneumatic spray and gave them a shot. "Good luck."

Alan and Phil stepped forward. "Can't say much more than Angus did really," said Alan. "Remember, this is irreplaceable, so make sure you know who you release it to and are certain of their motivations. If necessary, hold onto it for years until you find the right person."

Trevor said nothing, briefly touching each on the shoulder as they moved to the pods.

Neil sat back into the padding, watching the cover slide down as the drugs began to take effect. His skin tingled then burnt red hot. He tried to shout that something wasn't right, but a sense of floating and detachment overtook his fears and suddenly he felt like he was flying, then he was asleep. Over the next five minutes his pulse dropped to one beat per minute and respiration to one shallow breath every two minutes, the single breath taking the full time.

"Successful hibernation. Timer set for sixty years." Dr Moore looked up from the monitor console and activated the pod displays. "Time to leave, I think."

Trevor held up his hand. "Just a moment." From his bag he took a bottle of malt whisky and placed it on the console, along with three glasses upturned so they didn't get dusty. He placed a handwritten note... "Should be about mature by now!"

They took one last look and headed back to the surface, closing and sealing the blast door on the way. From now on it could only be opened from inside.

OP4 SE of Troywood
5 May 2028, 21:42 UTC

Higgins took advantage of the terrain and saw it would funnel the Neo-Comms directly into his ambush.

"On my command, stand by... FIRE."

His section opened up with volley fire, cutting the second half of the raid off at the head. Pressing fire virtually eliminated any reaction; there wasn't time.

"On me, charge," Higgins yelled, and ran toward the enemy, firing constantly from the shoulder and adjusting from target to target like an automaton. Several cries behind him indicated wounded but Higgins kept going. With his charge, his section, rapidly reinforced by the section from OP5, drove the Neo-Comms back to the beach.

"Grenadiers," he called.

Three soldiers moved up including, he was happy to see, Lance Corporal Sally Long, his best shot.

"The two boats out there, kill them."

For the next minute the pop-thwonk of 40mm grenades and their corresponding explosions sounded over the beach, and two flaming hulks slowly settled below the surface.

"Right, redistribute ammunition. We're moving up the road toward OP1 and we'll cut their knackers off there. Move..."

Troywood near Crail Fife
5 May 2028, 23:30 UTC

"We're mopping up, sir. Looks like we got all of them, although this isn't the last we'll see of them," Derek said to MacDonald, showing the brief battle on paper. "It was just wrong place and wrong time for us and them. I've got a couple of ideas I'd like to run by Colonel Sinclair, Major Carter, and yourself. Nasty sneaky stuff they'll love."

"My office noon tomorrow. Carry on, Major. I've one last job to do."

He turned and walked back toward the farmhouse, stopping at the Landrover to retrieve a bright orange box. He then proceeded to the main door. Kneeling down, he reached in and pulled a loop of black primacord free. Working carefully, he attached a small black box and, lifting a guard, flipped a small switch. A tiny green LED flashed three times then showed solid red. MacDonald stood and slowly walked back to the others.

"Time to move back," he said and walked to the Landrover. Around him the two platoons worked to load the trucks with the wounded and two dead. He waited until they pulled away and then drove halfway down the access road, where he stopped. He got out, taking a yellow EPC Digishot initiator with him.

"Anyone want the honours?" Nobody said anything.

"Okay, initiation in five, four, three, two, one... Detonation." He closed the trigger.

The primacord detonated with a crack and the building started to fall in on itself. As it did, white phosphorous charges detonated, starting a fierce fire which rapidly consumed the remnants of the building.

"Time to leave. We've all got work in the morning."

Deep below the collapsing walls and burning timbers, a timer clicked off and the main lights extinguished, leaving the three CHILSS pods illuminated only by the soft blue emergency lighting indicators. The built-in tablet-based instrumentation showing the sleepers' essential data.

STEPHEN DAVID HODNETT: D.O.B: 17/06/2001
STASIS:05/05/2028

KELLY ANNE STEWART: D.O.B: 15/02/2006
STASIS:05/05/2028

NEIL WESLEY BRIXHAM: D.O.B: 01/11/2005
STASIS:05/05/2028

Maximizing the Value of North Koreans

John Babb

Chapter 1—The Offer

Pyongyang, DPRK December 15, 2027
Although it was 2027 in the rest of the world, the Democratic People's Republic of Korea used its own annual dating system, which was based on the birth year of the country's first leader, Kim Il-Sung, who had been born in 1912. For the DPRK, that became year one, with all succeeding years following, therefore inside North Korea their calendar was year 115.

The founder's grandson, Kim Jong-un, the current leader of the DPRK, sat in his library in the once-luxurious Ryongsung Palace with his sister, Kim Yo-jong. Sitting in front of a coal fireplace, both of them still wore several layers of clothing to ward off the winter chill. The average December daytime temperature in the capital city was minus three degrees centigrade.

Previously, many of the homes and businesses in Pyongyang were heated for much of the year by using hot water from the nearby nuclear power plant. This was accomplished by funneling the heated water through a series of copper pipes which were buried under heavy concrete tiles in the floors. People in small towns and on small farms, however, burned coal in their fireplaces to heat, and often to use for cooking—at least, when there was anything to cook.

Three-fourths of the palace was now closed off to prevent having to heat the entire building. Also, the staff had been reduced to just a handful of necessary people.

The air in the library was filled with acrid smoke. Both

brother and sister had become thoroughly addicted to nicotine when they were grammer school students in Switzerland. But since the economic collapse, their cigarette choice no longer consisted of the fantastically expensive tobacco product from Yves St. Laurent, and now the only brand available was some fetid sort of cigarette from Uzbekistan.

Kim held up the smouldering ash of his Tashkent cigarette. "Time was I could get regular shipments of cigarettes from the Iranians. I even allowed the Americans to pay the ransom for the release of their pet prisoners with Yves St. Laurent." He curled his lip in distaste. "But now we're stuck with this." After this complaint session, the main topic of conversation followed. "I took the painful step of having gastric-bypass surgery at the start of this food shortage. I wanted our people to see that I was losing weight, thus proving that I was also having to go without the foods I was used to. I quickly lost almost fifty pounds, and at least for a short time, the people felt sorry for my obviously weakened condition. But I don't think that sympathy lasted very long."

His sister asked bitterly, "What have the United Nations and the World Health Organization done for us since the U.S. started to melt down almost three years ago? Nothing! Not a single grain of rice."

"What are the people saying about me now?"

"My two house servants always qualify their statements by saying this is what they hear in the markets. They say the people are impatient that nothing positive has happened for the last two and a half years, ever since the American economy forced the entire world into this depression."

"Are they blaming me for that?"

"Of course not. None of them have any idea that the multitude of secret attacks by the DPRK are what started this whole worldwide death spiral. One woman at the market spied the large amount of food that my house servant was buying, and tried to get her to take her two children. Can you imagine! I suppose she figured that the kids would get fed if someone who was able to buy so much food would adopt her children. It makes me worry about the safety of my staff going out to public markets."

"But are the people blaming me?"

"They say the DPRK no longer has any friends. They say that no country is willing to give us a helping hand. In previous food shortages, China and even the Republic of Korea has been helpful in providing at least some assistance. The average citizen interprets this as you personally no longer having friends that you can call upon during this extreme hour of need."

Kim Jong-un scowled. "Both the Russians and the Chinese had full knowledge of our attack plans, including the use of the nuclear weapon. But now they have conveniently forgotten their involvement, and it is we who are the world's pariah."

"One shopper said that we had spent too much of our nation's wealth on nuclear weapons, and what little wealth we had has now slowly disappeared. It was because of that, she claimed, that we now have nothing left." Kim Yo-jung stretched. "Were you able to speak to President Xi?"

"At least he took my call this time. As we had discussed, I asked what we could do for him in order to receive a suppply of food and a shipment of oil. I went through the whole litany of offers. I suggested that the DPRK Special Operations Forces was willing to go into the Chinese province of Xinjiang and wipe out the Uyghur population."

"But there are over twelve million Muslim Uyghurs. Surely that is almost impossible."

"Probably so, sister, but Xi has been putting hundreds of thousands of them in concentration camps for years. There's no telling how much he spends on such an operation, so I thought our offer might make sense. Unfortunately, he pointed out that the neighboring countries of Tajikistan and Kyrguzstan also had several million Uyghurs, and the Russians might not appreciate us attacking their allies on China's behalf."

"What about your idea to lay a radioactive cobalt line between India and China?"

"I actually stole that idea from the Americans. General MacArthur made that very suggestion after our war in Korea. He wanted to lay cobalt between the two Koreas to stop any future invasions in either direction. I think President Truman stopped that plan in its tracks."

His sister nodded. "Your plan would certainly discourage any further Indian incursions on their southern border."

"Oh, he loved that idea. Except for the problem that many rivers flow from that border region into both China and President Xi's good friends in Pakistan. He pointed out that we might end up punishing his own country and Pakistan as much or more than India. I even offered to supply any nation of his choice with nuclear weapons and intermediate range missiles."

"Surely he was interested."

"He said the world was in a perilous situation, that any further use of nuclear weapons could completely push it beyond any hope of recovery."

His sister shook her head. "So we end up with nothing—no food and no fuel? Our own country is in dire straits. We've been suffering from this terrible famine for the last six years. The last time we admitted the United Nations into our country in 2020, they cited their own definition of acute malnutrition. According to them, their definition is that at least thirty percent of a county's population is suffering from severe malnutrition, and at least one person out of five thousand are dying either from malnutrition, or because their nutritional status is so bad that they are dying from diseases and illnesses because their bodies are in such a weakened state.

"Even back in 2020, the U.N. claimed thirty-two percent of our people had severe malnutrition, and the death rate from related diseases was closer to twenty of every five thousand. And brother, we both know with this famine, the numbers could only be worse today. To complicate our situation, virtually no oil is being pumped out of the ground.

"Our population in 2020 was just over twenty-five million. Of course, no one has actually counted since then. But if what I hear is true from the countryside, some of the small towns are almost completely empty. That population number may actually be much less than fifteen million today. If nothing is done, I fear for your ability to hold our country together. Our southern kinfolk would like nothing better than to take us over."

"Our army is in a pitiful shape," said her brother. "Some of the commanders are claiming their actual troop readiness numbers are less than sixty percent. And they're probably lying about that! Whatever you say about our nuclear program, if not for that deterrent, those people in the south most assuredly would try to take over our country." Kim Jung-un displayed a slight smile. "President Xi did offer one small solution which our people might appreciate."

Chapter 2—The Chairman Mao Conglomerate

Pyongyang, DPRK December 5, 2027

"For sure, Xi made it crystal clear that the government of China was neither willing nor able to provide anything for our suffering populace. However, he introduced me to the grandson of Mao Zedong, the first chairman of the People's Republic of China." Kim puffed out his chest, preening at his next sentence. "He stressed the point that his grandfather and ours fought together at the very beginning of the cause. We then spoke at great length about his many projects in China, and how the people of the DPRK might be willing to contribute."

"Contribute? How does he plan to get blood from a withered turnip?"

"Hear me out, sister dear. The grandson is one of the wealthy investors in the ghost cities of China."

"Are you talking about those huge, modernistic cities that were built twenty-something years ago, with the expectation that several million Chinese would flock to these cities to work in a variety of industries? I thought they were a complete and utter failure."

"That much was true, sister dear, but the Chairman Mao Conglomerate purchased three of those cities for pennies on the dollar, and now they have plans in place to make those ghost cities come to life."

"And what benefit can that possibly have for the people of the DPRK?"

Kim smiled broadly for the first time in months. "He wants to employ between one hundred thousand and two hundred thousand of our people."

His sister interrupted. "I don't see how that helps us."

"That's more or less what I said at first. Here is his offer. His company will provide free transport for our citizens to the new Chinese cities of Zhangzhou, Urumqi, or Dongying before the end of January."

"Again, how does this help us?"

"For every able-bodied citizen of the DPRK between the ages of sixteen and thirty who agrees to this offer, the Chairman Mao Conglomerate will provide what is essentially a one-time sign-on bonus at the train station of one hundred kilos of rice, one hundred kilos of potatoes, fifty kilos of wheat, fifty kilos of kimchi, a hundred kilos of canned meat, and twenty liters of cooking oil. That amount of food is given to each family who provides a worker.

"The DPRK will provide an armed escort from the train station to the families' residences, as there may be bandits who will see this new abundance as an opportunity to steal these goods. When the new workers arrive in their new cities, they will be provided free living quarters in brand new, furnished apartment buildings. They all have indoor plumbing, running water, heat, and electricity. Also, they will be paid a salary so they can purchase their food and clothing. Each worker will be expected to serve their new employer for twenty-four months, and this may be extended if they and their employer agree."

She laughed. "I'll bet most of the new workers have never seen a flush toilet before, let alone used one. Maybe they'll need a class on using a toilet." She thought a moment. "Is there medical care available in these new cities?"

"Yes, and before any DPRK citizen is accepted for employment, they will be given a thorough medical exam here, prior to departure."

"Any idea how thorough this medical exam is supposed to be?"

"He talked about a long list of tests. I think their main worry was bringing diseases into the country. He mentioned venereal diseases, heart, liver, and kidney ailments, drug or alcohol addiction, and tuberculosis."

"TB may end up disqualifying a great number of our people."

"That worries me as well."

"What kinds of work will they be expected to perform, brother?"

Kim dug into his pocket. "He gave me a long list. Manual labor, working on a manufacturing assembly line, staffing grocery and clothing stores, office jobs, shipping, the entertainment industry, medical laboratories, and nurses aides."

"So how does this assist our citizens who are starving?"

"Think about it, sister dear. A minimum of a hundred thousand families will be collectively receiving ten million kilos of rice, potatoes, and meat; five million kilos of wheat and kimchi; plus two million liters of cooking oil. Not only that, but at least a hundred thousand citizens will be eating all their meals in China rather than the DPRK for at least two years."

"Hopefully we can convince these families to save back ten percent of this shipment of rice, potatoes, and wheat to be used to plant a replacement crop in May. Otherwise, they won't have food for next winter."

"That will certainly take some explanation on our part," said Kim. "This is only a one-time gift, and it won't be repeated again."

"What happens if one of our volunteers can't or won't fulfill their new duties?"

"Then a volunteer from that individual's family will have to take his or her place."

Kim Yo-jong cocked an eye in her brother's direction. "I can definitely tell you where you need to start looking for volunteers. You need to insist that the citizens you have been responsible for supporting these past years should be the first to sign up for such a program."

Chapter 3—The Pleasure Squad

Pyongyang, DPRK December 5–6, 2027

"Let's be honest, at least with each other, brother. The DPRK is a relatively small nation, yet we have more men and women in our military than any other country on earth—even including the Americans and the Chinese. What exactly are we afraid of? The last time one of the Korean security forces tried to enter the other's country, it was sixty years ago. And by the way, it was us who sent our special forces across no man's land and into Seoul to kidnap the South Korean president. Like it or not, our forces failed simply because they couldn't remember the code to enter the front gate of their president's mansion. In the confusion, they were quickly defeated by the South's much smaller force.

"So now we are trying to deal with a terrible and long-lasting shortage of food, yet we—our government—continues to feed and house this ridiculously over-sized military force. How can it be justified during this time of famine that we still have the largest army in the world?"

"You obviously don't understand the concept of military might, sister dear."

"It's like building a twenty-foot-tall fence around your garden in order to keep out the rabbits. It's foolish to waste scarce resources on maintaining such a large force. You should strongly encourage at least fifty thousand of them to sign up for the proposal from this Chairman Mao Conglomerate. Surely they can see the benefit of helping their own families obtain such a large amount of food. If that happens, we have three direct benefits. First, their families obtain these food supplies. Second, the costs of feeding and housing them as soldiers would no longer come out of the national budget. Finally, their paychecks, no matter how meager, no longer is paid from that same budget.

"Beyond that, keep your special forces units, your submariners, your nuclear scientists, and your missile experts, but dramatically cut your total number of men and women in the rest of the armed forces to well under a million. We simply can't afford it any longer."

"I'll take your advice under consideration, sister dear."

"Good. There is one more large problem which must be addressed, and if word got out to the citizens of our country as to what has been going on during a multi-year national food emergency, your very life might be in dire jeopardy."

"What are you getting at?"

"Tell me about your Pleasure Squad, brother."

"Oh, that's just a few girls to entertain our troops."

"Really? I have it on good authority that you have two thousand girls who are used in one way or another by you and high-ranking members of the military, as well as many of your so-called business associates."

"I don't know who your *good authority* is, but that figure is ridiculous."

"Have you decided to start lying to your only remaining sibling? These girls are divided into entertainers—like singers and dancers—plus masseuses and sex workers. So apparently, this is the way you buy the loyalty of your military officers and the senior people in some of your favorite private industries. And from my information, their housing, food, and a stipend are paid for by our government. I also understand that the members of the Pleasure Squad are promised an opportunity to marry a military officer at the end of their so-called service."

"You have completely distorted the information."

"So I assume your own wife is supportive of this arrangement, brother?"

"My own wife has not been able to provide me with a male

heir. Frankly, I'm tired of even looking at the woman."

"You and I carry exactly the same genes we inherited from our father and grandfather, and you speak about your wife as though she has betrayed you by not having a male child. It is widely acknowledged by scientists that the father is usually the determining factor when it comes to predicting whether a child will be male or female. What about my own son? He has the same genes from our family as any son of yours would have. What has he done to be ignored by you, his only uncle?"

"It's not the same thing, and you know it, sister dear."

"Is this why you maintain this group of prostitutes, so that one of them might bear you a son? What comes next? Is it your plan to divorce your wife and marry a whore so that you can claim you suddenly have a male heir?"

"I refuse to discuss this further."

"Then let's go back to the important topic of how your average citizen would feel about this relationship, particularly when they are enduring a famine, and for most, a total lack of electricity in their everyday lives. Yet here you are providing two thousand prostitutes for the entertainment of yourself, your officers, and your friends, as well as a place to live, food to eat, some money, and at least some access to electricity."

"So what is your solution to the situation you describe?"

"Send every last one of them to the Chairman Mao Conglomerate. After all, one of the job descriptions is entertainment. That solves your problem of two thousand totally unnecessary mouths to feed."

"I'll consider the ramifications of your suggestion, sister dear. However, you know our policy of not allowing children of mixed race to enter our country."

"So you're saying if one of our DPRK girls becomes pregnant in China, and tries to return home to our country in two years, that—what—she will have to prove that the father is also Korean?"

"The guarantee of maintaining a population unspoiled by other nationalities has been our policy for our grandfather, our father, and for myself."

"All I can say is, you'd best consider what you will say to your people if word gets out about this Pleasure Squad. It could mean your downfall."

He narrowed his eyes, "Are you threatening me?"

"I'm doing my best to give you good advice."

Chapter 4—The DPRK Response

Pyongyang, DPRK December 16–January 31, 2027

Once the offer from the Chairman Mao Conglomerate was made public, there was very little delay amongst the citizens of the DPRK. The original offer had been for 100,000 workers, then generously increased to 200,000. Kim Jong-un had been appreciative, but was highly doubtful that his citizens would meet that number, thinking their sense of loyalty would mean that most would want to remain in the country of their birth. However, within three days, 2.3 million people had applied for inclusion in the program.

Of course, the Conglomerate could not begin to meet that number, but realized they would be able pick the most ablebodied workers from such an overwhelming number of applicants. Three days after the application deadline, a train bearing twenty million kilograms of rice, potatoes, and potted meat; ten million kilos of wheat and kimchee; and four million kilos of cooking oil had departed central China.

China possessed quite a few high speed rail lines, allowing speeds of up to 200 kilometers per hour. Unfortunately, the rail system in the DPRK was poorly maintained, with many tight curves and loose connections, only allowing trains to move at a maximum speed of twenty-five kilometers per hour. This necessitated unloading all of this freight, which had traveled to a switchyard immediately west of the Sino-Korean Friendship Bridge, to be reloaded onto DPRK railcars, pulled by DPRK engines, to be able to proceed further into North Korea.

This would prove to be more than a two-week process, as North Korea did not own the necessary 2,000 passenger cars to move 200,000 people. In fact, they could only come up with a maximum of 380 passenger cars, and so six trips were necessary, spread over an eighteen-day period.

A group of workmen were hired specifically to accomplish the transfer of food products from Chinese freight cars to DPRK freight cars. Who knew that a half-dozen of those workers were members of the Wo Shing Tong? These triad mobsters were able to leave one of the railcars containing 110,000 kilograms of potatoes unloaded, yet still connected to the Chinese rail system.

When this was finally discovered upon the arrival of freight cars in Pyongyang, the Conglomerate had no choice other than to summon a replacement railcar, containing 2,200 fifty-kilo bags of potatoes. From that point forward, until the various trains and cars departed North Korea in the ensuing three weeks, everything was locked down and placed under twenty-four hour surveillance by the DPRK military.

The logistics of such an undertaking were nightmarish in complexity, and were overseen by two men, Major General Hye Hwang from the North Korean side, and Cheng Wang, representing the Conglomerate in China. First steps were to send Conglomerate representatives to each of six major DPRK cities—Wonsan, Nampo, Hamhung, Chongjin, Sinuiji, and Pyongyang—where they would begin the interview processes, to include determining medical status and performing laboratory studies.

Each location would be responsible for selecting 33,333 successful candidates. Each would be issued a Chinese work visa with a two-year expiration date. The workers would then be given a departure date, and told to report by six AM on that day with a single bag of clothing and personal gear. They were to be accompanied by a cart, wagon, or truck that could accommodate four hundred and thirty kilos of food. Once that food was handed off to each worker's family, the individual worker volunteer would be escorted to a passenger railcar to await departure within twelve hours.

Workers from Wonsan would then depart to the Friendship Bridge, where they would transfer from the Korean rail system to the Chinese Railway, and then leave immediately for Kangbashi, China, which was 1,200 kilometers to the west. When the workers from Wonsan arrived, their train would return to its starting point to await the arrival of the next group of 33,333 workers from Nampo, who would also be sent to Kangbashi.

The process repeated itself for workers from Chongjin and Hamhung, who would be sent to the city of Urumqi, located almost 4,000 kilometers to the northwest, perched on the edge of the Gobi Desert and immediately south of the highest elevations in China. Again, after unloading, their train would return to the Friendship Bridge.

The fifth city of departure would be Pyongyang itself, and

of those almost 34,000 volunteers, two thirds of them were members of the DPRK armed forces. Additionally, 1,920 volunteers would come from the Pleasure Squad. Unfortunately, eighty of them had been unable to pass the STD component of the medical exam and were left behind, much to the disapproval of Kim Yo-jong. The remainder were ordinary citizens both in and around the capital city.

This group would be sent almost directly south, 1,000 kilometers to the city of Dongying, China, which was located on the eastern shores of the Yellow Sea. The temperature in Dongying was far more temperate than any location inside the DPRK. Another 33,333 workers from Sinuiju were the last group to depart their homes in the DPRK, and everybody was immediately put to work.

The new workers from the DPRK were assigned two to a small apartment, fed two meals a day, lived in a comfortable environment, and luxuriated in having running water, an indoor toilet, sink, and at least some electricity. They also slept on two mattresses, and did what little cooking they needed in a small pressure cooker. They worked only six days per week, which they had not expected, and they were transported to and from work by either a subway or buses. Of course, they missed their families, but were almost universally proud that they had been able to contribute in such a tangible way to their relatives' food resources.

Chapter 5—The Ghost Cities

February 1–20, 2028

Between 2011 and 2014, China used more concrete in the construction of homes and industries than the U.S. did during the entire first quarter of the 21st century. The majority of this work was done in thirty to fifty medium-sized cities throughout China, where the government was trying to attract new residents from nearby small towns and farms. The construction cost was estimated at several trillion dollars U.S, and something close to half a quadrillion yuan.

In 2015, a handful of U.S. news programs reported on this new construction boom going on in China, showing video of hundreds of buildings at least fifteen to twenty stories in height, which would supposedly provide housing for all the

Chinese who would be moving to these new metropolises. The U.S. media, when they discovered that almost all these new buildings were empty, called the sites ghost cities. The Chinese were not amused.

In fact, the Chinese government immediately stopped talking about the building program, would no longer disclose the location of more than a few of the cities, and refused to publish or comment on whether or not all those new buildings were actually attracting new residents. Actually, by 2016, the program was beginning to be somewhat successful in at least some locations, but still there was no official comment.

About this time, several of the ghost cities attracted new money and new enthusiasm from investors who were able to purchase already completed apartment buildings and industries at a fraction of their cost. This is where the Chairman Mao Conglomerate entered the picture, and they began an aggressive marketing campaign of their own. When that failed to fill their newly acquired buildings with relocating Chinese, the Conglomerate finally approached the DPRK with their novel idea of trading food for workers.

The Conglomerate purchased buildings in both highly desirable areas and those which had real issues finding interested workers. Not every new resident was thrilled with their work assignment, let alone their new geographic location—particularly those sent to Urumqi, which was less than twenty kilometers from the Tian Shen Mountain Range (the so-called Mountains of Heaven). Their accommodations, however, were far better than they had ever experienced before in North Korea, except for a small number of girls from the DPRK Pleasure Squad, who had generally enjoyed desirable living quarters wherever they were previously assigned.

But for workers whose new jobs in Urumqi required that they spend significant time outside, they discovered the actual daytime high temperatures in February were around −6° Centigrade. They saw the sun less than fifty hours during the entire month, it snowed five times in those 28 days, and when the winds blew out of the mountains, the wind chill was frequently recorded at or below −35°C.

The day the group arrived in Urumqi, a special meeting was held for the 840 females from the DPRK who were included in the workers. The Conglomerate representative made his point quickly. "Each of you were brought here to serve for two years as reimbursement for the food shipment your family received, which, by the way, was worth approximately 3,500 Yuan. If any of you should require time off from work for any reason, that entire time will be added to your two-year commitment.

"We have items for sale in the commissary which are effective in preventing pregnancy. However, if you should become pregnant, whether through your negligence or that of your partner, you will be given the choice of terminating your pregnancy immediately or carrying the child until birth. But this facility has no facilities whatsoever for taking care of infants. Therefore, any child born here will be offered for adoption, and any work you miss will be added to your two-year commitment."

Several hands went up in the audience. The representative waved his hand dismissively. "There will be no exceptions."

Their first workday, all 200,000 new workers in each of their three cities were provided a bowl, a glass, and chopsticks. They were expected to bring these items with them each work day, and to keep them in clean condition. Each worker was fed twice a day at the job site, for twenty minutes in both mid-morning and late afternoon. For the most part, the Conglomerate made an effort to appeal to the North Korean diet with kimchi and rice, or rice and noodles, sometimes offering a more Chinese flair of noodle rolls.

To their displeasure, the Korean workers learned they would be paid in 'Conglomerate money,' which was actually entered as a credit at the Conglomerate commissary rather than being physically paid in Chinese Yuans. In contrast, the native Chinese who worked for the Conglomerate were paid in physical Chinese Yuans.

Most of the Koreans had no reference for the value of a Yuan. Back before the implosion of America, a Yuan was worth the equivalent of sixteen cents U.S. However, in the last three years of worldwide collapse, only the Yuan had maintained at least some of its previous value. Both the U.S. dollar and the North Korean won, on the other hand, were literally worthless.

The North Korean workers were promised that their weekly Conglomerate salary would supposedly be equal to two hundred Yuans. However, their salaries could only be spent at one of the Conglomerate commissaries rather than in the general economy of the city, nor could any funds be sent home to their families in the DPRK. This pay system was similar to the company store system used in the 1800s and early 1900s in America in some dominant company towns.

Even before their first payday, most of the workers sought out the commissary, just to see what and how much they could buy with their meager salaries. What they found appealed to both Korean and Chinese appetites, but the varieties were severely limited.

The Chinese found plenty of Tsingtao beer, and Jiuniang, which was a fermented sweet rice wine. The North Koreans, in contrast, discovered one of their favorites, Soju, made from fermented pine or acorn nuts, and Makgeoli, the thick, sweet rice wine they preferred.

Predictably, both nationalities sought out the snacks available. The Chinese found rice noodle rolls and pineapple buns, which were made from flour, oil, sugar, and eggs (they oddly contained no pineapple). The Koreans had to be satisfied with injo kogi bap—a cooked rice wrapped in thin soybean paste, or Ttŏk—their sticky rice cakes. Of course, even in distant Urumgi, there was room on the shelves for colas and various chips, which were now manufactured in China, but were a bit more expensive than other, similar items. Between buying a small amount of paper, a pen, a decent shirt or blouse, and the snacks they all craved, they came away convinced that it would not take long for their weekly Conglomerate credits to disappear in the commissary.

At the conclusion of their first work week, many workers quickly visited the commissary, spending almost their entire paycheck, before returning to their apartment buildings to gamble with their fellow workers. Rather than betting by using money, they all agreed on the relative values of various snacks and alcoholic drinks, and that was used for currency by both Koreans and Chinese during the gambling, which often lasted all night long. By the next morning, many workers were entirely without snacks or drinks, while a few had accumulated five times as much as what they started with the night before.

What everybody back in the DPRK had failed to foresee or didn't want to acknowledge with the food giveaway program, and the sudden absence of the most able-bodied members from receiving families, should have been obvious. Such newfound wealth among 200,000 North Korean families, versus the still-starving status of millions of their countrymen, created such an imbalance that it could not be tolerated.

Before the loss of access to electricity, people would have been using pressure cookers for their rice. However, now the daily smells of the charcoal cooking fires and the scent of rice and kimchi cooked in oil which emanated from the homes of the haves was more than could be tolerated by their neighbors, the have-nots, who were painfully watching their own children, with distended bellies and shrunken arms and legs and faces. Also, they observed helplessly as their elderly relatives denied themselves anything more than a morsel to eat in an attempt to at least allow the children to survive.

North Koreans in small villages and farms had traditionally all been in equally dire situations. Many times, neighbors had shared when someone harvested a decent crop, or if a farmer slaughtered a pig or even a dog. They knew they were all in the same boat, and inevitably would be in a position where it was they who needed help, and the neighbor would probably assist.

But now, the households who had received food had also been required to hand over their greatest asset—the family's strongest son or daughter. This meant those families had one less set of hands—the most capable of hands—to work, to farm, or to forage.

Despite their small gardens, winter had come early and harshly once again in the DPRK. The ground had been frozen rock-hard since early November. The storage bins of most families were already empty, or almost so, with nothing to look forward to until they could forage for food in the spring. Therefore, many were withering away from starvation. It was an intolerable situation, and human nature was about to show its worst and sometimes its best side.

Chapter 6—Brother, It's Cold Outside

Urumqi, China February 21–29, 2028

All the DPRK workers sent to Urumqi primarily came from the cities of Chongjin and Hamhong, both of which were in cold environments, but a long way from the extremely frigid air experienced in their new home situated between the mountains and the Gobi Desert of northwestern China. If it wasn't snowing, it seemed to be sleeting, or they were surrounded by a fog so cold it made breathing difficult. The workers whose jobs required that they be outside were issued insulated coveralls, caps, gloves, and a scarf which was to be wrapped around the person's face to filter the cold air. All of the North Koreans assigned to Urumqi commiserated with one another regarding the weather, but at least two of them wondered if there was something they could do to change their situation.

These long-time friends, Ahn Il-soong and Baek Dae-jung, had grown up on adjoining farms outside Hamhong, and began to quietly discuss the problems which would need to be overcome if they were successful in leaving such a place. The more they considered, the more daunting their idea became.

They were fortunate, after the fourth week of their work, to have been wandering around the commissary one Saturday evening, when they were approached by a swarthy-looking fellow. He spoke in broken Korean. "My name is Abaka Ganbaakar. I watch you guys for last two weeks. You hardly buy anything."

"I'm Baek Dae-jung, and this is my friend, Ahn Il-soong. We decided to save as much money as we can."

Ganbaakar slowly shook his head. "That not going to work here. We need to talk." His head turned on a swivel. "Somewhere with no people."

Baek glanced at Ahn, and they both nodded. "We'd appreciate that. We don't understand the rules at all." Baek looked at their new friend. "What do you drink? We're buying."

They managed to find a relatively isolated spot in the same building, near the entrance to a small video game emporium, and shared a carton of Tsingtao beer. Ahn looked at Ganbaakar. "Why do you sound different from the other Chinese?"

"Maybe 'cause I not Chinese. I from Mongolia—western part, near Hovid. Maybe you hear of Genghis Khan? I come from him and his land."

"So what are you doing here?"

"I come looking for work, but not like you. You guys get paid in commissary script. I get paid in Chinese Yuans."

"Can't we cash in our script for Yuans whenever we want to?"

"Maybe you think you saving money, but the only money you gonna get is script. That script only good in company comissary."

"Why do you get real money and we only get script? We're doing the same work."

"They don't tell you much, do they? Maybe they figure your families got plenty of money already with the free food they received, and you got nothing else coming."

"What about when we finally leave here?"

"You get nothing."

Ahn slowly scanned the room. "How can we switch commissary script for Yuans?"

Ganbaaker shook his head and lowered his voice. "That a very dangerous question."

"Why is it dangerous?"

"The Conglomerate gonna figure there only one reason for you to want to make that switch. Only reason you need Yuans is if you trying to leave here."

"Do you know of any way to make such a switch?"

Ganbaaker hid his mouth behind his beer. "First thing, my friends, you cannot speak about this to anyone. I've heard stories about what might happen if the Conglomerate finds out about this." He looked around again. "Since you can't actually touch the commissary credits, you would have to purchase merchandise, then trade the actual merchandise to someone else for Yuans."

"What good would that merchandise do someone?" asked Baek.

"Your buyer would then have to sell the merchandise to someone who has Yuans. Of course, there would have to be a big discount to make it worthwhile to the person buying the merchandise from you, as well as the person they would turn around and sell it to."

"So how big of a discount?"

"First of all, your script only buys half as much stuff as my Yuans." He held up his beer. "I pay fifteen Yuan for a carton of this beer, but you pay thirty script for same thing. So you miss out on fifty percent before anything else happens. I think the discount would have to be about thirty percent. Remember the person giving you Yuans is taking big risk, too."

Baek nodded. "Do you know someone with Yuans who might be willing to take merchandise which the two of us paid up to 330 in script for every week?"

Their new Mongol friend shrugged. "I might."

Chapter 7—Both Sides of the Same Coin

North Korea March 1-7, 2028

Baek Dae-jung and Ahn Il-soong would be proud to have heard what their families had decided to do near Hamhong, North Korea. There were five families which had lived in close proximity for as long as Baek and Ahn could remember. The fact that each family lived on a farm would be confusing to Western ears, as a farm in North Korea was almost never larger than one acre and seldom consisted of more than a large garden. Most of the landscape in the country is rocky, and practically or completely untillable, so access to land suitable for farming was difficult.

No one possessed any farm machinery, and the few mules and workhorses had been eaten out of desperation many years ago during previous food shortages. Therefore, the farms were no larger than what could be taken care of by two people. While one guided an old plow, the other pulled and strained in the traces to serve in place of a mule. The work was extremely demanding physically, and the older or more feeble the worker, the smaller portion of ground which could be plowed, planted, watered, and harvested.

Baek and Ahn's families lived almost on top of their neighbors, and they had been close friends for years. So when these two small families considered the huge amount of food they had received in compensation for their sons' labors in China, they couldn't help but recognize the painful difference between their new wealth versus that of their three closest neighbors.

The first night after their food supply had been delivered, they spent a few minutes considering, then invited their three neighboring families for a discussion. Their solution was to share the wealth, with five families enjoying their morning and evening meals together.

"We have known each other for over fifteen years," reasoned Ahn's mother, "some of us for our entire lives. What is ours is yours—at least under these conditions. Among our five families, we have seven adults and three children. The food will be divided according to each family's size. But when we work our gardens, everyone will pitch in, because our two families are without our sons. If you catch a few fish, or kill a pigeon or a rabbit, we expect you to share with all of us. If we are extremely careful, and work together, perhaps we can all survive the next two years."

At their first communal meal, Ahn's mother opened one of the half-kilogram cans of meat. It was clearly labeled PORK PRODUCTS, but upon inspection, at least twenty-five percent of the contents included a gelatinous goo which surrounded the actual meat. They didn't know if the goo was actually edible or not.

Ahn's mother remembered the last time they tasted pork some four years previous. They had saved their last small pig to be consumed for a feast to celebrate the birthdate of their country's founder. The animal had been confined in a small pen for several days, and on the appointed day, all were surprised to recognize the arrival of a small truck occupied by four DPRK soldiers.

The soldiers, somehow knowing of the impending harvest, quickly cut the pig's throat and were about to hoist him into the back of their truck. Ahn's mother spread out her hands to them. "Since you have already slaughtered our pig, why don't you allow me to gut and clean the carcass so you can fully enjoy what is edible?"

After some deliberation, the soldiers agreed to her offer, and she gutted the animal, cleaned out the body cavity, and removed its head. The soldiers were happy not to have gotten any of the gore on them, and they departed.

Ahn's mother then cleaned out the entrails, washed the heart and liver, and sliced thin slices of meat from the head. Those parts had been her family's last exposure to pork, so they were surprised at what was labeled as PORK PRODUCTS in their cans of potted meat. The families mixed in some rice and kimchi and ate it anyway.

After that first meal together, strangely, all five families felt stronger. All five of them suddenly had hope. And without question there was gratitude.

Unfortunately, this level of friendship was not at all common, as most families who received such a large amount of food could see no reason whatsoever for sharing with their neighbors. After all, they no longer had their strongest family member to help them in their farming. Worse, many of their neighbors had no patience for this stinginess. Food was stolen at every opportunity. Someone in the family had to remain in the cabin or hovel at all times to guard their larder with nothing but a sharp hoe to defend their treasure.

Two or three able-bodied men attacked people who couldn't defend themselves. Someone who tried to fight back—even an old granny—was often beaten senseless, or worse.

As the long winter dragged into early spring, everyone realized this was the hardest time of the year for starving families, as any production from gardens or even wild greens from the forest was still weeks away. The attacks grew ever more common and desperate. All that food was often regarded as a curse rather than a gift.

Chapter 8—Maximizing the Investment

Urumqi, China March 5–9 2028

Back in Urumqi, by mid-morning on Monday, word had spread like wildfire on the Chairman Mao Conglomerate campus. Two of the workers were missing. Their work supervisor was overheard on a radio to one of the housing units, asking that the quarters of the two men be searched—perhaps to discover if they were too sick to report to work, or was there evidence that they had fled.

Before the day was out, the missing workers had been identified as two North Koreans who had come originally from Chongjin. Neither Baek nor Ahn knew the men, and for that they were grateful, as it seemed a number of men in the housing units from Chongjin were interviewed in depth.

This was reinforced later that day by Abuka Ganbaakar. "If you knew them, say nothing. When they're caught, they are in deep kimche, and anyone who might have known something ahead of time will be guilty as well."

Late on the second day, an orderly reported that two men had been brought into the medical facility, secured to wheelchairs. The orderly could not confirm whether the men were alive or dead, but he claimed to have seen no evidence of wounds on either man.

The next morning, the physician in charge declared that it appeared both men had been infected by an unknown or suspicious virus when they were discovered in Jiayuguan at the train station, and the doctor was transferring both men to the large hospital in Urumqi. He continued that everything possible had been done to protect the workforce, but he was taking no chances that the men might spread some new disease.

The physician failed to mention that the railway agent became suspicious of the men, not because they were ill, but simply because they were unable to communicate in any Chinese dialect, and could not tell him where they wished to travel next. The agent called the Conglomerate, held the men until security finally arrived, and was rewarded with a small financial stipend.

At mid-morning a medical unit arrived, accompanied by security personnel, and the two escapees were whisked away, supposedly to the local hospital. Instead, the two vehicles departed directly for the small Urumqi airport, where a Lear 60XR jet was standing in the private aircraft area.

The Lear showed VV as its tailfin identity, which would lead one to believe the plane was at one time registered in Vladivostok, Russia. The small jet could transport up to eight passengers and two crewmembers. It possessed a cruising speed of 800 kilometers per hour and a range of 8,000 kilometers, at least under ideal flying conditions.

After the two North Koreans were fully restrained in their seats, the medical officer on board injected each man with a mild sedative. At the same time, the Conglomerate representative had business to conduct, and he retrieved a delicate scale from its container, weighing the contents of a small box which was presented by the Lear jet pilot. The representative studied the scale until it steadied, and he turned toward the pilot. "Perfect, Captain. Exactly fifteen troy ounces.. Now if you don't mind, there is one more formality." He extracted a gold purity reader from his briefcase, made a series of measurements of the small pile of nuggets, and concurred again. "Perfect at twenty-four karats. I believe that concludes our business. Have a good flight."

Prior to the economic collapse, fifteen troy ounces of 24 karat gold had been worth 160,000 Yuans. Because of the decline in world currencies, the same amount of gold in 2028 had a value of just over 375,000 yuans.

In ten minutes the jet was wheels-up and headed for its first stop—Novosibirsk, Russia, on the banks of the Ob River.

The next stop was near the Sea of Japan in Vladivostok.

The Lear spent no more than fifteen minutes on the ground at each stop. An ambulance pulled up at the loading area, and one partially conscious escapee was placed in the vehicle, then it departed the airport, driving a few kilometers before arriving at a specialty medical clinic.

Once more, the escapee was transferred into the facility, yet another confirming laboratory test was performed, and he was wheeled into a surgical suite, where he was placed under general anesthesia. In two minutes, a surgeon and surgical nurse arrived, scrubbed themselves and the patient, and began their tasks.

In forty-five minutes, six technicians, each carrying a temperature-controlled cooler, exited the facility, and were again escorted to the airport. The exact scenario was repeated with the second escapee in Vladivostok, and that was that.

In these difficult times, it was widely accepted in China and Russia that only five items now had any real value—precious metals, oil, food, people, and medical care. In the United States, when workers in critical industries discovered that the value of their paychecks were practically worthless, they simply walked away, and nothing could be done to force them to return to their jobs. In isolated cases, the cartels stepped in and took over the oil refineries in Texas and Louisiana, but this was solely for their own benefit.

By contrast, China and Russia were both fortunate that they each possessed oil wells and refineries where men, no matter their change in pay, could be forced to pull oil out of the ground and transport the oil to refineries, while others were forced to turn the crude oil into diesel, gasoline, and jet fuel. The amount of fuel refined was only a small fraction of what it once had been, but it was enough to at least partially satisfy the appetites of favored oligarchs and senior members of the Party.

As to people, they possessed two kinds of value—first as workers or sex workers, and secondly as the source of desperately needed replacement organs—lungs, hearts, livers, and kidneys for wealthy constituents. One thing was certain, enterprising men and women in both China and Russia had become expert at fully maximizing the value of "people."

It was later reported back in Urumqi that both men had been sent to prison as punishment for their escape attempt. That seemed logical, and life at the Chairman Mao Conglomerate soon returned to normal.

Baek and Ahn continued to work with their Mongolian friend, Abuka Ganbaakar, but all were more cautious than ever before. Each Saturday evening, Baek and Ahn assembled the results of their weekly shopping list at the commissary, and each Saturday evening, Ganbaakar presented them with a couple of fifty Yuan notes.

After Ganbaakar departed their small apartment, the two North Koreans would go to their hiding place. They knew it was unwise to leave the building every Saturday evening or Sunday morning to regularly visit a specific hiding place. Someone would undoubtedly be watching. Instead, with Ahn standing on Baek's shoulders, he discovered that the top layer of bricks on one wall of their room had a series of six holes in each brick, accessible only from the top of the bricks. Each hole was no larger than a little finger, so they began to tightly roll each pair of fifty Yuan notes into a cigarette shape and stuff them into one of those holes. Slowly they began to accumulate.

The two friends had agreed on resolving several issues before they would even consider the risk of leaving. First, they had to gain at least enough familiarity with one of the Chinese dialects to safely get them the 4,000 kilometers from western China to the border with North Korea. They discovered that the Chinese language had about 10 variations, and what was spoken in the west (Yan Lin Mandarin) versus what they would encounter on their trip (Tibetan, followed by Central Mandarin, followed by Jin Lu Mandarin), was not so important, but they did apparently need a basic understanding of Mandarin.

They agreed that they must wait for warmer weather to begin their journey, particularly since their strategy involved a great deal of walking. Riding the trains the entire distance was simply far too predictable, and thus too dangerous. They had decided not to catch the train locally, but to walk overland from Urumqui to Turpan (200 km), then catch the train there and ride all the way to Siping. At that point they would walk the last 300 km to the China/DPRK border, cross the river at night near Kanggye, North Korea, then walk the final 200 kilometers to the southeast toward Hamhong and home. Whatever happened, they both agreed they could not endure another winter at their current location.

As time went on, they began to hear rumors of other DPRK workers who had become dissatisfied with the cold weather, the constant harrassment from their Chinese supervisors, and perhaps the overpowering desire to return to their families—particularly those who sought the comfort of their wives back home in North Korea. At least one female was rumored to be showing signs of pregnancy, and very soon she and her male friend were found to be missing as well. Whether they or others were successful in their escape attempts was unknown, but they were never seen again.

By the middle of August, Baek and Ahn had squirreled away 2,200 Yuans in their hiding place. They knew that warm weather would soon be a thing of the past and colder weather might make it very difficult to complete the long walks, particularly in the mountains toward the end of their journey, which had to be included in their plans.

Ganbaakar began to ask thinly veiled questions about their plans, making both Baek and Ahn wonder about his motive. Perhaps it was just curiosity, but at least every two weeks he had mentioned their ultimate plan. The next Saturday night, Baek finally told Ganbaakar they had waited too late in the year to undertake such a journey, and had decided to wait until the next spring.

Baek and Ahn had no idea what the actual risk was if they were discovered, but after the Mongolian had departed from their apartment, Baek and Ahn looked at each other for confirmation, retrieved their stash of Yuans, put on a second set of clothing over their work clothes, gathered together their very small amount of personal belongings, plus their stash of food from the Commissary, and walked off into the night.

They Call Me The Breeze

Kevin W. Steverson

Chapter One

Rabun County, Georgia
January 1, 2028

"What do you mean, it smells like snow?" Staff Sergeant Givens asked. "What the hell does snow smell like?"

"I don't know," Sergeant Krayner answered. "Like... snow. Look, just trust me. It's going to snow."

Givens looked over to his partner. "Sounds like some ol' Yankee shit to me."

"He is from Minnesota," Staff Sergeant Traft agreed. "Still, it does feel kinda different today. It's not that unusual for this corner of Georgia to get some snow."

"You guys always bring that up, Tee," Krayner complained. "I haven't lived in Minnesota since 2018. That's like, more than ten years ago."

"Yeah, but you still have the accent, don't ya know?" Traft teased.

"I may have the accent, but I'm gonna freeze my ass off just like you guys. I'm a Southerner now. Give me the ninety-degree summertime weather over this, any time. How much longer do we have on this shift, anyway?"

"Another half hour," Givens answered. "Basim, Wilkins, and Nguyen will relieve us. Come on, help me get the tarp over the fifty. If it is going to snow, we don't want it getting on the gun or its tripod. It'll rust for sure."

The three NCOs covered the weapon, and then stomped their feet and rubbed their gloved hands to build up and maintain what body heat they could. They had been on guard duty for close to four hours. It was a long shift and unusual for those of their rank, but all the unit's NCOs had come together and decided to give the enlisted solders New Year's Eve and the 1st off. Kind of a late Christmas gift.

The ridge they occupied overlooked the narrow road into the valley where the headquarters for the 2017th Separate Infantry Battalion was located. Tucked away, beyond state and federal forest land, the armory was semi-secret. Not a lot of people knew exactly where it was located and the road in was heavily guarded the last year or so.

It was home to the unit members, their families, and many civilians in the northeast corner of Georgia. The local sheriff and those working with him were partnered with the last remaining unit of the Georgia Army National Guard. Whatever else remained of the state's military as well as the "Big Army" were stuck overseas or fighting in and around Texas.

The country and the rest of the world had fallen into total chaos, so there was no guarantee if the Army was still together as fighting units. These days it was every man for himself, or community, if folks could find ways to work together. In Northeast Georgia, some semblance of civilization remained, held in check by neighbors looking out for each other and the 2017th there to ensure things didn't get out of hand. A pocket of sanity within the growing apocalyptic world.

The next morning, Givens shook his head and laughed. "I should have known. You guys see that? Those three specialists just left to go to their normal guard position. They have a shelter with them... and a heater. I bet they set the fifty up in it and stay warm all day."

"You know they will," agreed Traft. "Leave it to a specialist to figure out the best way to do it. Why didn't we think of that?"

"Beats me. Probably 'cause we can't do shit like that when we are out on a mission. Snipers and their spotter can't be in a shelter with all kinds of heat signature rising off it."

"Yeah. I guess. Still."

"Hey, you ready?" Specialist Mulligan asked as he walked up.

"Ready for what?" Traft asked. "All we know is the LT wants us in on the meeting this morning. Something about a mission."

"Yeah," Givens asked, "what gives? What do you know? Is it the Sevens?"

"Can't be the Wayne Gang," Traft said. "We took care of them last year."

"Oh, I know," Mulligan said. "I know exactly what it is."

As the commander's driver, he was privy to many things. He was also trustworthy and never revealed things he knew First Lieutenant Rojas didn't want known until the time was right. For some things, that was never. Both members of the unit's sniper team knew that. They also knew it didn't hurt to ask.

Thirty minutes later, they knew what he did. They stared at each other in amazement and waited for someone in the room to make a comment. It didn't take long.

"Jamaica?" Staff Sergeant Flores asked in his heavy accent. "As in Jamaica, Jamaica?"

"The one and only," Lieutenant Rojas answered. He leaned back in his seat and put his hands behind his head. "It's going to be nice this time of year, too."

"Shoot, yes," Sergeant First Class Warren said. The unit's senior NCO was Jamaican on her mother's side, though there was no trace of an island accent. The only accent she had was that of a woman raised on a farm in middle Georgia. It often surprised those who saw her before they heard her speak.

"I get that we need to go get the Platoon Mama's mama," Flores said. "I mean, that's family. That's her mama. I'd kill someone who even disrespected mine and she is just across the valley raising chickens and hot peppers. So, like I get it. But... how the hell are we gonna get to Jamaica?"

"We're going to fly," CW4 Bonville said. The older man grinned and leaned back, like his commander beside him.

"I never claimed to be a genius," Staff Sergeant Green confessed. She wiped a strand of blond hair out of her eye. "But even I know a Black Hawk or that small plane you have is not going to fly that far. It's just not."

"We're not taking either of those," Rojas said. "Just where do you think the chief and Warrant Officer Jones have been the last few weeks?"

"I mean, on leave?" Green answered.

"We went down to Florida and acquired an airplane," answered newly promoted Warrant Officer Tyrell. "We took a squad for security and flew down to the Fantasy of Flight Museum in Polk City."

"And with all the craziness in the world right now, you just flew down and grabbed an airplane?" Givens asked. "Hell, there's planes all over the place in what's left of the Atlanta airport. Why not get one of them?"

"Maintenance," Bonville answered, as if it was plain as day.

"I know there are planes at the airport in Atlanta," the junior warrant officer said. "Remember, I was undercover near there for six months so we could get rid of those working locally with the Sevens. They thought I was one of them and going to spy on the 2017th."

"How did you get away with that anyway? And what did you do to take them out?" Tee asked.

"Save that story for some other time," suggested the commander. He waved his hand in dismissal. "Tell them what you brought back north from Florida."

"Roger, sir," Jones continued. "Anyway, those are all jets, and they need crazy maintenance. There are very few aircraft still airworthy these days, you know. Prop engines or not. We went down to the museum because I knew, for a fact, they had a plane with proper maintenance logs. My cousin worked on it for the last seven years. We brought him back with us, too."

"Well, what kind of plane is it?" Flores asked.

"A Catalina," Bonville answered proudly.

"A what?" Tee asked. "What is a Catalina? Sounds like a salad dressing, or something."

"A Consolidated PBY-5A Catalina," Mulligan said. "You know, a flying boat, and the damn thing is way older than the plane you jumped from in Winder, SSG Green. Way older."

"Just how old?" Green asked. She glanced towards her fiancé nervously. Flores shrugged his shoulders.

"Built in 1943," Jones said. "But it was rebuilt a little over ten years ago and has been maintained since. As a matter of fact, it went on its test flight just a week before the world fell apart. There are only a few intact planes at the museum now, or what's left of it, but this one was locked up tight deep in the hangar. We just had to do some stuff to her to get here ready again."

"I imagine," Rojas said. "I'm just amazed you were able to fly it here... or that the owner let it go."

"Well, with my cousin's help we got it airworthy again. The owner hated to see it go but knew it was the only way to keep her in the air. Besides, his health isn't the best these days and it doesn't look like any type of life-saving surgery is in his future. What little might be left for him."

The room was silent for a moment.

Lieutenant Rojas broke the mood. "So, we'll go down to Jamaica and get Sergeant First Class Warren's mom and bring her back here. Nothing to it."

"We'll have to find her, but yes, sir," Warren said. "Nothing to it. She was visiting family when it all happened. Daddy misses her... I miss her." The last came out almost in a whisper.

"Are we sure... I mean, is she still..." Mulligan asked.

"Yes. She will be there. I just know it," insisted Warren. "She has to be."

Toccoa, Georgia
Airfield

Twelve soldiers stood in formation on the tarmac. Behind them, a few of the unit members assigned to the airfield in Toccoa rolled three fifty-gallon drums full of fuel towards the airplane. They were full and ready to be "just a little insurance" as far as flight time in the old machine.

"We will be landing near Oracabessa," Lieutenant Rojas said. "Hopefully at Ian Fleming International Airport. Look, many of you know about Jamacia. Probably been there, on a cruise or vacation. What you don't know is the parts of Jamacia tourists don't see. The city of Kingston, Spanish Town... places like that. There is rampant gang activity, one of the highest murder rates in the Caribbean, hell, in the world probably. Per capita, anyway. We won't be near any of that."

"If we can't find a suitable runway, we will land in the water and coast into the shallows," Bonville informed the assembled troops. "It will be a long flight. A little over ten hours, because we will be conserving fuel and we're not in a hurry, but this bird has a toilet, so there is that. With the extra fuel, fifty-cal ammunition, and gear, we will be close to the max weight allowance for the distance we will be flying, but the calculations show we will be fine."

He cupped his chin in thought and continued. "We can go 2,600 miles. We're looking at 2,400 miles there and back. That gives us a little for maneuvering or weather. Plus, we have some extra fuel we will transfer before the return trip. It's not as if we have the weight of bombs or the anti-sub torpedoes they carried when they were first put into service."

A hand went up in the back. Private First Class Smith asked, "Sir, how many guns are on that thing anyway?" Shmitty, as he was known, always asked a lot of questions.

"Four. The bow, port and starboard on the waist, and ventral." Seeing the confused looks, he explained, "One up front, two on the sides and one in the rear. All are now fifty-cal. This particular model was modified; they removed and replaced the thirties up front and in the rear."

"Damnit, man!" Staff Sergeant Flores said. "And we have rounds for them, too? Heaven help some pendejo who wants to fuck around and find out."

The entire group burst out laughing.

"Check your gear one last time," Rojas ordered. "Yes, we have the guns on the plane and rounds for them. That doesn't mean we will use them. It's not like the rounds are easy to replace. I don't anticipate any type of action. The most we might run into is the type of lawlessness we see the farther we get from our little corner of the world. It won't be anything a fully trained squad-plus sized force can't handle. They will be able to tell the weapons in our hands aren't just for show. Besides, the criminal elements will be far from where we will be."

He paused a moment and then continued. "The entire island is probably doing just fine. What makes a gang a gang is no longer something anybody wants. Money is worthless and drug trafficking is a business that is... out of business. They may be shut off from the world like most places across the globe, but they were an island of fishermen and farmers long before modern technology. I bet they are doing better than most countries. Anyway, we get in, find who we are looking for, and we get out. That's the plan. Like I said, nothing to it."

Guantanamo Bay, Cuba

"Nothing to it," Presidente Juan Carlos Perez said. He tapped the hastily drawn map of an island with a stick. A smaller island than Cuba.

He looked around at the devastation of what was once an American base in his country. It had all but been abandoned early when the terrorists hit the United States. With no hope for any type of reinforcements, those remaining fought to the last man and woman, but the Cuban forces prevailed. Lacking their own support from outside countries, it didn't take long for the new occupiers to run it into the ground. Now, because it was a place with protection from the hills surrounding it and control of its shoreline, the leader of Cuba and hand-picked followers shut themselves off from the rest of their country for months. A country burning itself to the ground in revenge.

It was a situation that could not last, as supplies were running low. Seafood they could get. Other foods, not so much. It wasn't as if *they* would plant crops or raise livestock. Perez had a plan to escape the anger of the decades of mistreatment of the Cuban people completely. One to leave them to themselves and their fate.

"We hit the shore near Montego Bay and establish a beach head. The remainder of our forces will follow at best speed. Once we roll across Jamacia, then we will bring those loyal to me to our new home. They and their families, the right families, will help me to take Jamacia and remake it like it should be."

"What about Cuba?" asked a young general. He was the president's nephew.

"We can no longer count on the support of Russia and our brothers and sisters from Venezuela to keep the peasants in line, so the people can have it." He turned his head and spat. "The hell with the *people*. They are never satisfied. We tell them how to live and to be happy and, for years, all they want is more. More, more, more! I am sick of the peasants. They can have Cuba... and they can starve. We will be in Jamaica where we can convert the Jamaicans to the right way to live and kill those who will not bend to my will. I will no longer be just El Presidente. I will be a king."

"Do we have enough forces for that?" the same man asked. "Loyal forces, I mean."

"We have enough. Those who have been siding with the people can stay here and deal with them. When my forces leave to follow, they have been instructed to destroy what is left of the fuel and food here. There is little fuel anywhere else in Cuba. Others will not have the means to leave, unless they plan to sail. If we see any slow-moving ships on the horizon once we are settled... well, they can be taken care of, too."

El Presidente continued, emphasizing his point again. "The peasants can *have* Cuba; we will take Jamaica. Even with the few remaining troops I have... Jamaica has far less. They didn't have any type of real military before all this; I doubt they have one now. Anyway. What happens here does not matter. What will matter is what happens in our new home. One we will take."

He looked at his plan on the map and nodded his head to reassure himself. "Nothing to it."

"Hey, sir," Bonville said. "Can you come up front and take a look at this?"

Rojas took off his headphones, stood, and stretched. He had been seated in the navigator's seat in the compartment used for it and the radarman, a position Specialist Mulligan occupied as he'd played with the gear for the last several hours. A question by his driver to the pilot had caused them to fly at a lower altitude for the last few minutes. It would seem the answer was now revealed.

"What's up?" Rojas asked. "Man, the ocean is beautiful at this level. Look at all the different shades of blues."

"I'll bank around so you can see. I don't like it."

"What is it..." Rojas' voice trailed off. "Those are Cuban flags on those ships," Rojas observed. "I don't know what kind of ship that big one is, but it has guns on it. Big ones."

"Yeah, and those smaller ships have some, too," Jones commented. "Several swung towards us before we climbed. They're on a direct course for Jamaica. Looks like towards Montego Bay, if my charts are right."

"Damn. I wonder why?"

"I don't know, sir," Bonville said. "They aren't moving very fast, that's for sure. The way that big ship is smoking, I'd say one engine is out and the other is not far behind. Maybe the smaller boats are there to pull it if the remaining engine goes out."

"Is that a helicopter pad on it?"

"Looks like it. I can get lower to see what type, if you want. This thing was designed with some protection from anti-air rounds. The tanks are self-sealing, too."

"Maybe we should. If I didn't know any better, I'd say that

is an invasion fleet, or third-world troop transport. Look at the gear lined up on the deck. It looks like pallets of something. Give me a few minutes to get back to my seat and then make a low-level pass. It's risky but if it is an invasion, we need to let whoever is leading Jamacia know it's coming. We're not getting involved in third-world fights, but we can do that much."

He made his way back to where the rest of his troops were. "Hey! Get your flack vests off and put them below your seats. We may take a few rounds and I have no idea what this thing has for armor or whatever."

"Fuck me!" Flores said. "You heard him. Move, you shitbags! Get them laid out!"

Up front, CW4 Bonville called up to the mechanic's compartment. "Hey, Marcus. Keep an eye on things. We may take a few rounds."

"Wait! What?" Marcus asked over the intercom.

W1 Jones grinned at his brother's concern. "Hey, man, I told you when you agreed to enlist, shit could happen. You're a member of the 2017th now. You may be an aircraft mechanic, but you're a soldier, too. It'll all come back to you from your days in the Air Force."

"That was more than a decade ago! Shit." Corporal Marcus Jones paused and then said. "Roger, sir. I'm on it. Mechanic's compartment standing by."

The plane banked and descended for a closer look. Barrels swiveled. Rounds flew.

Rio Jatibonico
Cuban Revolutionary Navy

Capitan de Flotilla Juan Garcia watched through his binoculars as the strange plane slowly banked and came back around. It was clearly losing altitude and would come directly over the four ships he commanded. His ship, the converted frigate *Rio Jatibonico*, had no hope of maneuvering if fired upon. It was all it could do to keep moving forward with the one engine running. The other diesel and the gas turbine were both out of operation now. Only one of the three props spun.

"I do not like this. What if it is a Jamaican plane and they are gathering intel before we can land the majority of our soldiers?" he said to no one in particular. "Shoot it from the sky!"

"Yes, sir!" a young Alferez said. The junior officer relayed the orders to those assigned to the weapons systems. The ones that worked, anyway.

"Whoa!" shouted Jones. "They're firing at us!"

"Hang on!" Bonville shouted. He pulled back and banked away.

"Full thrust," Jones said as he helped to fly the plane. "Looks like they missed…"

Several rounds hit the underside of the plane. The impact could be both felt and heard. The armor plating stopped most of them from penetrating. One round made its way through, hit the steel seat Bonville sat in, and a piece of it penetrated his leg. He screamed and the plane veered. Jones took over flying the old plane completely.

"Medic!" Jones shouted over the intercom.

Sergeant First Class Warren took off her headset and shouted to Doc, the unit's medic.

He made his way forward, fighting gravity and the steep angle of the climb, his pack in one hand. "Moving, Sergeant!"

Bonville was made comfortable in the crew compartment, an I.V. hung above him. He grimaced in pain, the medicine just starting to ease it.

"He needs surgery," Doc said. "Soon. There is a piece I couldn't get to. I might be able to do it but not here, that's for sure."

"Jones says we will be on the ground within the hour. Maybe we can find a hospital still in operation… or a clinic or something."

"Once on the ground in a stable environment, I'm pretty sure I can do it. Just gotta make sure there's no chance of infection. I seen shit like this when we were in Texas and before that when I worked at Grady in Atlanta. Jagged wounds with debris inside."

"I imagine. That part of Atlanta was always in the news."

An hour later, Jones turned the nose of the plane towards the ocean. The airfield was in no shape to land on. There were several abandoned planes, some destroyed long ago, while others looked to be simply abandoned. Cars and trucks were on the runway, as well.

"Looks like a water landing, sir," Jones said.

"This will be a first for me," Rojas said.

"Me too," Jones confided.

"Great. Let's just keep that tidbit of information to ourselves."

They were able to taxi up to a long dock obviously designed for yachts. There were none tied up to it. Several men stood on the dock waiting for them. The men took a step back when Lieutenant Rojas and the rest of his troops stepped off the plain in full battle-rattle.

One held his hands up slightly in question. "What gives, mon? You plan to invade us too, den?"

"No," Rojas assured him. "Nothing like that. We're American soldiers. We came to pick up someone. Once we locate her, we will leave your country. We don't want any trouble. From the looks of things, it looks like you had enough of that."

"Dat we did, mon. Dat we did. But we got plenty more, for sure."

"Yeah?"

"Over in Montego, day got dem Cubans killing everyone like the gangs did last year. Dey say dey gone take de island. Dey just might, you know."

"What do you mean? You can fight them off. There can't be many here yet. We saw more coming, but it will be days before they get here. At least one, anyway."

"How we gone fight soldiers? Dey got guns. We got none."

"I can't believe there are no weapons here. None? I mean, the gangs have weapons, right?"

"Ders no more gangs. De people done took care of dat."

"What?"

"When de world went crazy, and dey were no more tourists, dey money dried up. No money. No way to ship drugs. Nuting. The gangs turned on each other to try and be the ones who took down de government. After dey kill each other off, dey was no bullets left. Dey had de guns, but nutting to shoot in dem. That's when de people rose up. De fight was fair wid no guns involved. Anyone wid de gangs was shark food, you know. Dats de way it is. De balance always comes back around. We all live in peace. Love your brother and sister. Das de way. Das de only way."

"So, no one is in charge?"

"Well, de government is still around, but dey are like de rest of us. De grow dey garden and dey fish, too. Nuting for dem to do, you know. Many of de people done moved out of de cities. Life is good now."

"'Cept for dese Cubans," the other man added. "Dey gone mess tings up real good."

"How many Cubans are in Montego?" SFC Warren asked.

"I do not know, but I know de man who saw dem. He on dat catamaran over der on de other dock. I'll take you to him."

"Wally Newark. Pleased to meet you, Lieutenant. What can I do for you?" the older man asked as he shook Rojas's hand. He flicked his head sideways to move the long greying hair from his eyes.

"I hear you have information on the Cubans."

"Yeah. Yeah, I do. I slipped out at night and sailed away. They have a platoon-sized element. Came in on an old corvette. Looks like something from World War II. Believe it or not, President Perez is with them."

"Perez?" Rojas asked, his eyes wide. "The Cuban dictator?"

"That's the one. A cousin of the original Castros, or some shit. Anyway, they are just gunning folks down and spouting their communist shit day and night. Got some loudspeakers set up on the boat."

"Damn. So, what's your story, anyway?"

"I'm retired. Air Force. Used to fly a little. Nothing as old as that thing you came in on, but you know. I flew a C-130 gunship for Spec-Ops. Nowadays, I travel the blue waters. I kinda miss the States, though. Thinking about going home. It'll be a long trip, but I'm prepping for it."

Rojas stared off for a moment. Then, his mind made up, he said, "Look. We can give you a lift back to the States. We need a co-pilot right now anyway. We have a man needing surgery and he won't get behind the stick for a while. But I need details on that platoon. We plan on putting a stop to it before it can begin. We know where the follow-on troops are and we can make a run on them, but I want to wipe out that platoon, too."

"I can do that. I have an idea for that ship, too. It's all about the angle when you fire down on one."

"You gone help us?" asked the first man they'd met. "You do dat and I can find who you are lookin' for. What is de name and where dey 'sposed to be at?"

Three hours later, SFC Warren was reunited with her

mother. They held each other tightly for several minutes.

"I didn't know if I was going to see you again," the younger Warren said.

She wiped an eye. The troops near her looked away. Their platoon sergeant was tough as nails. Never one to cuss and a strong Christian woman, but tough as nails all the same. They let her maintain that by giving her and her mother their privacy.

"Me too, baby girl. Me too. I was able to spend the last few months with your auntie before the cancer took her. Then the whole world changed the next week. I couldn't get home. Tell me how your daddy is?"

"He's fine, Momma. He has moved up to north Georgia with me. He heads up a lot of the farming in our valley. There was no way he could stay in middle Georgia with everything happening."

Her mother paused a moment. "Well, I'm going to miss my home… and the farm, but it doesn't matter. What matters is being with your daddy and you. I can make a home anywhere. When do we leave?"

"About that. There's something we need to do before we go."

"All right. Any questions?"

"No, sir," Flores said. "We hit the compound, take out the security, and clear the mansion. Fuck those commie bastards."

"Lord save us," Warren said. "And my ears."

"Sorry," Flores said. She waved it off.

"Let me hear you do it again," Rojas said.

Staff Sergeant Flores grinned and did his best impersonation of a Cuban in Spanish. "North side! They are attacking on the north side. Everyone shift over here. Protect El Presidente!"

"Damn, that's pretty good," Rojas said.

"What do you mean?" Mulligan asked. "It just sounds like more Spanish to me."

"It's hard to explain," Rojas said. "It's kind of like being able to hear Sergeant Krayner's Minnesota accent compared to Shmitty's Southern drawl, or someone from say… California. It's American English, but it's different. It's the same with

Spanish. Puerto Ricans, Mexicans, Cubans, most countries, really. They all have unique accents."

"Like someone British?"

"No, that's different than American English, like someone from Spain compared to Latin America. Way different."

"Well, as long as it's convincing, sir," Mulligan said, "So we can take those commies out. From what I've seen of Jamacia, it's beautiful. I'd hate to see it ruined."

"Me, too. Now let's board the plane."

Jones was able to land smoothly by moonlight, using the small whitecaps on the water as a guide. Everyone was wet from the waist down by the time they made the shore. They dropped their night vision devices on their helmets and moved out at a brisk pace. They had about a mile to go through what remained of a resort and an upscale neighborhood. The target was located on the end of a peninsula called The Lagoons on Calypso Drive. As they moved out, they heard the faint sound of the Catalina taking off after taxiing a long way from land.

Later, Rojas heard the call. "Red Six, Eyes."

"Go for Red Six."

"Hey, sir, we're set up here," Givens said. "We found an empty house across the cul-de-sac. We are on the third floor overlooking the gate. We can see two on guard. They are lit up like Christmas trees, chain smoking big-ass cigars. We have a good view of most of the front."

"Roger that. When I give the word, take them down. Break. Green Six. Sit-rep, over."

Staff Sergeant Green answered. "We have eyes on the boat tied up to the dock. Garner is rigging it now. They didn't even leave a guard on it."

"Idiots. Stand by for my signal."

Once the rest of the troops were in place, Rojas called out, "Eyes, you are a go at this time."

"Roger, Red Six. Ten seconds."

Givens turned to Tee. "Shooter. By eye, go to sector one."

"Contact," Tee replied.

"Go to seven o'clock. Approximately 8 mills."

"Contact."

"Go to glass."

Sergeant Pete Traft, or Tee to his friends, steadied himself and put his eye to the scope. His crosshairs were quickly centered on the side of the head of a man smoking a cigar. The glow lit his face as well as the man beside him.

With the Leupold Mark 5 HD scope on his rifle, the low light wasn't an issue. His target was easily seen by the light of the stars and bright moon. He spoke softly. "Two men. Cigar glow silhouetting his head beside the other man. Both are in sight."

"Those are your targets. Check parallax and mill."

Tee adjusted his scope and whispered, "One point four."

Sergeant Lyle Givens studied the small device in his hand to gauge the wind. "Check level." He paused. "Holdover. Three point eight."

Tee shifted slightly, moving the reticle to accommodate the wind, took a normal breath, slowly exhaled half, and said, "Ready."

"Left point two."

Tee shifted the reticles even less, back towards his target. His finger, with a will of its own, slowly squeezed. As always, the shot itself surprised him. The round entered one head, exited, and entered the next. Per the plan, both men dropped out of his sight. His scope never wavered.

Givens said, "Clean kills. Targets are down." He reached for his neck and engaged his radio again. "Red Six, Eyes. Targets are eliminated. Shifting to engagement area overwatch."

"Roger, Eyes," the LT said. "Acquire and eliminate targets at will when contact is initiated."

"Roger that, sir,"

Tee began shifting his body before he heard Givens say, "Shooter. By eyes, go to sector two."

"Contact."

"Go to six o'clock. Approximately twenty mills."

"Contact."

"Go to glass."

"Courtyard. Front porch with columns."

"Be aware our friendlies," Givens advised.

"Roger."

Staff Sergeant Flores and Private First Class Carter

slipped through the unlocked gate and ran in a low crouch to the downed men. Flores grabbed the radio off one of them and grinned, his teeth white in the night. Carter grinned right back as she held up four cigars. She tucked them away and gathered the men's rifles and magazines.

They slipped back out of the gate and Flores put the radio to his lips. He made the urgent call twice and then prepared to engage targets. It didn't take long.

Most of the Cuban troops went down as one when the troops from the 2017th initiated the ambush. It was L-shaped with the waist-high wall surrounding the front yard providing plenty of cover for them.

Those who didn't go out the front door tried to make it to the boat tied up at the dock. Garner triggered the charge before they got near and blew the boat literally out of the water when the fuel exploded along with the Claymore's explosion. The three men with rifles threw them down and raised their hands. It didn't take long for LT Rojas and his troops to surround them.

He recognized Presidente Perez on sight. The man stood shaking in fear and was nothing like the propaganda his country sent out a few years earlier.

Rojas shook his head in disgust. "It wasn't enough that Communism ruined your own country. You had to try and bring it here? These people have it figured out. Love one another and live in peace. There's no room for your lies."

"Yeah," Flores chimed in. He used a handful of carefully chosen curse words in Spanish, most of them aimed at the lack of manhood of Perez. The men standing with their hands raised widened their eyes at hearing it.

"The people of Jamacia will decide what to do with you," Rojas advised.

"They will do nothing," Perez stated, some semblance of fortitude coming back to him. "When my soldiers arrive, they..."

Rojas raised a hand to stop him. "They will never arrive. Not just because the ship they are on probably won't make it, but because they will become shark food in just a few minutes."

"Yeah, shark food," Flores chimed in. "That's what will happen to you, too. The Jamaicans are serious about living in peace. They fed enough gang members to the sharks, and a few more assholes won't bother them. You can kiss your commie ass goodbye."

Perez was shaking again.

"I see it, sir," Mulligan said. He was looking at the radar on the Catalina. "You should be able to see her lights any time now."

"There it is," Jones confirmed. He turned to the man beside him. "Are you sure about this?"

"Yeah, I'm sure. It's like riding a bike. Get up there and man the fifty. We got someone on one of the side guns and ol' Mulligan back there has his little surprise. Ready."

"All right," Jones said. "You seem to fly this thing pretty good, so I'm going to trust you. You might just earn a call sign from this."

"I already got one. Earned it decades ago in the Air Force."

"Yeah?"

"They call me The Breeze."

On the first pass, Mulligan shoved the barrel of fuel out the door. It tumbled into the darkness towards the well-lit ship below them. He pulled against the harness holding him back as he watched it stabilize with the odd nose he had strapped to it facing down. The big fins he had ratcheted to the other end of the barrel seemed to be doing their job; he hoped the nose did, too.

When the barrel hit the ship, the nose crushed against the lid and cut deep into it, shredding one side as it did. Fuel splashed everywhere as the rest of the barrel crumbled. Moments later sparks set off the liquid and what remained in the sliding make-shift bomb.

"Yes!" Mulligan shouted. "See! It didn't just bounce off and spill a little. Those pieces of steel shredded the barrel. We're gonna be able to save the other two for the return flight."

"Good job. Now man that fifty!" Jones ordered. "We need to sink it and the escorts. The Breeze is bringing us back around a few times."

"Who?" Mulligan asked as he pulled back the charging handle on the fifty.

Rio Jatibonico
Cuban Revolutionary Navy

Capitan Garcia looked up sharply. He recognized the sound. He dropped his fork and ran for the galley hatch. By the time he was through it and headed up the short flight of steps, the world lit up.

Rounds from a large-caliber weapon impacted on the deck of the ship and against the superstructure. The sparks ignited the fuel on the deck as well as what remained in the barrel sliding across the deck towards him. Everything became engulfed. His sailors couldn't get to the weapons to fight back. He retreated deep into the ship and waited. It didn't take long for him to decide he didn't want to wait on the crushing depths to take him.

He slid his pistol out of his holster.

2017th Armory

Lieutenant Rojas leaned against the wall under the eave of the building and watched the snow fall. Across the parking lot, his platoon sergeant... and friend, hugged both her parents as the snow fell on them.

The trip had been worth it, despite the long boring flight home in the cramped plane. One injury, no loss of life. He could accept the outcome of missions like that. *Nothing to it.*

"This sucks, sir," Krayner said, interrupting his thoughts. "I left Minnesota years ago to get away from this."

"It won't last long. Enjoy it."

"Easy for you to say, sir. You spent a week in Jamacia. Next time you go, I volunteer for the mission."

"I hear you. If we go back, I'll be sure to rotate who goes. I doubt we will, though. Fuel is a precious commodity."

Krayner looked over at SFC Warner and her family. "To see her like that, I'd say it was worth it."

"Yeah. Yeah, it was."

The Hare and the Hunter

Larry Hoy

2031

Maria caught her foot on a root and fell sprawling in the snow. The cold bit at her frozen hands, causing her to cry out in surprise and pain.

"She's over here." A man's voice called out from somewhere in the dark behind her. "This way."

Maria reached out and felt the ground fall away to her right. She crept towards it, lurched forward to rolling into the gully. The forest was thick, blocking out most of the starlight; the moon had already disappeared below the horizon. She was relieved that moving through the gully was more manageable; she didn't have to fight through the underbrush. The leaves still crunched as she crawled over them, but the men chasing her were making enough noise to hide her.

She kept her head low as she crawled along and missed seeing the hare, also hiding in the forest gully.

The hare leaped from its hiding place and ran; it leaped free of the gully and dashed from one bush to the next. Maria froze, unable to see where the animal ran, although she could track it from all the noise it made crashing through the brush. She guessed it was moving off to her left, the same side of the gully as her pursuers, but moving much quicker.

"There she goes. Hurry, she's running for it," one man called out. Maria flattened herself and waited as the man ran along, blasting through the bushes in pursuit of the hare.

Maria turned her head to the side and held her breath. A man crashed through a bush only a few strides from where she lay in the snow. He was dressed in a camouflage soldier's uniform; a long dark coat hung to his knees and he held a rifle to his chest. He paused, peering through the darkness; the forest was quiet. The hare must have stopped running.

She turned her head more, unable to look away. The man had thick black hair and beard, which needed brushing. He stood like a statue, waiting, listening. She lay in the snow, hidden from his view by the gully and some bushes, but if he were to look down... Maria knew if she could see him, he'd be able to see her.

She pressed her lips together to fight back a groan; her hands ached from where they landed in the snow. She pulled a quivering breath and let it ease out as she tried to slow her breathing, afraid it might be visible in the frosty night.

Then there was a rustle from the brush; further along, the hare was on the move.

"Keep going, you bitch," he said, voice low, but Maria heard him clearly. "You'll only be able to run for so long. I'll catch you, even if I have to follow you all night." He marched off, moving in the same direction as the rabbit.

Maria rolled onto her side and stuffed her hands under her armpits, praying that she might warm them enough that she could keep crawling. She wanted to get farther along before the man realized what he was chasing and doubled back. She pulled her fists into her coat sleeves and climbed to her feet.

She set off at a diagonal from where the soldier went. It was a challenge; the ledge was only a couple feet tall, but the snow made everything slippery. She grabbed a tree branch and heaved herself out. Her foot slipped, but her grip on the tree branch kept her from falling back. Now back at forest level, she was careful to gently push aside the branches that crossed her path; she was better off moving a little slower and remaining silent.

The man was calling for help. She recognized his voice, but he was so far away she couldn't make out the words. She ducked and plowed along; there was a glimmer of hope in her chest that she might get out of this.

She stumbled along an animal path moving in her general direction, and the way helped her move faster through the forest. The trail emerged into a small clearing; Maria stepped from the forest and glanced up at the sky, identifying the constellations of Orion, Gemini, and Cancer. She wondered just how far she had traveled through the woods. Still, the clearing didn't give her enough view of the stars to calculate her location, but she had been walking most of the day.

"That will be just enough."

Maria spun around and spotted a man stepping into the clearing, just as she had. Like the other man, he was also dressed in camouflage, but in place of the long dark coat, this man had a white and black mottled cloak with a hood. He wasn't carrying a rifle, but he had a long spear with a foot-long blade on its end. The spear and blade were both blackened. The hood hid his face, but she could see a white beard covering his chin.

"You did pretty well getting away from my boy, but you had a lot of help from the hare you spooked; if it hadn't been for that rabbit, he'd of found you."

Maria glanced around the clearing, looking for an exit.

"Please don't." He had been using the spear as a walking stick, but now brought it across his chest in a ready position. "If you run, I'll have to use this."

Maria nodded her head and held out her hands in surrender.

The hooded man pulled out a length of cord from a pocket. He looped it over her wrists and cinched it tight. "We're going back to the cabin. Then you and I are going to sit down and talk like civilized people. Do you understand?"

He gave a sharp tug on the cord, pulling Maria off balance; she stumbled and struggled to keep her balance with her hands tied. When he stepped from the clearing back into the dark forest, Maria lost sight of the man, even though he was only a few strides ahead. The cloak distorted his natural shape, making him disappear like a magic spell.

The cord pulled taut, and it jerked her along, crashing through a bush and slamming into the back of the man. He didn't respond, just kept moving through the darkness. Maria increased her speed and tried to follow in his footsteps, but the cloak made it impossible. She almost plowed into his back again when he came to a stop.

Maria glanced at the short natural walls on either side of them and realized he had brought her right back to the gully where she had scared the rabbit.

"The hare was lucky, but this was a good move, except for that." He pointed to the ground. "Do you see your mistake?" Snow collected in clumps as it filtered through the trees, but at her feet in a pile of snow was her handprint. "I'd of still caught you, but I do like the challenge. Come on, it's time we get back. I want to beat him back to the camp."

The man led her to his camp, a simple single-room hunting cabin deep in the woods; Maria guessed it was twenty kilometers to the nearest town. She was all alone, and there was no help coming.

"Over here." He escorted her to the fireplace and tied off the cord to a thick iron ring on the wall. "Wait here."

The man removed his cloak and hung it on a hook by the door. His long spear he carried with him as he moved around the cabin and paused, only to build a fire and light some candles. When the fire was roaring, he pulled a chair near the fireplace and sat down. He did not bring a char for Maria. "Let's talk while we wait for Maurus to get back." He leaned forward and rubbed his hands together near the fire. "What's your name?"

Maria looked at the cord that held her hands together, ignoring the man. She tried to loosen the lines on her wrists, but everything held firm.

"You can talk to me or don't. I don't really care; I was just hoping for some civilized conversation. My name's Giovanni."

Tied to the iron ring like she was, she leaned her back against the wall. "I'm Maria."

"Well, it's a pleasure to meet you, Maria. So what were you doing sneaking around our little hideaway?"

Maria shrugged. "I was hunting for food."

"So you must live around here?"

"I'm from the town; I didn't realize just how far I had walked."

The man nodded. "Are you a good hunter?"

"Better than some."

"Where is the rest of your family?"

"We have a house in town."

"Just to be sure I have this right. You started out early this morning to go hunting. You walked all day and into the night, and you brought no weapons and without cold-weather gear. Do I have everything correct?"

Maria brushed the hair out of her eyes but didn't say anything. She just locked eyes with Giovanni, waiting for the man to blink. The front door opened with a slam and bounced off the wall. Maria looked up and recognized the man in the doorway; the dark-haired man was back.

"Maurus, it's about time," Giovanni called out to the man at the door. "Look at what I found wandering around in the woods."

Maurus closed the door with a slam and latched it shut. "Yea, I figured you'd find her; I brought some dinner before we start the entertainment." He pulled a pair of hares out from under his jacket; they hung limp, strung together by their hind legs. He peeled off his coat and moved to the kitchen area of the room. He picked up a huge cleaver and lopped off their heads in two quick hits.

"Did she tell you why she was peeking around our place?" He started cleaning the rabbits as he talked.

"She was out here hunting," Giovanni said.

"Well, I guess it would be ungracious to kick her out without some food in her belly. Then afterward, maybe she could think of a way to thank us for our generosity." He punctuated his statement with a quick pull, stripping the skin off one hare.

"Maria was just telling me she is from Pinzolo. You are from Pinzolo, correct? That's the nearest town and a pretty healthy walk from here." Giovanni leaned back in his chair and stroked his beard. "Winter in the mountains, you might do better to stay with us till the spring."

Maria's blood turned cold. They would never let her leave here alive.

"You're probably right. The mountains can be dangerous in the winter." He turned towards the woman and used a bloody carving knife to emphasize his words. "I think we are going to be good friends. Do you like rabbit?" Maurus slammed the blade against the chopping board, dividing the hare.

Maria jerked against the cords securing her to the wall; the lines cut against her wrist, threatening to crush her bones. When she finally surrendered, she fell to her knees, her hands high above her head. "Please let me go; I'll tell no one." Tears ran down her face.

Giovanni rose and advanced on her. "Who are you going to tell? What were you doing here?" He grabbed a fist full of her hair and twisted her head around so she could see his face. "Don't lie to me, or the rest of your life will be so much worse than anything you could ever think of."

"I was looking for mushrooms," Maria cried. "That's all. I was just looking for mushrooms."

Giovanni shook her by her hair. "Lies. You didn't walk from the town for mushrooms."

"No, I have a cabin, higher in the mountains." She hissed through her teeth at the pain.

The man released her hair and returned to his seat. "That I believe. Now who is with you?"

Maria pressed her face into her arms. "There's six of us." Her voice broke through the tears. "They are going to come for me. You need to let me go."

Maurus appeared, carrying a thick iron pot; water sloshed at the lip. He lifted the handle and set it to hang from an iron hook over the flames. "What do you think? Is she telling the truth?"

Giovanni shrugged. "Does it matter? We can hide her away if anyone comes looking. Until then..." A smile split through the man's thick white beard. "...she's ours."

"No." Maria twisted like a fish on the end of the cord. "No, let me go, please."

"How long till the stew is ready?" Giovanni asked.

"Half an hour."

"Good," The older man stood up and untied the cord holding Maria from the wall. "You come with me."

"No." She collapsed to the floor when the cord came free of the wall. "Don't do this."

Giovanni grabbed a fist full of hair and pulled her to her feet, his other hand holding the cord tied to her wrists. He pulled her towards a bed along the wall. "Maurus, why don't you go for a walk outside." The man scooped Maria in his arms and tossed her onto the bed.

"Are you crazy? It's freezing outside." The man watched from his spot by the fire.

"Suit yourself." He wrapped the free end of the cord around one of the corner poles of the bed, pulling Maria's arms high over her head. She rolled away from him, so Giovanni pinned her in place with his knee as he unbuttoned his shirt.

With his shirt off, he grabbed the collar of her shirt and ripped it open. Buttons shot off in every direction. The sight of her pink breasts made him lick his lips; he grabbed her breasts, crushing them in his meaty hands. He bent towards her and bit into her neck.

Maria screamed, bucking and kicking, anything to throw the man off. He moved his knee onto her belly and pressed harder, preventing her from breathing. She saw blood on his lips, her blood.

"No." She gasped.

He rose and smiled at her. With a gentle touch, he traced the swell of her breast. Cupping the mounds against his palms, he bent again and this time bit into her cheek.

Maria let out a blood-curdling scream as he clutched and twisted her breasts. He reared up and bellowed, eyes hungry and wild. He slapped her hard across her face. Stars exploded behind her eyes. She tried to blink them away, and the room swam before her eyes. When the world stopped spinning, she was choking on a mouthful of blood.

"Shut up." His voice was low and savage. "Don't you say another fucking word." He rose off her lap and tugged at her belt.

Maria's ears were still ringing, and her hands were pulled tight from where they strained against the bed. She spat out the blood and turned the pillow red. She was exhausted from fighting. Her head fell to the side, and she closed her eyes, trying to block out what was happening.

Giovanni didn't notice; he redoubled his efforts on her belt. With a savage pull, he ripped the buckle away, and the belt separated. He grabbed her pants and tugged them down to her knees with a cry of satisfaction. He moved his knee leg, pinning Maria's legs flat against the bed. Then he bent to her belly and licked from her navel to the bite marks on her neck.

He grabbed her face. "Open your eyes."

She squeezed her eyes even tighter and tried to shake her head.

"Open your eyes, or I'll tear your eyelids off."

Maria struggled, but the rope held her arms tight to the pole, and he pinned her legs under his knee. She was defeated. Her body went limp, and she opened her eyes.

The man was over her; his white beard was now stained red with her blood. "This doesn't have to be painful." He started working on his own belt. "You might just enjoy it." He eased his pants lower when there was a knock at the door.

"What the hell?" He pulled his pants back up. "Maurus, did you hear that?"

The younger man was already scrambling after his rifle.

There was another knock. "Hello? Is there someone inside?" The voice carried a distinctive German accent. The knock was repeated a third time.

"Shit." Giovanni stood up and pulled a blanket over Maria, hiding her nudity. "Don't say a damn thing, and you'll live through the night. Open your mouth, and I'll break your jaw." Then he turned to the door and called out in a loud voice. "Who is it? What do you want?" He fastened his belt and retrieved his black spear.

"My name is Sargent Bastian; I'm with the First German Cavalry. I need you to open this door. My men and I require a room and nourishment for the night."

Maria tilted her head to the door. The two men stood on either side, weapons at the ready. "I don't have anything for you. There is only enough here for me."

"That is not for you to decide. If you do not open this door, I'll be forced to open it myself."

The two hunters looked at each other, seemingly unsure of what to do next.

The door handle exploded as someone outside fired into it, splinters of wood and metal flying. Maurus fell back with a curse. Giovanni readied his spear.

"Step back from the door, or I will deem your actions aggressive, and we will shoot you as a war criminal."

Giovanni took a few steps back, but Maurus couldn't stand; he slid back, leaving a trail of blood. His rifle hung forgotten from his shoulder. The door swung open with a freezing gust of wind. A voice called out from the darkness. "Lower your weapons now, or I'll give the order to fire."

Maurus tossed his rifle away, his hand pressing against a bloody spot on his shirt. Giovanni spat on the floor, dropped his spear, and held his arms to the side. "Won't you please come in?" His offer sounded far from sincere.

Four men in German battle uniforms entered the room, three holding rifles. The fourth had a pistol holstered at his side. He closed the door and braced it closed with a box sitting nearby. He stood with a smile. "Something smells wonderful; what's for dinner?"

"Sargent." One man pointed his rifle at Maria under the blanket. "There's someone else."

"You in the bed, please stand up. Move slowly, so we don't

get the wrong impression."

Maria shook her head. "I can't; they tied me up."

"Watch him." The sargent gestured to Giovanni as he made his way to the bed. There, he found Maria with her arms tied over her head. He lifted the blanket, and his eyes went wide when he saw her nudity.

Maria rolled towards the wall to hide from his leering eyes.

"Well, isn't that something?" The sargent slowly lowered the blanket; his eyes seemed to drink in her image. "Show me your hands, woman."

Maria twisted around under the blankets until she was facing him again. She presented her wrists to the sargent and waited while butterflies fluttered away in her stomach.

He drew a folding knife from his pocket and pressed a button on the handle. A gleaming blade sprang to life. He carefully slipped the blade between her wrists, and with a quick stroke, he pulled up on the edge, and her wrists flew apart.

Maria gasped and grabbed the edge of the blanket, pressing it against her. "Thank you, sir. You saved my life." One arm slipped below the blanket, and she worked her pants up over her hips.

"One step at a time, shall we?" He raised the switchblade and pressed a button, folding the blade back into the handle.

Maria's blood turned cold as she caught a better look at the knife; the handle was black wood with silver accents; in the middle was a silver eagle with his wings wide resting above the Nazi broken cross.

The sargent closed the blade and slipped the knife back into his pocket. "All right, miss. Get yourself cleaned up; there is much to do." He turned back to the room. "So I think I've already asked this question, but I'll repeat myself just this once. What's for dinner?" He waved a hand. One soldier escorted Giovanni towards the fireplace; the other two grabbed Maurus by the shoulders and left him by the wall.

"Hasenpfeffer," Giovanni answered, "but we only had two hares. There's not enough for everyone." He nodded at the pot dangling in the fireplace.

"You two look rather well-fed. I'm sure you won't starve by missing one meal, and I assure you the German Army appreciates your sacrifice." The sargent sat at the table. "So, how about a bowl?"

Giovanni dipped his head and gave a curt bow. "Please allow me to serve you." He moved to the kitchen area to fetch a stack of bowls. He scooped the rabbit stew into a bowl and set it before the sargent. "Bon appetit."

The sargent spooned a portion into his mouth and then slammed his fist on the table. "Hot," he sucked air into his mouth. "Hot." He struggled to chew and swallow the bite. "Water." He gasped.

Giovanni fetched water from a pump at the sink and set it on the table. The sargent drank down a mouthful and gave a sigh. "Wow, my compliments to the chef. The rabbit is most excellent. I have a bottle of wine in my pack. Would you mind going with my man to retrieve it?"

Marius caught Giovanni's eye, his face pale with fear. "Don't do it; he's just going to put a bullet in your back when you get outside."

Giovanni stepped towards his spear on the floor.

"That will not be necessary." He waved at his man, "If he takes another step towards his weapon, kill him." The sargent pulled his pistol and shot Maurus.

Maria screamed and quickly covered her mouth with her hand to muffle the scream; Maurus went limp and slumped to the side.

"Private, please take the man outside." The sargent set his pistol on the tabletop and took another bite of stew. "Young lady, if you have prepared yourself, perhaps you would be so kind as to join me."

Maria rose from the bed, her clothes mostly restored; she tied the bottom of her blouse closed now that the buttons were gone. "Why did you shoot that man?"

The sargent motioned for her to join him at the table. "I punished him for his crimes, or am I mistaken? Was your little tryst in the bed consensual?"

"No," she eased herself into the seat across from him. "It was not consensual."

"There you have it," he brushed off his hands. "Kidnapping, rape, torture, the penalty is death."

Giovanni lunged at the sargent with a guttural cry. He dove low and fast, moving below the tabletop to prevent the soldiers from a clear shot.

One soldier raised his rifle and fired, hitting the wall where Giovanni was standing half a second before; with one rifleman still outside, the remaining two started moving in opposite directions around the table.

"Hold your fire," The sargent said with one hand raised. "I apologize, miss; my men's reactions have deteriorated due to hunger." He placed both his hands flat on the table and, sitting at attention, continued speaking. "Very well, you have the advantage; what are your terms?"

"Tell your men to back up," Giovanni called from under the table. "I have a knife to your balls. If I get shot, you are going to lose your manhood."

The sargent waved at his men. "Please back to the doorway, gentlemen. Should the man under the table harm anyone, kill him slowly." The sargent waited for the soldiers to return to the doorway. "Very well. What's next? Shall I get you a helicopter and a Swiss bank account with a million dollars?"

"I was thinking you have your men set their rifles on the floor, for starters."

The sargent nodded, and the men pulled the rifle slings from over their heads and set them on the floor. As the soldiers were standing up, the table exploded upward. Maria fell backward and crashed to the floor; a blur shot out, running for the window. Giovanni grabbed his spear and cloak and launched himself through the window before the soldiers could retrieve their rifles.

The soldiers scrambled through after him into the dark through the broken window. A quick burst of gunfire sounded in the darkness as muzzle flares lit up the night like lightning bolts.

Maria scrambled away from her fallen chair and found the sargent looming over her with his hand out. "Please allow me." He helped her to her feet. "Well, that was fun, don't you think?"

Maria took a step back, realizing they were alone in the room. "What is to become of him?"

"Exactly what I promised, I will execute him for his crimes."

"What will happen to me?"

The sargent righted her chair and brushed it off with his hand before gesturing her to sit. "Before we were so rudely interrupted, we were about to get to know each other." He walked to the kitchen area of the room and pumped the water pump handle, and water flowed into the sink. "Look at that; it works." He returned to the table with a pitcher of water and two carved wooden cups. "It's the simple things. There is a working water pump, hot stew, and a warm, dry cabin in the woods. It makes a person long for the world we lost, where every luxury was at our fingertips." He filled the cups and set one before Maria. With his own, he drained it and then refilled. "My name is Sargent Bastian; my men and I are with the First German Cavalry."

"My name is Maria."

"Such a lovely name. I am most curious how you found yourself in the company of those most unsavory of fellows."

She took a sip of the water and considered the story she told Giovanni, but recalled how easily he picked it apart. "I live with a group about ten or fifteen kilometers further up the mountains. I went out this morning to collect mushrooms; I got curious and followed them back here. They must have found this cabin recently because I don't remember anyone living here before. It's sat empty for years."

The sargent glanced around the cabin. "That's fortunate, an empty hunting cabin. My men and I severely underestimated the challenge of crossing the Alps in the winter. This cabin would give us the place to wait till the season turns a bit more hospitable."

"If I may ask, why are you coming through the mountains?" Maria asked.

A half-smile slipped across his face, giving Maria a shiver. "That is the question, isn't it?" The man sat silently for a bit and answered. "For the moment, you could say we are sightseeing, simply passing through."

The three soldiers took that moment to return; they stepped into the room and started removing the rifles and coats.

"Gentlemen, how was the hunt?"

The tallest man shrugged off his coat and kicked the snow from his boots. "He got away by the time we got after him. He moved like a ghost, we never even saw a trace, and I didn't want to risk finding him in the dark."

The sargent nodded. "Smart, block up that window, and then you divvy up the rest of the stew among yourselves. We're spending the night. Bring the horses inside; I don't want that man going after them."

The tall man nodded; he sent the other two to bring in the horses while he went to work securing the broken window.

Sargent Bastian turned back to Maria. "Now, my dear, you were just about to tell me exactly where you are from."

"It's about fifteen kilometers higher in the mountains."

"Yes, you said that. Tomorrow, you'll lead us there and introduce me." He stood up and held out his hand. "It's going to be a big day; perhaps we should retire to the bed. Won't you join me?"

Marie shook her head. "I don't want to do that."

When the sargent smiled this time, Marie's breath caught in her throat. "My dear, you misunderstood me. This is not a request." His hand struck out with the speed of a viper and locked on her wrist. Before she even had the thought of resisting him, she was walking towards the bed with her arm twisted painfully high between her shoulder blades.

The sargent released her with a push that sent her crashing across the mattress. He grabbed the length of cord that was still tied to the corner post and rewound it around her wrists. "There we go; can't have you running off, can we? You stay there, and I'll be right back."

He turned back to the tall soldier. "Before the men sack out, I want this building inventoried, and collect everything on the table. We move out tomorrow at sunup; we are going to meet the neighbors."

The sargent returned to the bed, and he removed his uniform, folding it neatly on the foot of the bed. Then he slid beneath the blankets with Maria. "Gentlemen, if you would be so kind as to extinguish any extra candles."

The room grew dim, with just enough light for the men to move around the cabin.

Maria flinched when the sargent's fingers touched her, gently pulling at her clothes, different from the savage attack of Giovanni, but just as horrible.

"I thought you were here to save me?" she whispered.

The sargent chuckled at that. "My dear, whatever gave you that idea?"

When the sun finally broke through the gloom, the second in charge rose early and stirred the coals in the fireplace. Maria waved her bound hands to get his attention, but he ignored her. If she could get the man to cut her free, she might get away as Giovanni did. She kept waving, hoping he would help.

"My dear, please tell me what is so important?"

Her heart sank; she had woken the devil beside her. She could still taste him on her lips. Her stomach did a slow roll at the realization. At least she didn't cry; she held tight to that one slim fact. He hadn't been able to make her cry as he used her. "I need to use the toilet."

He took a deep breath and sat up. He paused, stretching. "Lukas, do I smell coffee?"

"We found some old moldy beans last night; I rinsed them off and ground them. So we'll see?"

The sargent glanced over to the corner; the horses were gone. "And the horses?"

"I had the boys take them outside. They are standing guard. I was about to swap out with them for a bit." The man pulled on his coat and went to the fireplace.

"Very well. Send someone to escort the lady. She wants to freshen up."

"Of course, I'll send them in." He slipped out the door, a steaming cup in his hand.

"Well, my dear, I think it's time we start the day."

The sargent tossed back the blanket. The cold air bit at Maria's skin, turning it to goose flesh. She didn't say a word, only holding out her wrists. The sargent admired her nude body, his eyes crawling up from her toes. When he finally reached her wrists, he pulled out his knife and pressed the button. The silver blade popped out with a soft click.

He slipped the knife carefully between her wrists. "Steady, I wouldn't want to accidentally cut you." With a quick jerk, her wrists came free. "Did you see the symbols on my knife?" He held it towards her; the Nazi cross glimmered in the morning sun. "Do you know what it means?"

"It is Nazi, the symbol for the German Army during the old wars." She curled her legs up and pulled a shirt over her head.

"World War Two, to be exact. My great-grandfather was an officer in that command. When the war ended, he lost everything, his farm, house, everything. The government even came through and confiscated all his war memorabilia. He hid the knife. Now it is the only evidence of his service. He risked being sent to jail to keep the knife. Do you know why I have it?"

Maria didn't answer him; she kept pulling on clothes. His hand moved in a flash and slapped her across the face.

"You will not ignore me; I asked you a question." He the

knife into his pocket. "I carry this to remind me of Germany's greatness and to not accept anything less than perfection: not from myself, not from my men, and not from those whom I have conquered for my country."

He laced his boots and straightened his shirt before he advanced on the fireplace and poured himself a cup of the stale coffee. He took a cautious sip and swallowed. "My, how the world has changed." He chuckled and took another sip.

There was a knock on the door.

"Enter."

A young man stepped inside the door and stood at attention. "Sir, I am reporting for morning detail."

"Yes, Private, the lady requires the use of the toilet. You will escort her; you will not take your eyes from her. Should she try to evade you, put a bullet through her, but do not kill her. We will be breaking camp soon, and she has a long walk ahead of her."

"Yes, sir." He swung his short rifle from his back and held it across his chest as he advanced on the bed. "Ma'am, please come with me."

Maria stood, cinching her belt and crossing her arms across her chest to hold her blouse closed. She walked through the door, the private following, his finger on the trigger.

Within the hour, Maria was leading them through the forest. The men pulled out some grain and made a portage with it; it was thin, but it was warm. She was not offered anything; her stomach was growling in the complaint; she hadn't eaten since she left for mushrooms the day before.

With every step she took, her disgust grew. She hated finding the cabin yesterday. She hated being spotted when she peeked in the window. She hated the two Italian men who ran her down and the Germans who trapped her. More than anything, she hated the sargent for everything he did.

She watched for a chance to run, but they were on horseback, and she was walking; she'd never be able to escape. The only thing she could think to do was to lead them home. The mother would know what to do; she'd have a plan. Maria just had to concentrate on walking. There was still a long way to go.

She pulled her thick cotton shawl tight around her and wondered whether she had only been away from home for one day. It seemed so very much longer. She gave a quick glance behind her; the men followed along with a single file. The private was in the lead, his rifle still across his chest.

The winter sun was setting. She led the group into her grove. Five simple A-frame cottages all faced a common area in the middle. A suspicious person might wonder if the arrangement of the houses to resemble a communal pentagram was coincidental.

Maria collapsed exhausted into a porch chair of her home. The Germans mounted on horseback followed seconds after her. Maria watched as they walked their horses around the perimeter of the center lawn, only to return to her porch and dismount.

"Such a cozy little hamlet you have here," The sargent said as he tied his mount to a corner pole. "Perhaps you should introduce us to whoever is in charge." He brushed away the grime that had collected on his uniform. "Private, assist her."

"Of course, Sargent." The young man couldn't have been sixteen yet; Maria thought he was more a boy than a man. He swung down from his horse and swung his short-barreled rifle from under his arm till it rested across his chest. "Lead the way, ma'am." He wasn't pointing the gun at her, but he was holding it at the ready, just in case.

Maria's feet cramped, and she stumbled a few steps. Her body ached all over, but she knew that there was much more to be done before she would rest. She grabbed a walking stick from the porch to lean on and headed towards a neighboring house.

The mother's house was identifiable by the collection of wind chimes; she claimed they were to ward off evil spirits. There was also a fenced-in area beside it, where they kept the community chickens. Maria knocked on the mother's door.

"I'll be right there," a voice called from inside. A few moments later, an older woman opened the door. It was impossible to guess her age; she stood straight and firm, with a wrinkled face and silver hair. She might have been fifty or she might be a hundred and fifty. Her face lit up when she recognized Maria. "Darling, I'm so happy to see you. They told me you didn't come home last night." The old woman glanced at the soldier standing with Maria. "Did you bring our lost daughter home?" she said with a smile.

"Madam, my sargent would like a word." The boy motioned with his rifle.

"Of course, just give me a moment to fetch my shawl." When she returned, Maria gave her the walking stick and took the older woman's elbow, while the private followed.

"Madam." The sargent gave a curt nod. "I sent for the leader of this community. Is that you?"

The woman returned his nod with a smile. "Yes, they call me Mother. Do I have you to thank for returning my daughter to us?"

"Are there no men here?" he asked.

Mother shook her head. "No, they all went off to fight or hunt. Now there are only my daughters and me."

"How many daughters do you have?" The sargent emphasized the word daughters.

"It's cold out here. Won't you join me for dinner? It's the least we could do for a group of soldiers."

The sargent smiled at the opportunity. "That would be most generous. Do you have a barn where we might secure our mounts?"

"Maria, would you be so kind as to find some help? Take their horses to the barn and tell the others to prepare dinner. We must celebrate."

Maria stood to her feet and bowed her head. "Of course, Mother. I'll tell the others." She disappeared into her house.

"Please, sargent?" She let the word hang until he nodded. "You and your men should join me; the women will be along soon enough." Mother stepped forward, looped her arm around the sargent's elbow, and pointed him towards her house. "I'm sure you are tired from your journey. I have refreshments inside.

"Please sit," and she motioned to the long center table. Each man sat with his weapon in reach. The mother went to the kitchen area and returned with a water pitcher and a stack of cups. She made her way around the table, serving each man before pouring a cup for herself.

"You are most generous," the sargent said. "But how do you manage without men?"

"We do all right. During the summer we have gardens; we also raise chickens and swine. Everyone helps, and the goddess provides."

"The goddess?"

"Aradia, she is the goddess of the moon; she watches over us."

"I'm not here to discuss your heathen ways. I want to know how you defend yourselves."

Mother smiled. "We are just a simple community. We mind our own business and leave the world to the men. We don't need much."

The sargent stood and raised his glass in a toast. "Well, I wouldn't feel right about leaving a bunch of helpless women alone in the forest. My men and I will camp here through the winter, and we'll be here to protect you from any intruders that might threaten. For the winter at least, I claim this territory in the name of the Mother Land. For Germany."

The other three men jumped to their feet; each raised his glass and echoed the cry. "For Germany."

"You are too kind," she said, and she too was smiling. "Please, let's discuss the trivialities in the morning. Tonight we dine in your honor."

This time the sargent motioned to one of the privates to refill the cups, while he told the mother about what an honor it was to become part of Germany. Within the hour, two women entered the room with a large pot of pasta. The smells of garlic, basil, and olive oil filled the room. The aroma stopped the sargent mid-sentence; all eyes turned to the steaming bowl of noodles.

"This isn't much, just simple seasoning," one woman said, clearly embarrassed at the attention. The other started dishing the pasta out with a large fork.

Each man dove into his meal as soon as the plate hit the table. The plates were emptied and refilled until the pot was empty.

"How were you able to make pasta?" the sargent asked, licking olive oil from his plate. It had been years since he had tasted such a fine meal.

Mother laughed. "Every Italian woman grew up at her grandmother's side. Cooking is part of our culture."

"Sargent," Lukas, his second in command, interrupted. "May I be dismissed?"

One woman was sitting beside him, holding the last forkful of pasta, teasing him with it. She touched the pasta to his nose and chin before Lukas lunged forward, catching the fork in his teeth.

"Dismissed. Let's meet tomorrow afternoon to discuss plans."

"Thank you, sir." Lukas all but leapt from the table; he scooped the woman up and left the mother's house.

"Please forgive my man; we have been traveling for a long while."

"There is nothing to forgive. It has been a long while since my daughters have seen such fine men in our little grove."

The door opened, and two more women entered. One was carrying a platter of roasted meat, sliced into thin strips. The other was carrying a platter of peppers, mushrooms, and cheese, drizzled with more olive oil and spices.

When the platters were emptied, the sargent sat back, licking the juices from his fingertips, unwilling to lose even the tiniest drop. He scanned around the table and noticed that the rest of his men had disappeared. He was so intent on the food, he didn't even remember them leaving.

"The meal is masterful," he told Mother.

She rose from the long table and dismissed the women with a wave. They gathered the plates and left.

"Please allow me to show you my treat." She pulled a dark bottle from a cabinet. "Have you ever had homemade grappa?"

"Never."

The woman pulled the cork from the bottle with her teeth and set two cups on the table. "Grappa is another long tradition of my family. They taught me to always have a bottle for visitors. This is my last bottle; I'll have to send some of my girls to bring more in the spring."

"You said this was homemade." The sargent sniffed at his cup. The pungent smell of alcohol burned at his nose.

"It is, but not my home. This is Luigi's grappa." Mother raised her glass and tossed the liquor back.

The sargent mimicked her. The liquid burned like fire; he struggled to swallow it before he coughed and risked losing the drink. The warm burn slowly moved down to his stomach before he started coughing.

Mother smiled. "I'm guessing it's been a while since you had a good drink?"

The sargent put his hand to his face and tried to stop the coughing fit. "Yes, and it has some bite." He sat up and took a deep breath. Between the drink and his coughing fit, he felt a little light-headed.

"Yes, Luigi's grappa has a little bite to it. It's an acquired taste." She pushed the cork back into the bottle, preserving the last bit.

The sargent smacked his lips as she walked off with the bottle; the alcohol had made his lips go numb; he wanted another taste, but he couldn't form the words to ask. Suddenly the seat moved on him, and he sprawled on the floor. He rolled onto his back. The room was spinning. He could feel his stomach threatening to vomit everything up, but he fought the urge.

"Matha." It came out all slurred, and he struggled, but couldn't keep his eyes in focus. "Wa." His eyes rolled back, and the world went black.

The sargent woke up all at once; adrenaline surged into his bloodstream. He shook his head to clear away the cobwebs and realized everything hurt. He was hanging from a rope, his feet dangling in the air, rope biting into his wrists, and he was naked.

He kicked out and set himself swinging. "Damn those fool women."

"You're awake?"

"Who's there?" The room was dark, a single candle providing just enough light to tell he was hanging in some sort of barn. Behind him was the sound of a door opening and then closing.

His arms and shoulders burned from supporting his weight for who knew how long, and he was suffering through a pounding migraine. He thought back, trying to remember just how much he drank the night before, but it was blank. He had been eating a wonderful dinner and then nothing.

A draft blew through the barn, reminding him he was naked and freezing cold. He tried kicking with his legs; he was facing a blank wall and wanted to see what else might be in the room. With every kick, he just kept moving back and forth. The strain on his shoulders was tremendous.

"Hello," he called out to the darkness. "What's going on?"

There was no reply; he guessed the first voice must have left to alert someone. The women must have poisoned him, and then the men came out and captured them. How had he been so careless as to let himself be captured? He heard the door behind him open, and a rush of blistering cold air bit at him.

"Wonderful, you're awake." Mother entered with a handful of women; they fanned around him. A couple lit candles, confirming he was indeed in a barn. Some faces he recognized from the banquet; many were not. Maria stood in the middle of the group, and she held a long-bladed knife with a savage-looking hook on the backside of the blade.

"What's going on?" he snapped at the women. "Let me down at once." He kicked out at the nearest one with his foot but didn't even come near to touching her. He scanned their faces; no one seemed worried or even considered. They regarded him as if he were merely another task they needed to accomplish.

The sargent felt the cold squeeze at his heart with icy fingers. "You need to let me down." He tried again.

The mother placed her hand on Maria's shoulder. "This is the man who raped you?" Maria nodded. The older woman stepped forward to address him directly. "Do you have anything to say?" she asked, but she was clearly not interested in anything he had to say.

"Release me; when my men find out what you are, they will kill every one of you. You'll die begging them to slit your throat."

Some women chuckled at that; his jaw went slack as he struggled to understand what was going on.

The mother stepped forward, taking a hooked stick from the wall. She swung it; he felt the hook bite into his leg, but the cold room had already numbed much of his body. The mother turned him so he could see the room behind him. "You aren't aware of what's going on. Let me help you."

The barn section had been re-purposed into a smokehouse; an open fireplace was unfortunately empty. Sections of meat hung from the ceiling; he hadn't seen so much in years. He was in shock, wondering how a small group of women could have managed so much. Then he saw it.

One of the meat sections was sporting a Nazi tattoo; it was the same tattoo on his own arm. The same tattoo that all his soldiers wore. "For all that's holy, what have you done?" His words were more of a whisper.

The old woman laughed. "You dare to speak of holy things

after you've branded yourself with the mark of the devil?" She crossed her arms across her chest. "Tell me again how you are going to protect us? You couldn't even protect yourself from a bunch of helpless women."

His mind raced; where did he miss the signs? Where did he go wrong? "There will be others."

"Maybe, maybe not." She smiled, and the sargent recognized her smile. It was a look he wore so many times before. "Either way, it won't change what's waiting for you." The old woman stepped aside. "Maria."

The women all gathered around in a semicircle. Maria stepped to the sargent and grabbed his testicles in one hand. It felt like a line of ice cut across his abdomen, and he screamed. The woman's hand came away bloody; she was holding something and laughing.

The sargent kicked out, and he felt a tearing pain that caused his legs to fall limp. He tried to crane his neck but couldn't see much, hanging like he was.

"Don't do this." His breath came out in a steamy whisper.

The mother stepped forward. "Some men learn slow, but you should know by now. There is always a bigger monster hiding in the woods." She took the knife from Maria and made a long slice across his belly. He screamed as she stepped aside and sent them forward to pull out his entrails.

Others went and started pulling tools down from the wall. Saws, axes, and long knives were passed around. Maria tossed his testicles into the firepit while the Mother merely looked on, a grim look of satisfaction across her face.

The sargent screamed, but this time his voice was weak. Dark circles popped at the edges of his vision, and his head grew heavy. It fell forward, and he saw the bloodstain spreading across the floor.

He closed his eyes and waited for the screaming to stop.

Pine Gap

William Alan Webb

Joint Defense Facility Pine Gap, Third Floor (Subterranean)
18 kilometers southwest of Alice Springs, Northern Territory,
Australia
3:29 PM, January 19, 2031

Hunkered down in the Central Communications Office, invariably called the Radio Room, Taylor Reston leaned forward as the gunfire at surface level died away. She kept waiting to hear from somebody about what had happened, but as the seconds slipped by, all was quiet. Sweat saturated the foam earpieces of her headphones and ran down her neck. With the air-conditioning system dry of coolant, the blower fans could only pump in fresh but warm air.

After a minute of nothingness, Reston couldn't stand it any longer. "Eddie, are you on?" she said into the microphone three inches from her lips. "Anybody, what's going on up there?"

The response was immediate, if hushed.

"They're Chinese, all right," said the low voice of Major Eddie Johnson. "Special forces, I'd expect. We gave them a few bursts and they went to ground. Testing us, I'd say, but they'll be back. They didn't come all this way for a walkabout."

"Any idea of numbers?"

"Can't be too many. They had to come in on helicopters, otherwise we'd have picked them up on radar. Maybe a platoon…"

"Anybody hit?"

"No, they didn't shoot back. Just showed themselves enough to draw fire, see if we'd noticed their approach. I reckon they'll wait to move under cover of darkness, but if they come in earnest... we need more firepower."

"I'm on my way up," Reston said.

"No, that's not what I meant," Johnson said. "You stay put."

"No offense, Major, but I'm trained same as you."

"No offense taken, *Captain,* and I know you can fight. I've seen you do it, remember? That's not the point. If the base falls, somebody has to make sure the enemy doesn't get control of the network. That's your job. If we all cark it, you've got to set off the self-destruct charges."

"There's a dirking for you," Reston said.

"There's no DS Solution here, Taylor, or none that I can see. Dead is dead, whether it's from a Chinese bullet or blown to bits by our own demo charges. At least your way it'll be over quick."

"I'd like to avoid it altogether, if I can." She tried to think of a way to argue the point, couldn't. "It's hard just sitting here, Eddie, knowing you might be in danger, knowing you all might."

"I know, but in the meantime we've got to keep monitoring the radios. You can never tell when deliverance might show up, or what form it might take. Maybe we can help it, though. Send out a message on the distress channel, open language, asking any ADF units still around to come to our aid."

"Open language? Won't the—"

"—Chinese pick it up? Probably, but if they think company's coming they might think twice about coming in."

"Or speed up."

"Either way, we need help. Send the message. That's an order, Taylor, if you need it to be."

"I'll send it, Eddie, but I hope like hell you're right."

"You and me both."

Measuring thirty meters square, the Radio Room was a warren of various-sized monitors, computer servers, laptops, desktops, keyboards, radio transmitters and receivers, microphones, long-silent telephones connected to secure landlines, desks, chairs, and anything else that had been needed in the pre-Collapse world to keep the base running at peak efficiency. Having begun as a control and communications relay station for American satellites, Pine Gap evolved first into a monitoring station for spy satellites directed at China and Russia, and later, during the War on Terror, into a war-fighting command.

Money had never been an issue for keeping Pine Gap supplied with whatever it needed to function, including the best radio equipment, and the means to keep it functioning *in extremis*. Pushing her rolling desk chair to a long table filled with various radios, she found the one she needed, thought about how to frame the message, and cleared her throat. Keying open the broadcast switch, she said, "I'm calling for any Australian armed forces who might be out there... this is the Pine Gap facility asking for assistance. We are being attacked by Chinese commandos, and they have damaged our communications array. Get here fast, we can't hold out long—"

"—Taylor, we've got movement," Major Johnson said, his voice blasting from the speaker connected to the base radio net. "What can you see on the video feeds?"

Reston switched off the broadcast and moved over to the video monitors.

"I think they've got a machine gun," she said.

Special Operations Command (SOCOMD) Compound NWT 4,
'Ricky Jick'
Near Yulara, Northern Territory, Australia
4:17 PM, January 19, 2031

Trudging over the red desert sands, Jonathan 'Dingo' Dooley felt clammy despite the high, hot sun. If he needed further evidence that he wasn't 25 any more, then he'd found it. He'd stayed out hunting longer than was safe, and run out of water. Once upon a time that wouldn't have bothered him much; those days were long gone now.

Mooney knew better, but he was sick of the constant diet of dried goanna they'd been living on for the past five weeks. A red deer or kangaroo would have been a welcome change, except the only worthwhile target he'd spotted had never come within range to risk using up a precious round of ammunition for the Highlander M85 rifle. Chambered in .223 caliber, it had been common in the days before the world fell apart, so common that thousands of Australian hunters owned them. Once the world economy collapsed, and hunting was for survival, not sport, such rounds became the favored currency in place of the Australian dollar. Paper money became a fire-starter.

Dooley knew that such a small bullet would not have put down large prey. However, they had even less ammo for the

Tikka T3x Lite Medium NT, which used caliber .308 cartridges, and since he was far more likely to get a rabbit or goanna than something bigger, it made better sense to take the smaller gun. As for the other firearms... they had a different purpose. There were plenty of guns and ammunition in the outpost's armory, but those were for war, not hunting.

Dust clogged his nostrils, forcing him to breathe through his mouth, but that only dried it out more. Dooley also had to keep blinking to clear his vision. Temperatures during Central Australia's hottest month often exceeded 100 degrees F., and nearly four years of living in the Outback had taught him to recognize the warning signs of heat exhaustion, if not heat stroke. He needed water and a place to cool down.

The days of the combination barracks/headquarters building being air-conditioned were long gone. It wasn't that they didn't have electricity; they did, thanks to the military-grade solar-power system. Nor were they lacking spare parts to fix the evaporator coil in the compressor, which had a hole; Parker had scavenged one off the abandoned health clinic in Yulara that matched perfectly. What they didn't have, and never would again, was the correct refrigerant.

With dragging footsteps, he made it to a hillside some 80 meters from the barracks building, and stopped by a steel door. The sun had sunk far enough so it no longer shone directly on the metal, otherwise it would have blistered his bare hand. After digging a key ring out of his pants pocket, Dooley ducked inside the base greenhouse. Cool air washed over him. Stripping off his sunglasses, he leaned against the nearest wall and sucked down breaths.

The greenhouse had been designed to feed twenty people for twenty years. On Dooley's left, rows of plants lined a series of plastic terraces filled with enriched dirt. Sunlight still lit them, despite the hillside itself being in shadows cast by the surrounding hills, due to a complex series of openings in the hilltops, with mirrors strategically placed to direct the lighting onto the growing vegetables, fruits, and legumes far below. Water came from the same well system that supplied the base, with a large supply of replacement soil in an interior storeroom. With only two people left at the base now, keeping the place functioning required constant attention. On the plus side, there was plenty to eat.

By gulping the cool air, in ten minutes Dooley felt normal

again. After checking a few gauges on the compressors and humidifiers, he locked up and crunched over the sand to the barracks. He was hungry, and while there wouldn't be meat for supper, even beans sounded good.

The door nearest the hillside greenhouse led into the kitchen area, with storage rooms on the right and laundry on the left. Directly ahead down a short corridor were the lavatories, beyond which lay the combination mess hall/entertainment room. When Ricky Jick had first opened in late summer of 2025, with all twenty of its permanent garrison drawn from both the Army and Socomd, the barracks had been a noisy place. The hum of electric appliances, clatter of cookware, snores during nighttime, whispers, shouts, and every other sound that twenty human beings made during the course of living and working in one confined space, it had all combined to make Ricky Jick sound and feel like a typical military facility. But now, with no TV or radio programming, and only two people living there, it had the ambiance of a mausoleum.

Satellite internet remained, although the signal was rarely strong enough even to download messages. Having been part of the communications net set up primarily by the United States and the United Kingdom, with double and triple redundancy, and with thousands of satellites in orbit, the system lasted longer than most other methods of communication.

Formed as one of more than fifty such places across Australia, Ricky Jick was established as a combination supply depot, rest and refueling stop for convoys moving through the Outback, a relay station, and also a Quick Reaction Force in case of nearby trouble. Nobody knew what was going to happen as war became inevitable, but the government wanted military forces throughout the country.

"Silvie?" Dooley's call echoed in the empty space. He'd hoped she was in the kitchen preparing supper. It was her turn, after all, but when nobody answered, he headed out the front door. "Where's she got off to?"

His eyes hadn't had time to adjust to the darker interior, so the sunglasses were enough to protect his vision against glare. The top of his wide-brimmed hat, however, felt like someone had a high-powered laser trained to burn through to his skull.

The other main buildings in the compound were the armory, the garage, and the headquarters, all some fifty meters from the barracks. With the outpost thrown together quickly there were no hard paths connecting them, so Dooley inspected the dirt for recent boot prints, found them, and followed the trail to the headquarters. Sheltered near the eastern edge of a hill, the building lay within the lengthening shadows of late afternoon, and so provided some relief from the heat.

Captain Sylvia Champion sat in the swivel chair behind the array of radio and computer equipment to his left. As the door squeaked open she held up a hand for silence, although how she could hear him wearing headphones seemed uncanny. Maybe she just *sensed* him. She was a captain, after all. But when he took a step she turned in the chair and slid off the headphones.

"Stop, not another step."

"I just—"

"Bloody well fucking listen for once in your life!" she cried. Moving slowly, she showed him where she'd used a computer cable as a tourniquet on her left leg, above the knee. Calming herself, Champion continued. "There's a snake in here, Dingo. I think it's a brownie."

"Western?"

"I don't think so. I only got a glimpse, but I'm pretty sure it's an Eastern."

"No worries, Captain, we've got to—"

"Sergeant Dooley, shut up! He got me when I sat down, and I sat down because I heard a message on the command net. That message takes priority over all else, and I have to hear if there is more, so I am monitoring. Right now, you need to go get the snake gear and the antivenom. I know it's expired, but it's all we've got. When you get back, find that snake and either catch or kill it. I'd fancy eating the damned thing, just out of spite."

Adrenaline cut through all traces of Dooley's hunger and fatigue. After a fast glance for any sign of the snake, Dooley ran to the storage shed for the snake-handling gear. It being Australia, where nearly everything that crawled, walked, flew, or swam wanted to kill you, training courses on how to use the equipment had been mandatory. Not that Dooley needed them. Twenty-one years in the Army, with most of those in Special Forces Command, meant that he'd dealt with venomous snakes not only in Australia, but throughout Southeast Asia, New Guinea, various Pacific Islands, and the Middle

East. He'd even once caught what the Americans called a cottonmouth during a training exercise in the Florida Everglades.

After pulling on a special pair of thigh-high snake-proof boots made from heavy denim, Dooley grabbed the two-meter snare pole from its place on a shelf, and a bucket with a screw-on lid. He'd make a second trip for the antivenom, since administering it wasn't as cut and dried as the captain thought. For one thing, she had to first exhibit symptoms of reacting to the bite, because a bad reaction to the antivenom could kill her as easily as the venom could. So they also had to have adrenaline ready to inject. Then the antivenom had to be kept refrigerated until used, mixed properly, and administered intravenously.

Cracking open the headquarters door and seeing no sign of the snake, Dooley entered and began hunting the serpent. Champion remained hunched forward, elbows on the radio table, her headphones blocking out Dooley's entrance. Her legs remained propped on a second chair so that she sat at an angle to the table.

Dooley knew that time was of the essence, so he moved about the room faster than you normally would with a venomous snake present, and the inevitable happened; from the shadows under a desk, the snake struck him on the calf. Eastern Brown snakes have short fangs, however, and it did nothing more than leave a smear of venom on his boots. Now that he knew where the snake was, Dooley went into capture mode. Very slowly, he moved the end of the pole that had the noose until it circled the snake's head, and then he snapped it shut.

Although slender, Dooley could feel the power of the snake's muscular body as it thrashed at the end of the pole. Several times, it nearly caused him to drop the pole. But strong or not the snake was still a snake, and Dooley swung it squirming into the bucket. Holding it at the bottom, he slammed down the lid, released the noose, and screwed the top closed. Panting from the exertion, and the adrenaline rush of dealing with such a deadly elapid, Dooley barely had time to blink before Captain Champion was out of her chair and limping toward the door.

"Come on then, Sergeant," Champion said, "we've got to be on the road within five minutes… maybe ten. Top off the G-Wagon, load up with food and water, and bring enough firepower to discourage any nasties we might meet along the way. Oh, and where is the antivenom?"

"Ma'am, I... I... what's going on, Sylvie?"

"None of that Sylvie stuff, not now, we're back in the game. We're moving out."

"Back in *what* game? Moving out where?"

"What do you mean, what game? The *Army* game, what do you think? Looks like we're not the last of our lot. Now where did you put the antivenom?"

"I didn't bring it, I was afraid it would get warm. We need to splint and pressure wrap that bite, Syl— Captain. You need to stop moving around; that's just getting the venom moving through your body faster."

"There's no time for that now. Pine Gap is under attack."

"Under attack? I didn't even know it was still open for business," he said.

"Me either, but it is, and they need our help."

"How did they know *we* were still in business? I mean, there's only the two of us left."

"They didn't call us in particular; it was a general call for help from anyone who could hear them. I only heard it twice, and they never acknowledged my response. If Pine Gap's still open, that would be a nice landing spot for us."

"Forgive my asking, Captain, but who could possibly be attacking the Pine Gap facility? Not saying you're wrong, or you misheard, but it's in the middle of the country. The *exact* middle of the country. Who is attacking it, a mob of roos?"

Champion stopped, leaned against a desk, and coughed. "That's exactly what you're saying, Dingo, that I've gone troppo. But it's not as bad as a bunch of kangaroos going off," she said. "It's only the Chinese."

Outside Joint Defense Facility Pine Gap
18 kilometers southwest of Alice Springs, Northern Territory, Australia
4:48 PM, January 19, 2031

Like white hot air balloons tethered to the ground, Lieutenant Colonel Xia Jie focused his binoculars to inspect the radomes of the Pine Gap facility. Swarming bush flies left him constantly swatting them away as he examined the target he'd come so far to destroy. Concealed inside the white metal orbs were satellite dishes used to control spy and targeting satellites up to 40,000 km above the earth. The Sino-American war was going into its fourth year, and Pine Gap had been a primary target for destruction the entire time. Missiles aimed at the facility had been destroyed on multiple occasions, including strategic missiles as well as cruise missiles. Given that it was the most important American intelligence base outside the United States, the automated defenses had so far kept it safe.

What the enemy had not expected was a man like Xia Jie leading a special forces attack using helicopters for a means of ingress, since escaping from the exact center of Australia seemed unlikely. Even with the effective dissolution of Australia's central government, more than enough other dangers made getting back to China hard to imagine. Put another way, Jie considered it a suicide mission, which was why he led an all-volunteer strike team comprised entirely of non-volunteers. Not that he particularly cared; since the death of his family during the lockdown in 2022, living sometimes seemed like more trouble than it was worth.

Technically under the command of the Leishin Commando Airborne Force, the Thundergods, in reality Xia Jie led an ad-hoc force drawn from numerous special forces teams. Every man had, in some way, run afoul of either the leadership of the People's Liberation Army, or the Communist Party bureaucracy. Completing the mission would lead to their redemption, or so they were promised. Any promotions or honors would probably be posthumous, however, since even getting to the base was a long-shot *before* one of the three Z-20 Stealth helicopters suffered catastrophic engine failure and crashed into the Arafura Sea.

With the aircraft having a range of only 500 kilometers, the mission depended on a series of refueling stops, either along the coast of an unoccupied island, on New Guinea, or in a remote section of Australia itself. Setting up the operation strained China's remaining resources to the limit, which showed how important they considered destruction of the Pine Gap facility. What began as a war for leadership of the world had devolved into a death match for national survival.

The lost helicopter carried 4,000 kilograms of explosives, machine guns, and RPGs in external pods, and 1,000 kilograms of aviation fuel internally in specially designed pump containers to facilitate refueling in the field. That left Xia Jie with 27 fully equipped soldiers and no heavy weapons or way to blow up the radomes, which were his main target. To accomplish his goal, the colonel would have to not only fight his way inside the base, he would have to stay there long enough to figure out how to destroy his targets. As Xia Jie stood atop the hill thinking of ways to do that very thing, the strike team's second-in-command, Captain Xi Din, climbed the short rise to face his commanding officer. Sweat poured down Xi Din's face as afternoon sunlight baked the ground around them.

"The enemy defenses seem weaker than I would've imagined, sir," he said. "We encountered machine-gun fire, 12.7mm I think, but it wasn't accurate and didn't seem to be handled by someone who knew what they were doing. It's very strange, almost as if the regular military who should be guarding the base are gone. This might be easier than we thought."

"When things seem easy, Captain, that's when we must be extra careful. I would think you should've known that by now, given your combat experience."

"Yes, sir, you are of course right."

"Did you suffer casualties?"

"No, Comrade Colonel."

Xia Jie nodded. As mission commander he had access to the undoctored records of all the men in his team. Xi Din had supposedly been part of a dozen or more such covert missions, but something about the way his after-action reports were written made Xia Jie think they inflated Xi Din's role. Could that have anything to do with the captain's father having been a three-star general, now disgraced after the debacle in Vietnam? Until then, the father could have covered up for his son's incompetence. Xia Jie had nothing to prove his theory, other than his own observations. But if Xi Din endangered the mission in any way, Xia Jie would not hesitate to shoot him. The colonel had no intention of dying in some remote part of the Australian Outback... even on a suicide mission.

"It is possible that Australia withdrew the garrison for use elsewhere," Xia Jie said. "Perhaps for use in Malaysia, perhaps to put down riots at home... who can say? But if there are no American security forces, that surprises me. The Americans are not usually so stupid."

"It is their arrogance, Comrade Colonel. They felt safe in

their isolation."

"Did you discover if the fence is electrified?"

"It is. I crawled within thirty meters of the compound," Xi Din said. "From there I could hear insects coming in contact with the fence wires, and the electric sound as they were vaporized."

Xia Jie squinted, his only reaction to the captain's lie. Xia Jie had watched the entire effort through his binoculars, and the captain never got closer than 200 meters. One of the enlisted men did get close, however, and no doubt told the captain what he'd seen and heard. One more bit of evidence that his second-in-command was the coward Xia Jie believed him to be.

Before the colonel could say anything more, from several meters down the opposite slope, the team's radioman signaled for Xia Jie's attention. The colonel held up a hand to stop the captain from saying anything more. "What is your report, Sergeant?" he said.

"Comrade Colonel, Pine Gap just sent an unencrypted request for help."

"Unencrypted? Was it scrambled?"

"No, it was in plain language, on a single frequency."

"Did they receive a response?"

"Not yet."

"They are desperate!" Captain Xi Din said. "We must attack immediately!"

"*Must?*" the colonel said. "*Must?* Do you forget who is in command here?"

"I— no, Comrade Colonel, you are in command."

"You would do well to remember that, *Comrade* Captain." Something bit Xia Jie's neck. He slapped at it, inspecting his palm for signs that he'd killed the stinging insect, but found none. "I hate this country." Turning west, he studied the sun for a few seconds, considering the timeline of deploying his men, attacking, and overwhelming the Pine Gap garrison before night fell. Along with everything else on the lost helicopter was their night vision gear. "This day is nearly over. We will therefore time our assault for tomorrow at dawn. Set the watch, Captain, tell the men to eat, while I devise a plan for the morning."

"Comrade Colonel, if I could just—"

"You have your orders!" Xia Jie put more force into his

snarled half-shout than was his wont. While examining the enemy base, some part of his brain had begun to form an alternate plan to the one he'd been sent to execute, one where, instead of destroying Pine Gap, it became his new home. What he needed now was time to think.

Special Operations Command (SOCOMD) Compound NWT 4, 'Ricky Jick'
Near Yulara, Northern Territory, Australia
5:34 PM, January 19, 2031

By the time Dooley helped Champion limp to the barracks, she was too dizzy to walk and lay down on the nearest bed. She insisted that he get the G-Car ready, but he pretended not to hear and she soon quieted. Although the entire garrison had gone over snakebite procedures numerous times, Dooley took out the instruction card specific to prepping Eastern Brown snake antivenom. Warnings in bold red letters indicated that it should not be used unless there was clear evidence of envenomation to the victim, since allergic reactions could actually be more dangerous than the venom itself. He prepared it anyway.

Ten years in Special Forces trained him to be a good field medic, and as Dooley worked to prepare the medicine that might save his captain's life, all of that practice lent confidence to his actions. Ricky Jick had a medical section designed to administer the needs of twenty people, up to and including minor surgery.

First, Dooley slid an Epinephrine pen into his top pocket, because in some cases of an allergic reaction, the antivenom could prove more dangerous than the venom itself. The dispensary closet had more than two dozen intravenous bags of Hartmann's Solution, a combination of sodium chloride, sodium lactate, potassium chloride, and calcium chloride, dissolved in water. Removing one vial of the precious antivenom, Dooley mixed it into one of the bags, which had been premeasured at the correct ratio of ten parts solution to one part antivenom. Once that was ready, Dooley tore open a packet containing the needle and hose, attached that, wheeled one of the two IV stands to Champion's bedside, hung the bag, and inserted the needle into her right forearm, below the elbow. After taping it in place, he knelt beside the now unconscious woman.

Gently stroking hair away from her forehead, he noted the sallow appearance of her usually flushed cheeks. Champion was only three years older than his own 37 years, and while they had never been lovers—regardless of their situation she *was* an officer—a deep affection had grown between them. He wasn't sure how she felt, but for him the collapse of the Australian government, and its armed forces, meant that expressing his feelings for her no longer seemed like he was breaking any rules. Before he could do that, however, he had to first keep her alive.

After checking her splint, he wrapped the wound in a pressure bandage. Then there was nothing to do beside making some coffee and pulling up a chair to keep a vigil for signs of an adverse reaction. Champion drifted in and out of consciousness. The room grew dark as the sun set, but Dooley didn't move until three hours had passed, leaving him to debate the best next move.

As far as Dooley knew, no medical facilities were still running anywhere in the country. Had Pine Gap not called, there would have been no choice except to stay put and do his best, but was Pine Gap really still functioning? It seemed possible. Given its importance as America's second most important base facility outside of the Continental United States, if anything was still running, Pine Gap was a likely pick. And they would also no doubt have a full hospital setup that could deal with a severe envenomation. With a glance at Champion, Dooley rose and headed back to the headquarters building.

Having taken off the clumsy snake boots, he used a torch to make sure he didn't step on another one out looking for an early supper. Inland Taipans weren't supposed to be in the area, but a few years back one of the other garrison members reported seeing a Taipan near Yulara. A bite from one of those would likely prove fatal since Ricky Jick had no antivenom for Taipans venom, and a death adder wouldn't be much better.

Once inside, he weighed using the lamp near the radio. Decisions about whether to use electrical devices were constant since replacements were unlikely to ever be available again. From LEDs and fluorescent overhead bulbs to computers and radios, there had to be a good reason for justifying turning them on. Dooley didn't waste time thinking; he clicked on the overhead lights, sat in front of the radios, and turned on the desk lamp.

Slipping on a pair of headphones, Dooley switched the radio to monitor all five Voice Control Nets, or VCNs, which were broadcast at different frequencies by the Australian Defense Force Modernized High Frequency Communications System. The VCNs had been active until early 2027, when Chinese submarine-launched missiles took out the nodes in Darwin and Townsville, leaving the status of the other two, in Riverina and the North West Cape, unknown. Incoming messages had all but disappeared during the previous year. Now, as the system scanned for broadcasts, Dooley heard what he usually heard: static. Fortunately, the incoming message had automatically triggered the computer log, so Dooley was able to pull the earlier message, and the technical details, too.

The sender used 5696 KHz, the military distress frequency. That surprised him, since in the presence of the enemy, procedures called for frequency changes according to one of the pre-established patterns. Why would the most secure facility on the continent, with the most sophisticated communications array in the country, broadcast on an open frequency? It made no sense.

Until he heard the message. The voice was female, high-pitched and thin, and with a faint but distinctly Western Australian accent.

"I'm calling for any Australian armed forces who might be out there... this is the Pine Gap facility asking for assistance. We're being attacked by Chinese commandos, and they have damaged our communications array. Get here fast, we can't hold out long—"

The message ended abruptly. There was nothing further. But after listening twice, there was no doubt about the speaker's identity. He'd once heard the same voice pronounce the same word, *we're*, in the same way, making it sound like *we-ah*, except followed by *finished* instead of *being attacked*...

Prior to listening, Dooley's only concern was keeping his superior officer alive. He wasn't sure about his feelings toward Sylvie Champion, except that he considered her his closest friend, a mate in the truest Australian sense of the word. Maybe there was more there, and maybe not; all Dooley knew was that when he looked into those pale blue eyes set against the darkly tanned skin, something changed in the rhythm of his heartbeat. His only motivation for risking a dangerous drive down the Lasseter Highway to the A87 at Erldunda, and then north toward Alice Springs, had been to get Sylvie Champion proper medical care. But now...

Now Dooley had the voice of his first love and one-time fiancée echoing in his brain, and if Taylor Reston needed rescuing, nobody had better get in his way of doing it. It wasn't rational, she had bumped him without explanation or warning, but since when was love rational? And if he could help Pine Gap, too? Sure, why not?

As the world beyond the Outback collapsed, Ricky Jick's exterior floodlights had not been switched on since the camp's numbers dropped into single digits more than two years earlier. In a post-civilization world, where candles became more valuable than gold, the hours of darkness once again became the time of predators. Lights attracted attention from everything that crawled, walked, or flew, including humans. To those attuned to such things, the glow of Klieg lights could be seen from a distance of twenty kilometers, or more.

Dooley no longer cared about any of that. His sole focus was getting Silvie Champion to Pine Gap for medical treatment... Taylor Reston being there was nothing more than coincidence. Or so he told himself. And if he had to fight through the Chinese to do it, then he would.

Ricky Jick's G-Wagen dated from 2009, when the Australian Army bought 1,200 of the vehicle's new version. Once dark green, the brutal Australian sun had since bleached it leaf-yellow, with rusted pinholes along the edges of the engine bonnet. Over the previous three-plus years, long stretches of inactivity had left Ricky Jick's chief mechanic, Scott Daltrey, with plenty of time to keep it clean and well maintained. Whether or not it could stand up to the 450-kilometer trip to Pine Gap, on roads that hadn't been maintained since 2026, was a question that only driving the route could answer.

Nor could Dooley be certain of the distillate fuel. It had been treated with biocides and diesel stabilizer, and the tank was underground to maintain a cool temperature, but the only way to be certain that it remained viable was to drive. Under the harsh glow of the Klieg lights, he packed the G-Wagen with two F88A-1 Austeyr rifles; ten magazines loaded with thirty 5.56mm rounds each; two Browning GP-35 pistols; ten F1 hand grenades; and five CRM5 ration packs. He filled bottles with enough water for four to five days. Pine Gap was a 450-kilometer drive, but he planned in case the G-Wagen broke down.

Examining the vehicle to visualize packing, Dooley realized there wasn't much choice. Since he would need the entire backseat for Captain Champion and her IV setup, Dooley had to load the fuel containers, six in all, each filled with twenty liters, into the same compartment with the food, weapons, ammunition, and grenades. Then, with an IV needle stuck into Champion's arm, he had to drive at top speed over highways that hadn't been maintained for four years, avoiding potholes that might break an axle, shred a tire, or rip out the needle. He had to do it during the dead of night, and with gangs of criminals reportedly infesting the countryside. And *if* he made it to Pine Gap in one piece, he then might have to fight through a cordon of Chinese troops, or find the base in their hands.

On the front passenger seat, Dooley loaded two more rifles within easy reach, each with a round in the chamber, plus four additional magazines and four grenades. Taking one last look inside the weapons room, he was about to turn out the light when something caught his eye—an FGM-148 Javelin Anti-Tank Missile System. The stout tube weighed 19 pounds and would fit on the seat, but did he need such a powerful weapon? Probably not, yet if Pine Gap really *was* under Chinese attack, then could having too much firepower be a bad thing? Decision made, he wedged the Javelin into the G-Wagen.

"Guns, grenades, fuel, and missiles all packed into one car. What could possibly go wrong?" he said, scratching his cheek. Turning to the barracks so he could start loading Champion, on a whim he added one list item—the bucket containing the snake. "I'm not the one gonna hurt you, mate. That'd be Silvie Champion. You might wind up bein' her dinner."

Outside Joint Defense Facility Pine Gap
18 kilometers southwest of Alice Springs, Northern Territory, Australia
8:29 PM, January 19, 2031

The Pine Gap perimeter was tiny compared to its strategic significance, with no visible defenses aside from an electric fence. Nor did the Chinese see more than a handful of base personnel, which led Captain Xi Din to continue his argument for an immediate assault, which Colonel Xia Jie steadfastly refused to authorize.

As Xia Jie told his subordinate, he didn't believe that a place so critical to American interests would be so lightly defended, and assumed that in addition to unseen troops, there were also automated weapons systems ready to cut down any attackers, mostly likely connected to sophisticated thermal imaging equipment and vibration sensors. Moreover, since the base had called for reinforcements, it would be disastrous if those showed up while the Chinese were in the middle of their assault, and with the town of Alice Springs within twenty kilometers, that seemed a very real possibility. If the third helicopter hadn't crashed, taking with it their heavy weapons, explosives, and night vision gear, that would have changed the situation. As things were, he announced, they would wait until dawn the next day and judge the situation then.

What Xia Jie did *not* tell the captain was his burgeoning idea of surrendering to the Australians, not killing them. The death of his family had first made him question the decisions of the Communist government, and begun the erosion of his loyalty to the regime. Eight years later, having so far survived a global economic collapse and subsequent war between superpowers, Xia Jie wasn't sure there was anything left in the world that he believed in enough to die for. What he was pretty sure about, though, was that even if there *was* something worth dying for, a remote enemy base in the middle of nowhere wasn't it.

Adopting a passive deployment to buy himself time for his decision to harden, by two hours after nightfall, the Chinese had Pine Gap entirely surrounded. With only two dozen men left, the colonel assigned five soldiers to the north and east sides, with seven on the south and west. That allowed enough firepower to cover the road that entered the base from the southwest. Satisfied, he slumped to the sand beside the sergeant with the radio.

"Have you eaten yet?" he said.

"No, Comrade Colonel. I was awaiting permission."

"Did Captain Xi not see to this?"

"Uh... no, Comrade Colonel, it was not convenient. Comrade Captain has been very busy."

"Well, it is now convenient for me to give you permission to eat. And if you see Captain Xi, please inform him of my desire that all of the men eat in place immediately. Do you understand?"

"Yes, Comrade Colonel."

"In fact, radio the men to eat."

"Will not the enemy overhear us, Comrade Colonel?"

"Keeping up the men's strength is more important."

"Yes, Comrade Colonel."

"I will be on that hill over there," Xia Jie said, pointing to his right. Under the dim starlight, only gradations of gray differentiated one terrain feature from another. Near the sergeant was a canvas satchel filled with Type 17 Individual Soldier's Self-Heating Meals. Xia Jie grabbed one and stalked off.

He chose a place atop a small hill, from where he could inspect the Australian-American compound. Exposed as he was, Xia Jie recognized that a sniper with night vision gear could pick him off at their leisure, but in the moment he didn't care. Tearing open the brown paper bag, he removed the various smaller packets to assemble his meal. First he laid aside a small cardboard tray with spoon, and placed a plastic-wrapped raisin-energy bar on top. The main course came in a large pouch containing all elements for the Flameless Ration Heater, needing only water to activate. There were also packets with dried blueberries, spicy mushrooms, tomato-egg soup, some chewing gum and chocolate, and finally a chicken-flavored sauce.

Pouring water from his canteen into a pre-measured pouch, Xia Jie added that to his main course of Chicken Fried Rice. Shaking the FRH pouch, he would have to turn it every two minutes for the next twenty minutes before it would be ready to eat. In the meantime, he munched on the energy bar and thought. As it had so often lately, the oath of a PLA member came to his mind.

I am a member of the People's Liberation Army. I promise that I will follow the leadership of the Communist Party of China, serve the people wholeheartedly, obey orders, strictly observe discipline, fight heroically, fear no sacrifice, loyally discharge my duties, work hard, practice hard to master combat skills, and resolutely fulfill my missions. Under no circumstances will I betray the Motherland or desert the army.

Chewing and flipping the FRH and thinking, after a while

Xia Jie realized that he'd finished the meal, although he didn't remember anything after the first few bites of the energy bar. Many times in the months after their deaths, he had conjured up the faces of his wife and child, pretending their spirits were still with him. In difficult moments, nothing ever brought him comfort like his beloved Jing. Even after she died during the Shanghai lockdown, he found solace in speaking to her. But as he tried to do so now, to picture not only Jing's radiant smile, but the giggling laugh of his daughter Ai, nothing came. In a panic, Xia Jie tried to force his mind's eye to bring their faces into focus, and couldn't. He saw only darkness. Like flower petals on a breeze, they were gone.

Xia Jie wanted them back.

Joint Defense Facility Pine Gap, Operations Building
18 kilometers southwest of Alice Springs, Northern Territory, Australia
11:13 PM, January 19, 2031

When war with China broke out in 2026, more than 1,000 people staffed Pine Gap, not including a dedicated Mechanized Infantry company from the Australian Army, anti-aircraft batteries, and various other security forces. Within a year most were gone, either shipped overseas, or re-assigned to domestic missions ranging from escorting supply convoys to putting down food riots. Within two years, the Australian economy had collapsed, most of the population was dead, and Pine Gap had fewer than fifty people still on base. Only three Americans remained, the rest having scrambled to get aboard one of four CIA flights that evacuated them back to the States. The last had been in March of 2028, and those left behind at Pine Gap learned via short wave that the plane went down somewhere between Australia and Guam.

Now, as Captain Taylor Reston stood at the front of an assemblage of the remaining non-military personnel, eleven in total, she tried to think of how to calm them in the face of an imminent Chinese attack. Three had been sent to join Major Johnson's small defense squad, comprised of the last eight members of the security detachment. Of the other noncombatants, the ones Reston addressed, none were younger than 70. They were technicians, experts in fields such as integration of LIDAR into the analysis of Synthetic Aperture Radar

Telemetry. Reston knew what that meant in theory, but although trained in communications for the Australian Defense Force, the science of how it worked transcended her understanding.

The meeting took place in the once bustling cafeteria two floors underneath the Operations Building. Built to seat 500 people at a time, with most of the lights shut down to conserve energy for the perimeter fence, Reston couldn't see the back wall hidden in shadow. Five of the eleven in the room were too infirm to stand for more than a few minutes, so she had everyone sit at one of the dining tables.

"I think you all know there's a Chinese commando team outside the perimeter," she said, not bothering to mask the gravity of the situation by her tone. They were the last of the last. Everyone knew each other too well at that point for deception. "And it's a good bet they aren't here for a late Christmas bash."

"How many are out there?" said Dr. Chastain LeMoyne, the oldest person left on site at 82 years. In meetings, by default the others usually let him act as their spokesman.

"We don't know for sure," Reston said. "Not too many, I wouldn't think."

"No chance of someone popping in to our rescue, I take it?"

"I broadcast a call for help, but..."

"Nobody heard you."

"I can't say *that*."

"Did anyone answer?"

"No."

"Because nobody heard... Can you keep them out?"

"I honestly don't know, Chastain. We're certainly gonna try. Electrifying the fence should help."

"About that. It has put quite a load on the solar batteries. I doubt they can power it much beyond another hour."

"That's all?"

"You need to remember they were meant to be on the grid, and have generators for backup. The solar system was only for emergencies. Honestly, I'm rather surprised they have lasted this long."

Reston bit her thumbnail, thinking. "We can't have it draining all of our power. Go ahead and shut it down now. If the Chinese were coming during nighttime, they'd have already done it. I'll inform Major Johnson."

LeMoyne pushed up from his seat and shuffled off to another room. Moments later he returned. "The deed is done, Captain. There is nothing for us to do now except wait." Turning in his seat, LeMoyne lowered his glasses and scanned the others. "Or perhaps have a bit of chess. Who's up for a match?"

Stewart Highway/A87
47 Kilometers Southeast of Pine Gap
3:29 AM, January 20, 2031

"Brekkie up yet?" said a hoarse, weak voice from the backseat of the G-Wagen. "Avo on toast would sit well. Or do a Maccas run."

"I was thinking more snags of the barbie."

"Spicy meat," Sylvie Champion said. "No way I'd chunder that up."

Outside the vehicle while refueling, Dooley leaned sideways to look in the back window, although with night still heavy over the landscape he couldn't see much. "How ya' feeling, Sylvie?"

"Fair dinkum, and that's *Captain* Sylvie to you, mate."

Dooley smiled. "Fair dinkum? Haven't heard that for a while."

"I feel like shit, Dingo, which I suppose means I'm still alive. That's gotta count for something. Where are we? Have long have I been out?"

"Mind you're careful not to pull out that IV needle. I'll check it here in a minute. We're on the road to Pine Gap, been gone from Ricky Jick near seven hours. I've been havin' to take it slow; the road's in rough shape. We're maybe fifty kilometers out, so I figured to top off the tanks and get ready. You want some water?"

"Couldn't find a servo?"

"Passed quite a few, but none were open."

"I can't imagine why not. Water would be nice."

"Sure thing. I've got some eats along if you really are hungry."

"No, thanks. I was just joking about that. By the way, if you're ever thinking about getting bit by a brownie, I don't recommend it."

"I'd say pull a sickie before we get to Pine Gap, but you're kind of the reason we're going."

"What about the Chinese?"

"There's two of us, Sylvie. Not two hundred—two. Now sure, I'm a badass, but not *that* bad. It's not like we're significant reinforcements. No, we're going because you need a real doctor, and I figure if anybody's still got one, it's probably them. If the Chinese get in our way, well, that's bad luck for them."

"Says the not-so-badass. But look here, Dingo, if it gets too hot, you light out, understand me? I'm half dead now anyway, my leg's the size of a beach float... you make a dash for it, and I'll cover you."

"Like hell you will."

"Then that's an order."

"You can press charges later, but I ain't runnin' out on you, Sylvie." Even in the darkness, their eyes met. In those few seconds, Dooley's feelings for the older woman crystalized into something more, something deeper. "I'm not doin' it."

"You'll live to regret those words. If you don't die."

"I'm not planning on dying any time soon."

Before pulling off for the final run to Pine Gap, Dooley checked the IV setup. The bag of antivenom was dry, so he removed the needle and bandaged Champion's arm. Helping her into a sitting position required sliding his hand under her buttocks, which both of them pointedly ignored. When she was situated with the injured leg propped sideways on the other seat, Dooley handed her an Ausgeyr and two magazines.

"Got one in the chamber already. Try not to shoot the driver, Captain."

"I'll try not to, unless he keeps talking and doesn't start driving again."

Earlier in the drive, Dooley had risked using the G-Wagen's headlights. Forty minutes after stopping, as the hunched shapes of trees began to stand out over the dark, flat ground on either side of Stewart Highway, he switched them off. Lights attracted attention, and with Chinese in the general area, attention was the last thing he wanted. That forced him to slow down even more, though, because while the road ran straight, with no curves, and even pushed by his ever-present sense of urgency, Dooley dared not risk slamming into an unseen hole in the pavement.

Then he sensed the road widening. Flicking on the headlights for less than a second, in the flash he saw faded lines indicating a lane to the right, where another road merged with the highway. That meant two turn-offs coming on the left, the first of which he spotted moments later. Dawn was still more than an hour away, but even the imperceptible lightening of the sky helped his night-adjusted vision pick out details. Turning onto the smaller road, Dooley knew it was time to be extra careful. Within one meter, the road ended in a fork.

Although unmarked, the old military map indicated that to the left ran past the Alice Springs Correctional Facility, which he saw as crouching shadows in the distance. That wasn't his route. Turning right, he had barely straightened the car before he had to turn left. Towers for electricity marched away on his right at regular intervals. It was the last run to Pine Gap, maybe the last run of his life.

Joint Defense Facility Pine Gap, Southwest perimeter corner
18 kilometers southwest of Alice Springs, Northern Territory, Australia
5:44 AM, January 20, 2031

Nobody ever expected Pine Gap to be under physical ground attack, which explained the lack of any defenses beyond crowd control. The only danger had ever seemed to be from peace demonstrators. Any threat from enemy action was assumed to be in the form of air attack, probably cruise missiles or nuclear weapons, with airplanes considered a remote danger. The compound's air defenses were formidable, as was proved by the multiple missile attacks that had been defeated without damaging the complex.

Building the rudimentary defensive positions for Pine Gap's two .50 caliber machine guns taxed the facility's remaining manpower to its limit. They had plenty of empty burlap sandbags, but people to shovel them full of dirt was a different story. Only after 4 AM did Major Eddie Johnson consider them adequate, much to the relief of his exhausted soldiers and the civilian volunteers.

Taylor Reston leaned against the interior wall of the gun position at the corner of the southwest perimeter, beside a radome. The giant metal orb provided protection to the northwest from small arms fire. After pouring water down her forehead, Reston wiped dirt away from her eyes.

"Sun's almost up," she said. "They'll be coming soon."

Equally exhausted, Johnson nodded and drew a deep breath. "Yeah."

The two men manning the gun both looked at the officers, and with the coming of dawn Reston could make out their anxious expressions. Both were past 30 years old now, but unlike Johnson and Reston, they had never been in combat.

"Major, why didn't they come last night?" said the loader.

"Maybe they don't have night vision gear, or maybe they didn't feel confident about our defenses. There can't be too many of them, so I'm thinking their CO didn't want to risk casualties by stumbling over unseen defenses. They also might think there's more of us than there really are. Otherwise, I've got no idea."

"I wish it was over with, Major."

"I don't think we've got much longer to wait."

Against the pale grey sky, Reston admired Johnson's profile, even the little sags under the chin that weren't there two years earlier. Somehow, it only made him more handsome. When she pulled on his sleeve, he leaned over so she could speak into his ear.

"If I don't ever get a chance, Eddie," Reston whispered, "I want you to know that I—"

He pulled away to stop her from saying anything more. "Save it for after, so I can repeat it back to you."

Outside Joint Defense Facility Pine Gap
18 kilometers southwest of Alice Springs, Northern Territory, Australia
6:09 AM, January 20, 2031

Colonel Xia Jie watched a speckled brown lizard skitter across the road leading into Pine Gap, wondering if the creature could feel the coming violence and went looking for shelter. If so, it was the more intelligent species. In a dying world, he was preparing to order men to die for something that no longer mattered. His family died because the government mandated their fate. The war began because the government commanded the reconquest of the lost province of Taiwan. His men would die because the government told them to. In service of a lost war to control a lost world, it was all as useless as it was inevitable.

But some time during the night, Xia Jie not only accepted

the surety of his own death, he came to desire it. The government said there was no god, and for his entire life Xia Jie had repeated the mantra like a priest. The one thing the government could not do, however, was monitor his deepest, most private thoughts, where Xia Jie wasn't nearly as certain of the words he mouthed. One thing he *did* know, without reservation, was that life without his wife Jing and daughter Ai was no longer worth living.

Removing his QSZ-92-9 pistol from its holster on his belt, Xia Jie chambered a round and stepped to the middle of the road. Still crouching nearby, four soldiers and Captain Xi Din watched him without moving.

"Comrade Captain," Xia Jie said, knowing that for all this bravado, the other man was essentially a coward. "I'm ready to attack now. Will you join me?"

"Attack, Comrade Colonel? Surely you do not intend to march down the road? They will have many weapons aimed there."

"Probably, yes. So what? You are known to be a brave, resourceful officer, are you not?" Smiling at the man's discomfiture, he went on. "Be led by the inspirational words of your oath, Comrade Captain Xi Din, as I am. 'I promise that I will follow the leadership of the Communist Party of China, serve the people wholeheartedly, obey orders, strictly observe discipline, fight heroically, fear no sacrifice...' Stand next to me, my comrade, and let us attack together." The colonel bent his elbow, pointing the pistol at the sky.

"Comrade Colonel, as we are the only two officers, should not one of us stay behind in case the other falls?"

"Are you offering to attack in my stead, Captain?"

"Oh! I... you are more of an inspiration to the men, Comrade Colonel."

"Nonsense, Comrade Captain, the men love and respect you. Join me now." When Xi Din still didn't move, Xia Jie lost some of his smile. "That's an order."

Joint Defense Facility Pine Gap, Southwest perimeter corner
18 kilometers southwest of Alice Springs, Northern Territory, Australia
6:14 AM, January 20, 2031

"Here they come!" cried the machine gunner. When he

pressed the trigger, the big weapon spat .50 caliber shells at figures moving forward over the desert outside the perimeter.

Despite herself, Taylor Reston had fallen into a stupor. The gunfire startled her awake. Resting her Austeyr on the sandbag wall, she saw founts of dirt kicked up around the Chinese, who went to ground and returned fire, all except one man, who rolled down a hill and didn't move.

A stitch of incoming bullets ripped into the sandbags, spraying dust into her eyes. Crouching low and blinking, it took twenty seconds to clear her vision. When she could finally see again, Reston saw Major Eddie Johnson lying next to her, eyes staring upward, with a hole in his forehead.

"No!" she screamed.

Dropping the rifle, she brushed away hot shell casings ejected by the machine gun that bounced and landed on Johnson's chest. The bullet had entered above the left eye and left a golf-ball-sized exit wound. From the first glance her brain knew he was dead, but that didn't stop her from listening for a heartbeat, or feeling for a pulse, and even trying CPR. She worked for minutes as the battle went on around her, without hearing the staccato explosions of firing shells, or the answering rifle fire. Only when the machine gunner yelled out between bursts did she come back to the present.

"Who the hell is that?" he said, pointing at the road.

The road leading to Joint Defense Facility Pine Gap, half a kilometer from the front gate
18 kilometers southwest of Alice Springs, Northern Territory, Australia
6:14 AM, January 20, 2031

With better light, Dooley accelerated past 70 kph. The G-Wagen topped a low rise, which led to a shallow valley until the road rose up another small hill, beyond which Dooley could see huge white globes shining in the morning sun. To either side he saw men flittering from tree to tree, rock to rock, using them for cover as they moved toward Pine Gap. Tightening his left hand on the steering wheel, Dooley maneuvered an Austeyr out the driver's window. He was about to open fire when he spotted two men standing in the road less than 100 meters ahead. At the sound of his engine they turned. The taller of the two didn't move, while the shorter one ran for cover. He didn't get far.

Dooley could tell by the uniforms they were officers, and watched as the one standing in the road twisted and shot the other one in the back. The pistol recoiled multiple times, while the shorter officer dropped to his knees, toppled forward, and twitched. Forty meters distant, bouncing over dozens of small pits in the roadbed, Dooley couldn't process what he was watching... did one Chinese officer really just kill another Chinese officer?

But then the man turned the pistol and aimed it at the speeding G-Wagen, and he forgot about that. With ditches on either side, and the Chinese officer standing astride the center lane marker, there was nowhere to go except right through him.

"Hang on tight!" he called out to Sylvie Champion, and pressed the gas pedal to the floor.

Metallic *thunks* indicated bullets hitting the G-Wagen. Steering with one hand, he opened fire at half-seen targets with the other. Shell casings clanked and clattered into his lap and out the window. Champion fired from the back seat, screaming as she did so. Then he struck the Chinese officer at a speed of 86 kph and the G-Wagen skewed sideways in a cloud of black rubber smoke.

The road leading to Joint Defense Facility Pine Gap, one quarter kilometer from the front gate
18 kilometers southwest of Alice Springs, Northern Territory, Australia
6:16 AM, January 20, 2031

"You are insane!" Captain Xi Din yelled. "We are going to die!"

Pistol at his side, Colonel Xia Jie laughed. The enemy vehicle was accelerating toward them. "Yes, Comrade Captain, a glorious death is only seconds away. We are doing our duty, as we face the enemy in battle. There is no greater honor, is there?"

Xi Din rocked on his feet, clearly wanting to get off the road, but aware of their men watching him from both sides. "Our deaths will be useless!"

"Of course they will. That does not matter; only obedience to our oath matters. Now ready yourself to fire at the enemy.

That is my order."

With the racing Australian truck less than 60 meters away, Xi Din broke for the cover of the roadside ditch. Colonel Xia Jie had been ready for that, however, and shot the captain between his shoulder blades. Knocked forward, Xi Din fell on hands and knees, turning a shocked face toward his killer. Xia Jie emptied the pistol's magazine into his cowardly subordinate. Turning, he pointed the empty weapon at the truck.

"Be looking for me, beloved," he said. "I am coming to you."

For his last two seconds of life, Colonel Xia Jie's mind conjured up a clear image of his smiling family.

The road leading to Joint Defense Facility Pine Gap, 200 meters from the front gate
18 kilometers southwest of Alice Springs, Northern Territory, Australia
6:17 AM, January 20, 2031

The G-Wagen drove the Chinese officer's body backward and down, dragging it thirty meters down the pavement as the vehicle skidded to a stop. There was a moment's lapse from incoming fire, no doubt because the Chinese soldiers feared killing their own commander. That gave Dooley time to step out of the driver's door and wrestle the Javelin out with him. Then the shooting started up again.

Tire smoke that reeked of rubber hung low over the pavement as bullets webbed the windshield from hits and ricochets, while multiple *thunks* rattled the truck's frame. As rounds skipped off the pavement, he ran for the ditch on the opposite side and jumped in. Some dark stained his upper left arm, but there was no time to worry about that now. Behind him, still in the G-Wagen, Champion changed magazines and kept firing to the left. Caught in a crossfire, there wasn't much he could do to help.

During his dash to cover, Dooley had seen multiple muzzle flashes 300 meters away behind a cluster of bushes. To use the missile he would have to expose his head and upper torso, aim, and fire, all while risking being hit, but that couldn't be helped. The danger to Sylvie Champion was greater now than mere snake venom.

Intended for top attacks against tanks, being an infrared

acquisition weapon the Javelin had a secondary use against aircraft. Dooley intended to fire at the ground, since for the missile to detonate it needed either something to lock onto, or something to strike. Without wasting motion, Dooley raised, placed the targeting cursor at a waist-high boulder between the bushes, and fired.

The backblast flashed across the highway and scorched the front of the G-Wagen. The missile left its tube in a soft launch, which minimized recoil, deployed its guidance fins, ignited the secondary thrust, and raced toward the target. Dropping the now-useless firing tube, Dooley ran back to the G-Wagen and pressed down the accelerator.

Joint Defense Facility Pine Gap, southwest corner machine gun position
18 kilometers southwest of Alice Springs, Northern Territory, Australia
6:14 AM, January 20, 2031

Lost in fury, Taylor Reston fired off magazine after magazine at anything that moved. She would have gunned down the two men who appeared in the road, standing still and presenting a perfect target, except she was out of ammo. She'd run to a pack ten feet away to grab more when she saw them.

"There!" she yelled to the machine gunner. He swiveled the gun, but didn't fire. Confused, Reston watched as one of the Chinese killed the other one, who had sensibly tried to get out of the middle of the road. Then, transfixed at what she was seeing and oblivious to incoming fire, she spotted a speeding vehicle racing at the remaining Chinese officer. He didn't move.

The road passed her position at a distance of forty meters as it wound toward the main gate, so Reston had a clear view of what happened next. The vehicle, a G-Wagen in faded Australian Army markings, hit him directly. Something from the man's uniform must have caught on the truck's underside, because it dragged him along as it careened sideways. It didn't roll over, though; the wheel base was too wide for that.

Chinese riflemen poured fire at the G-Wagen, which snapped Reston out of her trance. Switching out magazines for her Austeyr, she took aim at an enemy soldier who half-stood to get a better shot at the G-Wagen. A three-round burst put him down. In her peripheral vision she saw someone dash from the G-Wagen into the drainage ditch. Seconds later the figure rose, shouldering what looked like a Javelin missile, and fired.

About 120 meters out from her position, the missile hit a boulder and exploded. Rock shrapnel ripped through some bushes. Three men rose and tried to run away, but Reston and the machine gunner cut them down within five paces. While she did that, the driver got back into the G-Wagen and sped toward the main gate.

No substantial fortification of the gate against hostile ingress had ever been thought necessary. The gates were similar to the fence itself, and intended to be electrified. Now, with the power off, they were too flimsy to stop the shot-up G-Wagen from crashing through.

"Shit!" Reston said. The rage fueled by Johnson's death found vent at whoever the idiot was that breached their perimeter. Like the gates of a medieval castle, once down the entire defense was compromised. "Inform—" Reston stopped. She was about to say inform the CO that the gate had been destroyed, but the CO was Johnson, and after him it was... her. "Cover the gate," she said. "Tell the northeast position to send two men to the gate." Carrying her own rifle, Reston ran to see who the idiot was that wrecked their defensive position.

Pine Gap wasn't a large facility, but it wasn't small, either. Using radomes and buildings for cover, she ran until her legs burned. Sweat soaked her uniform by the time Reston saw the G-Wagen hissing steam outside the Operations Building. Black scorch marks covered the front right fender, while the matching tire had gone flat. The windows had all been shot out, and dozens of bullet holes riddled the truck's frame. The gates both hung askew, although neither had fallen. Reston would try to chain them back together when help arrived. Some part of her mind noted that, for the moment, at least, all shooting had stopped.

On the driver's side, the figure of a man in Australian Army uniform was bent over the rear seat. Trotting toward the G-Wagen, she saw a body there, also in uniform. Stopping beside him, she leaned the Austeyr against the vehicle and put hands on hips, gulping down breaths.

"Help me get her out," the man said. He looked up at her and Reston gaped back.

"Jon Dooley?"

"Grab her feet. I'll go around and get her shoulders."

"Is she wounded?" Reston said, although the blood on Dooley's hands made clear that she was.

"Yeah, in the shoulder, but that's not the bad part. She took a bite from a brownie, needs a doctor."

Despite the chaos swirling around her, Reston didn't hesitate. She tried to hold Champion up, but the weight proved too much. Fortunately, two younger men joined them and took over. Reston instructed them to get her into the base hospital, but when Dooley started to follow she stopped him.

"They know what they're doing. We've gotta defend the gate!"

Dooley hesitated, watched the two soldiers carrying Champion inside, and nodded. Taking up position behind the G-Wagen, he collected all the guns into a pile, ready to shoot. Reston moved behind a metal shed to one side. She fought down the memories that seeing Dooley again brought to the fore, and couldn't help wondering at the synchronicity of losing Johnson only to find Dooley again. It was too much for the moment, though, so she concentrated on seeking targets that never came

---

Joint Defense Facility Pine Gap
18 kilometers southwest of Alice Springs, Northern Territory, Australia
11:27 AM, January 26, 2031

With their officers dead, demoralized and with nowhere to go, over the two days following the initial attack, the 18 surviving Chinese commandos surrendered. Thrust into the role of camp commander, Taylor Reston put off grieving to bury the dead and repair the main gate. Initially she intended to leave the Chinese dead for the dingoes, but the prisoners requested the chance to dig a shallow mass grave and cover it with stones, and Reston relented.

She avoided Dooley as much as possible, and he did the same. Her feeling for him had never fully faded, and she sensed that he might feel the same way. With all that had happened, it was too much, too soon, and so she found reasons not to be alone with him. But by the sixth day, Reston could no longer hold back the tears, and spent the first hours after dawn crying in her quarters. Only four hours after sunrise did she feel empty enough to get started on the day's duties, the first of which was visiting her newly arrived fellow captain.

Sylvie Champion had healed enough to start moving around again. Although Pine Gap had no medical doctor, it did have a fully-equipped hospital with enough equipment and supplies to provide care for a garrison of 1,000 or more people. The remaining base occupants shared enough knowledge of human anatomy and had a large enough reference library to deal with less complicated medical emergencies. Champion's shoulder wound had been a through-and-through, while a second bag of antivenom, followed by bed rest, negated the snake venom.

Reston found the captain sitting on the edge of her hospital bed. "You're up. I'm glad to see it," she said.

"No more than me," Champion replied. "That brownie got me good. If it wasn't for Dingo and your people, I wouldn't be here."

"They're not really my people, Captain. Our commander, Major Johnson, kept them all alive this long. He was quite a man."

"More than that to you, I think."

Reston looked down and smiled a sad smile. "I tried to tell him when the Chinese came, and he said to wait, we'd say it to each other, after..."

"And now there's no after..."

"No."

"If it makes you feel better, I think he'll hear you if you still want to tell him."

"I did."

They both fell silent for a while, each staring off into space.

Finally, Reston turned for the door. "I'll send Dooley round to see you," she said.

"Oh?"

"Captain... may I call you Sylvie?"

"Of course."

"Don't repeat my mistake, Sylvie. Life's too short."

"I don't know what you mean."

"I think you do, and I'll tell you now. I've seen the way Dooley looks at you. He feels the same way."

"Weren't you two, once... you know..."

"Yes, we were engaged. It was a long time ago. Tell him, Sylvie."

With that, Reston walked out the hospital room door. At her back, she heard Champion yell after her, "Don't forget to send him 'round!"

Triple Frontera

Gustavo Bondoni

2032

"Ah, the promised land," Zaeim Kimball said, breathing in the humid air. Ciudad del Este's airport was just a single cleared runway of ancient concrete and a terminal building that looked like it would soon be overrun by vegetation. His first impression of the Kingdom of Paraguay was positive. "Green, isn't it?"

Judging by the way Mustafa looked up at him, Zaeim knew he must have said or done something that ran roughshod over the New Prophecies. Again.

But what did they expect? He'd been born Malcolm, not Zaeim, and he'd worked his way up the ranks in an independentist group from Alabama. He'd never read a word of Armstrong's prophecies before they recruited him for this mission and made him change his name.

He didn't care. If Mustafa got any ideas, he could be sentenced to death.

"What's the situation?" Zaeim asked the man.

"Our convoy is ready. Four CSK-181 assault vehicles. Twelve Brazilian Guaraní APCs and two Challenger tanks. We have no idea where those came from, but they were for sale cheap in Argentina including a few dozen shells, so we grabbed them."

Zaeim grunted. The area where the borders of Paraguay, Argentina, and Brazil came together, called the Triple Frontera by the locals, was one of the most lawless areas in all of South America. The permeable jungle borders were once a clearing house for everything from weapons on their way to Islamic terrorists and Afghan opium about to be processed for the markets in the Northern Hemisphere to cheap knockoff electronics to be consumed in South America itself.

Apparently, it was still a place where one could buy war materiel, and Mustafa seemed to have done well with his purchases.

It was old equipment, and mismatched, but it was built to last. Only one thing concerned him. "Will it be enough?"

"In Paraguay?" Mustafa scoffed. "We could probably conquer everything from here to Brasilia with that much firepower."

"I'll take your word for it. You are the expert, and I think you've done a fantastic job."

His new second-in-command nodded, apparently mollified. Nevertheless, Zaeim made a note to keep an eye on the man; he was reported to be fanatically devoted to the cause, the kind of man who brought fear to the heart of the Caliphate's enemies by his mere presence. But also the kind of man who might flinch from the Realpolitik of actually taking territory and holding it. They needed to take the area, true, but it would be just as important to hold it for several weeks, and that could prove bloody.

From the briefings, Zaeim knew the countryside around Ciudad del Este had been important for fifty years, all the way back to the 1990s. The porous border between Paraguay, Argentina, and Brazil had served as the perfect clearinghouse for Islamic terrorist groups operating in the early 21st century. It was a place where they could easily access the two large, stable democracies of South America, and from there, reach out to the rest of the world.

They boarded a battered minivan that reeked of some kind of alcohol fuel. Mustafa took the driver's seat and Zaeim and his three companions sat in the back. Two of the men were heavily armed and armored bodyguards, while the third, Basaam Al Alamo, was a beefy Texan who spoke for Armstrong.

They rode in silence for some minutes.

"No customs?" Zaeim asked Mustafa.

"I pre-cleared your flight with the gate. These infidels are very easy to bribe."

"What do you bribe them with? I imagine that none of our currencies work down here."

"Everyone accepts small electronic devices," Mustafa replied with a sneer.

Of course they do, Zaeim thought as the gate opened and their van rolled onto an empty two-lane road. *They can trade them for food.*

They drove for less than ten minutes, avoiding potholes and crawling over places where the road had eroded away before turning onto a dirt lane that led to a dilapidated warehouse of corrugated steel that resembled a Quonset hut grown to ten times its normal size.

The door opened to reveal a dark interior and they descended from the minivan to find the vehicles promised huddled near the entrance: a mismatched set of assault vehicles whose camo ranged from the bright green of the Chinese off-road vehicles to the dark green and grey of the British tanks.

"Are they ready to run?" Zaeim asked.

"Ready, fueled, and the ammunition is loaded. We're just waiting for you to give the order."

"And the men?"

"The barracks are behind the vehicles. We have two hundred believers."

"And the police? What are we up against?"

"About the same. But there's a difference," Mustafa replied.

"And what would that be?" Zaeim steeled himself for a long speech about them doing the work of Allah. He would nod along and congratulate Mustafa for his piety, but the man surprised him.

"We have ammunition. They don't, or at least not enough to stop us."

Zaeim smiled. "Then let's do this."

"Now?"

"We are doing the work of Allah," Zaeim said. "It should not be delayed."

Mustafa smiled. "Are you coming with us?"

"Of course. Allah is my shield."

"And which vehicle would you like to ride in?"

Zaeim pointed. "That one."

The Challenger III was an impressive tank. If he'd had a few of those in Alabama, the Caliphs would be working for him as opposed to the other way around.

This must have been how Rommel felt, Zaeim thought as he watched the city pass by. He stood in the open hatch of the Challenger tank as they rolled through Ciudad del Este. The roar of the enormous diesel engine drowned out the voices of passersby, but he could see the awe in their faces. The sidewalks teemed with people walking slowly from one place to another. Most carried bundles.

What he didn't see were too many cars, not even as they approached the city center, with its five or six city blocks of high-rises—in this case most of the buildings were about fifteen or twenty stories high, nothing to write home about. The vehicles that could be seen consisted mainly of minivans and small buses which were overloaded with large-eyed people, and which meandered at a snail's pace.

Even the largest of the buses would have been crushed beneath the tank's tracks, but he'd given specific orders to avoid civilian casualties. Holding a city this size would take more than just men... he needed the citizens cooperative, or, at the very least, passive. Killing them was not a step in that direction.

Of course, the Caliphate had made contingency plans to get all the muscle they needed if things didn't quite work out with the civilian population. But that would cost money, and money for that particular job meant gold, not small electronic devices. He preferred not to spend it if possible.

His map told him they were approaching the river, and the driver cut across a park, churning up the red dirt into thick dust.

Zaeim enjoyed every minute of it. What good was having a tank if you stuck to paved roads?

They ground to a halt. Before him was a stretch of dusty, potholed tarmac road. On the other side of that, a ten-foot-tall brick wall painted a faded red blocked their way.

"What's that? Why are we stopping?"

The other tank pulled up alongside, and Mustafa's face popped out of the hatch. "That's the municipality. Once we take that, we're in control of the city." The young man was smiling eagerly, evidently enjoying their run down from the warehouse as much as Zaeim himself.

"So why are we stopped here?"

"Because if we go in through the main gate, they'll immediately know we're here and maybe they'll find some guns or get resistance together. But if we just go through the wall, we'll have a clear run to the mayor's palace."

"Mustafa," Zaeim said, shaking his head, "I may have misjudged you."

"So we go through the wall?"

"Absolutely."

The fanatic smiled. "Then it is I who may have misjudged you."

Mustafa went back down, slamming the hatch behind him.

Zaeim followed suit.

The two tanks crashed through the wall like it was made of paper, and Zaeim felt the adrenaline rush he always got when moving into combat.

Leaving the rest of their vehicles to get through the opening as best they could, the two Challenger tanks raced each other towards the center of the walled compound, where a single white building stood.

For a municipal seat, it was anything but impressive, with the paint flaking off and the exposed wood covered in greenish-gray mold.

Even more disappointing was the attitude of the guards: faced with a tank bearing down on them, every single man broke and ran for the front gate.

Except one.

One glorious bastard stationed at the door holed up behind a three-foot-tall flowerpot with a palm growing in it and opened fire on the two Challengers with what looked like an old FAL rifle.

Zaeim wanted to give the order to capture the guy alive and offer him a commission in the Caliphate's army, based on either having the biggest set of balls he'd ever seen or the smallest brain—either would serve.

But, short of waiting for him to run out of ammo, there seemed no realistic way to grab the guy.

And Mustafa, it seemed, had less admiration for desperate gestures than Zaeim. The other Challenger opened fire with its chain gun.

The pot exploded into shards in the barrage, and the guy was soon lying dead and bloody on the doorstep.

By the time they'd dealt with the guard, the troop carriers had caught up with the tanks and began disgorging jihadis.

Well, most of them were jihadis. A few were men Zaeim actually trusted, motivated by money as opposed to blind faith in the new prophets.

They poured into the building, and soon emerged herding about a dozen scared-looking men and women.

Once he was convinced none of the guards would choose that moment to reappear and try to play hero, Zaeim approached the group huddled under the guns.

He spoke in Spanish to the oldest of them, a man in his fifties, balding and sporting a mustache that would have made a Civil War general proud. "Who's in charge here?"

"I am," the man said. "What is the meaning..."

Zaeim shot him in the head. Though he didn't want to antagonize the locals, he had to make sure of two things: that the major political figures were out of the way, and that his men understood he was not to be trifled with. This murder was a way to do both at once.

"Wrong answer," he said. He was about to continue the clichéd charade and ask the next-most senior member of the group the same question when he realized they might not know to give him the right answer. So he saved them the mental effort. "As of this moment, I'm in charge. I formally declare the city of Ciudad del Este as a protectorate of the Caliphate." He nodded to Mustafa. "You may tell your men to put up the flag."

Mustafa nodded and gave the orders. Zaeim turned back to his prisoners. "The main question is, will you work for the new head of the municipality, or will you join your deceased friend," he gestured absently at the corpse, "wherever he is."

One man spoke up. "We..." He looked at his companions. "We will serve."

"Good. You'll be confined to this compound, of course, until we can establish order on the streets, and will help us get the police working correctly to aid in the transition."

"Will you be the head of the municipality?"

"I am merely the military commander. I think you already know the new municipal boss."

From out of one of the Brazilian armored personnel carriers, a man stepped forward, impeccably dressed in a light tan suit. His mustache was nearly as impressive as the dead man's... but the full head of hair was sleekly black. He certainly looked like an upgrade over the recently deceased mayor, anyway.

"But in case you haven't had the pleasure," Zaeim continued, "this is Ronson Ermindez. He is an eminent businessman and is honored to have been offered the position of mayor. He accepted it this morning."

The cluster of bureaucrats mumbled amongst themselves, but none of them spoke up. They all knew exactly who Ermindez was—the man who ran the largest drug cartel in Paraguay, operating on all three territories in the triple border area: eastern Paraguay, northern Argentina, and southern Brazil. His family used to run weapons for Islamic terrorists in the early part of the century, but he'd found it much more profitable—and safer—to concentrate on the drug trade.

Zaeim was just happy that they'd managed to take the municipality without the man's help. He was going to be an expensive ally as it was... better to limit his involvement to where it was really critical. His large army of enforcers would play an important role in the next phase of the operation.

Finally, he pulled out his satellite phone—one of the few remaining anywhere in the Caliphate's possession—and made a call.

"Staging area secure. We'll start stage two right away. It shouldn't take more than a few more hours."

Belén Castrense watched the little girl as she disappeared over the hill. She hated to let Carina go to school on her own but, at six, she was old enough to walk the two hundred meters to the schoolhouse.

Besides, she had to walk a much longer road in the opposite direction: her shift was about to start at the dam.

She stayed to the red dirt beside the road, not for safety considerations—trucks were few and far between—but because the earth was soft and yielding, and she'd be standing guard on a concrete structure all day. In eight hours' time, her feet would be thankful for small mercies.

Rodrigo, the guard at the gate, smiled as she approached.

She smirked. "How come you always get the easy jobs?" she said.

"Merit," he replied with a straight face. "The commander

knows I'm the most trustworthy man in the detachment."

She blew a raspberry at him and walked on, his laughter trailing behind.

Sergeant Jiménez was a big man, bouncy and permanently smiling. His grin widened when she entered.

"You've got turbine duty today," he said.

"Will they be running?"

"Nope."

She returned his smile. "Thanks." The wall near the turbines was a flat concrete area just like any other, except that when the dam was producing electricity, it was the loudest place she'd ever been to. Legend had it that, back when Itaipú was the second largest dam in the world—at least considering its generation capacity—trailing only one in China, the turbines had spun all day every day, sending their electricity to the teeming masses of Sao Paulo and Rio de Janeiro.

Back then, there had been earplugs for the guards, and they'd been rotated every two hours.

You couldn't do that now, of course. There were barely enough guards for their current eight-hour shifts. And not every day.

The Brazilian revolt of 2031 had, apart from killing countless millions of people in the two megacities, severed the power lines that ran to the populous coast, and no one had bothered to rebuild them.

That meant the Itaipú Dam only had to supply Paraguay and a few tiny Brazilian cities. It had gotten so bad that there was serious talk of cannibalizing some of the idle generators for parts; the engineering crew had thus far been reluctant to do so, but the bean counters in Asunción and Brazilia were beginning to choke off access to new spares.

Anyhow, she was responsible for a hundred-meter stretch of dam with nothing to do but sweat in the sun and look out over the river.

"Hey, Belén," a voice called out. "Do you think we're going to get rain today?"

Belén rolled her eyes. Santiago had pulled duty on the next sector over, and he stood right on the edge of the zone he was patrolling to shout over to her. He wasn't a bad guy, certainly not like some of the other creeps she pulled duty with sometimes, but he was a little too chirpy. He was Brazilian, from the other side of the dam, and he had that nation's child-like attitude towards enjoying life. He was probably looking forward to the rain, but he'd be equally delighted if it remained sunny.

"I don't think so," she replied, walking closer. The boy—he couldn't have been more than eighteen or nineteen years old—was tall and lithe, with beautiful skin the color of almonds. They stopped about ten meters apart, close enough that they could talk without shouting too much, far enough away that they each stayed within their assigned regions.

"That's great. I heard they're putting the Seleção back together."

Leave it to a Brazilian to be thinking of the country's soccer team when the entire nation was in danger of splintering into warring states and tribes and races. "Where'd you hear that?" she asked.

"I was playing for Aguilas do Foç on Saturday and a man came. He said he was from Porto Alegre, and that they were looking for players."

"You think you might be selected?"

And suddenly the boy was bashful. He kicked at the concrete. "I don't know. I've never really expected to." Then he held her gaze. "Do you think they'd take someone like me?"

"I can't really say," Belén replied. "I've never seen you play."

Santiago's smile turned impish. "That's true. And you're from Argentina, so you don't really know anything about soccer."

"What I know is that the Argentine National Team is still playing and would probably wipe the floor with Brazil right now. But, more importantly, so would Paraguay."

It was true. Her native land, Argentina, had managed to hold things together through The Collapse... barely. It was still a democracy where the rule of law held some semblance of sway. The reason everyone gave was that Argentina had two characteristics which saved it: it had tons of food and very few people. The main fear was always that one of the large powers—particularly China—would invade for the land and resources.

But China had its own problems, including the sudden unexplained meltdown of several nuclear reactors, and couldn't be bothered to extend its reach to South America... although the Australians should be worried.

Like Argentina, Paraguay had survived intact. Chile, of course, had torn itself to pieces. Their ridiculous constitution—unwisely redesigned in 2022—had created chaos even before the Fall.

Best of all, though, was what had happened in Peru. In the midst of the economic depression, as the government was teetering, the Shuar tribe had suddenly appeared out of the Amazon armed with modern weapons, reminded everyone that they'd never formally surrendered to the Spanish—or accepted Spanish rule—and calmly began to slaughter everyone who resisted their push to reclaim ancestral lands.

The Shuar were headhunters, and they caused a panic when they started harvesting anyone who couldn't prove their ancestry. Photographs of piles of human heads waiting their turn to be processed were the sensation of the internet, before the entire Amazonian region of Peru and a good chunk of Ecuador went dark.

The rest of those countries had splintered shortly thereafter.

But nothing compared to the collapse of Brazil. A collapse which, if Santiago was right, seemed to be reversing itself. He glared at her defiantly. "I would never let Paraguay beat us. I play against Paraguayans every other weekend. They have nothing. Nothing, I say."

"If you say so."

Her late husband—her second husband, following her disastrous marriage in Argentina—had been Paraguayan, and proud of the fact that life had gone on pretty much as normal there while the rest of the world fell apart. The fact that the democratic government had been replaced by a despotic monarchy fazed him not in the least.

He'd never wanted to face the fact that things remained the same mostly because Paraguay never really had too far to fall.

"And we'll beat Argentina, too." He said it like he was discussing moving to the moon: something so far away that no one would ever be able to prove him wrong.

Belén held up a hand. "Did you hear that?"

"What?"

"It sounded like cracking concrete. There it is again."

Suddenly Santiago's face went from dreamy to alarmed. "That wasn't the concrete. That was a gunshot. Look." He pointed behind her.

Belén turned to look. A large convoy of vehicles was in the process of driving through the main gate. They stopped by the main admin building and she could see men—tiny in the distance—storm inside.

"We need to go help!" Belén shouted.

Santiago said nothing. He just ran up to her and pulled her behind the nearest of the refrigeration columns, a ten-meter-tall white cylinder streaked with rust. "No. What we need to do is run for the Brazilian side of the border and tell them what's happening."

"We're guards," she said, "we need to stop them."

"With what? That?" He indicated her sidearm. "Have you ever fired that? Do you have bullets in it? It will probably explode if you pull the trigger. You're not going to stop that many men with fifteen bullets."

"Thirty," she replied. "I'm counting on your help."

He shook his head. "The sergeant gave me a gun, but no bullets. He says I can have them when I become a man."

"Damn." Belén was thinking of the dam, but even more, she was thinking of Carina. She wasn't going to be able to get across the dam if those guys were holding the Paraguayan end. "Give me a second."

She pulled out her cell phone and dialed. María Marcos was the woman who took care of Carina after she got out of school and until Belén got home.

"María," she said, "I can't talk right now, but listen to me. Keep Carina away from the dam. There's something happening."

"All right."

"I might not be home tonight. Please keep her safe."

"I'll guard her with my life."

"Thank you." Tears flowed down Belén's cheeks. She knew María would be true to her word. Then she turned back to Santiago. "Okay, now I can listen to you."

"We need to run to the Brazilian side and have them send in the Army."

"The Brazilian Army, or whatever might be left of it, has better things to do than come save a dam they're not using any more. They probably have Zombies in Sao Paulo."

"The police..."

"Would die. There's a tank over there. How many officers

do you have in the town?"

"Seven. One of them is in a wheelchair." She saw in his eyes that he knew she was right. "We have to tell someone. We need to do something."

Belén sighed. "Dammit," she said. "Dammit, dammit, dammit."

She pulled out her phone and dialed again. This time, it wasn't a local call on the Ciudad del Este mobile infrastructure. This one took a hell of a long time to connect and when it did, a voice she absolutely hated said, "I had a feeling you'd be calling me someday."

She almost hung up. "Don't," she said. "Just don't."

"Whatever." She could almost hear him shrug. The only reason she'd even kept in touch with the creep was that Carina deserved to have a father. Even one as defective as Germán. "What is it? You need money? You want me to go pick you up? Tired of living in the jungle?"

"No. Stop being a jerk for one moment of your life and listen to me." She took a breath. "There's a bunch of men on the dam. They seem to be taking it over. They've got armored personnel carriers. And tanks."

"Tanks? You're kidding."

"Not kidding. I'm stuck on the Brazilian side. I can't get back to Carina. I don't know what's going on on the Paraguayan side. But I'm afraid."

This time, the silence lasted some moments. "Is she all right?" His voice was suddenly soft and reasonable, with no sign of mockery.

"As of five minutes ago, yes. But I can't get back to her. She's with a friend." Belén rattled off María's number from memory.

"How far are you from the bad guys?"

"Not far enough. I'm on the dam, over the turbines. They'll be here to check."

"Get out of there. I'll call you in a while."

⇀⫟⇁

Germán cursed. That woman had a capacity for attracting chaos that went beyond anyone else he'd ever seen. When he first met her, he'd found it attractive... but now, it grated on him the way everything else had over that last hellish year when they'd tried to make each other miserable. It had been a relief when she crossed the border one night, deserting the Argentine armed forces and her husband.

He thought he'd seen the last of her, but he should have known better. She had called him less than two months later with the news that she was pregnant and that yes, she was completely sure it was his. He'd been sending her money ever since; it wasn't Carina's fault that her mother was a natural disaster.

But this time it didn't appear to be Belén's fault. Not even she could summon mechanized infantry out of thin air.

He entered the HQ building and stormed into an office.

Colonel Javier Balzano looked up at him. "Is everything all right?"

Germán put him up to speed on what Belén had told him.

"Why would they need the dam? There's nothing up there that needs that much juice. Hell, the thing has been pretty much mothballed for years."

Germán sighed. "It's the aluminum smelter," he said. "I told you we should have bombed the hell out it. With the juice, they can process the mountain of ore they have sitting around... and once you have the aluminum... you can restart the Dao Feng plant. It can build forty all-terrain-amphibious jeeps every single day."

"And who would want to do that?" Javier asked. "You'd need transport ships to get them anywhere. And no one with a transport ship would move anything but food."

"Not if they can drive where they're going."

Javier raised an eyebrow. "You think they're coming for us."

"They're coming for the harvest," he replied. "With enough of those jeeps and a few hundred machine guns, you could take every ton of soy sitting in Rosario, and mount them on ships going down the river. The Argentine Army doesn't have anything that can stop them."

"No. They don't," Javier replied.

"But there's us."

"No one knows we exist," Javier replied.

"Maybe it's about time we showed them."

His superior sighed. "You know how you're always saying your ex is trouble on the hoof? Well, I wish you wouldn't let your personal life spill over into your work."

"Don't I know it."

"Get out of here. I'll see if anyone in the command structure can tell me what the hell is going on over there."

A long hour later, Balzano caught up with Germán as he was smoking a cigarette on the thin grass verge between the concrete parking lot of the base—kept short by dozens of conscripts—and the encroaching jungle looking to take back what once belonged to it.

The colonel didn't look happy. Not even a little bit.

"I hate you," Balzano said, gesturing for a cigarette.

Germán chuckled and handed it over. "Bad news?"

Balzano lit the cigarette. Germán rolled them himself, and his superior almost never went near them.

"Very bad. As far as anyone could tell me, an armed group stormed the mayor's complex in Ciudad del Este early this morning. They shot the mayor, installed a new one, told the Paraguayan government not to bother sending tax collectors any more, and drove down to the dam. You know the rest."

"No, I don't. Who are these guys?"

Balzano took a long puff. "No one in Paraguay seems to have any real idea."

Germán peered at the colonel long and hard. They'd been steaming in the godforsaken jungle together for nearly ten years... he could almost read the older man's thoughts. "But you do," he said.

Balzano nodded.

Germán could almost feel the reluctance coming off the older man in waves. "Tell me."

"I'm not entirely sure," Balzano hedged.

"But you have a suspicion."

"It's the Caliphate."

"The crazy people in America?"

"Yeah."

"What are they doing here?"

"Trying to corner the food market," Balzano replied. "At last count, Argentina produces a third of the world's beef, half the world's soy, and a quarter of the wheat. If they can raid the storehouses, they can send it to whoever they want and keep it from whoever they want. Both in Asia and in North America."

"They need ships for that. A lot of ships."

"That's how I figured out who it was. There's a fleet of ships coming this way, hired through shell companies by the Sinaloa Cartel, but…"

"But they work with the Caliphate."

"Exactly."

"Damn. How much time do we have?"

"Three weeks for the ships to arrive."

"And how much can they build in three weeks? They'll need to start the smelter, and the factory…"

"They already did that. The military aspect of the operation was the final part."

"Who told you that?" Germán said.

Balzano smiled sadly. "You're not the only person who has contacts in Paraguay."

"Then it's time," Germán said, putting into words the thought they'd been skirting since the conversation started.

"I wish it wasn't."

"We've been waiting for this ever since we started the project."

"I'd have been much happier to keep waiting. Is this really such a bad life?" He gestured around them, to the sunshine, the endless green, and a toucan sitting on a nearby branch.

"We always knew it would end someday."

And the day had come. They needed to get their team together, and pronto.

The only consolation was that, unlike the enemy, Balzano's team wouldn't need to build its gear. They had plenty of equipment ready to go.

As Zaeim Kimball looked across the factory floor, he could see the light of TIG welders making their way across aluminum panels. He nodded towards Mustafa. "You were smart to get the factories running before we took the dam."

"I thought it would give our enemies less time to react."

Zaeim chuckled at that. "I suppose you might be right," he conceded. "But I find it hard to believe that our enemies are organized enough that it will make any difference in the end. Paraguay has no armed forces to speak of. Their equipment is pitiful."

"They have people, though, and rifles. If they get together enough of them, they can overrun us through sheer numbers.

While we're mobile and they're not, there are also potentially millions of them and just a few hundred of us. And they aren't the only players in the region."

"Has Brazil given any sign of life?" The entire mission depended on the dormant giant to the east taking too long to respond. They needed to be out of the area by the time the big bad Brazilian Army got too interested.

That, in turn, depended on them deciding to prioritize the situation in Cuidad del Este over their own humanitarian crisis in the cities. Zaeim expected to have to fight off at least one exploratory mission—probably from some kind of special forces unit—before the Brazilians would accept that the problem needed a serious investment of forces.

Hopefully, the back-and-forth in Brasilia would give Zaeim enough time to get himself and his people out of Dodge before then. If they could get a foothold in Northern Argentina, and manage to supply it via the Paraná river... no one was going to dig them out, and they could guarantee the Caliphate's food independence forever, no matter how far it expanded. Argentina was still capable of producing the same amount of food as it always had... except there were fewer markets for it now.

"Nothing yet. My men are waiting for them, though. They will hit us in the deepest, darkest part of the night one day."

"They will. Keep them vigilant."

"Of course. No one will take our dam offline. So far, the only person who's even approached from the Brazilian side is a woman who said her kid was on the other side. We checked her for weapons and let her through."

Zaeim wasn't worried about physical threats to the dam as much as he was worried about the power plant and the lines. Those would be much easier targets to disable... but he was out at the head of a very long supply line, and power plant transformers might be just as impossible to source as a gigantic hydroelectric generator.

If those were damaged, replacing them might mean leaving the city without power... which could destroy their mission as easily as the Brazilian Army. Right now, the citizens were going about their life peacefully. All they knew was that the mayor had been replaced by a local businessman—a shady one, granted, but they were used to shady politicians in these climes—and that the city was now in some kind of conflict with the central Paraguayan government.

But the lives of the citizens themselves had changed very little. If anything, they enjoyed a few more freedoms than before... and they now had, thanks to the new mayor's first decree, free electricity. No one was looking the gift horse in the mouth.

Unfortunately, the situation could change very quickly if he had to cannibalize the civilian grid to keep the factories online: there was no way they could control the population if they became disgruntled.

Or actually, there was, but putting Ronson Ermindez's thugs on the street seemed like a good way to lose command of his own forces. The coalition was a fragile one; the true believers among the Caliph's troops would never look kindly on men whose main objective appeared to be to live a life of the senses as fully and quickly as humanly possible. Drugs, alcohol, and women were not the pleasures of the Caliph's troops.

"Good," he said. "Keep me informed of anything that comes up."

Another man approached. "We've got the first pre-production example off the line. Want to take it for a spin?"

Arthur Jenkins didn't even pretend to be one of the Caliph's converts. Short and pudgy, he wore his hair in a ponytail and wasn't so much clean-shaven as incapable of growing a beard, even at over forty years of age. Mustafa's troops looked upon him with grave misgivings, but the man was a genius at what he did.

"Of course," Zaeim replied. "Lead the way."

Jenkins preceded him through the factory. While the men Mustafa hired had done excellent work on the machinery itself, the building had been maintained just enough to keep the roof from falling in on them... which was exactly what Zaeim had expected from a factory in Paraguay. The place was a huge shed of corrugated steel. The glass sections in the roof were covered in greenish mold, which forced the crew to illuminate the interior with floodlights.

Which didn't matter. They had more juice than they could ever use.

After leaving the production area, they walked through a darker zone where piles of old machinery rusted in the corner. It smelled musty, like everything else in the jungle climate.

He blinked when they reached the inspection area. The light here was really bright, and there was no sign that they were in an underdeveloped part of the world. The place was immaculate, bright white floors and walls and ceilings.

The monochrome of the room was broken only by the polished silver of the attack buggy in the middle of it, fiercely reflecting the lights into Zaeim's eyes. He focused on one of the tires—black as the deepest night—while he waited for his vision to acclimatize itself.

"Let me present to you," Jenkins said with a flourish towards the shiny vehicle, "the first of our Haqq buggies. These babies are based around the design of the old Rally Raid racers before the Fall and they're capable of moving a hundred miles an hour over rough terrain. If these things can't get through something, only a tank will make it."

"And if the enemy has tanks?" He'd read somewhere that the Argentines had a few old hulks from the 20th century. He doubted they would be much use, even if they were still running... but he wanted to be sure.

"The kind of tanks people have here? You can outrun them."

"Show me."

The little man's smile broadened. "My pleasure."

Belén watched the factory door from a sturdy branch in a tree about a hundred meters from the facility, just outside the perimeter fence. She had binoculars in her backpack, but she didn't dare use them. The canopy hid her from sight, but the sun was at a bad angle, and even the dumbest guards would investigate a reflection from a tree.

Though she'd spent a good chunk of the previous days in the branches, trying to spot anything Germán could use, she'd gotten very little for her pains. A few deliveries of raw materials, trucks coming in and out, but no inkling of what they might be building in there.

Suddenly, however, a raucous sound broke through the muggy air, an overpowering buzz like the sound of a million angry hornets.

Out of the darkened hole that was the large doorway, a silver buggy emerged.

"Uh, oh," she said.

It was a big thing, insectoid with four wide wheels, unpainted in polished metal. It roared down the access lane, out the opening in the fence, and right into the drainage ditch on the other side of the road.

It didn't even slow.

Wham!

By the time the sound reached her perch, the buggy was in the air. It landed on its wheels and accelerated along the unkempt strip of undergrowth alongside the potholed tarmac.

The long suspension travel absorbed bumps, canals, and even bushes and small trees without slowing—in fact, it went faster and faster all the time. When it was almost out of sight, the buggy turned hard left and, fishtailing along the actual road, accelerated back towards her position.

The thing was fast. Scary fast.

Belén stayed only long enough to take a couple of pictures of it and then climbed down from her tree and returned to her house through the wood paths to avoid being seen from the factory.

Only when she reached her home did she take out her phone and send the photographs to Germán, fuming as the dead-slow network struggled to upload them.

Javier Balzano cursed. "That's a Gordon-Fabcar chassis. They won a bunch of Dakar Rallies before the Fall."

"Race cars?" Germán asked, scratching his head. "What good is that?"

"You obviously don't know a lot about what happened in Africa in the 2030s, do you? These chassis were used in huge numbers by the Sub-Saharan alliance. They're unbreakable and they can carry a lot of armor, not to mention four men and a fixed machine gun. Some were even modified for light artillery. They won a lot of bush wars by themselves."

"And how come this factory is building them?"

Balzano laughed. "No one ever figured out where they were being supplied from. Paraguay makes sense. This used to be a rally hotbed way back when."

"Why do you know all this stuff?"

This time, Balzano's laugh was tempered with sadness. "I'm older than you are. In my day, kids used to love auto racing, and we'd follow everything about it."

"I've never seen the point," Germán replied with a shrug. "Just a bunch of guys going round in circles while polluting the air and burning up our fuel reserves."

"That's just because you're a philistine," Balzano replied. "It's a good thing you're also a good soldier, because we're going to need to think about how to deal with a couple of hundred of those things coming at us."

"The first thing we need to do is to call our friends from the Andes."

"Already done."

Germán looked surprised. "That was quick."

"The phrase 'the quick and the dead' applies more to war than to any other human endeavor."

"I don't think that means what you think it means."

"Maybe you aren't such a good soldier after all. Things always mean what the officer with the highest rank in the room thinks they mean." Balzano paused. "So what do you think we need to do?"

"Those buggies look faster than our tanks," Germán said. "We need to either disperse them so they can't act in a coordinated way or we need to bunch them all together so we can shoot at them."

"What about both, one after the other? Get them into a bottleneck, kill as many of the vehicles as we can, and then force the rest to scatter."

"A good trick if you can pull it off, but if they can go off road..."

"Well, we know where they're coming from, right?"

"Sure. They have to come over the bridge from the Brazilian side." Germán's eyes widened. "Wait! What about if we just take down the bridge?"

"That would be a terrible idea," Balzano replied.

"Why? That bridge is the only way across the Paraná for a hundred kilometers in any direction. It will cost them a lot of time to get around."

"Hours, maybe. Those buggies can cover the ground in a couple of hours over rough terrain. On paved roads? They'll be at the next bridge before we can get there. Worse, they might split their forces and come at us from both sides... or they might skip a bridge and take the next one down the line, which means we'll lose them. Right now, our only advantage is surprise. They have no idea we're here, and even less that we're waiting for them. If we take out the bridge, we lose that advantage immediately."

"So it's settled? We ambush them at the bridge?"

"We let them cross the bridge. And then we hit them."

Balzano could tell Germán didn't like it. That was fine; Balzano hated it. Doing it this way would allow a large enemy force to enter Argentine territory before engaging them. A force that was much more mobile than what they could field. If they lost containment, it was blades and manure time. "If you can think of a better alternative, I'd love to hear it. I would love to bomb the hell out of their factory, but we have exactly two functioning military airplanes, and no bombs. And we can't call for help, because if we did…"

He didn't need to finish the phrase. They both knew that if the Argentine government got wind of what they had here, they would confiscate the whole base. The only reason they hadn't was Balzano's insistence on taking on only local recruits who had zero connection to the central government or even—when possible—relations in the capital. Kids so poor that they often had to be taught to read while they were taught to drive tanks.

They were loyal. To the last man and woman of them. Balzano had been betting his career on it for a decade. And he'd be betting his life on it soon enough.

His officers, of course, were more loyal still. After all, every single one of them had been on the raid he'd organized, a raid on a transport ship headed towards South Africa carrying everything Argentina needed to secure its northern border from the kind of ground incursion that could actually happen in the region—a small one.

Of course, what they'd done that day was piracy: the hijacking of a ship owned by a sovereign nation, carrying weapons purchased legitimately from another foreign nation.

Every single one of his officers had been a part of that. Two of them hadn't returned. That kind of thing created a blood bond.

"How many tanks?" Germán asked.

"For this? All of them."

Germán nodded. "The government will learn about us."

Balzano shrugged. "This is the reason we've been hunkered down here all this time."

"We'll have to emigrate. We won't be able to come back for years… it'll take Buenos Aires a while to forget this."

"You got anything holding you back?" Balzano asked. He

knew Germán had been avoiding relationships since the thing with Belén crashed and burned.

"Not really."

"So maybe we'll just join our Peruvian friends and fight off the outside world for a few years. That's what old warhorses like us do best, after all."

"I don't know. I might just walk away. It wears on you."

Balzano just nodded. He wouldn't know what to do if he didn't have the discipline and order of military life to fall back on. His one true love had lasted all of six months... and it had been with a Russian woman who had been completely wrong for him, despite which she'd ruined him for other relationships forever.

"I guess," he replied.

The airplane shuddered as it descended and Pahuac grinned at the fear in his men's eyes. These were supposed to be the most feared jungle warriors in the world, yet they trembled like little boys on their first hunt. They'd been terrified ever since the plane left the ground in Lima.

"If the spirits wish for you to die," he shouted over the roar of the engine, "then you shall die on the field of battle. They will give our enemy the strength to take your heads and the wisdom to shrink them. If the spirits are against us, many of their troops will become men when we fight." He looked around. "But they will not kill a group like ours in a rattly tin can. The spirits do not act that way."

He knew he was telling the truth, but the men were harder to convince; most of them were too young to remember a time when riding in airplanes was a matter of course.

They landed without incident and he strode across the pulverized tarmac to where his old friend Balzano was waiting. "You still haven't made general?" he said as he shook the man's hand.

"I had more important things to do."

"Tell me."

Balzano grinned. "You won't have coffee first? Rest from the trip?"

"Tell me over coffee. You might have gone soft sitting here in this warm little place out of the way of everything, but I've had my hands full trying to keep the outside world from carving our national lands back into Peru and Ecuador."

Balzano gave a sergeant instructions to billet Pahuac's men and they walked over to the headquarters building, a couple of hundred meters distant.

"And yet, you could fly off on twelve hours' notice."

"For an old friend, yes. And besides, this is part of the same war, the war that started when that bastard Colón arrived and brought his smelly Spaniards with him."

"I'm not exactly indigenous, my friend," Balzano said with a smile.

"I know that, you idiot. But you are more indigenous than the people coming after you. Even crappy European bloodlines are infused by the nobility of the soil after a century and a half. In another thousand years or so, your descendants will almost be human."

Balzano led him into a small, grey-painted room with a single table in it, with an ordnance map spread out on the wood. Pins marked the map.

"High-tech as always, I see. Thank you." An aide had brought him coffee.

"What we're doing doesn't need fancy electronics or GPS. Look, here's the bridge which the enemy is going to be driving over. This is the jungle on the far side of the bridge. I suggest we park our tanks here, along the road."

"How many tanks do you have?"

"We have seventy-four of them fully mobile and eight sitting in the shed, mostly cannibalized for parts. We're thinking of taking fifty of the mobile ones here and holding the other twenty-four in reserve."

"Crewed?"

"Crewed, fueled, armed, and ready to go."

"If it works, we shouldn't need them."

"If it works."

Pahuac nodded. The plan was simple enough. But then he did some numbers in his head. "You have a total of eighty-two tanks. We kept fifteen from the original shipment, which brings us to ninety-seven. What happened to the other three?"

Balzano sighed. He wished he didn't have to explain "They were stolen eight years ago."

"And..."

"Two of them were sold to the Caliph's people. We don't know what happened to the other one. I suspect they built two complete tanks out of the three they stole."

Pahuac nodded. He didn't blame Balzano for the situation. This kind of thing happened all the time in South America, even before the Fall. Even among his own people, the closely-knit tribe that had emerged from the jungle and taken over large swaths of Peru and Ecuador, corruption of this kind wasn't unheard of.

"So we'll get to fight the Challengers we risked our butts to steal from the British."

"Two of them, at least. The good thing is that they can't have much ammunition..."

"That's something, at least. Unless you happen to be in one of the tanks that gets hit."

"Yeah."

Pahuac shrugged. "War is always in the hands of the spirits. It could have been worse. When do you expect them to strike?"

"Four days from now at the earliest. Seven at the latest. Our person on the ground tells me they're building the buggies at an enormous rate."

"All right. Let me think about the terrain a bit." He pointed at the map. "What do you plan to do about this open area here?"

"We'll put five tanks in these trees," Balzano replied.

And they got down to the serious discussion about how to deploy their forces.

The heat and humidity reminded Zaeim of summer in southern Alabama, only more so. The air was even heavier on your skin, and the mosquitoes were uniformly enormous. Just that morning he'd watched a couple of ants nearly the size of his thumb take on an armored beetle like a child's fist in a battle for some kind of insectile dominance. He wondered if it was a sign that Allah was preparing the world for war.

He shook his head. He was beginning to think like Mustafa.

But maybe it was time to think like the man. Mustafa was many things—fanatical, dedicated and perhaps a bit naïve as to the ways of the world—but there could be no denying that the man was a true warrior. He'd even declined the relative safety of one of the Challengers so that he could ride at the head of the buggy brigade. They weren't expecting too many losses, of course—Argentina's ragtag military would never be able to put up much of a fight—but the first few buggies would bear the brunt of any minor casualties they might incur. Mustafa had just shrugged those considerations off.

All of that was in the future, however. Right now, they were moving across the Itaipu dam at the Challenger's top speed—about eighty miles an hour—with the column of buggies behind them. The second Challenger brought up the rear.

There was a reason for this layout. In order to reach the bridge to Argentina, they had to drive through the city of Foç de Iguazú, a place they didn't control. If anyone reacted badly, or if the Brazilians had beefed up their presence, having the two hundred buggies surrounded by tanks was the best way to deal with it.

They sped through the city—there was almost no traffic at six in the morning—and approached the bridge, which also served as a border crossing.

The two guards on the Argentine side dove out of the way as the tank drove over the flimsy metal barrier.

"Park beside the road," Zaeim said to his driver.

The man complied and Mustafa's buggy pulled up alongside them. They watched ten of their soldiers capture the Argentine guards to keep them from radioing ahead.

"May Allah be with you," Zaeim said when the excitement was over.

"I have lived my life for Allah's glory. He will not abandon me," Mustafa replied. Then he accelerated into the distance.

Zaeim watched him go, wondering what Mustafa would say if he knew just how badly the Caliph, a man who'd never had a religious thought in his life, had lied to him and to all the rest of the men who thought like him.

If there was an Allah, he certainly wouldn't be on Mustafa's side.

But that didn't matter. They had more vehicles and more armed men than the entire Argentine Army. Allah would stay out of this one.

Germán popped out of the turret of his tank and ran the five hundred meters to where Balzano was concealed in the undergrowth, shaded by the trees.

"Belén said they're on their way," he shouted. He was out of breath, but they didn't know if the enemy was monitoring the radio waves. "They should be here in an hour. Probably less."

Balzano looked down on him. "If you happen to see her after this is all over, could you tell her how much we appreciate this? If we win, it will only have been because of her."

"We have to win first," Germán replied.

Mustafa shouted, the battle cry torn from his throat by the glorious wind.

His buggies advanced, five wide, down the two-lane blacktop, along the red dirt beside the road, and even through the lush green vegetation further from the road.

Argentina. Enemy territory at last! The objective was just a few hours away, and with any luck, they'd be able to seize the four depots—bursting with food bound for Asia—and hold them for the couple of days they would need to load the ships.

Once that was done, they'd see about turning their beachhead into a true invasion.

"Faster!" he shouted down at the driver. The buggy had a hatch in the roof. The passenger could stand on the seat and operate a pivoting machine gun. Though the instructors had droned on about how it was a Brazilian design designed to function in the heat and humidity of the Amazon forest, Mustafa had paid them no attention. All he cared about was that it would cut down his enemies in their prime, for the greater glory of Allah and the Caliphate.

The driver grinned up at him and the acceleration pushed him back into the roll hoop. He shouted again.

It became a race. Ibrahim's buggy, to his right, squirted ahead. Then Bassam's shot forward and roared into the distance.

Mustafa watched the buggy go, wondering why it was faster than his own.

Before he could turn to ask the driver if they couldn't go any faster, Bassam's vehicle exploded. Mustafa watched, uncomprehending, as it barrel-rolled, shedding parts, wheels, and glass before coming to rest on its side.

His mind couldn't quite process what he'd just seen. Had the engine blown? The driveshaft?

"Stop the car! We need to see if they're all right!" he shouted.

And that was when Ibrahim's buggy blew up and he realized that they were under attack.

The driver must have come to exactly the same conclusion. He wove and suddenly hit the brakes to go into a long curve. Mustafa gripped the roll cage as the buggy slid on the tarmac. Behind him, two more of the vehicles exploded.

He slid into the seat and got on to the radio. "We're taking fire!" he shouted. "Proceed with extreme caution and run evasive maneuvers."

"Where is it coming from?" Zaeim's voice cut through the sudden jabbering. "I don't see any aircraft?"

"I don't know! Bassam and Ibrahim just blew up."

"Stay calm. Look for cover where a few guys with RPGs can hide. Remember that the Argentines don't have anything major in the area."

"The trees... Give me a minute."

Mustafa switched off the command channel and onto the frequency for his lead cars. "Get closer to the trees and drop off a few men with rifles. Find the bastards who are doing this and bring them to me. I'm going to skin them alive."

The five buggies that remained in the forward group split and headed for the trees.

"Go right," Mustafa said. "It looks like there's a gap between the trees there. I think that's where they're hiding. Go."

The problem with the tropical vegetation near the border was that it was extremely dense on the surface and the canopy, but extremely dark within. There could be an army of men hiding within, and he wouldn't be able to spot them until the last....

"No! Get back! Turn away."

The driver swerved right and then looked at him quizzically.

"There's a tank in there. I need to warn the others."

Even as he spoke the words, Mustafa had the awful feeling that it was too late. To his right, along the tree line, a Challenger tank that could have been the twin of the one they'd driven into the mayor's palace in Ciudad del Este broke out of the greenery and slammed into the buggy just ten meters ahead of Mustafa's position. The man on the machine gun and the two men in the rear compartment were thrown clear with the impact, but the driver was still inside as the tank rolled over the buggy, turning steel and aluminum into a flattened crumpled mass.

"Fall back!" Mustafa shouted into the radio.

Only when he saw the second wave approaching up the road—there were a full fifty vehicles in that formation—did he realize he was still on the local frequency. He switched to the command channel and spoke to his officers. "Everyone fall back. It's a trap. There are tanks here. Fall back."

"How many tanks, Mustafa?" Zaeim's voice came through. He sounded calm.

"I... three. No, four. Oh, Allah, there are too many of them."

"How many? Can you count them?"

But Mustafa was watching the nearest tank as its turret turned and pointed towards the buggy. He heard his men returning fire. They'd dismounted from the buggies and were following the manual that they didn't think they'd need down here: engaging tanks on foot, spreading out to give them too many targets. The tanks' machine gunners were getting kills in the dozens.

And then the muzzle flashed and the world spun. The buggy lifted up into the air and the force of the explosion tore Mustafa's grip from the roll cage.

Free from the vehicle, he felt a moment of utter bliss as the air flew past slowly. Then the reddish tarmac came up to greet him, and he hit it with a crash that shattered bones. He felt the agony as they broke, and then the continued pain as he slid across the rough road, his skin peeling away in chunks.

Then all movement stopped and he lay there, panting in agony. Though the sun above blistered his skin, the tarmac below was even hotter, burning at his exposed nerves.

He wanted to scream, but he couldn't. All he could do was lie there, trying to move as little as possible as the hot road slowly cooked him.

The shooting had stopped long minutes before. Something approached. Footsteps. Voices.

"Water," Mustafa croaked. Then he realized the voices were speaking Spanish. "Agua."

Two sets of boots—one polished and black, the other scuffed and tan—stopped before him. Mustafa couldn't turn his head, but by moving his eyes, he saw two men, both dark-haired, one clearly indigenous, the other probably a descendant of European colonists.

"What did you want me here for? We can't take any of these guys with us. Our orders were to destroy their machines. We're not supposed to try to capture anyone."

"I need you to witness."

"Witness?"

"Today, by Shuar tradition, I become a man in front of the spirits."

"What... you're going to take his head? Just take one from the dead men."

"No. If I do that, I'll never be sure I killed him. This is the way."

The sunlight glinted off steel. Mustafa tried to scream, to beg Allah to intervene on his behalf, but his broken body couldn't muster the strength.

The blade fell and he knew nothing more.

"Go faster," Zaeim shouted down to his driver. The tank rumbled over the highway at an enormous clip, but they still hadn't reached the engagement zone. He spoke into the command channel. "Everyone retreat back toward the bridge. We've got to go around them."

"We're cut off," one of the squad leaders replied. "There are tanks behind us as well as in front. Get us out of here."

"Drive around them," Zaeim replied. "We'll try to hold them off."

How he was going to do that was a mystery. Even if he disregarded the more wildly exaggerated reports from the drivers, the Argentines had pulled a couple of dozen tanks out of their asses... how had they done that?

He might need to have a serious talk with the intelligence geeks when he made it back.

If he made it back. He was currently attempting to attack a much larger force with two tanks. That kind of thing was not conducive to extended longevity, but it was the only way to help his troops. If he lost them all, the Caliph would kill him himself.

He was close enough to see the columns of smoke rising over the trees, and he gritted his teeth. He needed to get there *now*.

A bend in the road revealed...

"Stop the tank!" he shouted. And he sent the same order to the other Challenger under his command.

The behemoth groaned to a halt as the treads slid on the asphalt before digging in. The other tank slewed sideways a bit before also stopping at an angle.

Ahead of them, four enemy tanks faced away from the two from the Caliphate. These must be the ones that the drivers reported as boxing them in. He admired the neatness of the ambush: the Argentines had let everyone through, and were now simply shelling the trapped buggies. Shooting fish in a barrel.

"Head back towards the bridge," he told the trapped buggies. "We'll deal with the tanks behind you." Then he leaned into the interior of the Challenger and said, "Fire at the two tanks in front of us. Aim for the base of the turret." At this range they couldn't miss. He relayed the order to the second tank.

"Firing in three, two, one," the voice of the loader emerged from the cabin. Was he supposed to get inside for firing? Zaeim didn't know, so he stayed where he was... but held on.

The tank bucked beneath him and the muzzle spouted flames and smoke. Ahead, the enemy tank began to pour smoke from every hole. A hatch opened, and a single man staggered out and collapsed onto the tarmac. A second later the other Caliphate tank fired as well. This time the bad guy actually exploded, launching its turret into the air as its ammo went.

"Shoot the next one!" he said.

The two remaining enemy vehicles turned towards them, caught by surprise. Now it was a race to see who could get their charges off first.

It was no contest. The Argentine crews had obviously been training with their vehicles forever. They both fired before the Caliphate tanks. Unfortunately for them, they both fired at the same tank, the one sitting next to Zaeim's vehicle.

A moment after his comrades exploded into hot shrapnel, his own tank fired and scored a hit on one of the Argentine Challengers, tearing off a tread.

"Get us out of here," he called into the interior.

The driver needed no further encouragement. The man knew the odds, and no one wanted to face twenty tanks at once. He executed a quick turn, grinding the tarmac to powder, and shot off at ninety degrees.

The four tanks barring the way had been reduced to one. Buggies began to pour through the gaps, zigzagging to avoid enemy fire, while the crew of the remaining Challenger struggled to acquire targets.

"Move, move," Zaeim whispered, egging them on. There were a lot of them, all passing him as they shot through.

But after fifty or sixty buggies passed, the stream became a trickle, and then only individual stragglers, damaged and broken, went by. Zaeim cursed. If that was all he had left, the plan was pretty much scuttled.

"Regroup on the Brazilian side of the bridge," he ordered. "And send someone back for us. This tank can't outrun the Argentines all the way back. We're going to have to abandon it."

A crowd had gathered on the shores of the Paraná. It was mostly composed of Zaeim's own troops, but some locals had come along to watch the fevered preparations as well. One of them looked like a woman they'd seen walking across the dam a few days ago but, to be honest, she could have been any one of the thousands of local women in the area. They all looked similar to him: slim, dusky-skinned, with lank black hair.

They'd crossed the bridge ten minutes before, and now his demolitions crew—or what was left of it—was setting charges in the center of the bridge. They needed to hurry, to drop that span or at least weaken it enough that the pursuing tanks couldn't cross. Once the tanks arrived, it was too late.

The men must have disregarded every single security protocol on the planet, because another ten minutes later, the work was done and they were sprinting across the bridge, dragging a detonator line behind them. Zaeim wondered why they wouldn't detonate the thing remotely, but he supposed they weren't taking any chances.

Just as the tanks rolled into view around a bend in the road, the crack of explosives sounded and a small section of bridge crumbled into the Paraná.

The tanks on the other side rumbled to a halt.

The road was out of sight of the bridge, and the Argentines couldn't see them. He hadn't seen any sign of air support, so he assumed they wouldn't be able to find them either.

Good.

They'd have a very long head start. Their plan to invade might be scuttled, but they could still grab enough food in Rosario to feed the Caliphate for a year.

They'd think about what to do next when the time came.

Zaeim waved at the tanks and walked calmly back to rejoin his men, well hidden behind the trees where the tank commanders couldn't see them.

"They're heading east," Belén said as she watched the column head deeper into Brazil. "They have exactly seventy-four buggies left."

Germán thanked her, but he didn't sound too happy about it.

"Did your people take anyone prisoner?" Balzano asked as he observed Pahuac's men. Each had a sack or bundle wrapped in paper and dripping gore. Part of the agreement was that the Shuar warriors would be permitted to hunt one head per combatant. Balzano hated it, but he needed the battle-hardened tank crews.

Pahuac shrugged. "A few. But maybe we should have killed them all. From what they've been telling my men, these soldiers aren't warriors. They're thugs that work for the local drug traffickers, reporting to some guy called Ermindez." He chuckled. "They throw around Ermindez's name like he was some kind of boogeyman, and that we'll regret ever having crossed him. I had to explain that I have a special display case in my house where I keep the shrunken heads of the druglords I've met. We used to have a lot of them up north. Not so many around now. But they still wouldn't believe me. They only shut up when I showed them the photos on my phone."

"Any of the Caliph's men?"

"Only a few, and they don't speak much Spanish. Most of the muscle appears to have been local. Brazilians. Paraguayans. A few of your countrymen. What are you going to do with them?"

"I'm going to turn them over to the police."

"The police?"

"Sure. They're in the country illegally and, unless we can move a lot quicker than I expect, we won't be able to catch their friends. So the ones that got away are going to become a serious problem for Argentina... and the authorities will probably shoot these guys for war crimes. Even if they don't, Buenos Aires is going to be pissed. They'll most likely dump these guys in the deepest, smelliest dungeon they can find and throw away the key."

Balzano knew the operation, by any objective measure, had been a spectacular success. They'd disabled or destroyed more than a hundred of the enemy's vehicles. How the hell they'd managed to build so many in such a short time, even with a functional factory, would be a question for another day.

The Argentine troops had captured about eighty men, a number of them wounded badly—getting shelled or rammed by a main battle tank was not particularly conducive to good health. Pahuac seemed to have a couple dozen more.

Unfortunately, no one was going to be lining up to congratulate Balzano. If anyone in Buenos Aires had been informed that a column of several hundred technicals would charge his position, the colonel and his troops would have been expected to defend their positions for a few minutes and then die like heroes. They weren't supposed to have a metric buttload of recent-generation battle tanks stolen from the British, and they especially weren't supposed to call in foreign troops—especially not foreign troops famous the world over for headhunting their enemies—to help man them.

So Balzano had broken every law in Argentina. Worse, he hadn't quite stopped the enemy. Sure, he'd destroyed most of their vehicles and killed most of their men. Hell, they'd even recovered one of the stolen Challengers and blown up the other.

But the speed with which the survivors retreated, regrouped, and headed off in a different direction was a clear sign that someone was still in charge.

And that meant they would be heading towards Rosario at twice the speed Balzano could chase them.

Worse, fueling the tanks for a 600-kilometer chase was not something they could manage. He'd need to split his forces into several columns and suck every truck stop along the way completely dry. And even so, he'd lose vehicles as they ran out of diesel and had to be abandoned.

But what choice did he have? Even though he'd already ignored several calls from Buenos Aires, calls that probably brought pointed questions about a pitched battle that should never have happened, he was still an Argentine officer. For now. Technically.

As such, he needed to do the best he could to minimize the damage.

He held out his hand to Pahuac. "Thank you for the help. Your men were invaluable. As promised, you can have twenty-five of the tanks. How are you going to get them to Peru?"

Pahuac looked at him like he was the village idiot. "We'll drive them up that road over there," he replied, pointing to a two-lane that headed west. "Until we come to a bridge that hasn't been blown up. Then we'll drive north to Peru. Do you think anyone in Paraguay or Bolivia is going to mess with a column of tanks that actually work? If it weren't for one annoying Argentine colonel in possession of an even bigger force, I could declare myself Emperor of South America."

Balzano laughed. "Good point."

"What about you?" Pahuac replied. "You have the look of a man about to do something incredibly stupid. You've done your part. Those buggies will be in Rosario in five hours, and they'll have their ships loaded in fifteen. You can't arrive in time to stop them."

"I have to try."

"And if you fail?"

He shrugged. "I'll drive off into the sunset."

Pahuac gave him a long look. "If you do, you are always welcome in Peru. But something tells me you won't do the smart thing." He shook the proffered hand and embraced Balzano. "It's been a pleasure, my friend."

"Always," Balzano replied.

―⚔―

"That's the last of the wheat. The soy ships are already full," the lieutenant reported. "We also got fifty of the buggies loaded, and booby-trapped the ones we couldn't get aboard, as ordered."

Zaeim grinned. "Good. Let's get out of here."

Rosario was a big city, and the Argentines probably thought that was where they were headed, so they ignored the obvious urban target and hit the port of San Nicolás, a smaller city but a place where endless rows of silos full of wheat and soy awaited a convoy of ships that had been delayed without explanation.

Zaeim knew the explanation. The ships were under new management: the Caliph had had them all hired away from the original contractors.

Of course, that would have been worthless if the people on shore had refused to fill them, which is why pointing guns at the port operators and making a few examples of men who dragged their feet was so important.

It was ironic that the speed with which the port facilities could deliver their load had worked against the Argentines. By dawn, the loading was done, and the authorities had only sent a single police cruiser to investigate. An RPG had made quick work of that.

The ship moved and Zaeim breathed a sigh of relief. He'd half-expected to see a column of tanks rolling into the port.

But it hadn't happened, and now they were on the way back to the Caliphate with their mission at least a partial success. The food had been secured and, more importantly, denied to everyone else. The best of it was that the operation had been essentially free, except for the initial cost of the APCs and the two tanks, which had been ridiculously cheap. Everything they got was profit; both the food and the materials to build the vehicles had been stolen from the host countries. Even the druglord's men came free, in exchange for the chance to have an outside force do the dirty work of killing the mayor and giving Ermindez Ciudad del Este. The only thing the Caliphate had lost was men, a few fanatics.

Men were the easiest thing to replace.

As the miles drifted behind the ships, Zaeim relaxed. They'd pulled it off.

The green coast punctuated by the occasional town and the muddy waters reminded him of home. It was the right kind of river, although bigger than the ones he'd grown up around, the right kind of weather. He gazed dreamily over the water and the column of vessels ahead.

They had no warning. No sound of shells whizzing overhead, no reports from the far bank. The first evidence Zaeim had that they were under attack was that the bridge of the ship in front of him in line suddenly exploded.

Less than a second later, the bridge of his own followed

suit. Glass shattered and sprayed all over the foredeck. Only the size of the ship, which meant he was quite far from the explosion, kept him from being cut to pieces. As it was, a couple of shards stung his leg.

He took cover behind a steel bulkhead and looked out to the right. Muzzle flashes lit up the left coast on the warm morning.

The tanks had arrived.

Zaeim sprinted to the rear of the ship, hoping to find someone with a working radio or someone who could steer the ship nearer to the right bank. They'd said something about a deep-water channel, but he hadn't paid much attention. The maritime portion of the operation wasn't his responsibility.

Except now, he needed to get these ships away from the tanks.

Explosions, one after another, never letting up, pounded the ship in rhythmic succession. It was like hearing the drum section of an enormous orchestra.

His ears rang with the noise.

When he reached the bridge, he found nothing but mangled steel. There was no one alive in there.

He was thrown forward as the ship slammed into something. He lifted his head to see that they'd whacked the vessel ahead. He wiped his forehead, and his hand came away bloody. But he felt all right. He wasn't seriously injured.

It was time to abandon ship. He could swim to the right coast. At this point, both banks of the Paraná river were in Argentine territory, but at least he would swim away from the enemy forces.

He ran towards the deck, trying to jump clear enough that he wouldn't be sucked down if the ship went under, but he never made it. A shell hit the deck a few feet from his position.

Zaeim felt the shrapnel tear through him in midair and he hit the water in pain, too injured to swim.

The muddy water drowned him in agony.

"Hold your fire!" Balzano shouted. "Enough. They're not going anywhere. Maybe we can salvage some of the food."

The tanks stopped firing, except for one straggler on the end who fired off a final round before obeying the order.

Javier studied the ships. They were jammed up and disabled. The one at the head of the line, the one they'd had to sink to block the rest, had nearly disappeared under the brown water.

He dismounted from the tank and leaned against it. He was so exhausted that he barely looked up when a green jeep stopped beside them fifteen minutes later. A frightened-looking man in a major's uniform descended. "Colonel Balzano?" he said.

Balzano nodded wearily.

"I have a message from General Tanoia. He says there had better be a really good explanation for all this."

"There is."

"He also said that I should write down anything you said to use as evidence in your court martial. He told me not to tell you, but I think it's only fair you should know."

Balzano laughed. "You're a brave man, Major. What's to stop me from having my tanks blow you to pieces?"

The man shrugged. "The general said you wouldn't do that. He said you might have dropped both yourself and our country into the deepest level of crap, but that you wouldn't turn traitor. Hell, he even said you wouldn't even try to run."

"He's wrong about that. I would definitely have run. Except I'm out of fuel."

"It's a good thing I didn't hear that last part, isn't it?" the major said. "It would cast a pall over the fact that you came willingly. Now is there anything you'd like to say for the record?"

"Yeah. My men and my officers were only following orders. None of them knew this wasn't sanctioned."

The major nodded. "Duly noted."

"Also, the tanks are a gift to the Argentine Republic. No charge."

Carina skipped a stone under the watchful eyes of both her parents.

"They just let you go?" Belén said.

Germán nodded. "All the officers said the same thing. We acted to defend our borders with the materiel at hand. And we all denied knowing where the tanks came from. In the end, they stowed us in a prison in Cordoba for a few months and, when the public eye turned to the Argentina-Brazil match, they quietly let us go."

"And Balzano?"

"I don't know. They can't keep him locked up too long. Now that the story is out, everyone in the army knows he saved the country. If they shoot him, the government will fall. We'll see. He hasn't asked for clemency —he just told the story as it was, except he never named a single member of the crew that stole the tanks. And we swore an oath not to tell of our involvement." He shrugged. "I hope he'll be all right."

"You think he won't?"

"I think he knows it's over for him, one way or the other. I think he feels he did what he was supposed to do. I hope I'm wrong." He looked over to where Carina was tossing stones. "And I think our girl needs both parents."

"You think you can just…"

He held up his hands. "None of that. I think I'll settle here and see her when you let me."

"And nothing between us?"

"Not unless you want it. You were very clear when you left me. I know I wasn't the best husband."

She looked at him for a while, looking surprised. "I don't mind seeing you. Not now that you are a retired war hero. And especially not now that you left everything behind to spend time with your daughter." She paused. "As for anything else, we'll need to give it time. We were really, really terrible together."

He laughed. "But we had our good times, too."

"Don't start."

They sat in silence, watching their daughter. Both of them smiled as rocks fell into the water, one after another.

Los Banditos

Jason Cordova

2032

"Here they come!"

Once more the *soldados* of the cartel attempted to push through the breach, laying down withering gunfire as they moved. Teams of two, leap-frogging past one another, trying to provide enough cover for the next team to continue its advance. Their movements appeared well-rehearsed, an abrupt change in tactics after their last failed attack on our outpost. Before we had faced rabble, the lowest-ranking *soldados*, the street thugs. Those poor bastards hadn't stood a chance.

These new ones? They moved like real *soldados*, wore similar body armor to us, and even had equipment like what Major Diaz had brought with him. We still wore the old Mexican National Army uniforms, even though they were practically threadbare and see-through by this point. We'd learned the cartels targeted us by rank early on, sniping at our senior NCOs and officers whenever they had the chance, so they stopped wearing them. We also stopped saluting officers as well, since a salute of any type was usually followed by a sniper's round. Fortunately, while they were well equipped, the cartels didn't really have anyone in their ranks who would be considered a skilled shooter.

Not yet, at least. Who knew what next week would bring?

Using the ruined vehicles from their past attacks to hide from our shooters, the cartel *soldados* almost made it to the concrete barriers before their initial good luck ran out. One of them, not paying attention to where he was walking, stepped on a toe-popper. The tiny anti-personnel mine exploded and the *soldado* dropped to the ground, screaming in pain and clutching his foot. Or rather, what was left of it. His teammate, clearly distracted by his partner's injury, stood upright and forgot to remain behind cover. His head was removed in a shower of bone and brain matter. A sharp *crack!* echoed from behind us immediately after. Inwardly I smiled. Marla had tagged him with a single shot to the head from the watchtower three hundred yards away. The *soldado* flopped to the ground atop his wounded teammate, his strings cut like a marionette. The wounded man lay screaming on the ground, partially pinned down by his dead compatriot. The other five groups continued to move forward, apparently undeterred by one of their teams being taken out.

"Sappers!" Senior Sergeant Montoya shouted from nearby. I shifted the barrel of my M240 machine gun a few centimeters but held off on firing just yet. They weren't in my sector. Right now they were Montoya's responsibility. Ten meters left, though, and they were in for a rude welcome. While I scanned the field, I thought about this latest tactic the cartel was trying.

Sending in sappers made sense. The cartels, in four years of constant probing attacks on our compound, hadn't managed to breach the outer gate since the early days of the war. The gate had stood defiantly against everything they'd thrown at it—including a big rig truck, which had *almost* made it to the gate before we'd taken it out with our final Javelin anti-tank missile. The cartel quit trying to use big vehicles after that, afraid of what we could throw at them. They had no idea we'd shot our last one in taking out the semi.

I continued to watch my sector as my loader Pedro kept an eye on the gate. The cartel was sneaky and liked to try to create diversionary attacks. Whoever was in charge of the cartel thought themselves to be a cross between Pancho Villa and Alexander the Great. While they appeared to be a very efficient cartel drug lord, they were shit when it came to commanding *soldados*. Well, typically. Today's excursion looked more professional than we were used to seeing.

"Hey, Pedro?"

"*Sí?*"

"These *putas* seem more coordinated than normal?" I asked my loader.

"*Si, un poco,*" he agreed. They *were* acting a little more coordinated. It made me wonder if there'd been a shake-up in the ranks of the cartel.

A second shot came from the watchtower and another cartel *soldado* dropped, dead before he hit the ground. I risked a glance up to the watchtower. Marla, a local who'd joined us after the cartels burned her town to the ground, was arguably the best shot I'd ever seen. She'd proven her worth time and time again since joining us. We had no idea where she'd learned to shoot like that, though. Marla never spoke of it and, after a few tries, Major Diaz quit asking. Naturally, this stopped none of the rumors.

"Movement," Pedro's calm voice jerked me out of my reminiscing. We'd burned back the treeline from the gate months ago and then mined everything in between. There was some dense underbrush over a hundred meters away—which is where the annoying cartel snipers loved to hide—but anyone who stepped out of the treeline and tried to cross the open field would die. It was almost a flawless defensive position for us.

Flawless except for the goats, at least.

The goats were a recent addition. Once the mines had been laid down, it was nearly impossible for us to keep the bushes and grass low. Major Diaz had suggested flamethrowers but we didn't know if the heat would trigger the explosives or not, so nobody wanted to risk it. Lieutenant Casteñeda, the hapless but well-meaning idiot, had tried to come up with a weedeater extension pole. Fortunately, nobody lost a limb when the makeshift tripped a mine. Then Marla came up with a brilliant idea. Goats.

I thought it was some sort of urban legend but it turned out to be true. The goats somehow sensed where the mines were and stepped around them. They still ate the grass which grew on top, though, so there weren't any obvious tall clumps of grass or shrubs to point out where the mines were hidden.

No, the problem came from the paths the goats walked. What had started as a few goats had, over the months, grown into a small herd as more just seemed to show up. With the goats all walking the same path, eventually we could see the trails wandering around the mines. If we could see it, then the spotters and snipers of the cartel who were hiding out in the jungle could definitely see them. It was only a matter of time before they tried to push my sector, which was why we had the tripod-mounted M240 pointed this way and not at the main road.

"Got them," I murmured as I spotted dark forms moving in the jungle beyond the goats. It was hard to get an exact number in such dim lighting but it was easily more than a dozen. The sapper attack on the main gate was both a diversion and an assault. "They're at marker two."

"*Si*," Pedro agreed. "Warning shots?"

"They already know we're here," I reminded him. "No point in warning them. Patience."

Pedro muttered a string of curses under his breath. "Stupid cartels."

I silently agreed with him. There was no rhyme or reason for them to want anything to do with the Yucatan. Outside of being able to say "I own Cancun," at least. Which, in the grand scheme of things, really wasn't much. Most of the tourists who'd gotten stuck here had died of the typhoid outbreak a few years ago. The majority of the survivors had moved into the jungles towards Chichen Itza. Those poor bastards had never been heard from again. The rest of us had joined up with the scattered remnants of the Mexican National Army and holed up at Firebase Cancun, our home. It was nothing more than a makeshift, last-ditch effort built by Major Alejandro Diaz to protect the town.

It was weird how things worked out. I never thought me, a Hispanic kid from Imperial Beach, California, would end up on the Yucatan peninsula protecting some tourists and innocent Mayan villagers from rampaging drug cartels during the end of civilization.

My family was from California but we had relatives right across the border in Tijuana. I'd always been a bit of a rebel when compared to my older brothers, and moved away when I was 18, joining the Navy. I'd enjoyed Pensacola and being in Virginia during my time in, so I decided to stay in the south after my five years was up. Built up a little tech start-up company, sold it a few years later, and decided I wanted to spend a month in Cozumel and Cancun to treat myself. I'd earned it after working five years straight without a single day off.

Of course, that was when everything went to shit and the world ended.

At first, they told all of the tourists to stay in their rooms while the police figured things out. Most of the tourists had complied. A few had tried to sneak out, though I still don't understand what they were thinking. Was there some secret boat trip they could make across the Gulf of Mexico to reach Texas? Considering I had a pretty good idea how many people had died crossing a narrower gap between Cuba and Florida, their hope of making it up to Texas from Cancun was... *ambitious*.

Eventually the police disappeared and we were left to our own devices. It hadn't been pretty. There was an old joke my department chief used to say about how, when the United States catches a cold, the rest of the world gets pneumonia. So when the States died, the world went to hell in a handbasket. For the most part the locals left us alone, preferring to kill one another for things going back generations. Mayans really hated everyone not Mayan. However, they really despised anyone who came to the Yucatan during the *Porforiato*. I used to think my *abuela* could hold a grudge better than anyone. After dealing with the local Mayans, though, I now knew the truth. They never forgot a transgression.

My loader Pedro was Mayan, one of the many villagers who'd joined Major Diaz's attempt to keep Mexico safe and functioning. He hadn't had any formal military training but there was nobody as sneaky when it came to moving in the jungles. I was pretty sure if Delta Force or some SOCOM operators came down here, he could teach them a thing or two. There was just something about how the short *hombre* moved silently. It was unsettling. On top of that, he had much better eyes. His trigger discipline sucked, though, which was how he ended up being my loader.

"They're moving away," Pedro hissed quietly in Yucatec. I'd picked up quite a bit of the language in the years since the end began, but I wasn't really fluent in it yet. Fortunately, Pedro also spoke Spanish, so I wasn't completely hosed. His Spanish, though, left much to be desired. I couldn't complain. It was still better than his English, which consisted of "Fuck yeah!" and "Hang loose."

I swear to God if I ever find the tourist who told him these were the everyday greetings of Americans, I will gut them like a pig.

"Contact front!" Lieutenant Casteñeda screamed out as a wave of cartel *soldados* erupted from the treeline between the main fortified gate and our position. These new arrivals were following the path shown by the sappers. It was well over five dozen men, each armed with an AK-47. The *soldados* fired as they ran forward, which forced the others along the wall to keep their heads down.

Not Marla, though. Her rifle immediately opened up once again and the *soldados* died as fast as she could pull the trigger. Every round found a home, and none of the *soldados* moved after being hit. The only reason any of them were getting close to the gate was the rifle's magazine. The magazine was short, only good for six shots before it needed to be reloaded. In those scant seconds between reloads, the *soldados* made excellent progress and breached the outer wall.

It wasn't really a wall. It was a knee-high concrete barrier we'd "borrowed" from a local construction site in Cancun. Since they weren't going to need it any more, Major Diaz figured we could find some use for all the building materials we'd found. Crude, but effective in slowing the advance of the *soldados*. Out of the corner of my eye I watched one of our fire teams shift position to meet the advance. The toe poppers weren't on this part of the road, mainly because past *soldados* had tripped them. We hadn't had enough to replace them all.

As much as I wanted to turn the barrel of my M240 towards the oncoming horde, I knew my responsibilities. The front gate was actually not our sector, but covered by Marla, up in her sniper's nest, and Fire Team One—which was really just Senior Sergeant Montoya and our giant German tourist turned rifleman, Rolf.

Rolf was a quiet guy. I think he didn't speak much because he had a really strange accent. Not like they did in the movies, though. It made you take a second look at him because when one is almost seven feet tall and built like a linebacker, you don't expect him to sound the way he does.

With Montoya, Rolf, and Marla covering the primary assault sector, and Lieutenant Castañeda's team backing *them* up, we were in pretty good shape. Granted, the *soldados* getting past the concrete barrier was annoying, but it wasn't the first time. The trick was to get them pinned down between the outer gate and the concrete barriers.

Meanwhile, shadows continued to move about in the jungle just outside our cleared range. It was annoying and I *really* wanted to do some hedge trimming with my machine gun, but I didn't want a two-hour lecture from Senior Sergeant Montoya about my lack of trigger discipline. Ammunition was not in great supply and eventually we'd have to figure out a way to gather more ammo.

"How many do you see, Pedro?"

"Eight, nine, maybe more," my loader said slowly, his eyes flickering back and forth between the reinforced compound entry, our sector, and the jungle beyond. "They keep moving around. Could be more, could be less."

"Hmph," I grunted and pulled back the cocking handle of the M240. The bolt and carrier assembly locked into place. I pushed the button for the safety on and waited. The odds were good they would try and push through the trails in the grass left by the goats, but I knew we could cover it well. The sandbags which protected my position, combined with the elevated view of our sector, meant the *soldados* of the cartels would be fed to the meat grinder if they pushed us.

"Unless they brought grenades," I muttered under my breath. Pedro turned and gave me a weird look. Politely ignoring him was the best option for me at the moment. After all, it wasn't right to mention worst case scenarios right before a battle. No need to tempt fate, karma, or any other superstitious entity. I was pretty devout but Pedro made me look like some yanqui atheist. With Pedro? You never, ever, mentioned how bad it could be. It was almost as bad as if a black cat walked in front of him. He'd make some weird hand gesture to ward off the evil eye, draw something in the ground in front of him, then wipe it all away and say a quick prayer. The *hombre* was, well, fucking crazy.

After years of constant warfare trying to keep the Yucatan peninsula out of the hands of the cartels, though, we all were a little *loco en cabeza*.

The sappers were finally down. Marla had quit waiting for perfect headshots, deciding instead to simply wound the sappers and kill them later. A bit cold-blooded but nobody would blame her. The main wave of the assault had slowed their approach, trying to use the cars for cover the same way the sappers had. Senior Sergeant Montoya and Rolf had better lines of fire on them than Marla, but weren't nearly as accurate. Still, seventy *soldados* against a few real soldiers, an American, two Mayans, and a German was not normally a recipe for a win.

However, Firebase Cancun hadn't survived this long by

pure luck. Major Diaz was a brilliant commander in his own right. He knew how to defend our makeshift home, understood every angle of attack and how to counter them. The main push of the cartel's *soldados* was out in the open, between the concrete outer gate and the reinforced inner one. With cars blocking the only easy access point in, the *soldados* believed they had cover for their assault and were safe.

They were sadly mistaken.

Lieutenant Castañeda was your typical young officer, true, but he was also a bit of an explosives guy. More accurately, he was a firebug. He loved to see stuff burn, but in a constructive sort of way. Dangerous? Oh, yeah. To us? Sometimes... maybe a little? Not as much as expected. He hadn't blown anything important up accidentally yet, but there'd been a few close calls. Still, he'd gotten better with practice. Major Diaz had made certain of this.

The lieutenant had figured out how to create some type of napalm early on, using packaging peanuts and diesel fuel to mix the stuff up. To make it interesting, Major Diaz then suggested adding a fuel additive to thin it out. Unsurprisingly, the makeshift napalm burned hotter with the additive. Of course, it was Rolf—a self-professed history nut—who later asked if it was possible to make flamethrowers out of old steel piping, an air compressor, and the dead vehicles around Firebase Cancun.

Long story short, Casteñeda could. And did. But he didn't create any old flamethrower, no. That would have been too easy. He wanted to create a blast furnace out in the open. The psycho...

Jets of flame erupted from beneath two of the ruined cars, catching the cowering *soldados* and igniting their clothing. The napalm clung to everything as the flames spewed forth into their midst. Every single one of them who were lit on fire jumped up and started flapping their arms wildly. Screaming, they tried to run and get away from the flames. It was horrifying to watch and I looked away, sickened.

Marla, though, was having a field day with her suddenly flaming targets. One by one the burning *soldados* dropped. The sniper did not waste a single round. *Crack! Crack! Crack!* It was as steady as a heartbeat. Though dead, the bodies continued to burn hard as the pipes poured more flames out of the piping.

"Contact!" Pedro suddenly shouted. I looked back into our sector and spotted a dozen *soldados* breaking from the treeline. Expectedly, they followed the worn-down goat trails. I aimed the M240, whispered a silent prayer, and squeezed the trigger.

The machine gun opened up. Remembering the lessons I'd received from Major Diaz, I kept the bursts between six to ten rounds with every squeeze of the trigger. Since every fifth round was a tracer, I could easily correct if I was off. Which wasn't often. Even though I'd been Navy, the M240 and I were a good fit.

A *soldado* exploded violently as he stepped on one of the mines in the field after I tagged him with a few rounds. His leg flew one way and the rest of him went another. I instantly dismissed him and focused on a trio of cartel *soldados* who were getting close. The M240 chewed through them and they all fell. One of them continued moving, so I gave him a second burst. He twitched again, but there was no reason to continue pumping him full of lead. The *soldado* was clearly dead.

The remaining *soldados* attack was shattered as the second M240 opened up from the other side of the base. We'd never had to fire both in the same battle before. The ones who'd survived the attack were clearly broken. A whistle blew from somewhere in the nearby jungle. The attackers stopped and began running away. I managed to stitch a half dozen rounds through a particularly portly *soldado* before the survivors melted back into the jungle. Pedro knelt next to me, his eyes scanning the treeline for any sign of them doubling back. I kept my finger close to the trigger of the M240. The safety remained off, though. It would stay that way until Captain Diaz gave the all-clear signal. The cartels had feinted before, acting like they were retreating before doubling back and launching a second attack.

However, this was possibly the worst bloody nose we'd given them to date. At least forty died during the attack, and I was pretty sure all of them had been wounded to some degree or the other. The first sapper who'd been the winner of "find the hidden toe-popper" had died sometime during the firefight. Surprisingly, it wasn't from blood loss from the toe-popper or the makeshift car bomb/flamethrower Lieutenant Casteñeda had built.

Someone, I thought and looked back towards where the

watchtower overlooked the entrance, *put a round right through his heart.*

A shrill whistle pierced the air. Two more shorter ones followed. The "all clear" typically changed after every attack, just in case some *soldado* got a little too clever. Fortunately for us all, the whistles were loud enough to hear over the steady ringing in our ears. Earplugs, much like toilet paper and disposable razors, had been used up pretty quickly in the first year or so after the Mexican government fell. We had to make do with what was on hand. Which, at the moment, was nothing.

I pushed the safety button on my machine gun and leaned back. As the tension left my body, I became aware of a severe pain in my shoulders and neck. Crouching down in the heat of battle, you typically don't realize how uncomfortable you were when the M240 was hammering away in your hands. It's only after the fact when the pain really hits home. I rolled my head left, then right, trying desperately to get ahead of the tension headache which would inevitably follow. Pedro began shaking his hands and massaging his forearms. Running the machine gun was tough. Being the loader, though, was far worse.

"Medic!" someone cried out from near the other M240. I cursed loudly. We had been lucky during the last few attacks and nobody had been seriously hurt. The worst injury we'd seen was when Lieutenant Casteñeda tripped and sprained his ankle.

"Go," I told Pedro. I motioned at our machine gun. "I can handle it for a few minutes if they come back."

The Mayan nodded and hurried towards the other machine gun nest. He wasn't a trained medic, not by a long shot. He was, however, the one Major Diaz had begun to train to become a medic to back up Senior Sergeant Montoya. Unlike the other surviving members of the Mexican National Army, Montoya had fought the cartels before in Sinola. He'd been the medic for his unit there, and was pretty much all we had here.

Unlike what we used to see on TV, there hadn't been a doctor in Cancun on vacation with their family during the end of civilization. They'd all bailed out long before, when the nukes went off in the U.S. Only idiots and poor people were taking vacations after that.

You know... people like me.

"Gio," someone called out from nearby. I turned and spotted one of the other tourists who'd joined in with the army to try and protect the town. Fernando was a good guy, if a bit older than most. He had been pudgy when this had all first started but a serious lack of sugars and carbs had cut his waistline to almost half.

"Yo?"

"Major Diaz needs you," Fernando said. "He wants me to man your duty station."

No rest for the wicked. Rolling out of the nest, I let Fernando get situated with his loader before heading out to the command building—which, in reality, was nothing more than an old appropriated Paco's Tacos building. Greasy Tex-Mex knockoff tacos in the Yucatan… okay, I'll admit I ate there a few times during my initial vacation stay. *Everyone* ate there, according to the locals. It was only later I learned it was a nasty tourist trap which didn't even serve beef but something… else.

Let's just say there wasn't a rat problem in Cancun for a reason.

Inside, I spotted Pedro helping Major Diaz bandaging up Private Gutierrez's arm. The former dining area had been split into two sections. One was where Major Diaz had his "office." The other was a makeshift triage center. There was a bit of blood but the young enlisted didn't appear to be in too much pain. Which was odd. It was clear he'd been shot. I expected much more screaming. Looking around, I caught sight of a disposable needle near the sink. Suddenly the young private's lack of pain made more sense.

Back in the early days of the Fall, we'd had quite a few injured come into this very room. Most didn't walk out alive. It wasn't that we didn't try to save them. Without a doctor, though, we didn't really know when stomach gas was actually appendicitis or how badly a wound was infected. Major Diaz had done his best but I knew—hell, all of us knew—it weighed heavily on his mind.

"Gio," he murmured as he stepped back from the wounded soldier. "Good shooting today."

"Could have been better, Major." I shrugged. "How's Gutierrez?"

"He'll live," the major replied as Pedro finished tying off the bandaging. He pulled me aside, out of hearing range of the two. "Fragment scratched him. We got lucky. We have another problem, though."

"Stupid cartels," I growled.

The major flashed me a smile but shook his head. "Yes, but not what I had in mind."

"Oh?" I raised an eyebrow. "What's up, Major?"

"This," and he jerked a chin towards Private Gutierrez. "The cartels are in a war of attrition with us. We only have so many people. They seem to grow stronger with every attack."

"Where are they getting their recruits?" I asked.

Major Diaz shrugged. "Good question, but not our concern."

"It's not?"

"No. My concern is our supplies."

"Food?" I scratched my chin. The fishing was going well off the pier, and the few old charter boats still running were catching plenty out in the sea. Granted, they were all old sailing vessels which had been converted for fishing, but they were better rowboats. Safer, too. "As long as nobody complains about the fish, we catch enough to feed everyone and have some to smoke for jerky afterwards. Plus the foraging in the jungle brings in some fresh fruit. Pedro and Maria seem to know where to find all the good shit, sir."

Major Diaz shook his head. "We need medical supplies. Bandages. Painkillers. Penicillin."

"Yeah, that makes more sense," I agreed. Looking over at Gutierrez, I wondered how much longer it would be before we couldn't bandage wounds any more. Worse, what if it became infected? If we were out of penicillin, he could die of blood poisoning and there wasn't much we would be able to do about it. "What did you have in mind, sir?"

"There's a petting zoo about an hour down the road," he began and walked over to the "office" side of the room. Behind me I could hear Pedro muttering something to Gutierrez, but it was low enough I couldn't understand. Major Diaz stopped at his desk and pointed at the map of the Yucatan pinned on the wall. "You see this village here? Punta Allen?"

"Yeah." I nodded, not sure where he was going with this. He'd sent a few men down there after the last hurricane had hit six months before. None of them had really talked about what they saw there, but it must have been pretty bad. The group hadn't brought any survivors back with them.

"One thing the lieutenant noticed while down there was

they had a petting zoo of some kind," Major Diaz continued, a sour look on his face. "None of the animals there were still alive, so he didn't think to check the buildings much. He was looking for survivors, not supplies. If they had a petting zoo, one that served *turistas*, then there was someone there to take care of the animals. Gringos don't want to pet sick animals, right?"

He had a point. "Okay..."

"If someone was there to take care of the animals, then there might be something there we can use," Major Diaz explained.

I suddenly saw where he was going with this and smiled. "Drugs like penicillin," I said.

"Plus bandages and who knows what else." Major Diaz was excited now. "Stitches, rubbing alcohol..."

"You want me to go down to Punta Allen and check it out?"

"Lieutenant Casteñeda's been there before," Major Diaz said. "So has Pedro. If you think you're up for it, I'd like you and one other civilian to go along with them."

"With all due respect, sir, why me? Why not real *soldados*, like Sergeant Montoya?"

Major Diaz let out a long sigh. "Try not to be offended by this, but... well, you're expendable."

"Huh?"

"How many regular *soldados* do we have left?" he asked me. "Real ones, I mean. The ones who were with me from the start?"

"Uh..." I tried to remember how many had been with Major Diaz when Firebase Cancun was first built. It had been quite a few, though we'd lost almost half of them when the cartels had attacked the first time. I wasn't sure how many soldiers were in a Mexican Army company, but I knew it was more than a hundred. I finally shrugged in defeat. "I don't know, sir."

"Nine."

Ouch. I knew we'd lost a lot of guys, but I'd had no idea it was so bad. Looking back, it should have been obvious. There'd been a lot of quick memorial services. So many, in fact, that I couldn't remember many of them specifically. *I bet Major Diaz does.*

"Damn," I whispered.

"I can't afford to lose any more if we're going to keep

standing firm against the cartels," he continued. "However, I'm not going to force you to do anything you don't feel—"

"I'll go, sir," I interrupted. "I get it. The three of us should be able to get the job done."

"Four," Major Diaz corrected. "I want you to take one other person..."

"*B double e double r-u-n beer run!* Woo!" Rolf sang out happily as the ancient pickup bounced down the uneven road. The shocks were worn to nothing and the tires shouldn't have held air in them, and don't even get me started on the alcohol we'd filtered and added to the tank. Yet somehow the reliable old truck was still going. Fate, it seemed, was not done with us quite yet.

I glanced over at the man-shaped mountain but he was ignoring me. His singing was atrocious and the lyrics worse. It sounded like some country song, which was weird. I didn't know Germany even had country music. I know some of my cousins who lived out in San Bernardino were big into country, but they were *very* distant cousins. Plus, *Tejano* music was more gangster than some gangsta rap.

Rolf was right here and now, and his singing voice reminded me of an old garbage disposal with a fork stuck in it. He was pretty enthusiastic about it, though. I had to give him props for that, even if I could feel a minor migraine starting to form.

"I didn't know Germans liked country," I said as he took a breath.

The big man paused, looked over at me, and smiled. "Germany loves American country music!" Rolf said. "Garth Brooks is amazing."

I had my own doubts about that but what did I know? I hated country music. I was more into EDM myself. "I thought you guys listened to polka?"

"*Pah*," and he spat out the open window of the truck. "Polka? Fucking Swabian pigfuckers."

"Oh. Okay." I had no idea what he was talking about. The only thing I knew about Germany was they played soccer more than we did, loved bratwurst and beer, and hated Russians.

"Beer run! Got going on a beer run! Woohoo!" Rolf started back up, belting out a mishmash of lyrics which sounded oddly made up and only moderately rhymed. I shook my head and tried not to smile. It might not be normal, but people like Rolf found the good in everything. Even if this wasn't really a beer run.

"This is not a beer run, Rolf," Lieutenant Casteñeda said from the driver's seat.

Rolf paused and shrugged. "No matter. We get medicine, I find beer. Everyone wins!" The singing resumed.

"Any sign of the cartels?" Pedro asked, leaning close so I could hear him over Rolf's raucous singing.

I shook my head. "Nothing."

"They saw us leave," Pedro muttered quietly, his voice barely audible over Rolf's caroling. I silently agreed with his assessment. The cartels would have decided to simply give up on us otherwise. No, their scouts in the jungle saw the four of us pile into the last working pickup and drive off. Firebase Cancun wasn't undefended, not by a long shot. However, with the exception of Lieutenant Casteñeda, none of us were part of the original Mexican National Army, which mattered.

Major Diaz was a cold, calculating man. He knew what the cartels would do to any soldier they caught. Foreign *touristas* and some Mayan villagers, on the other hand? We could simply say the army gang pressed us into service. Granted, we'd still probably die, but at least they wouldn't torture us for information we probably didn't have.

Or they might. Who knows? There was something to be said about wanting a clean death when the time came.

Lieutenant Casteñeda slowed the truck down. Taking my eyes off my area of responsibility for a moment, I noticed the road ahead was partially washed out. Frowning, I looked around for any sign of an ambush. There was nothing obvious, but it wasn't like I knew what to look for. Pedro, on the other hand, seemed at ease.

"Nobody around?" I asked him.

He shook his head. "Birds went quiet when we stopped. They were loud before."

It made sense. "So... no cartels?"

"Probably not."

"Where'd all this water come from?" Lieutenant Casteñeda grumbled from the driver's seat. Since he was the only one who knew the way to the petting zoo, he'd been tasked by Major Diaz to drive us. It was clear he wasn't happy about being beyond the wire. "We haven't had a storm in weeks."

I looked around. He had a point. This part of the jungle, which should have been flooded with thick green undergrowth, had a surprising amount of dead foliage. The air smelled strange, brackish. The area was swampy, with pockets of dirty water pooling in the midst of the jungle plants. The sight tickled a long-forgotten memory, but for the life of me I couldn't put a finger on it. Frowning, I quickly hopped out of the truck's cabin and onto the pockmarked road. Pedro and Rolf got out of the other side while Lieutenant Casteñeda stayed in the truck. Part of me wanted to tell him to shut it off to save fuel, but if it were some kind of cartel ambush, then we'd be sitting ducks.

Instead, I inspected the marshy ground which was currently where the road had once been. We were used to potholes in the pavement—this was Mexico, after all, and everything ran on graft and corruption—but these were ridiculously oversized. If I were a more imaginative man I'd say they were made by some massive sea creature walking along. Since I wasn't, I suspected the limestone beneath the road collapsed into a sinkhole.

Or, I thought as I continued to look around, *a lot of sinkholes.*

Major Diaz had talked about this. It was one of the reasons why maintaining roads in the Yucatan was a pain. Everything was built on top of limestone here, which means large pockets of water were a constant danger due to the rock being porous. I only know this because it's the same reason Kentucky was such a good area for producing bourbon.

"Was it like this the last time you came down?" I asked the lieutenant.

He shook his head. "No. But there's been a lot of rain lately."

"Yeah," I reluctantly agreed. The winter had been a wet one, more so than normal. Apparently having dozens of nukes explode around the world changed the weather more drastically than an aerosol can. Who knew? And all the worry about my dad's big old diesel truck...

"You don't think this is natural?" Rolf asked.

"No clue," I admitted quietly, "but it sure seems weird."

Crack! The distinctive report of an AK-47 rang out from somewhere close by. All our heads pivoted simultaneously to the south. We'd been under enough gunfire the past few years to recognize not only the type of rifle fired, but its direction. I didn't even realize I was moving back to the truck until I was halfway inside. All of us were inside in less than three seconds with our weapons.

It took Lieutenant Casteñeda even less time to get the truck moving towards the sound of the shot. I kept the safety on my combat weapon as we bounced painfully down the pothole-filled road. Major Diaz had given me the spare FX-05 that we had, and the last thing I wanted to do was to have a negligent discharge inside the truck's cabin.

Less than two minutes passed before we arrived at the outskirts of a small village. Lieutenant Castañeda slowed down just as we passed the first stop sign. I knew from experience he wasn't actually going to stop, but it made sense to at least slow down, in case someone else came barreling along.

Slowing down cost him his life, but it saved all of ours.

The driver's side window exploded inward as a fusillade of rounds slammed into the truck. The lieutenant's head practically exploded as multiple rounds struck him. More hit his neck and shoulder, nearly severing the remnants of the poor young officer's head from his body. The truck immediately dipped to the right as the front tire was blown out at the same time. The engine began smoking as gunfire continue to pour into the truck. Rolf, in the passenger's side front seat, was already out of the truck and rolling away with Pedro right behind him.

I was in a bad spot. Somehow none of the rounds fired had hit me, but it was only a matter of time before they shifted their aim towards my position. I scooched down as low as I could and grabbed the duffel bag filled with extra magazines for our weapons. More rounds impacted the side and two punched through the door. Fortunately they fragmented when they hit so instead of taking a round in the spine, my ass was peppered with bullet fragments.

"Motherfucker!" I screeched in pain and dropped my rifle. Even though they were fragments and not moving nearly as fast as they had been before hitting the door, the bullets still hurt. Reaching back with my free hand, I found blood. I grimaced as a wave of nausea rolled over me. I'd never been shot before. Nobody ever told me what to expect. It was icy, burning, and very painful. It also smelled bad. "Fuck!"

"Get out!" Pedro yelled at me as he and Rolf moved alongside the slow-moving truck. They were using the frame as cover while waiting for our attackers to pause and reload.

"I'm shot!" I protested and held up a bloody hand.

Pedro rolled his eyes. "You're not dead. Out! *Andale!*"

"You prick," I snarled under my breath, but dragged myself along the back seat to Pedro. The helpful Mayan grabbed the duffel bag and hoisted it easily over his shoulder. Something snagged my boot, preventing me from moving forward. Growling, I yanked, hard. Searing pain raced across my back and down my leg. More swearing followed. The boot came loose, though. I gasped in relief as the pressure on my butt eased.

Strong hands grabbed my shoulders and finished pulling me out of the shot-up truck. Rolf had pushed Pedro out of the way to help me. Wriggling for all I was worth, I finally managed to escape from the death trap. Something warm and sticky dripped into my eye as I landed on the ground.

The truck came to a stop at an elevated curb. We were momentarily safe. I rolled onto my back and groaned as fresh pain washed over me. The lead fragments were hot and just beneath the skin, right in the meaty part of my butt. Not the worst place to be shot, but it was still painful. Pedro rolled me onto my side and dug into my pants. More pain.

"Ugh!" I grunted. It really hurt.

"Quit whining," Pedro muttered as he continued to check the wound. After a few moments he shrugged. "Can't see much between the blood and your hairy ass, but I think you're okay."

"Thanks, *pendajo*."

"*De nada.*"

"*Soldados!*" Rolf interrupted as he brought his rifle up and began firing single shots towards the direction of our ambushers. Rolf barely spoke Spanish but he'd picked up enough to know I wasn't going to die just yet. He switched back to English. "Come, little man. Let's kill drug cartels!"

"Castañeda's dead?" Pedro asked, risking a quick look inside the truck. His dark face paled and he shuddered. "*Si.* Dead."

"Rolf! How many?" I asked as I managed to get back to my knees. I felt a little woozy but the adrenaline was kicking in. Being shot in the ass felt like nothing more than an inconvenience at the moment. I snorted. Shock combined with adrenaline was an interesting thing. It was a terrific drug, but there were some side effects. The most noticeable? I felt like I was freezing.

"Three? No, four," Rolf replied as he flipped his selector. He fired off a quick burst. In the distance, I heard a scream. "Three."

Nice, I thought. *We can take them.*

They'd ambushed us, sure. They had even managed to take down our only real Army officer with us, though that was probably by accident. There was no way they knew we were coming.

Then who were they shooting at? I wondered as I ignored the throbbing pain in my butt cheek and peeked over the bed of the truck.

The cartel *soldados* were not supposed to be down this far. Nobody had ever seen them this far south. Granted, it meant little in the grand scheme of things, since we couldn't ask Lieutenant Castañeda if he'd seen any the last time he was down. His brains all over the dashboard—and on us—emphasized this point. Something had drawn them down here, but what?

I doubted it was beer. In spite of Rolf's earlier singing, any beer we found at this point would probably have turned. Alcohol was probably still good, and the wine—if it hadn't been left out in the sun—might actually have improved. Who knew? That hot Italian chick I'd been hitting on before the world had ended loved sweet reds.

Pull it together, ese. I rested my face against the metal of the truck. The shock was affecting my thought process. I shivered as a cool breeze washed over me. Or maybe it was just my ass flapping in the breeze? Hard to tell. Glancing over at Rolf, I noticed he was remarkably calm under fire. "Grenades?"

"Two," Rolf said and patted his pocket. "Want me to use them?"

"Fuck, yes!" I screamed. What sort of idiot asks whether he should use a grenade in the middle of a gunfight? I gave myself a mental slap. I'd apologize to the *hombre* later. He'd understand.

Rolf popped both M67 grenades and tossed them in the direction of the shooters. Surprised shouts could faintly be heard before the distinctive explosions of the frag grenades ripped through the air. The incoming gunfire abruptly ceased. The big man risked a quick peek before he sprinted forward, his rifle at the ready the entire way.

He would have made a Marine Corps Gunny proud.

Two of the shooters were down, the frag grenades having shredded their torsos and legs. The third was trying to crawl away but, judging by the blood smear he was leaving behind him on the ground, he wasn't going to get far. Without even slowing Rolf aimed and popped the lone survivor twice in the back of the head. Kicking the fallen *soldado's* weapon away, he pivoted and popped each of the dead in the back to make sure. I blinked.

I sometimes forgot that our big, goofy German was turning into a bit of a badass.

After a few moments Rolf came trotting back over. He didn't look too upset by the carnage he'd just wrought. "Cleared."

"No shit?" I asked sarcastically.

Apparently, he was immune. "No shit."

"You need bandages," Pedro told me as he helped me to my feet. The burning sensation came back with a vengeance. I gritted my teeth and did my best to ignore it. "But you're not dying."

"Infection?" I asked.

He shrugged. "Maybe... probably not, though. Clean it, bandage it, and you'll heal."

"What do we do about the lieutenant?" I wondered, my eyes drifting to the ruined truck. I limped over to the door and risked a look inside. My stomach roiled. It was just as bad as I remembered it being not a few minutes before. There was no rhyme or reason why I did it other than the simple need to *see*. "We can't leave him here."

"Can't bury him," Pedro replied. His face was stoic in spite of us being shot at mere minutes before. The post-battle shakes hadn't gotten to him yet. "No shovels."

"Shit," I muttered, looking around. I didn't know what village we were in, but it definitely wasn't Punta Allen. That village — and its petting zoo, and potential medicines—was still hours away. This place wasn't even marked on the map in Major Diaz's office, it was so small.

From out of the shadows of the buildings came men and

women. They were wearing clothing similar to what Pedro had worn when he first showed up at Firebase Cancun, only these were clearly in ill-repair and threadbare. They also looked emaciated. For some reason, these people were on the verge of starvation.

I didn't understand. The jungles had food if one knew where to look. Maria and Pedro both had shown us where to find the edible fruits. Plus, the sea was nearby, and the swampy marshes around us had fish, mammals, and all sorts of reptiles like crocodiles. There was no good reason why these people should be in the shape they were.

Unless... my mind drifted back to the problem with the cartels. They always appeared to have fresh *soldados* amongst their groups, and they looked like they weren't starving. It was possible—no, probable that they were forcing all of the local villagers who weren't being protected to pay a stiff tax in both people and food. These poor people were probably just one group of many the cartels had under their thumb.

"So what do we do now?" Rolf asked quietly. His eyes were staring at the dozens of people gathered around our partially destroyed truck. Old Reliable was not going to make it back to Firebase Cancun. Or anywhere, for that matter. "We can't carry them all back to the base. It's a long walk, too."

He was right, of course. There simply was no way we could pull this sort of evacuation. Especially since our only transportation had been taken out. Could we leave them behind so we could go and get help?

This place looks like hell, I thought.

I looked around. This tiny village was like every other one we'd seen in the years since Firebase Cancun sprouted up. Dilapidated, crumbling buildings being held up by the sheer force of nature itself surrounded by overgrown jungle—which, come to think about it, was odd. When I'd first come to Cancun as a tourist, it hadn't been surrounded by an overgrown jungle. It made me wonder just how much of the local brush and growth had been held back by man.

Nature could be one unforgiving bitch sometimes.

Oddly enough, none of the villagers seemed bothered by us being covered in Lieutenant Castañeda's blood. Or that none of us really "looked" military. Instead, they were focused on Rolf. It was possible they'd never seen a blond white guy before. More than likely, they'd never seen anyone as big as he was. I wasn't short, but Rolf made me look it.

There was something else off about the villagers, though. I just couldn't put my finger on it. The men and women all looked impoverished and underfed, but most of us lost some weight since the world ended. There weren't a lot of elderly in the group, either. Again, not surprising. Dysentery was a stone-cold bitch and, without modern medicine, the elderly were usually the first to die off when the disease ran through them. It was hell on anyone's guts, but particularly on old people. Those who'd survived this long were of a different breed entirely.

I limped along behind Pedro and Rolf, keeping an eye out for any sign of the cartels, though I doubted we'd see any. There was nothing but stunned villagers watching us. The silence was disturbing. There wasn't any noise other than the quiet murmurs of the men standing nearby. There wasn't any sound of kids crying. I looked around again. Suddenly it clicked. "Hey, where are all the kids?"

It was as though the dam had broken. The villagers immediately began babbling in a dialect of Spanish I'd never heard before. It took me a moment to realize it was some Yucatec version, which—fortunately—Pedro seemed to understand. My loader replied to what sounded like a very pointed question and all of the surviving villagers' heads turned towards him. He began nodding as the crowd surged forward, trying to answer as many questions as he could.

It took a while but eventually Pedro got them more or less calmed down. He was answering questions rapid-fire, barely taking a breath as he tried to help the villagers. The longer they spoke, the more I was able to understand. They were speaking so fast their Spanish had sounded like an entirely different language. There was the occasional word I didn't catch but for the most part I was able to keep up.

These were not the original inhabitants of the village, but transplants of sorts. They'd only moved in recently, taking over the destroyed ruins of the town and fixing it back up to livable conditions. Mayans, like Pedro, but from a different area. They had simply wanted to be left to their own devices. They'd existed in relative peace—until the cartels had arrived and forced them to gather food for them.

They'd done so for months, practically starving themselves to meet the demands of the cartels. One day before, the cartels had shown up to collect their monthly tax and the villagers had, unfortunately, been unable to meet their demands. Instead of killing them all, though, the cartels had simply taken their children. Pedro translated that if the villagers wanted their children back, then they needed to meet the quota set by the cartels. If they couldn't do that, well…

The cartels hadn't explained explicitly what would happen, which was far worse than gory details.

We had all the information we needed. Pedro had a panged look on his face. Mine wasn't much better. I looked over at Rolf. The big German was bothered by this turn of events. It was clear on his bearded face, though, what our next step should be. Silently I agreed. It was one thing to go after people and conscript them into the cartels. Kids? An entirely different beast altogether.

I can't explain why there was a difference in my head. There just is. Deal with it.

"What do we do?" Rolf asked. He was clearly concerned by it all. "What can we do?"

Looking around at all the villagers, it was easy to see they were scared, frightened. Beneath it, though, I could almost *feel* the anger. They had been attacked. They'd been hurt. Worst of all, their future had been taken from them. It was hard enough to come to terms with the fact the world ended. To have the possibility of a better tomorrow taken away? Desperation drives even the most stoic of men to action.

The answer was right before us. "We help them."

"How?"

"Bring them back to Firebase Cancun," I decided. The villagers looked at us and, for the first time, I could sense just a hint of hope emerge from their despair. We *needed* to help them. "We train them. We arm them. Then we help them go rescue their children."

We'd been simply *surviving* at Firebase Cancun for seven odd years. Without a mission, an objective other than survival, we were a vine withering away under the hot and unforgiving Central American climate. I looked back at the Mayan villagers. They'd been frightened, alarmed at our arrival. This had been replaced by hope. They no longer appeared to be beaten, downtrodden. I nodded.

Screw surviving. We now had *purpose*.

And as it's been proven many times in the past, purpose

could change the course of human history.
"Let's move out."

To Kill a Brother

Christo Louis Nel

Chapter 1—The Tunnel

Monday, March 14, 2033
Du Toit's Kloof Tunnel
Cape of Good Hope, after secession from South Africa

    Cyril, the driver of the heavily loaded tanker, yelled and pumped his fist out the window. "Where did you buy your freaking license?" The Hilux pickup crossed the solid white center lane and passed the tanker on a steep incline and dangerous curve on the Du Toit's Kloof mountain pass. The entrance to the tunnel lay only a few kilometers ahead. The tanker moved slowly as traffic backed up behind him. Cyril didn't care.

    "Idiot!" Fanie, operative of the Wine Producers Co-op of The Cape of Good Hope, and driver of the pickup, yelled back. He stuck his arm out of the window and shook his fist at the other driver.

    Gerhard leaned out the open window on the passenger side and made eye contact with the tanker driver. He extended his hand to the driver, pointed the index finger at him with the thumb up like he was holding a gun. He smiled, lowered the thumb onto the index finger, and jerked his hand up in a quick motion simulating a gun shot.

    Cyril did not like the gesture and grabbed the machete on the dashboard and pointed it at the pickup truck. Fanie swerved in front of the truck, did a brake check and sped up to stay in front of the tanker. The other driver took the bait and stepped on the gas. The huge tanker was slow to gain speed and Fanie made sure he stayed a few feet ahead of the tanker.

The road leveled out as they crested the hill and saw the entrance to the Huguenot tunnel. The four-kilometer-long tunnel, completed 43 years ago, reduced travel time over the mountain by an hour. The only alternative was the long winding mountain pass. A road not maintained in over 50 years.

The two vehicles entered the tunnel way above the posted speed limit of 60 km/h. The tanker driver responded exactly as Fanie hoped when he did another brake check inside the tunnel. The driver did not slow down and kept his foot on the gas pedal and got right on the bumper of the Hilux.

"Hold on," Fanie said. "We're almost there." He moved his eyes between the rear-view mirror and the road ahead, making sure they did not get run over by the tanker.

Gerhard turned his head and looked through the back window at the other driver. "Jou ma se moer," *your mother's mother*, he cursed with a grin before he turned his head back to see where they were.

"Ready," he said and tightened his grip on the handlebar.

Fanie accelerated to open the gap between the two vehicles, and then slammed his foot on the brake. The smell of burning rubber filled the tunnel. He released the brake and stepped hard on the gas pedal to get away from the tanker.

Gerhard pulled the pin from the smoke grenade, sprung the lever, and dropped it out the window. It exploded right between the two speeding trucks.

"What in the hell..." Cyril said, and instinctively slammed his foot on the brake pedal and locked the brakes. He broke through the wall of smoke and realized he had crossed into the other lane and was headed towards the side rails. He overcorrected and the truck started to swerve. He fought with the steering wheel, tried to straighten it and navigate around the bend. He missed the side rails by a few inches but was heading back to the other side of the tunnel. The driver of an oncoming white Corolla swerved, crossed over the center line, avoid a collision with the car behind the tanker, but could not maneuver around a blue Golf and crashed into it.

Chaos erupted in the tunnel with a mixture of blaring horns, squealing tires, and metal scraping on metal. The sounds intermingled with the smell of smoke and burning rubber. Traffic came to a screeching halt inside the tunnel—the main artery for traffic between the western coastal areas of

The Cape and the Karoo on the northern side of the Cape Fold Mountain range.

With the wheels still locked and tires heating up, Cyril managed to control the truck without hitting a car. The trailer behind the tanker jack-knifed and blocked both lanes.

Exactly as planned.

Fanie and Gerhard jumped out. Fanie grabbed a bag from the back of his truck and walked towards the tanker. He took a smoke grenade from the bag, pulled the pin, and rolled it to the side of the road. The smoke blocked the view from the south side of the tunnel.

Drivers on both sides of the accident realized something was wrong and did not want to get involved. They just wanted to get away as soon as possible.

"Turn around! Turn around!" drivers started to yell at each other.

"I smell gas," somebody else shouted.

"The tanker's going to explode! Get out!"

Drivers knew from experience the implications of an accident in the tunnel. It would take hours to get a tow truck to clear the road and they didn't want to get stuck inside the tunnel. Traffic on both sides of the accident made U-turns and headed back to the exits.

Kraai Bosman, driver of an old run-down pickup truck, did not turn around. He had witnessed the crash between the Corolla and the Golf and rushed towards the cars to make sure the occupants were okay. He scanned the scene of the tanker, saw smoke coming from the smoke grenades, and did not like what he saw.

"Get out as fast as you can," Kraai instructed the drivers of the damaged vehicles. They grabbed some personal belongings, abandoned their vehicles, and ran towards the exit.

As a rum-runner for the Mampoer Traders Union, Kraai used the tunnel daily. An accident inside the tunnel would impact his deliveries of illegal moonshine to customers on the other side of the mountain. The alternative route would cost him time and extra money for gas. He ran to his truck and turned around. He stopped at the drivers of the damaged cars. They jumped onto the back of his truck and hitched a ride into town.

"You bastards!" Cyril, the truck driver, yelled and reached for his gun below the seat. He opened the door and jumped out. The first bullet hit him in the stomach. The second in the chest, and the third in the face as he went down.

Fanie ran to the passenger side, opened the door, and looked inside over the barrel of his Vektor R4. The cabin was empty.

"Is hy dood?" (*Is he dead?*) Fanie asked as he walked up to Gerhard standing next to the body of the driver.

"Soos 'n mossie," (*Like a dodo*) Gerhard replied without emotion.

"Timers are set for seven minutes," Fanie said and handed two devices to Gerhard. "Back wheels." He crawled under the front of the truck and stuck one of the devices to the engine. He pressed the button to start the timer.

"All set," Gerhard said, and they scrambled to the Hilux. Fanie accelerated hard and the six-cylinder engine roared loudly in the empty tunnel as they raced south. Gerhard looked at his watch.

"Six," he said and looked up. Half a mile down the road in the middle section of the tunnel, Fannie slammed on the brakes and skidded into the emergency parking zone. They jumped out and ran to the yellow door of the engine room.

"Five," Gerhard said as he slammed the door behind them.

The construction of the tunnel was completed in the early eighties. Escape rooms were built into the walls of the tunnel to keep trapped drivers safe in case of an emergency or when stuck inside the tunnel. Over the years, it was only used a few times. Neglect caused the rooms to never be used in the past 30 years. A total of six escape rooms were spread throughout the tunnel. Four were for public use and two were marked as engine rooms. The engine rooms also had a more sinister purpose and only a handful of people still alive knew about it. Access to these rooms were hidden behind the huge engines that were used to suck fumes from the tunnel and blow it through chimneys to the outside. From inside the engine rooms, there were ladders next to the pipes carrying the fumes to the top of the mountains. No normal person wanted to climb up a narrow dark enclosure to try and escape from whatever danger existed inside the tunnel. They'd rather wait in their cars for the tunnel to clear.

During construction, two secret safe rooms were built towards the top of the mountain where air from the tunnel was blown out. Roads to the top were used to ensure the extractor fans were in working condition. Road access to the safe rooms were shut down in the early nineties when the apartheid regime came to an end and a rockslide made the road inaccessible. The only remaining access to enter the safe rooms were the ladders.

"Four," Gerhard continued the countdown as they climbed up the ladder. Two streams of light from the mining helmets they brought with them jumped from side to side. Both panted for air as they made their way up the steps.

"I can see the platform," Fanie said and stopped for a second. "I think we'll make it." He took a deep breath and resumed his ascent.

"Three," Gerhard said and quickened his pace.

"Two," Gerhard said as they stepped onto the first platform. Fanie took a key from his pocket, wiped the dust from the door leading into the secret escape room, and unlocked the door. The door was old, but still solid. He put his shoulder to it and forced it open. They stepped inside and for the first time in 36 years, light entered the darkness of the room where the Tokoloshe was stored.

"One minute," Gerhard said as he shut the door behind him. "Let's hope and pray the whole mountain doesn't collapse."

They waited.

Standing side by side, they kept their eyes on Gerhard's watch as he counted down the last few seconds. They felt the shockwave before they heard the distant sound of an explosion. The tanker was ripped to pieces as the gas it carried exploded. The entrance from the north collapsed and blocked access to the tunnel permanently. The mountain shook and the ceiling collapsed on the tanker and vehicles abandoned by its drivers.

"We're alive!" Fanie said and lifted his hand to high-five Gerhard.

"Yes! We made it," Gerhard said with relief. He looked at Fanie. "What now?"

"Let's see what's in here," Fanie said. From his backpack he took out an old mining lantern and turned it on. The safe room lit up and they could see the inside of the whole room.

It was bigger than they thought. On the opposite side of the room, they noticed the doors that would take them to the road down the mountain. To their left a forklift was parked next to a row of stacked wooden crates. Against the opposite wall were 3 huge crates marked with the letters A1, A2, and A3.

"You think that is the Tokoloshes?" Gerhard asked.

"I think we struck gold," Fanie said with a smile and walked towards the crates.

Chapter 2—Cabinet Meeting

Wednesday, March 3, 2033
Cape Town
Cape of Good Hope
10 days before the tunnel accident

He slammed the gavel a few times.

"Orde Asseblief! Order, please!" Herman Visser, president of The Cape of Good Hope (The Cape), slammed his gavel one more time. "I know the Stormers won last night, but we have business to take care of. We can discuss rugby later. Please take your seats so we can start."

The CapeXit movement got momentum after the events in the USA in 2029 caused a collapse of international trade and the world economy. The sudden spike in the gold price resulted in chaos in the South African government. Gold fever overwhelmed every member of parliament. The newly elected president, Jonas Limama, and his hand-picked cabinet made an executive decision and ruled that all ministerial functions had to be relocated to the Union Building in Tshwane. He wanted to be "close to the action." Everybody knew it was only an excuse to have more control over mining activities and government funds. The prestige of an office in the Union Building would better fit his ego. The emergency declaration to place all mining activities related to precious metals under government control infuriated everyone.

President Limama inherited a struggling gravy train from the previous government, and he needed a new source of funding. Control over the gold mining activities would give him free access to the proceeds from the operations. He ordered the military to control and guard mining facilities and the government seized all existing precious metals. Limama had his eyes on the benefits from gold. Other members of his cabinet realized there might be a spike in the future demand for uranium. They used their influence to get the president to include all precious metals in his emergency declaration. The gold grab by the government did not sit well with the rest of the country. Limama made more enemies than friends.

Age-old tribal rivalries resurfaced. Gang wars resumed in the mining communities and spread to remote areas. The struggle from the mid-eighties resumed. This time there was one more complication added to the fighting. Identification of friend or foe by skin color did not work well in the rainbow nation and gang affiliations were made based on language.

In the 1830s the British government forced the Dutch settlers to learn English. This resulted in the Dutch farmers leaving The Cape of Good Hope to seek a place to live. In the 1970s, the Apartheid Regime repeated the mistake and forced all schools to teach English and Afrikaans as the primary languages. Afrikaans became the language of the oppressor and the country rebelled against it. In 1994, a complex decision was made. English became the un-official business language, and 11 official languages were declared in the new constitution. In the new tribal wars, a person's decision about his mother tongue became a life and death choice.

The Western Cape Province decided they had enough of the infighting and corruption in the central government. In early 2032 a referendum to secede from South Africa was held. The outcome was an overwhelming YES. On the 1st of January 2033 they declared their independence and the new country of The Cape of Good Hope was established. The leader of the Democratic Alliance, and the main force behind the secession, Herman Visser, became president of The Cape.

As president, Visser had the responsibility to form a new government. It consisted of an Executive Council, a National Council, and a Local Council. The Executive Council included the president, a minister of defense, and a minister of finance. Visser appointed General Johan Skipper, a close friend and confidant for many years, as the new minister of defense in charge of the military and the police. A prominent businessman, also an old friend, Willem O'Neil, was named minister of finance. The threesome built a reputation of quick decision-making and was nicknamed the Three Kings, or 3K.

The six district leaders under the previous government were renamed district governors and assumed membership in the National Council. Each one was assigned a role in the new

Cabinet. Cabinet meetings, a combined meeting of the Executive and National Councils, controlled the central government functions and made national decisions. The lower chamber of the government, the Local Council, was formed by the mayors of the 25 municipalities.

Under the new government, the issue around language became controversial. The Cabinet decided to stick with the three most commonly used languages, Afrikaans 53%, English 27%, and Xhosa 20%.

The declaration of independence by the Western Province resulted in many citizens from the northern areas migrating to the southwestern area of the country. Soon after the secession of the Western Province, a group of Afrikaans-speaking settlers in the Karoo also seceded from the central government and formed their own country, and named it Orania.

The only comment from President Limama on behalf of the central government of South Africa was "Good riddance. Now they are closer to the beach, and we can chase them into the sea!"

"First item on the agenda." President Visser started the Cabinet meeting. "Electricity. We're all tired of load shedding. We need to find a solution and fix the problem once and for all. Maintenance of Koeberg power plant had been neglected for many years. It is our main source of supply for electricity, and we need to take care of it. We have no choice but to increase the output capacity to stop the load shedding. We'll continue to search for alternative ways to generate electricity. So, let me hear your opinions." He sat down and a lively debate followed.

Maintenance of the electrical grid had been a sensitive topic of discussion for many years. Under the previous government ample funding were approved and everybody knew most of it went towards the gravy train.

"Can we stop the feed to the north?" one of the members around the table asked.

"We have reduced the supply, but we cannot stop it," Visser responded. "Limama threatened to cut off uranium supplies if the feed to surrounding areas stops. We have fuel rods for about three to five years. If we increase output, we will burn through the supply in half the time. We're bartering with South Africa to exchange electricity for uranium pellets."

"Are the fuel rods secured?" another governor asked.

"Yes," General Skipper answered. "We increased the security at Koeberg and formed a separate task force to guard storage facilities. We're looking for alternative storage space that will be easier to protect."

The meeting continued till late in the evening. The members of the Cabinet, the G6, and the 3K battled through a tough budget discussion and how to fund it.

During the dinner break, the Governor of the Winelands, Pieter Brand, approached Willem O'Neil. He pulled him aside and made sure they could not be overheard.

"Are you aware of the rumors about what is really stored in the Huguenot tunnel?" Brand asked.

O'Neil looked around before responding. "There are many. Which one?"

"The Tokoloshe," Brand said and looked O'Neil straight in the eye. "Your family were part of the Blood Brothers. Mine too. I'm sure you know what I'm talking about."

"I can't confirm or deny. Do you have any proof?"

"Yes," Brand continued. "I know the term WP doesn't only refer to the Western Province rugby team. It also refers to a secret organization you're involved in."

O'Neil stared at Brand. He was used to being challenged about his involvement in the Wine Producers Co-Op, but not in public or at a cabinet meeting. He slowly lifted his glass and took a long sip from it. "And you know that how?"

"I was approached a while ago to join the organization. I had my doubts, and it took a while to accept the invitation. The reason I got invited was based on my great-grandfather's involvement in the Blood Brothers. Only after I joined did I find out who you really are."

"You know the penalty for lying to a brother?" O'Neil said and watched Brand closely.

"Yes. I know and I accepted the consequences of my actions."

"Good. Welcome to the club," O'Neil said and stretched out his hand. Only those familiar with the Wine Producers Co-Op code of conduct would know about the secret handshake. Brand stretched out his hand and slid his pinky between the pinky and ring finger of O'Neil. He gave him a firm handshake and with his thumb pressed twice on the hand of O'Neil.

O'Neil responded likewise and smiled at Brand. "Who would have guessed," O'Neil said and forced a smile. "You know I will verify your membership. Let's talk about the tunnel. What do you know?"

"One of the rumors is that there are some sensitive materials stored in it. Apparently, there are some secret storage spaces accessible from the safe rooms in the tunnel. Another rumor has it that a Tokoloshe may live there."

"That's a wild rumor and an old myth."

"Maybe, but I may have somebody interested in buying one. We met in Angola after the war. He's originally from Portugal and stayed in Angola after his unit returned. He married a local and was involved in the negotiations with the Chinese when they acquired oil rights from the Angolan government. He was compensated well for his vote in favor of the agreement. He was part of the enemy during the border war in Angola and I met him during a visit to Cuito Cuanavale in 2013. He invited us to his home, and we stayed in touch. He visited Cape Town a few months ago and mentioned he still has good contacts in the Chinese government in Angola."

"How will that help our electrical problems?"

"In two ways," Brand continued excitedly. "If the Tokoloshe really exist, I am convinced there will also be fuel rods in the same place. The one is worthless without the other. When De Klerk and his government signed the international treaty, a lot of questions were asked about clerical errors. It may be worth it to have a look at what is really in those safe rooms."

"You may be onto something," O'Neil said. "Let me do some investigation, and we can discuss this again. I'll talk to Visser. He knows a lot more than he'll say. Excuse me, I have to use the restroom," O'Neil said and walked out of the room. In the hallway he made a phone call.

"Hallo," a voice on the other end said.

"Rooi of groen? (*Red or green*) Pieter Brand," O'Neil said, and provided some basic details about Brand to the person on the phone.

"Groen (*green*)," the person said and ended the call.

As a senior member of the blood brothers, O'Neil only had to make a call to verify membership of the Co-Op. Nothing else was ever discussed. Although the membership of Pieter Brand was confirmed, deep in his gut O'Neil had an uneasy feeling. He walked to the bathroom and a few minutes later returned to the meeting. The president started the next session with his gavel.

"Next item. Sales tax." A big groan could be heard from the crowd. The president could not be swayed, and the debate started.

Chapter 3—Braai

Saturday, March 26, 2033
Blouberg Strand,
Cape of Good Hope
2 weeks after the tunnel blockage

"Any damage to the safe rooms?" President Visser asked as he leaned forward and flipped a piece of wood in the fire. Four sets of eyes stared into the fire. The wives had sensed the tension around the fire when the normal chit-chat was absent. They decided to go for a walk along the beach and let the men discuss whatever they needed to. They knew they would eventually be consulted in private. The cool ocean breeze added a chill to the atmosphere.

It was Brand's idea to block the tunnel. He approached the Executive Council a few days after the Cabinet meeting and met in O'Neil's office in Cape Town. He explained the purpose for blocking the tunnel and requested quick action.

"If the tunnel is damaged," he reasoned with the 3K—O'Neil, Visser and Skipper, "the military will have the perfect excuse to step in and occupy the tunnel. It will be in the interest of public safety and the military will be tasked to secure it. At the same time, they will have a safe place to stockpile uranium pellets needed for Koeberg. I don't have proof, but I've heard from a trusted source that there may be enriched uranium in one of the secret safe-rooms in the tunnel."

"I've heard about the rumors," Visser said. "At some point there was documentation, and I've seen some of it, but it was destroyed in the early nineties."

"I'll agree on one condition," O'Neil said. "Nobody should be able to point a finger to us or the government. How are you going to achieve that?"

"My district will benefit if we can stop the rum-runners using the tunnel," Brand continued in his efforts to convince the 3K. "Union members are relentless and becoming more aggressive. They have a cheap product and it's impacting liquor sales in my district. There's a lot of demand, and shebeens are popping up everywhere. If we block the runners from Worcester, local and national wine sales will increase again. We've discussed this at the cabinet meeting and it's time to do something."

Willem O'Neil looked at the three men in his office. "We can make use of WP operatives," he said. "But I don't like the idea. If they fail, we can blame the Union. I'll make sure they know how to keep us out of the picture. Sorry, Pieter, if something goes wrong, they'll claim you approached them and paid for the task. Are you okay with that?"

"Yes. I'm good with it," Brand said. The Wine Producers Co-Op had tight control over liquor sales and with it came control of the government. The Mampoer Traders Union, on the other hand, were seen as the opposition and an illegal organization who paid no taxes to the government. It was a longstanding territorial war and with the collapse of the world economy, the conflict and fighting escalated. The new government needed the tax revenue, but the man on the street preferred the cheaper alternative. Finding an alternative way to strengthen the government funding would also benefit their own individual businesses. If the rumors were true, they might have struck gold in more than one way.

The 3K agreed to Brand's plan. They needed proof that the rumors about uranium hidden somewhere were true. With Brand bringing the plan to them, they found a perfect scapegoat in case something went wrong. In exchange, Brand wanted access to one of the safe rooms inside the tunnel to store his own products.

"Didn't sound like there were any." Johan Skipper responded to the question from President Visser. Skipper and O'Neil were part of the founding members of WP Co-Op. Skipper's military experience, as commanding office of Bravo Group 33 in Angola, made him an easy choice as 2IC in charge of security and a militia group of WP operatives.

"The roof collapsed 400m from the north entrance and blocked all traffic. Our team made it to the escape room in the mid-section and accessed the east storage bunker using the escape ladders. The west bunker should be fine. Fanie and his team will investigate when the media frenzy calms down. It's further away from the collapsed site and should be fine."

They sat in their beach chairs overlooking the cold water of the Atlantic Ocean. It became their regular meeting spot when something of high importance had to be discussed. The constant assault of the ocean waves on the beach made enough background noise to ensure prying ears would not be able to follow their conversations.

"I still think it was a bad idea," O'Neil said after a long silence.

"We had to do it," Brand chipped in. "We need funding for electricity, and we may have struck gold with what we found. The additional storage is a bonus and we'll be able to store some extra wine barrels in there. It will be easier to protect than at the wineries. The rooms are ideal for aging whiskey. Oh, and don't forget, we managed to make life difficult for the rum-runners."

"That's one side of the argument," O'Neil snapped back. "You forgot we also need the routes to move our product. We're basically cut off from our markets to the north. We may have ample supply of wine and whiskey, but what are we going to do about meat supplies? People are already complaining about the spike in meat prices and availability." Frustration dripped from every word O'Neil said. He looked at Herman Visser sitting on the other side of Brand. "What do you think, Herman?"

"We'll be fine," said Visser, the eternal optimist. He became president for a reason. He was one of only a few living souls with knowledge about top secrets from the apartheid regime that ended in 1994. As an aid to De Klerk, he had insight into many things that happened behind the scenes. "It's only a bump in the road. We don't have the funds or the appetite to repair the tunnel. We'll just blame it on the illegal traders. Our meat supplies are still secure. The Overberg has enough grains and lamb. Beef from the Karoo will need to be rerouted. This is an ideal opportunity to strengthen our relationship with our meat suppliers."

"I'm sure they have more than enough meat and would welcome some liquor," Brand threw in his two cents to support the president.

"The benefits may outweigh the loss of access to the north," Skipper said. "But we have bigger problems on the eastern border to consider. Poaching of livestock has escalated, and more people are fleeing to The Cape. We can shift some of the resources used to control illegal trade through the tunnel to help defend the onslaught from the East Block."

O'Neil did not respond, and for the rest of the afternoon he was very quiet and busy with his own thoughts.

Chapter 4—Beach

Saturday, March 26, 2033
Blouberg Strand,
Cape of Good Hope
10 weeks after the tunnel blockage

Fanie stood on the beach with a fishing pole in his hands. He had a line in the water, but there was no bait on the hook. He liked fishing in his spare time, but when duty called, he was focused on the task at hand. As a team leader of the WP Operatives, he seldom backed away from a challenge. He kept the 3K in his peripheral vision as he scanned the beach area towards Table Mountain. Half a kilo down the beach, on the other side of the 3K, Gerhard stood in a similar posture. Waiting, observing, and ready.

O'Neil manned the braai with tongues in one hand and a glass of wine in the other. Brand stood on the other side of the fire in deep discussion with Franco De Santos. Negotiations proceeded better than planned and De Santos, the middleman with a potential big pay day waiting, negotiated on behalf of a Chinese government official in Angola. The Chinese officials were very excited to hear about the possibility of acquiring U235 and were willing to pay for it. Their military urgently needed the refined uranium to fuel their submarines. There was also the possibility that it could be used to expand their nuclear capabilities. It all depended on how much they could get their hands on. Negotiations with President Limama from South Africa stalled. Limama saw an opportunity when demand for uranium pellets increased, and he added a special handling fee as the president of South Africa. The one thing that irked the Chinese was handling fees and they looked for a source. When De Santos approached Lani Wenjonk with a potential opportunity to secure U235, they were open for negotiations. The only problem was De Santos also wanted a handling fee.

Pieter Brand negotiated on behalf of The Cape government. Selling part of the stash of uranium discovered in the tunnel would provide the much-needed cash to maintain the electrical infrastructure in The Cape. Boosting the output of the Koeberg power plant would put The Cape in a stronger position to barter with the South African government for uranium pellets to fuel the power plant.

The 3K was split on the deal. President Visser and his finance minister, Willem O'Neil, agreed about the deal with the Chinese. Defense Minister Johan Skipper objected to it. According to the 3K agreement, he had to go along with the majority vote.

Visser liked the opportunity, as the people were tired of years and years of load shedding. Improving the Koeberg power plant output would benefit the country and boost his popularity.

O'Neil knew how terrible the financial situation had become for The Cape. They needed the cash, and he also knew the Chinese would come back for more. His biggest problem was the same as the Chinese. He did not like the handling fee Brand and De Santos demanded. If he could bypass them, they could save a bunch.

Skipper's objection was part personal and part professional. He learned that De Santos frequently bragged about his involvement in the battle at Cuito Cuanavale, where Skipper lost a good friend. He thought many times about revenge.

His professional objection against the deal was based on the lack of benefit to the military. He would prefer selling uranium to NATO allies, but since the West had shunned South Africa for many years, he was still bitter about it. It would not be difficult to look the other way. The offer from the Chinese was a way out of a financial situation for The Cape. He agreed to the deal with China on one condition.

Skipper was fully aware of the Chinese activities in Angola.

In 2000, the Chinese agreed to assist Angola in rebuilding their infrastructure in exchange for the oil rights of the Angolan west coast. Part of the infrastructure improvement deal included a launch site for missiles. The target was the USA east coast across the Atlantic. The oil agreement included a weapons deal and the Chinese used it to stock pile uranium at the launch site.

Skipper made sure enough uranium would remain to keep

Koeberg running, and for use by The Cape defense force. With the confirmation of the existence of the Tokoloshe and knowledge about the content of the safe rooms, he was interested in the resurrection of the nuclear capabilities in The Cape. De Klerk and the apartheid regime agreed to dismantle the South African nuclear weapons in exchange for an end to sanctions by the West. De Klerk's decision was partially driven by his desire to prevent the new government from getting their hands on nuclear weapons. Multiple questions were asked about the discrepancies in documentation and the real number of A-bombs the government had. No answers were given, and rumors started about the Tokoloshe, the slang term used for A-bombs.

The infantry stockpiles in Angola were another consideration for Skipper. The Cape defense force was in urgent need of weapons to fight off the threat of an invasion from the different tribes in the north. The solution lay in the arsenal of small infantry weapons and ammo supplied to the Angolan military. With the end of the civil war, the need for weapons became redundant. The Angolan government could not find a buyer and Skipper was willing to agree to the trade deal if it included a supply of weapons and ammo.

Something about the beachcomber seemed odd but also familiar to Fanie. He faked a bite on his hook and reeled in. His action was the agreed-on signal to Fanie that something needed their attention. He picked up his tackle box, with no fishing equipment inside, but a loaded 9mm, and walked to the rock formation where Gerhard stood.

As he passed the stranger on the beach, he greeted the person with a friendly smile. "Good morning. Nice day for a beach stroll," he said.

"Ja, really lekker out here," the person responded without looking up.

Fanie stopped in his tracks when he heard the voice and recognized the man. It had been a few years since he had been on a hunting trip to the Kalahari. Before his dad passed away, they visited the same place at least once a year. An old military buddy of his dad, Kraai, was a professional tracker on a hunting ranch. They fought together during the South African border war in the 70s and 80s. His dad was a captain in the

Special Forces Group 33 and Kraai was one of the trackers. After the war and the change in government, his dad kept in contact with Kraai and introduced Fanie to his Bushman friend.

"Hi, wag-'n-bietjie (*wait a minute*). Ek ken you (*I know you*)! Kraai? Is dit jy (*is that you*)?"

The other person stopped, hesitated and turned around, a big smile on his face. "Fanie? My wêreld, is dit rerig jy?" (*My world, is it really you?*)

The two men rushed to each other and embraced in a bearish hug.

"Where have you been all these years? Look at you. Just as skinny as always."

"How's your dad?" Kraai asked.

A sad expression appeared on Fanie's face. "Passed away in 2022. Covid."

"Oh, man. So sorry to hear. Would've loved to see my old buddy again. Best sniper in the whole world."

"Ja, he knew how to handle a rifle. He taught me to hunt, as you know, and told me lots of stories about you. I was only a little boy when you stayed with us after they disbanded your unit. What are you doing at the beach? Do you still live in the Kalahari on the hunting ranch?" Fanie rambled along with lots of questions.

Kraai looked at his feet and kicked in the sand. "No. Life is tough, man. Not doing so well. Had to leave the Kalahari when the hunters stopped coming after what happened in the US. Moved to Worcester in 2031 and found a job there. Became a driver for a courier service. We're suffering, and food is expensive."

"What brings you here?" Fanie asked. Although Kraai was a longtime friend of the family, Fanie knew being so far away from his home and family was not like him.

Kraai ignored the question. "You live here on the beach?" he asked, and looked at Fanie.

"No. Just stopped by with a friend to see if we can catch something. No luck today." He pointed at Gerhard sitting on the rocks not far away.

"You know the group over there?" Kraai asked, and looked in the direction of Visser and his guests around the grill.

"Some, not all. Why? Do you know them?"

"One. The guy with the long sleeves. Seems odd to wear a

fancy shirt like that on a beach at a braai."

"Ja, it's odd. Where do you know him from?" Fanie continued his line of questioning.

"Long story. Don't wanna talk about it," Kraai said.

"Why don't you stay and have something to eat with us?"

Kraai looked at the fire and the food on the tables, then back at Fanie. "Maybe not today. Another time."

"Well, that's okay. Why don't you come visit me and we can catch up?"

"That would be nice. You still live at the Winery in Stellenbosch?"

"Yes. Dad left it to me to take care of when he passed away. Forever grateful."

They exchanged numbers and walked in opposite directions. Fanie walked to Gerhard and sat down next to him.

"Who's that?" Gerhard asked.

"An old family friend. Seems like he's going through a rough time with the economy."

"Seems like the food is ready? Let's go eat," Gerhard said, and he picked up his tackle box and fishing pole.

Fanie hesitated for a moment and looked at the lone figure of an old man walking along the Atlantic Ocean towards Table Mountain. Deep inside, he had mixed feelings about seeing Kraai again. *Maybe he needs some help*, Fanie thought with dearness in his heart.

He picked up his gear and caught up with Gerhard. As they approached the group around the fire, he looked down the beach again. Kraai was gone. Deep in his gut he had the same uneasy feeling as when seeing Kraai on the beach the first time. *I knew he was up to something. He doesn't belong here.*

He touched Gerhard's arm and looked at him. "Something is wrong. I'm not sure what, but be on the lookout."

Chapter 5—The Tracker

Worcester, Cape Winelands
East from Tunnel
6 weeks after the tunnel explosion

When the SADF disbanded the Special Forces Group 33 unit, operational in the Southern Angola during the South African Border war, Kraai found himself without an income. He returned to his hometown of Hotazel in the Karoo and found a job at a local mining company. He did not fit into the routine lifestyle and quit after a short period. An opportunity to become a guide at a hunting ranch close to the Botswana border was more in his nature.

With the change of government in 1994, international sanctions were lifted against South Africa. It resulted in a boom for tourism and the hunting ranch of Jesse Alan. Guests were more interested in the photo-op after a kill shot than any proceeds from it. Jesse kept the meat the guests couldn't consume while staying at the ranch.

Jesse hired Kraai as a guide and tracker. Fanie's father and Kraai were buddies in the special forces and he vouched for his skills and character. Kraai became his star tracker and returning guests insisted on Kraai's services. He lived on the ranch and became a close friend of Jesse.

Kraai observed the way Jesse treated guests and how he bartered with anything and everything to make extra cash. Jesse had the gift of the gab and mastered the art of negotiations. Kraai learned from him and soon became an attraction for guests around campfires when he mimicked Jesse's behavior. As tracker, Kraai entertained hunters with stories from his ancestors and demonstrations of traditional Bushmen tracking skills. His tips increased as the years went by, and life could not be better for him.

Kraai got his share of the meat hunters were not interested in. He made jerky from it and sold it back to hunters, guests, and local customers. He also made miniature bows and arrows in his spare time and sold them as souvenirs.

And then his income dried up in a matter of weeks in 2029. The attacks in the US and the collapse of the world economy stopped the inflow of international and local hunters to the ranch. Kraai's income streams dried up and he once again was looking for a new job. Jesse had to scale back his operation to ensure the survival of his own family.

An acquaintance knew about a courier job in the Worcester area that would fit Kraai's lifestyle and skills. It did involve driving a truck, something Kraai hated, but it also involved bartering with a new type of currency—mampoer. The negotiation skills he learned from Jesse came in handy.

In the wine-producing areas, grapes were available in

abundance. Wineries used the choice grade of grapes to produce only the best wines. The lesser quality grapes were used to produce cheap wines or ended in the human and animal food chains. Some were just thrown away. With the economic collapse, a lot of grapes ended up drying on the stalks. Enter the geniuses of the illegal liquor traders. Mampoer, the Afrikaans name for moonshine, was called the same thing in all eleven official languages. Each region had its own blend and flavor.

Government officials turned a blind eye on the illegal trading since they mostly enjoyed it themselves. Tax authorities felt different and were concerned about the loss of tax revenue. Wine and beer producers were concerned about their market share. The public didn't care. They enjoyed it, hated the aftereffects, but couldn't let a good deal pass by.

Unfortunately, this became one of Kraai's flaws. The new job helped him to survive the harsh conditions and provided him with a permanent supply of mampoer.

And then it happened again. For the third time in his life, circumstances outside of his control made him homeless and jobless. The blocked tunnel cut him off from his customers and he had to spend a lot more hours in his truck to reach his market. He hated every minute of it. He used to travel back and forth through the tunnel almost daily. His supplier was in Worcester and his market was on the other side of the tunnel in the Paarl Valley area. He traded mampoer for anything and everything to sustain his lifestyle. As an old man, single with no immediate family, his needs were small. He slept most of the time in his truck or wherever he found a place to lay down.

The nightmares, from his time in the special forces as tracker, was the main reason for his need of alcohol. Like many other soldiers from the apartheid era war from 1963 to 1989, he also suffered from PTSD. Talking about it had a stigma attached to it and a person was labeled as 'bossies'—an Afrikaans slang term used for somebody suffering mentally from a traumatic event. Nobody recognized it as an illness, admitted to suffering from it, or sought treatment. Victims just learned to live with it.

Kraai's skills as a soldier were not only for tracking the enemy. He was a skillful marksman with a bow and arrow. As a child he learned to stalk wildlife and get within a few feet of his prey. In the military, he switched from a normal Bushman-style bow and arrow to a miniature bow and arrow to hunt and kill the enemy. As a child he learned how to make his own poison from flea beetles found in the Kalahari. The poison would not kill a small animal instantly, and the sting of the arrow scared the animal and put it on the run. That was where his tracking skills were honed. Sometimes the poison took a while to take effect and paralyze his prey. Following the spoor of the animal became a skill he used many times.

The military provided Kraai with a more potent toxic mixture from a lab. He called it beetle juice. Using his 9-inch bow and 6-inch arrow, Kraai could crawl to within a few feet of the enemy, shoot the little arrow into the neck of the guard, and wait for the poison to take effect. The sting of the arrow felt like a mosquito bite. The time it took for the guard to pull out the arrow, study it, and realize what it was, was long enough for the poison to take effect and paralyze him. The follow-up actions were the ones that caused Kraai's nightmares and drove him to mampoer. In a swift movement he would leap from his cover and in one move cut the throat of the enemy.

Kill or be killed. The words from his drill sergeant echoed in his mind every time he had to kill somebody. After the kill, he used an owl call as the signal of his success to the rest of his peloton waiting in the dark. He would stay in the background during the surprise attack at the break of dawn. Although they had many victories, he did not always share in the celebrations.

One guest on Jesse Alan's ranch remembered Kraai. It was a cool night in the Karoo and the hunters were reliving the hunt for the day. The guests for the hunting trip were a group of Chinese officials stationed in Angola. They had just clinched a deal for the oil rights in Angola. As an incentive, one of the Angolan negotiators, Franco De Santos, arranged for the hunting trip in the Kalahari on the prestigious ranch of Jesse Alan. After a fair amount of alcohol, Kraai and De Santos reminisced about the war of many years ago. They discovered they were both involved in the battle at Cuito Cuanavale. De Santos bragged about the success of the event in 1988 during the Angola Civil war, and how they defeated the SADF. Kraai remembered how disappointed his peloton was when they were given the order to retreat. The SADF declared the battle a success, as they did manage to destroy the bridge over the river. FAPLA declared victory as UNITA and the SADF were forced to retreat. To protect his ego, Kraai in his drunkenness bragged about how he managed to kill many FAPLA soldiers with his small bow and arrow.

Lani Wenjonk, one of the Chinese negotiators, listened intently to the back-and-forth between De Santos and Kraai. Wenjonk knew the small talk and bickering was the alcohol talking. Kraai's stories were far more intriguing and believable than those of De Santos. Before he left the game ranch, Wenjonk made sure he had a brief personal discussion with Kraai. His main interest was in his willingness to use his hunting skills and military experience again in the future if needed by his government.

"For the right price, a lot of my skills are for sale," Kraai responded in a whisper.

"We have deep pockets," Lani said and winked at Kraai. "How do I get hold of you if I may need you in the future?"

Kraai smiled and with his head gestured in the direction of Jesse Alan. "We're old friends and Jesse will know how to get hold of me."

Twenty years later, Wenjonk made the call to Jesse. The price Wenjonk offered for the special mission was far more than Kraai had earned since the collapse of the world economy in 2029. His only source of income came to a screeching halt when the tunnel was blocked and his government pension from SASA was barely enough to buy food. He spent most of it on gas and mampoer. The opportunity to make some quick money came at the perfect time. He needed it and the Chinese indeed had deep pockets.

"What will you do with the money?" Jesse asked Kraai as they discussed the opportunity.

"Find the one responsible for blocking the tunnel. A lot of my friends worked for the Traders Union, lost their jobs, and are now homeless. It's a long way to drive around the mountain and gas is expensive. We don't make a lot, but now we have nothing."

"I know what you mean. We had to switch our business also. Biltong seems to be still in demand, and with the load shedding, fresh meat doesn't last long. You can always come back to the Kalahari and work for me again."

"If this job doesn't work out, I'll take you up on that." Kraai said, lifted his glass of mampoer, and emptied it with one gulp.

Chapter 6—Revenge

Worcester, Cape Winelands
East from Tunnel
6 weeks after Tunnel

The darkness of the night reflected the mood mourned around the fire. Each one was busy with his or her own thoughts, staring at the crackling fire. The usual laughter and loud discussions were absent.

Wessel De Bruin, owner of the mampoer distillery on a farm outside of Worcester, sponsored the event. A last get-together for the drivers he had employed as rum-runners for his illegal mampoer business. Their clients were located on the other side of the mountain, and with the blocked tunnel became out of reach. Tomorrow they would leave the farm, go back to their families, and hope to find a new job. Others would become homeless.

The influx of people from The Cape increased the demand for cheap liquor. Wessel saw an opportunity and took advantage of it. The mountain areas had a permanent natural supply of fresh water and he had access to an abundance of grapes in the local market. All the ingredients he needed to expand his production were available and his market was only a short distance away. That was until the tunnel got blocked.

The illegal distillers formed their own organization, the Mampoer Traders Union. They split the market into different territories and Wessel was assigned the Wellington area west of the tunnel. He competed with the Wine Producers Co-Op for market share. The governor of the area, Pieter Brand, used his political influence and engaged the police in his efforts to stop the illegal selling of mampoer that directly competed with his market.

The blocked tunnel impacted Wessel's operations. The alternative route around the Cedar Berg mountains was expensive and time consuming. The old mountain pass had become too dangerous for frequent use. Profits and morale suffered, and he had to scale back his operations. The decision to let his rum-runners go was not easy.

"I know who's responsible for blocking the tunnel," said Dawid, one of the drivers around the fire.

Kraai looked at him. "Who?" he asked.

"Pieter Brand."

"And you know that how?"

"I have my sources," Dawid said with a grin on his face. "I don't want to get him in trouble. He works for the government. He overheard Brand and the president discuss something about the tunnel before it happened."

"What's in it for him? Why would he want to block the tunnel?" somebody else asked.

"From what I heard," Dawid continued, "he is concerned about the impact of mampoer on his cheap labels."

"Where's his winery?" Kraai asked.

"In the Paarl," Dawid responded.

"Sounds about right to me then," Kraai said and starred into the fire. All eyes turned to him.

"You know something?" Wessel asked.

Kraai used a stick to stir the flames that were fading away. Sparks flew up and reached for the sky before dying and disappearing into the night. They sat in silence, waiting for a response from him. He was by far the oldest in the group and they had great respect for him. He outperformed all the others in deliveries and retaining customers. His stories were legendary during the good times. His wisdom about life was practical and came from experience. When he spoke, they listened and paid attention.

"I've been doing my own investigation," Kraai said after a long silence. "What Dawid says confirms what I found. Brand met with the 3K before the tunnel was blocked. They discussed the illegal trade and he wanted their help to stop it. Rumor has it that Brand wants to use the tunnel for wine storage. Apparently, he's a jakkals, a real two-faced bastard. He's got his own stills on the other side of the mountains. With us gone, he will be able to control the whole area on the other side of the mountain."

The reaction from the group was expected and they all started to express their feelings of disgust and gave their opinions about what should be done.

"Very interesting," Wessel said when the chatter faded. "The rumor I heard is that the Co-Op is tired of the increased tax on liquor sales and started to sell cheap wine in shebeens. The only problem is people prefer mampoer. It's still cheaper and taste better. We all know it's illegal and you know we don't pay taxes on our sales. Just think about all the food and other stuff you trade for mampoer. Of course they will want to stop us."

"Wish I could get my hands around his neck," someone said.

"Me too," a choir of voices echoed the sentiment. Everyone expressed what they would like to do to Pieter Brand.

"Talk is cheap," Kraai said with a loud voice. Silence fell on the group. They had never heard him raise his voice. He took his time and looked at each one directly while asking his next rhetorical question. "Who of you have actually killed somebody before? Looked him in the eyes while life slowly drained from him? Felt his body go still while your hand is on his mouth to keep him from making a sound?"

Far away they heard the howling of a jackal in the night. Nobody moved or made a sound.

Kraai stood up and walked from person to person. "Who! Who has done that?" He stood over Dawid. "So, you want to squeeze life from Pieter Brand? How will you do that? Grab him from the front and look him in the eyes, or sneak up to him from behind and choke him with a rope?"

"Agge nee, man!" Dawid said. "We're just expressing our frustration. I'm sure you had the same feelings."

"I may or may not have the same feelings. Thing is, you don't say something if you're not willing to do it." He turned around and walked to his seat, sat down and stared into the fire. Nobody said a word.

"So," Wessel said after a long silence, "what do we do? Say goodbye and go our own way, or are we actually going to do something?"

"Can't we find somebody who will actually do it?" Dawid asked.

"I know somebody that may be willing to do it," Kraai said and looked up. "It will cost us. He's not cheap."

"Are you serious?" Dawid said. "I was just joking. Didn't think of actually doing it."

"Then don't say it. If you're not interested, then maybe you should leave."

The group fell silent again, each contemplating what Kraai said.

"Remember," Kraai continued, "if you stay, you will be just as guilty as the one who does the job. We will all put something in. We will be hiring a hitman to kill somebody. If he kills Brand and is caught, we are just as guilty."

Nobody left.

"Drinks on me," Wessel said and opened a cooler box with bottles of mampoer. The chatter around the fire gathered speed and by midnight, they had a plan. Everyone would contribute the same amount. Wessel would secure additional funding from the Union, and Kraai would negotiate with the hitman. He refused to give any details about the person.

Chapter 7—Decision

Saturday, March 26, 2033
Blouberg Strand,
Cape of Good Hope
10 weeks after the tunnel blockage
Beach

Willem listened but did not participate in the casual conversations around the fire on the beach. In his hand he held a glass of Cabernet from his private collection. Named after the family patriarch, he not only inherited the farm from his great grandfather, but also the money from a family trust. Willem was not yet born when his father died in a motor accident. His grandfather raised him and taught him the intricacies of winemaking.

The required military service in the 1980s interrupted his career. His grandfather had no objections when Willem decided to join the special forces. As a WWII veteran, he in fact encouraged it.

Something in his peripheral vision attracted his attention. His training, and constant awareness of danger in the country he lived in, allowed him to stay calm. He stood up and made his way to Fanie, always keeping the area around him in sight.

"Caught any fish?" he said, and with his left index finger pulled on the bottom lid of his right eye and scratched his chin. One of the secret codes used by the WP operatives to indicate that something required investigation.

Fanie recognized the signal and nodded to acknowledge his understanding. "Nope. Do you think we should try another spot?"

"There may be a good one about two hundred yards down the beach towards the mountain. Behind the sand dune and the tall grass." For any bystander it would mean nothing. For Fanie, it indicated where he should focus his search.

"Will keep it in mind for next time. Excuse me for a minute? I'll be right back. Gerhard and I need to put our fishing gear in the truck before dark. Seems the party will last a while."

"Sure. No problem," Willem said and moved over to join the conversation between Franco De Santos and Pieter Brand.

Fanie walked over to Gerhard. "Something's brewing. Grab your gear. Willem saw something about two hundred yards south. If somebody asks, we're putting our gear in the truck. We'll be right back."

They stepped away from the fire and with his back to the spot Willem had indicated, he checked his 9mm, stuck it in his belt, and covered it with his sweater. Gerhard did the same.

As they approached the dune, Fanie noticed some movement in the grass. They walked past the spot, and he whispered to Gerhard.

"We passed him. In the grass on your right." He suddenly stopped and said out loud. "Oh, man, I forgot the fishing rod. Watch my tackle box. I'll be right back." He turned around and, in the process, glanced at the spot where he saw the movement. He was just as surprised as the person trying to hide in the tall grass and shrubs.

"I'll be damned. Twice on the same day." He walked towards the skinny figure of an old man curled up behind a bush. "Kraai?" he said.

Kraai slowly rolled over and got up. Guilt was written all over his face as he tried to drop the object in his hand without being noticed.

Fanie saw the movement but did not turn his eyes away from Kraai's.

"You found my sleeping spot." Kraai attempted a lie.

Fanie laughed at him. "Worst lie I've ever heard in my life. What're you doing here? I was surprised to see you on the beach, but now I know you're up to something." He pointed to Kraai's feet. "You dropped something." They both looked down.

When Fanie saw the miniature bow and arrow, he pulled the gun from his belt, took a step back, and pointed it at Kraai. "Don't touch that thing!" Fanie said in a tone that made Kraai freeze. "I've seen that before and you are very good with it. Wanna explain?"

Gerhard stepped away from Fanie and covered Kraai from the other side.

Kraai kept starring at his feet. He moved a few feet away from the bow and arrow, his trademark in the border war. Fanie had seen him many times hunting small game with it. Fanie and his father were frequent guests at the hunting ranch of Jesse Alan in the Kalahari. Kraai had explained to Fanie in detail the art of tracking, hunting, and killing animals. He had showed him the effects of the different mixtures of beetle juice and how to use it. It was very important for survival in the Kalahari. If you planned to eat the meat, just enough beetle juice was used to paralyze the animal. A strong mixture of beetle juice and snake poison was needed to kill something. Kraai always had multiple arrows prepped with both mixtures in case they ran into a predator. The same applied to humans. The mixture used on the arrow tip was determined by the purpose of its use. Fanie knew the facts and had seen the results. He didn't know for what purpose Kraai had prepared his arrows. To kill, or to paralyze?

Kraai hunched down. Fanie put his weapon away and sat down on the dune between Kraai and the arrows. Gerhard lowered his pistol but kept it at his side.

"He took away everything!" Kraai whispered.

"Who?" Fanie said with a frown.

"Brand," Kraai said, and looked in the direction of the fire. "Hy's 'n twee gat jakkals." He looked back at Fanie. "Do you know that?"

"A jakkals? Why?"

Kraai looked Fanie straight in the eye, clenched his teeth, and took a deep breath. He shook his head slowly. "I may be old, Fanie. But I'm not stupid. We have known each other for a long time. You know I won't lie to you," he said. He turned his head back to the group of men. "I walked with him and your dad in Angola. I'm not sure if you know that. I didn't expect to see him with Brand."

"Who are you talking about?" Fanie asked.

"Willem O'Neil. I wonder if he knows Brand is a jakkals?"

"Why's he a jakkals?" Fanie asked.

"He drinks wine from two fountains. One he swallows, the other he spits out."

"Which two fountains you're talking about?"

"Wine and mampoer. He's a wine producer and joined the Co-Op. Secretly, he's also making mampoer."

"How do you know that?"

"Doesn't matter. I was a rum-runner for the Traders Union until the tunnel got blocked. Lost my job, friends, income, everything. My market disappeared in the blink of an eye. And what do you know? Suddenly Mister Brand's mampoer is available everywhere. His winery sells wine to liquor stores, but his distillery runs mampoer to the Cape Flats and shebeens. I know he is the one behind the tunnel thing. He's responsible for blocking it and ruining our lives!" The anger in his voice couldn't match the shock on Fanie's face.

"So, this is revenge?" Fanie said and pointed to the bow and arrow. "Kill or torture?"

Kraai took another deep breath. "That's not for him."

"For whom, then? Willem?"

"Wow, you are stupid. You know I will never hurt him. We were together in Angola. He was my buddy and we're brothers for life. You don't kill a brother."

"So, who then? De Santos?" Fanie asked.

Kraai nodded slowly. "Yes," he said after a moment.

"Okay. Now I'm confused. Brand is the jakkals, but you want to kill De Santos. What has De Santos to do with the tunnel? He's from Angola. He knows nothing about it."

"Ja, but he's not here for mampoer or wine," Kraai said with a smirk.

Fanie did not know how to respond. He realized Kraai knew a lot more than he anticipated. He wondered if he was on Kraai's list, too. It took him a moment to respond. "Who hired you?" It was a long shot, but he knew he had to ask.

Kraai didn't blink. "The Chinese. They have deep pockets."

"How deep?"

"A hundred grand."

"In exchange for?"

"Killing the middleman."

"Middleman? For what?" Fanie asked, trying to hide the

fact that he knew what was being discussed around the fire.

"Whatever deal they are negotiating right now."

"I think it's time we need to join the discussion," Fanie said. He picked up the bow and arrow and stood up. "Let's go talk to Willem."

Kraai didn't move. He looked up and stared at Fanie. "Why?"

"He's my boss. I'm sure he would like to say hello to a long-lost brother."

"I don't want them to see me," Kraai begged. "I need the money."

"It will be okay. Come with us. We'll get Willem to come say hello to his old friend. I'm sure you know you can trust him."

Kraai slowly got up and walked with Fanie. He looked back and saw Gerhard walking a few feet behind them, his hand in his pocket.

Chapter 8—Payday

Cape Columbine Lighthouse,
Paternoster, The Cape
2 hrs. north of Cape Town
12 weeks after the tunnel

Lani Wenjonk selected the meeting place and changed it at the last minute. The location of the cattle truck, loaded with weapons and ammunition, was only provided after verification of the content in the wine barrels loaded on a fishing boat. The exchange took place on the beach two hours north of Cape Town in Paternoster.

The cattle truck was parked behind an old beach house fifteen minutes away. The Chinese representative provided the keys and location to Fanie. He left with two WP operatives and returned an hour later with the truck following him. He got out and gave the all clear sign to Gerhard and another operative waiting on the pier.

Gerhard handed the keys for the boat to the skipper. He untied the rope from the pier and threw it into the boat. They joined Fanie and the other operatives and left the beach.

The skipper had no idea what was in the wine barrels. He was paid for delivery of the cargo to a ship a few kilos offshore.

He couldn't leave yet. His passengers were still on the beach waiting to make one more delivery.

The deal was finalized seven days prior to the exchange. It was preceded by some unexpected events. The death of Franco De Santos and Pieter Brand, the key brokers and negotiators of the deal, forced the main sponsors from Angola and The Cape to step in at the last minute. Lani Wenjonk and Johan Skipper signed the trade agreement between the two countries without the brokers.

The terms of the agreement were finalized by Brand and De Santos. As a special reward for their success, they were offered a hunting expedition in the Kalahari with compliments from The Cape minister of finance, Willem O'Neil. The hunting trip to the luxurious ranch of Jesse Alan included the services from one of the best Bushman trackers in the Kalahari, Kraai.

The celebration trip turned tragic when they were both found dead the morning after a successful hunt for a Kudu and a night of heavy drinking. Brand brought with him some wine and cheap mampoer. De Santos liked the mampoer better and in their drunkenness, they wandered away from the camp and had an encounter with a puff adder.

The official cause of death on the coroner's report indicated it was snake poison from the very poisonous puff adder, common in the area, that killed them. The coroner's report noted that De Santos was the one who may have stepped on the snake based on the bite marks on his leg. Brand then tried to grab the snake and was bit in the arm. No mention was made in the report about the small wound both men had in the neck. The wounds were very similar to a stab from a sharp object like a miniature arrow. No foul play was suspected.

Jesse Alan confirmed they had frequent encounters with snakes in the area and showed the coroner, a good friend of his, where he had killed a snake that might have been the one that bit De Santos and Brand. It was found inside the cabin they slept in.

Fortunately for the two governments involved in the trade, all the arrangements for the trade deal were completed, and the final execution was a formality.

In Paternoster, Kraai waited behind a dune until the trucks had departed. He snuck up to the men sitting on the beach looking over the Atlantic Ocean, the arrow of his traditional hunting bow pulled back and ready. The three men never saw him coming.

"I believe you have a package for me," he said in a whisper.

They spun around to face him and froze when they saw the arrow pointing at them. "What the heck? Where did you come from?" one of the men stuttered.

"I was here all the time," Kraai said with a smile. "Don't make any sudden moves. I have backup. Just give me the package."

"What package?" The man in the middle faked a lie.

"You know what I'm talking about. The Chinese man said one of you will have it. You're dead if you don't have it, and the boat will go nowhere. Your choice." Kraai took a step closer and pointed the arrow at the person on the left. They stared at each other and Kraai squinted his eyes, lifted the arrow, and took aim at the man's throat.

"I... don't have it," he said, his voice almost failing, and he lifted his hands.

Kraai quickly moved the arrow to the man on the right.

Without saying a word, he pointed at a canvas bag lying in the sand. "It's right there," he said.

Kraai did not move or look away. "Pick it up. Slowly! The poison on the arrow will torture you for a long time before you die. Any sudden moves and... I think you know what I mean."

The man picked up the bag and held it out to Kraai.

"I'll take that," Gerhard said from behind them. The men were so focused on Kraai and the arrow, they did not notice Fanie and Gerhard making their way on the beach towards them. He took the bag, opened it, and looked inside. "Payday for you, Kraai," Gerhard said and handed him one of the gold bars from the bag. "Six bars and some cash. That what you expected?"

"Ja," Kraai said with his eyes fixed on the bar in his hand. "First time I ever held one of these. Wow! It's heavy for its size." He could not stop smiling. He looked at Gerhard. "Let's get out of here."

"This is how it's going to work," Gerhard said, and looked at the men. "You're leaving right now. Lani kept his promise, and we'll keep ours. The boat is loaded as agreed. The skipper has the keys. Now, take your stuff and go. Don't try anything silly."

The three men picked up their backpacks and when they reached for their guns, Fanie stepped closer. "Leave the rifles," he barked, and pointed his R4 at them.

They walked to the pier and got in the boat. The skipper started the engine and took off. They left without looking back.

Fanie, Gerhard, and Kraai watched as the boat rounded the corner of the bay. Fanie lifted his hand in the air and waved at somebody on a dune. A few minutes later a driver stopped next to them in Fanie's truck. He got behind the wheel and turned the truck around. The cattle truck was waiting at the main road. He stopped next to the truck and leaned out.

"Got the package. Let's go home. We'll follow you."

The trucks turned onto highway R399 in the direction of Vredenburg where they turned south on the R27 towards Cape Town.

Kraai sat in the back of Fanie's truck. The gold bar was still in his hand and the bag with the rest of his reward sat between his feet.

"Die Jirre is goed!" (*God is good*) he said, and tears ran down his wrinkled face. "I hope He can forgive me for what I did." He learned forward and put his hand on Fanie's shoulder. "I know you were only following orders. I forgive you."

Fanie tapped his hand. "Thank you. Just remember, you've changed sides now. You cannot kill a brother."

Do Unto Others

Jamie Ibson

2033

Avery Todd raised his rifle to his cheek, got a good weld, and placed the crosshairs over the bull moose. It was just a hundred, maybe a hundred twenty yards away, broad as a barn and chewing on swamp grass. His finger twitched off the frame, for just a fraction of a second, then he lowered the barrel.

"Dammit," he cursed. "Of all the days, has to be today?"

His boots crunched through the snow and ice as he went tree to tree, closing each tap and disconnected the tubes individually. Miss Olivia Fletcher, whose father had owned these lands, expertly installed each one of them by hand, starting well before "can't see" and not stopping until it was "can't see" again. He wouldn't be the one to remove the taps—that was up to the expert. But he could disconnect the tubes without any difficulty and prep them to be hauled down to the river for their initial rinse. Todd wasn't even sure of the month, let alone week or day, but given that the sap was done flowing, it must be late February or maybe even March.

It flowed down the same tubes Miss Fletcher had used since before The Collapse, seven long years ago—or was it eight? Since before tubes became a scarce commodity, at any rate. Since before *sugar* became as rare as an honest politician, and maple syrup became the only viable sweetener to be found for a thousand miles in any direction.

Since before the VAC cheques stopped, even though the nightmares hadn't.

For four weeks, Todd and a handful of others had dutifully followed Miss Fletcher, from can't see to can't see, hauling the blue tubes back and forth across Mister Fletcher's three hundred acres of sugar bush. They'd made a massive plate of blue spaghetti out of the purpose-built hoses and plumbing elbows, down to the creek bed's pump, and then to the shack where they boiled it down. But with the final thaw, the snow and ice had been churned into sloppy mud, the cycle ended, and with it, harvest season.

Olivia's three hundred acres wasn't entirely given over to maple trees, but what she did have still used miles and miles of hose, hundreds of taps, and Todd was the man tasked with disconnecting the tubes so they could be dragged clear. He had exactly no time to waste dressing and quartering a moose. Doing so would take most of the day, it would leave a lot of taps still hooked up, and it wouldn't be professional. Instead, he lifted the disconnected tubing and passed it through a wide-gated carabiner that kept the tubing elevated off the forest floor and prevented it from getting snagged as they retrieved it.

When he emerged from the treeline, muddy and sweaty, steam rose from his hoodie and a sheen of frost had developed on his shoulders. Lyndon, Amy, and Sean stood ready. He waved to them, and the three teens started hauling. Avery made for the shack to change out of his sweaty clothes before he froze. The trio heaved on the tube, dragging it and its many, many T-junctions from the forest. That part was a younger body's work, and Todd had done his part. He peeled off his hoodie as he trudged down the path and let his body cool some, so he wouldn't sweat in his next change of clothes. He'd seen too many friends die of hypothermia over the last seven (eight?) Canadian winters, friends who hadn't been able to adapt to the new normal and take his winter survival lessons to heart.

"That's the last of them, Liv," he said as he joined the group huddled under the cedar shed roof. It had had walls, once, but they'd disassembled them that first thaw, after the Madrid Fault bombing, to open the structure up and get proper airflow. They didn't use reverse osmosis or pressure vessels to boil the sap down any more. It was back to the old school, like Avery had done as a kid on a school field trip. Low, open-flame fires, with broad metal trays of sap boiling away.

"That's great, Avery, thanks," Olivia said. "Grab a seat, Kyle is bringing up some garlic venison sausages for dinner."

Of the natural food resources still available in New Brunswick, deer meat was among the more plentiful, and the Mennonites who lived a couple miles away had whole fields of spices. In a world where global supply chains had collapsed, it was a luxury.

Avery was starting to feel the chill again, and went to his kitbag. Old habits died hard, and he threw open the top flap of his old ruck and pulled out a fresh, if a little threadbare, polypro thermal top. He stripped off his own shirt and dropped it next to his hoodie, and pulled the new shirt on. He winced as he heard a few more threads rip, but so be it—it was that, or he'd trade for scratchy, homespun wool. When his head emerged from the old shirt, he caught sight of the teenagers, dragging the sap tapline with them. They'd coiled it in an enormous loop, ten or fifteen feet across, with the little tap splits sticking every which way like blue porcupine quills.

That would've been fine, except Lyndon, who was only kind of helping drag the line, tripped.

Maybe it was the snow, maybe it was a patch of clean ice, maybe he was a klutz whose feet were dragging, but his foot got caught in a loop of the line, which jerked him off balance. That threw Sean and Amy's careful cadence off, so when Lyndon stumbled sideways, he crashed into Sean. Sean went flying with half a dozen coils of sap line still in his hands, caromed towards the sugar shack, and tripped over the raised concrete lip. With a cry, he twisted and fell face-first into the open fires and boiling sap.

Just like that, Sergeant Avery Todd was back in Afghanistan.

Screams. Shouting. The chaos and sizzle of burning flesh.

Just like that, he was back. "MOVE!" he shouted and straight-armed one of the teenagers he didn't know aside. Those tending the fires had leaped back as the sticky, sugary sap and glowing hot embers scattered. Avery picked a route through the bodies like a running back. He pulled the sleeve of his thermal down to protect his right hand as he went, and the instant he was in reach, he grabbed the back of Sean's jacket. Sean writhed in agony, and threatened to pull himself out of Avery's grasp, but then the older man got his hand on Sean's belt and bodily lifted him clear in a deadman's lift.

"Make a hole!" he shouted and carried Sean a few feet back from the fire pit as the group made room. He searched the faces and found Olivia. "Warm water! Not cold, not yet! As much as we have, now!" Fletcher dragged two people with her as they went in search of water. Avery pulled his crash knife from his pocket and used the seatbelt cutter to slice away Sean's jacket, then shirt. He found Lyndon in the crowd next. "Blankets, now!"

Lyndon opened his mouth but stammered some incomprehensible gibberish. *Useless.* Avery found Amy's face next, and she dashed away towards one of the waiting wagons. Avery turned back to his patient. The teen's skin was covered in molten sap, and it had already blistered in spots. His hands and face were swelling up and there was a charred spot on the palm of his left hand. He moaned in pain and writhed on the ground. "Sean, it's Avery. I know it hurts. This is going to suck, but I need to wash the sap off of you before you can open your eyes. I'm right here, it's going to be okay." Olivia returned with pitchers of water in both hands. She passed one over, and Avery tested it with a finger. Warm, but not hot. Good.

"Hold your breath, this will only be a second," he said, and Sean let out a whimper. Avery slowly poured the warm water over his head, letting the it rinse his face and carry away the sticky solution that glued his eyes shut and was scalding him. Sean was coughing by the time Avery finished, but he wasn't done. "And now cool water, to bring your skin temp down and mitigate the damage. This is going to be... worse." After a pointed look, Olivia joined him, took hold of Sean's shoulders, and braced the back of his head, so he couldn't pull away. Avery poured the cool pitcher of water over him next, sluicing away more of the sap but, more importantly, cooling his skin's surface temperature down. Amy returned, an armload of horse blankets in hand, and Avery placed them on the ground next to his patient.

"More," he instructed her, and handed over the pitchers. She took them and ran for their rainwater collection barrels. In the meantime, Avery mopped up more of the cool water with Sean's ruined shirt and pressed it into his hand. His fingers were claws, drawn tight by the damage they'd suffered, and Avery grimaced. The teen's face was reddened and swollen like a bee-sting allergy sufferer who'd just been zapped, and his eyes were almost entirely hidden behind the puffy blisters.

What Avery hadn't noticed was that Sean had taken his

coils of tubing into the sap fires with him. Amy swore—and to his knowledge, Avery hadn't ever heard Amy swear—and yanked the sap tubes out of the fire where they'd fallen. The tubes had melted down into a puddle of blue glop in one section, the same section for each coil. As Amy spread them apart, the plastic dripped in rivulets; instead of one long line of hoses, she now had a dozen or more fifteen-foot lengths, with slagged, disconnected ends.

"Oh hell," Olivia said when she saw the damage. The tubes were irreplaceable. Todd marveled at the woman's self-control; he could almost see her mentally count to ten. On cue she blew out a deep breath of resignation and shook her head. "Nothing to be done for it right now, I guess." She motioned for Avery to follow her aside.

"What do you think?" she asked in a low tone.

"I think he's crippled," Avery replied bluntly. "I worry about the damage to his face, and most especially his eyes. They're so swollen I can't tell how badly damaged they are. A guy I knew in the sandbox lost an eye to burning diesel after a mine strike. His wounds looked bit like Sean's."

"Worse than that?" Olivia asked, her eyes widening.

"No, Sean's are worse. Like, a lot worse. Who's he living with these days?"

Olivia pursed her lips. "He and Amy were a couple for a few months, but they broke up last summer. I think he was crashing at the old Grant homestead with a couple of other teens there. Mama Grant has them working her fields."

"Well, she isn't going to be in a position to care for him and still get the spring prep ready. Those burns... I don't know. Burns were awful before everything went to shit. Now, I kind of feel like the kindest thing would be to give him a smidge too much of that opiate we've still got at the clinic and let him drift off to sleep."

Fletcher's features hardened. "Really? You'd euthanize him? He's not some horse with a broken leg!"

Todd shrugged in response. "Really, I'd euthanize him. And save him the agony of trying to regrow a new face without the benefits of modern medicine, antibiotics, skin grafts, or, you know, *doctors*. That presumes that his eyes are okay, which we can't be certain of, but I'm leaning towards partial blindness at minimum."

Fletcher shook her head. "Maybe I'm just a foolish optimist, but it's gotten me this far. We'll find somewhere for him to convalesce and roll out as soon as this last batch is bottled. Get your gear."

"As you say," Todd agreed.

In their absence, Lyndon, Amy, and a couple of the other teenagers had already hacked down a pair of stout branches, trimmed them, and had run them through the sleeves of a pair of jackets to make a stretcher.

"The Prices will take him," Amy informed them. "They've got a spare room, a rainwater barrel, and a water filter for cleaning linens."

Olivia nodded. "That's very kind of them; please thank them for us. Are you still planning to come on this trip down to Saint Stephen?"

"I'd like to, yes," the teen replied. "I've got a bunch of coyote and fox skin belt pouches I've been making in my spare time, and I'd like to see what I can trade for them. Dad had an SKS and *crates* of ammo; I've been practicing."

"Good," Avery said. "Meet the rest of us at the wagons at sunup tomorrow. Bring your cold weather travel gear. You'll need it. Twice as many socks as you think you'll need, and then some more. You have snowshoes? We'll be gone ten days, maybe two weeks."

It was a finger past sunup when Amy arrived with her stuff. She dragged a modified hand truck to the crest of the hill and the old on-ramp to the freeway, the freeway that hadn't had a gas engine operate on it since she was twelve. The hand truck had a wooden chest strapped to it, and a weather-beaten ruck tied to it above that. The clunky old wheels had been swapped out some time ago for larger ones that looked like they may have come from a ride-on lawnmower. She wore a ragged, faded-but-colorful snowboarding parka, a proper bobble-hat toque, and had her dad's SKS slung over her back. Her snowshoes were mismatched, but they seemed to work just fine—the snow was a couple feet deep here, but the shoes let them walk around on the surface without falling in.

"You're late," Avery said. He finished hitching up the horses to the wagon and moved to the rear of the wagon to hand her gear up to Wei, one of the other guards and the only other veteran on the team. "What have I taught you about being late?"

"That on-time is late, and early is on time," she replied glumly.

"So why are you late-late? Instead of being on-time-late?"

"No excuse, Sergeant Todd," she said.

"That's the right answer, but not a complete one. Seriously, what happened?"

"I'm all the way down by the river," she said. "Sunup comes later in the valley than up here by the old freeway. I didn't realize my mistake until it was too late."

Avery nodded thoughtfully. "Fair enough. You've got horse manure detail first up, and last watch tonight."

"Understood, Sergeant Todd."

Amy was the only new member to the guard crew, and Avery did introductions. Wei was a vet like him, born and raised in Toronto. Jaroslav was Czech, having come to Canada when Czechoslovakia imploded. Lionel was a black Frenchman—*France* French, not Quebecois, and Avery privately suspected he'd served in the French army, but Lionel would neither confirm nor deny. Kyle was one of their best hunters, and Summer was a young lady on her second trip down to the coast.

With the last of the gear stowed, Wei took Amy to the back of the column to show her the job of the trailing scout. Their group totaled ten—a pair of scouts in the lead, two per flank, one tail-end Charlie, and three drivers for three wagons. They rotated through the scout slots to keep everyone on their toes. By noon, Amy and Todd had moved into the point slot, and they reached the stretch of the old freeway Avery Todd hated most.

The Eel River passed below the freeway. It meant a long slow descent, followed by a long, knee-busting ascent on the far side. At the top, they'd crest the ridge and depart the freeway for the remnants of Meductic. One could see the entire freeway from the ridge, more than three klicks distant. Any sensible scout with a horse on that ridge could fall back, bring friends, and lay on one helluvan ambush with that much warning. It made Todd's skin crawl.

They halted the horses and their wagons before committing. Todd sent Wei and Jaroslav across the northbound bridge, while he and Amy crossed the southbound. The wagon drivers—Elena, Juan, and Michael—waited with the wagons until the lead security gave them the all-clear. Only then would they send the wagons, as fast as they could manage, and then the trailing three guards would race after them.

Halfway across the bridge, Avery caught a glint off something up in the treeline. He lifted his rifle to his shoulder and dialed the magnification on the scope up to 9x. When he looked again, the glint disappeared. "Shit. Ambush." He waved Elena, Michael, and Juan over and shared his concerns.

"So... what do we do?" Amy asked.

"Ideally, no one shoots anyone. I'd like to talk our way through this, hand over a toll. But if it goes loud, you've got two options. If they're far away, find some nice big rocks to hide behind. Not snow, not the wagons, not the horses, *rocks*. Cover is anything that'll stop a bullet and they could be shooting .22 or .338. We try to throw enough lead downrange that the horses can get turned around."

Juan shifted uncomfortably. "And if they're close?"

"We do unto them before they can do unto us. Charge them, screaming and shooting all the way. Keep your hatchets at hand and if your rifle runs dry, get your Viking on. Don't stop until you're well past them and regroup."

"Uh, my family was from Ecuador, Sergeant," Juan objected. "I'm not really Viking stock."

Todd rubbed his brows in obvious frustration. "So help me... Brute violence and an aggressive counterattack, Juan. Ambushers won't expect an immediate, violent response, so give 'em one."

They crossed the bridge and began the long slog to the ridge ahead. Once the two halves of the freeway came together again, he warned Wei, Jaroslav, and the other three.

"*Nous serons prêts*," Lionel said. He and Summer covered their right flank—this next hike was going to be a ball-buster. "We will be ready."

"*Tres bien*," Avery replied with a smile. Lionel laughed. Avery knew his accent was appalling, but it didn't stop him from trying.

The march to the crest of the ridge was agonizing. Keeping his .308 in hand meant Avery couldn't use his ski poles as walking sticks, and more than once the teeth on his snowshoes skidded off the icy surface rather than biting in. Even the horses were struggling. They neared the ridge, and he gave

Lionel the nod. He and Summer disappeared off through a break in the rock escarpment. Avery took a moment to catch his breath and let them gain some ground.

"Ready?" he asked Amy.

She seemed grateful for the break too but wasn't about to complain further. She took a swig of snowmelt from her camelbak and nodded. "Good times."

They were maybe fifty metres shy of the crest when a figure stepped out of the woodline and onto the road. He wore CAF-issue white snowpants, and a CADPAT Goretex winter jacket. More importantly, he was cradling a belt-fed C9 light machine gun, with its linked ammo coming from a green plastic box. It even still had the C79 scope mounted on the feed cover.

Shit.

That was rather more firepower than he'd been expecting.

"Hey, Juan, remember what I said earlier?" Avery called over his shoulder.

"I do," he replied cautiously.

"Forget all that."

Amy got closer to Todd as they approached the stranger with the machine gun. "Why?"

"Because unless those are blanks, he's got us all dead to rights. If he starts blasting, get off the X left and kill him before he kills everyone else. And believe me, he can. I'm hoping the fact that we're not dead already means he'd rather talk than fight."

"That's close enough dere b'y," the stranger shouted. They were still twenty or thirty meters away. "Been watchin' you some time now."

"I bet you have," Avery replied. "That you with the binos earlier?"

"As if I'd tell you," the man replied.

Avery held his hands out to his sides. "Worth a shot." He gestured to the machine gun in the man's hands. "Hope you're lubing that with graphite."

"Huh?" the man grunted. "Like, a pencil? What're you... never mind, I'm asking the questions. Where you headed?"

"Saint Stephen, for a bit of trade. Then back home again."

"That's a long walk, stranger. What're you hauling?"

"Maple syrup. Is this a toll? Or a robbery?"

"Ain't decided yet."

"Ideally, no one has to shoot anyone, Master Corporal." Avery looked pointedly at the rank slip-on on the front center of the man's jacket, which bore two chevrons and a maple leaf. The kid glanced down at the jacket's front, as if he hadn't known the rank slip on was there. The kid—and Avery was pretty sure he was just a kid—looked way too young to have earned a leaf in the CAF. "Tell you what, I'll let you... tax us, a toboggan's worth of syrup, for passage through your turf. You must have toboggans for hauling gear, right? In exchange, you let us pass through unmolested."

"Or?"

"Or we shoot it out, and one or both of us winds up dead."

The man in camouflage chuckled. "You think you can take me, old man? You do realize this is a machine gun, right?"

"I do. It's a C9 light machine gun, also known as the Minimi, also known as the M249. Shoots five-five-six in disintegrating link or, God forbid, from standard C7 mags. It tends to get cranky about jamming at the best of times, and in a frigid winter like this, graphite is the better lubricant. I'm curious whether the C79 sight still works, since it's radioactive and all, but I have no idea what the half-life of tritium is. Also, you haven't actually readied it yet."

"I— wha?" The man stammered and looked down at the gun in his hands. He gripped the handle and racked it back, and when he looked up, Avery was looking at him over the scope on his rifle. "Yes, it was!"

"Ah, but you weren't sure," Avery said. "Nor did you know about maintaining it in wintertime, nor what the rank tab on your jacket means. Three strikes tell me you're just a kid cosplaying soldier. Now do you want your damn syrup? Or shall we do this... uncivilized-like?"

"All right! All right," he said and let the machine gun hang on its sling. He turned to face the treeline and waved. He frowned and waved again.

"Someone missing?" Avery asked and allowed a smirk across his face as the kid's backup—a woodsy bearded man in red flannel and orange hunter's toque—marched out from the treeline, hands in the air, followed by Lionel and Summer.

"What—how—shit!" The kid cursed. "Oh dammit, you were just buying time..."

"Got it in one," Avery said with a smile. "Aren't you glad you didn't start shooting? Now unload that thing so we can talk all civilized-like. I wasn't kidding about the toboggan full of maple syrup, don't mind that at all."

The older man had refused to provide his name and had been disarmed for his trouble. They took the freeway offramp towards Canterbury and very quickly came upon what the kid—Dylan—and his orange-toque'd partner called Camp. Unoccupied houses and fences had been salvaged for viable lumber, and the residents had built a rough but serviceable barricade that blocked the road. They stopped well short of the barrier, far enough away Avery could be certain he'd hit someone he was aiming at, but far enough away they couldn't hear conversation.

Avery sent Orange Hat forward and kept Dylan close. The LMG couldn't be quickly loaded or readied, and any shenanigans on Dylan's behalf would quickly earn him a sucking chest wound. Strange as it seemed, it was safer to keep the machine gun close.

"Where'd you say you guys are from?" the kid asked.

"I didn't," Avery said. "Up the freeway some."

"Is that where all the Amish live?"

"Nearby," Avery allowed. "Not really Amish, but whatever. They've been real life savers. Nobody does low-tech farming like they do. You guys get a lot of carrots? Leeks? Cabbage?"

"No," the boy replied. "I don't even know what a leek *is*."

"Kids these days..." Avery sighed. "It's like an enormous green onion. You can make a pretty great soup with just leeks, potatoes, and some spices, you know. Oh, look, here comes your buddy."

Orange Hat returned. "Dey say, no foolin' wit' de toboggan o' syrup? You just give it up, no trouble?"

"No trouble," Avery replied. "Call it a toll, or a tax, or whatever makes you happy." Orange Hat turned and waved, and a young woman came forward dragging an old CAF sled.

Avery shook his head. The sleds were meant to be hauled by two humans up front with rope harnesses, and the folding push bar went to the rear for a third soldier to steer. This poor girl was pulling it backwards, struggling the whole way. When she got the toboggan close enough, half of Avery's guard crew got to work unloading the first wagon's supply. Orange Hat didn't help; neither did Dylan. Avery watched, and the longer he watched, the worse the gnawing in his gut got.

The woman refused to make eye contact with Orange Hat or Dylan at all. It was like she was trying not to see them. She wore a heavy wool skirt, and her boots were patched with cardboard. The sweater she wore was baggy, with sleeves that were too long, and she had the hood pulled up to hide her features. When he caught sight of the woman's shiner, he waved Amy and Summer over. "Hang on a sec," he said, and he voiced his concerns to his teammates.

Amy understood immediately. "Excuse me," she said to the woman, but Orange Hat interrupted.

"No *Anglais*," he said. "*Seulment francais.*"

"*Pas de problème*," Lionel replied, and Orange Hat's eyes flashed in surprise. "*Madamoiselle, ici, s'il vous plait?*"

Orange Hat put an arm out to stop her—and squeaked, as Avery's gloved hand closed on his throat like a vise. Dylan cursed and took a step back, but Wei was there on top of the wagon, brandishing his lever-action carbine. "Don't," he warned, and Dylan put his hands up. There were shouts from the barricade, but since these two were the 'guards,' there was little else they could do.

"We're just talking, *comprends?*" Avery told Orange Hat, and the man nodded. "Lionel, as you were."

"*Oui*," his guard said, and took the woman aside with Amy and Summer to talk.

Avery released his grip and reached back for one of the precious jugs of maple syrup. "Maybe you should help," he said, and jammed it forcefully into Orange Hat's chest. The man sullenly accepted the bottle and placed it in the toboggan. Avery kept shoving syrup at him, and the man kept loading it.

Lionel returned. "'Er name is *Josée*. She won't say anyt'ing. '*Non, non, pas de probleme,*' she say. Is bullshit, but..."

"But there isn't much we can do about that right now," Avery finished. "Shit. Not our business, not our problem. Let's finish this and go."

When the toboggan was full, the woman started dragging it back.

"*Josée? Arrête, une minute.*" Avery called. She froze. He went to the toboggan and reversed it, so it was pointed the right way and the skis on the sled would help, instead of interfering. "*Comme ca.*"

"*Merci,*" she said quietly, and began pushing the laden sled back towards the barricade. Avery gestured for Orange Hat to proceed. When there was enough separation between them, he gestured for Dylan to follow, and got his people moving again.

"You guys are a bit of a mystery, aren't you?" Avery asked.

"How's that?" Dylan replied.

"You're new here, obviously, you weren't here last year. I'm just curious how that machine gun came to be hanging out in this neck of the province without a proper owner. You know, someone who'd been trained in the care and feeding of belt-feds."

"It's my dad's," Dylan said—and froze. "Shit! You do this a lot?"

"What, the casual interrogation thing? Not lately, I'm rusty. Normally by now I'd have your birthday, home address, favorite food, and girlfriend's name. I bet Dad would be pissed, huh? That some random got the drop on you?"

"You have no idea."

"Not to worry, I won't tell if you don't. I just want to get to Saint Stephen without having to kill anyone, trade the syrup for scrip, trade the scrip for whatever useful kit I can get, and get home. You guys wouldn't happen to have antibiotics or something for burns, would you?"

They were approaching the barrier. Avery nodded to the men manning it and eyed the barricade. It looked good from afar, but it was far from good. Most of the beams had just been notched with an axe so they kind of leaned against each other. Whole wall sections were just sheets of rotting drywall, still on their stud frames with just the paper holding them together. It would trip up horses, and could damage the wagon wheels, so it did its job, but it was pathetic against foot-bound humans.

"No, nobody's had medicine for a long time," Dylan said. "The best we've got is some willow bark tea. Tastes rancid."

Avery nodded. "Well, Mary Poppins always said a spoonful of sugar helped the medicine go down. Just think, now you've got maple syrup instead!"

"Who?"

"Kids... Never mind."

Past the barrier, Avery got his first good look at the rest of the Camp's inhabitants. Josée pushed the toboggan down a laneway to a large farmhouse surrounded by empty horse paddocks. A dozen men had come to the end of their laneways, each of them armed with a rifle or shotgun of some kind. Other than Josée, there wasn't a woman to be seen anywhere. Or children, for that matter.

There was a second barrier, a hundred meters past the first, oriented the other way. The men guarding it had already opened it.

"Mount up, everyone," Avery called over his shoulder. "You too, Amy."

Amy frowned, and Avery silently urged her to just go with it. She did, hopping up onto Elena's wagon, and repeated his orders down the line. Wei flashed her a thumbs-up from the last wagon. "All aboard, Sergeant Todd!"

"Hey Dylan," Avery began. "What *did* your old man teach you about that thing? Do you know how to do a proper field strip? Or how to swap the barrels? Or was it just 'here's the cocking handle, here's the trigger, don't blow your foot off?'"

"Kinda," Dylan admitted. "I didn't even know the barrel comes off; we've only got the one."

"Oh, that's easy," Avery said, and let his rifle fall on its sling. "Here." In one motion, he clamped his left hand on the machine gun's receiver and thumbed the barrel release. At the same time, he rapped the barrel-carrying handle with his right, and the barrel popped loose.

"Hey!" Dylan objected, but it was too late.

"Nothing personal, kid," Avery said by way of apology, and he winged the barrel off into the bushes to their left. He hopped up onto the wagon next to Amy, and Elena snapped the reins. "Can't have you shooting us in the back on our way out!"

The men at the south barrier dove out of the way of the now-galloping horses, and the wagons thundered through the gap unimpeded.

When it became clear none of the Campers had opened fire, and none of them were pursuing, Avery waved for the wagon drivers to slow the horses to a canter. He leaned over the seatback and tapped Elena on the shoulder. "Nicely done back there, glad you caught on."

"Hell, I was as confused as anyone when you ordered everyone aboard. Amy clued me in," the wagon driver said.

"Well done, both of you." He fist-bumped Amy and climbed over the seatback to join Elena. "Now, here's the next bit of trickery..."

Their tracks were as obvious as obvious could be. So long as their pursuers—if there were any—remained persistent, they'd catch up. Thus, a bit of subterfuge was in order.

Dylan, Orange Hat, and the others had been new to the area. Todd had made the trip to Saint Stephen on the coast five years in a row now, and this was the first time anyone had set up barricades. He had no idea how they were feeding themselves, and it was clear they were abusing Josée, whether she was willing to discuss it or not. The whole thing left him very unsettled.

Do unto others, before they do unto you was one of Murphy's laws of combat. It was with that in mind that Avery'd had Elena go past the old Canterbury high school and pull in behind it. The other wagons dutifully followed.

The building had been stripped of useful salvage years ago, but it was still a structurally solid red brick building. They tucked the horses and wagons in a nook behind the building to keep them out of the wind, blanketed the animals against the cold, and got all ten of the people up on the roof. With their white tarps as a windbreak and for camouflage, all ten members of the trip cuddled together in their sleeping bags. It was brisk, but the sleeping bags were the best Woodstock had left.

Avery established a watch schedule and tucked in until midnight—his assigned watch block. It seemed he hadn't hardly closed his eyes when Wei shook him.

"They're here."

Avery came instantly awake and cold adrenaline filled his veins. "How many?"

"All of them, I think. I counted fourteen."

Shit.

"Wake the others."

"Already doing."

Avery wriggled out of his sleeping bag and slipped his feet into his boots. They were *cold*, and he struggled to tie the frozen laces. An involuntary groan escaped his lips as he tried to convince his back and knees to move as they should. He clamped down on it, did his best to ignore the pain, and picked up his rifle.

The Campers, he couldn't think of another term for them, were walking down the road in a... gaggle. They made no attempt at a formation, or tactical movement, or anything else resembling proper military teamwork. Amateurs, like he'd suspected.

"They're ready," Wei whispered.

"Good. Remind them, if this goes hot, no more than one or two shots from the same place, then they slither to a new spot. Ideally, no one shoots anyone."

"You keep saying that."

"And I mean it, every time," Avery said. Then he raised his voice and shouted down at the mob of Campers. "Stop right there!"

To their credit, almost half of them froze in place. Most of the rest looked around stupidly, trying to source the voice. One fool panicked, squeezed the trigger on his weapon, and the stillness of the night air was rent by the *boom* of a shotgun. As little as these men knew about military ops, it seemed they at least knew the rules for a safe hunt, because the blast failed to hit anyone. "Shit! Sorry, sorry!" the man shouted.

"Tabarnac!" another cursed in Quebecois. *"Idiot!"*

"If you're quite done?" Avery shouted, and the mob stilled. "Who's in charge?"

"I am!" a man shouted.

"It's *dark*, you idiot, wave your hand or something so I can see who I'm shouting to!"

One of the men did so. He wore white, from head to toe, including a white knit cap that Avery suspected was actually a rolled-up balaclava. It looked an awful lot like the one he'd had, once upon a time.

"You Dylan's dad?"

"Who wants to know?"

"Retired Sergeant Avery Todd," he shouted.

"No shit?" the man exclaimed. "Todd? It's Dan Van Der Beer. Retired, warrant, in 2019."

"Get the fuck out!"

"Man, I haven't seen you since you shipped out for Pet in, what was that? 2006?"

Interesting, Todd thought. *I guess we don't talk about Kandahar. Fine, we'll play it your way.*

"Technically, you still haven't, and I'd like to keep it that way, I think, unless you're going to take that murderous little mob of yours home so we can go on our way."

Van Der Beer seemed to think it over. "Fair enough, Todd. We'll go. My boy says you're heading down to the coast for some trade. Maybe we can do some trade on your way back?"

"We'll see. Now, forgive my directness, but kindly fuck off back home, Dan. It's been a long day."

"All right, Todd, no need to be a dick about it. Come on, boys, we're going."

A week later, Avery and Wei loaded one last crate of medicine onto the back of Elena's wagon.

"You look like you've got something to say," Avery said.

"Heh. Yeah. It's been bugging me for a while now. Guess I didn't know how to ask. You never told me you served under that piece of shit."

"You never asked," Todd replied. "And I didn't. We were both of the same generation, more or less. Did battle school together, went to a few courses together. I told off one or two too many prickly NCOs to get recommended for warrant school, while he was always a cock-gobbling yes man. Fuck Dan Van Der Beer. It surprises me not one bit that he's wound up king of his own little camp."

"How are we going to get through their little barricade? They're going to be pissed after last time. And on their guard."

"I'm not sure yet."

They stopped for lunch at a little town that had been called Andersonville. The few residents had been friendly enough on the trip down, and Avery wondered if that was because they didn't have a machine gun. Over spiced fried potatoes, Amy asked "Why don't we just, you know, shoot 'em?"

"You ready to kill them all?" Avery asked right back. "Cuz, make no mistake, if we start shooting, it won't stop until they're all dead. And then what? We didn't see any women with them, save the one, and no kids. You think it's just a bunch of bachelors hanging out? Or do you think it's more likely they're keeping the women and children at home under lock and key?"

"I hadn't looked at it that way," Amy admitted.

"No, and that's because we've kept our little patch of farmland and riverfront from turning into some dystopian shithole. There's enough farmland to keep everyone working and fed, there's moose in the woods and maple syrup in the trees." The whole region around Woodstock was potato country. Once upon a time, it had supplied most of Canada's freezers with French fries, courtesy of the big processing plant just up the road, and potatoes had been a carbohydrate staple for centuries. Maple syrup might have been the cash crop for trade, but it was the potatoes that kept his people from starving.

"Make no mistake, the shitholes are out there, especially where food gets scarce. Consider—what if we wind up shooting all the guys? Do we take the women and children in? That's likely to get bloody as well, don't kid yourself. Do we leave them to die? If they really are being... *kept*, like Mister Van Der Beer thinks he's the hero of some shitty *Handmaid's Tale* fanfic, then the women and children won't know the first thing about survival. Not *real* survival, at the tail end of a Canadian winter, and either way are they really going to want to integrate with the people who slaughtered the men?"

"Even if they're being *kept*?" Amy repeated. She spat the last word with as much distaste as she could manage.

"Of course. Stockholm Syndrome is a thing. However this thing goes..."

"Ideally, no one shoots anyone?" Wei asked.

"Got it in one." Avery groaned as he got to his feet and scrubbed his plate with a handful of fresh white snow. "That C9 is the greatest threat, assuming it works. Obviously, I don't know how much link it's got, but there was enough there to do all of us in. Even just a burst into one of the horses would ruin our day."

"Can we take it out somehow? Like you did with that barrel trick?" Amy asked.

Avery tucked his gear away in his pack and signaled for the rest to hurry up and get back on the road. "Maybe. Maybe this evening we'll have a little shooting competition, see who can hit a target at distance."

"I thought you said you didn't want to shoot anyone?" Amy said, puzzled.

"'Ideally' still leaves a lot of room for flex," Avery said. "Let's go."

The charred ruins of a gas station wound up being their final wait point. It was halfway between the old high school and Van Der Beer's camp. Avery had considered trying to sneak up on the guards and disabling them quietly, but for two problems. One, the crunch of snow under their snowshoes would give away their approach long before he got to hatchet range, and two, that shit only ever happened in old Chuck Norris movies.

It was well past midnight when they made their approach. Avery had traded his rifle for Jaroslav's shotgun, which was more easily concealed beneath a parka. He had a hand axe head-down in an oversized hip pocket, and prisoner-taking supplies in the other. One by one, the other guards fell behind, strung out in a line every couple hundred meters. They wore dark clothes, to better contrast with all the snow and make hand—or whole body—signals viable.

The last three were Avery, Lionel, and Wei. As he had on their initial approach, he opted for the direct route, choosing to walk straight up to the barricade, counting on the darkness to conceal their identities until it was too late for the guard to do anything about it. Two hundred meters shy of the barricade, once it was clearly visible in the distance through a scope, Lionel wordlessly stepped off the road and found a tree to hide behind.

"Remind me why I let you talk me into this?" Wei asked.

"Best chance we get through unharmed, with the loot intact," Avery replied. "Granted, not much of a chance, but it's a chance."

They were just twenty meters from the barricade when Avery saw the first sign of life. Woodsmoke was in the air, and he noticed a small hut he hadn't seen during his mad dash through the last time. Someone inside was stirring as they approached.

"*Allo?*" came the voice. "*Qui est la? Ou vas tu?*" *Who are you? Where are you going?*

"*Montreal?*" Avery replied. He remembered enough of his French to get by with that, at least.

"*Quoi?*" The man was clearly confused—Montreal was a three-week march west of them, on the far side of Maine.

Avery took advantage of his confusion to kick his snowshoes loose and close the last of the distance as the guard zipped up his parka. He stepped out of the hut and froze.

"*Merde!*" the man gasped, and Avery recognized him. It was Orange Hat again.

Avery tackled the man and they both went to the ground. They wrestled, made more difficult by mittens and snow getting everywhere, but he managed to get a forearm over Orange Hat's mouth to muffle his cries for help. The man drove a knee into Avery's gut, and he let out an *oof* with the impact. That gave Orange Hat the chance he needed to roll over, so he was on top of Avery. Then the pressure eased up. Wei had Orange Hat in a rear naked choke and dragged him off. The man flailed, grasped at his throat, and then went limp.

Wei rolled him onto his front as Avery moved in to help. He yanked the man's hat down over his eyes and pulled a sock from his parka's pocket to use as a gag. It only took a few seconds for the man to regain consciousness. "Mmph! *Mmmph!*"

Avery pulled the hatchet from his pocket and rolled the hat up just enough for the man to see. "Shut it. You have two options. One, you stay here, all quiet like, while we pass through. Two, I open your throat to the wind and your friends find you frozen in the morning. Live or die, it's your choice."

"Mm hmm," the man whimpered, and shifted so he was face-down in the snow.

"Signal the others," Avery said, and Wei got up to wave down the line at Lionel. Avery got busy with a bit of twine he'd secured in Saint Stephen. It was thin twine, the kind you'd use to tie up a pot roast, so it cut deep into the man's wrists as he bound them together. The moment his hands were secured, Avery rolled him into a seated position. "I'm going to stand you up and we're going to go down the road a bit, so you're out of the way. Don't make me kill you."

He frogmarched Orange Hat past the barricade, back down the road to a driveway. The snow was surprisingly hard packed, and he found he could manage without his snowshoes at all. "Sit."

The man sat.

It took a few minutes for the 'clear' signal to make its way down the line and confirmation to come back, but it seemed to work. Amy collected Lionel from his hide, and they joined Avery with his prisoner.

"The wagons are on their way," she said.

"Good. I'm getting too old for this bullshit... getting in scraps, rolling around in the snow," Avery complained. "Once

Kyle is here, we'll go clear the second barrier, and then we're through. We'll leave him here, he'll be fine."

One by one, the other guards caught up. Avery unloaded Jaroslav's shotgun, to make a better first impression, and made sure the tube mag was topped up. He could just barely see the first of the wagons trundling into view. "All right. No wasted time here. Jaroslav, you and Amy watch the prisoner. If he gets squirrely... stop him. Lionel, cover us from this barricade. Kyle, Wei, you're with me. Move."

The barricade at the other end had a hut as well. It glowed orange from another wood stove inside, and the entryway at the doorway glistened with ice. Avery slowed his approach, put each foot down carefully, and leaned around the doorway where the 'guard' was sleeping.

He racked the shotgun, loud and aggressive.

"Huh? Wha? Shit!" Dylan cursed. He surged to his feet, took one step out the hut, and his feet went out from under him. He fell in a heap, his slung rifle trapped beneath him. Avery planted a knee on his chest and pointed the shotgun aside.

"They say a shotgun racking is the second scariest sound there is," Avery said. He kept his voice low, but hard. "That true?"

"Ohhh no, not you again!"

"Me again. Keep your mouth shut and we'll be on our way."

"Man, my dad's gonna be so pissed. Like, he was pissed last time, but this time he's gonna be *really* mad."

"What part of 'keep your mouth shut' was unclear? Do you need a sock, too?"

"No, sir."

Kyle and Wei moved the barricade out of the way. For a few minutes, the only sound was the gusting wind, the crackle of the wood stove in the hut, and Dylan's breathing. To Avery's ear, it sounded like he was on the verge of panic. Then the soft crunch of the horses' hooves in the snow grew audible, and the first wagon loomed out of the darkness. Michael was in the lead and drove by without saying a word, just a quick wave of thanks.

"I'm so fucked," Dylan whispered.

"Right, you get the sock, too," Avery said, and he reached back into his parka for another gag.

"No, please," Dylan whispered. "You don't know what he's like. *He'll kill me,* seriously. Not joking."

Avery paused, sock in hand. "Okay, start talking, but keep your voice low. Is that hyperbole or will he actually murder his own son?"

"Hyper-what? Is that like exaggerating? Because I'm not. He will kill me. He said so, after the last shitshow. Took me like, three hours of searching to find that barrel and now he doesn't trust anyone else with the gun at all. Said I should have just opened up with the belt-fed, killed you guys, captured the women, and kept all the syrup. Said if I fucked up again, he'd banish me, even if it's minus twenty out."

"Captured the women, huh? It's like that, is it?"

"Yeah, well... you saw Josée, right?"

"I did. She said it was fine, she wanted nothing to do with us."

"She's Marcel's wife. Marcel's the guy in the orange hat."

"She seems a bit young for him."

"Right? But that's how Dad is. He arranges these marriages, promises the older guys they'll get these younger women if they back him. The girls don't get a say. Dad's got like, three girls of his own, they're barely older than me. Dad's already lined up Josée's younger sister for me when I get older, but she's only like, thirteen. It's fucked up."

The second wagon rolled past with Summer and Jaroslav on the back. Jaroslav flashed Avery a quick thumbs-up, and then they were through the barricade, too.

"How did you guys come to be here? Avery asked. "You weren't here last winter."

"We were just outside Fredericton, up on Keswick Ridge. Dad and some of the other guys were... hell... yeah, they were raiding some of the other towns nearby. Picked a fight with a group of vets. The wrong guys to fuck with. Most of Dad's buddies got whacked and we had to run."

The third wagon approached.

"So what do you want, kid? This sounds an awful lot like a plea for help. But the way I have it figured, we start killing, everyone dies. I have worked *very* hard not to kill anyone this trip."

"Take me with you?" the kid asked. "I'm dead, no matter what now."

"*What the fuck is going on out here?*"

Van Der Beer's voice bellowed through the trees, and then the silence was shattered by a burst of machine gun fire. Elena's horses whinnied in panic and broke into a gallop. The wagon raced past, moving too quick for Avery, Wei, or Kyle to hop on. Avery couldn't even tell if Lionel or Amy were on board. Instead, he rolled down into the ditch, then scrambled a few feet into the treeline to disappear. He lost sight of Kyle and Wei.

"*Who the fuck is on duty? Why are there wagons rolling through my camp? Dylan? What the hell is going on?*"

"I'm here, sir," Dylan called meekly. He'd gotten to his feet and stood unsteadily in the middle of the road.

Van Der Beer stormed up to him, half dressed in flannel pajama pants and a blue parka that hung to his knees. Without waiting for an explanation, he slugged Dylan in the jaw. The young man fell to the ground. "Explain yourself! Who was that?"

"Mmmph!" Orange Hat Marcel shouted through his gag from behind them. Van Der Beer swore again, stomped over to him, and pulled out the gag.

"Eet was dat soldier you knew," he said. "Dey who came t'rough a week ago, wit' de syrup."

"And you let them *go*?" Van Der Beer shouted.

"No," Dylan whimpered. "He surprised me."

"How?" the older man yelled. "How could he have *surprised* you?"

"I don't know, ask *him*!" Dylan shouted back, and he stood back up. He pointed at Marcel, whose hands were still bound behind his back. "*He* was watching the south gate! I was just sitting in the hut when the older guy was like, right there! Racked a shotgun in my face and told me to shut up!"

"*Not good enough!*" his father raged. He turned to Marcel next. "I suppose he jumped you, too?"

"*Oui*," Marcel admitted, and his shoulders slumped. "'E t'reatened to kill me wit' an axe if I talk'."

Van Der Beer poked Marcel in the chest, and the man stumbled backwards. He lost his balance and fell, without his arms to catch him. "What did I tell you? He's a punk, all show, no go! You didn't call his bluff? What's wrong with you?"

"Easier say den done," Marcel growled. "You try it next time, when 'e's got an axe a few inch' from your face."

Others of the camp were coming out from their homes

now; the machine gun burst had apparently awoken the whole camp. "Yeah, *Dad*," Dylan snarked, in that snide tone that kids use to drive their parents nuts. "When was the last time *you* even took an overnight guard duty? It's been pretty fucking cold out here. *We've* all been pulling nights, in minus ten, minus twenty, while you've been curled up with Victoria, and Nicole, and Annie-Claire! Must be nice!"

"Don't you take that kind of tone with me, boy," Van Der Beer bellowed. "I brought you into this world, and I sure as hell can take you out of it."

"Oh, shut the fuck up, Daniel," Avery said. He had the shotgun leveled, and those who'd gathered around Van Der Beer all took several steps back. "You're not impressing anyone."

The camp leader sputtered with impotent fury but raised his hands. Todd had him dead -to rights from barely fifteen meters away; at that distance the buckshot would pepper his whole torso.

Todd stepped down into the ditch, then climbed one-handed up the other side onto the roadway, keeping the barrel pointed at Van Der Beer. "A punk, am I? All show no go? Go fuck yourself, *Warrant.* I seem to recall a time where your ass got ambushed outside Kandahar delivering bottled water. You hid as your driver did what fighting he could without support. Who was first on scene to push the Taliban back, Daniel?"

"You were," Van Der Beer replied sullenly.

"Not just me. No, I was merely one sergeant in a whole platoon. What unit was that, Daniel?"

"The... The Spec Ops guys."

"The Canadian Special Operations Regiment! You got that right. Now, I've got sweet fuck all I need to prove to you or any of your little goon squad here. Their opinion of me means squat. But it seems to me maybe you've been playing up your little role in the war on terror a bit? Huh? Telling war stories about how much of a badass you are? And look, you managed to steal a fucking light machine gun from the armouries right when the wheels came off the big green machine? Real fucking heroic."

The furtive looks around the group told Avery he'd guessed right.

"You stolen valour goatfucker," Avery breathed. "You're a disgrace. And you've had all these guys doing your bidding, keeping you safe and warm and fed, while you're collecting 'wives' and handing out spares like they're Pokémon?"

Wei emerged from the shadows on the other side of the road. He pointed to Kyle, now on the far side of the barricade. "We gotta go."

Dylan unshouldered his shotgun—an old single-shot break-action twelve gauge—and pointed it at his father. "Go ahead, I'll cover you."

Avery nodded his thanks and turned to go. He was well past the barrier and heading down the off-ramp when he heard Van Der Beer shout something indistinct—and then a shotgun boomed.

Avery swore and turned to go back. Wei and Kyle followed. To his surprise, Lionel, Amy, and Summer had dismounted and were jogging back to them, too. On the other side of the barricade, Dylan stood over Van Der Beer's body. The rest of the campers had taken a few steps back. No one said anything.

"He didn't think I'd do it," Dylan whispered, and gestured with the empty shotgun at the LMG, where it had fallen next to his father's body. "He was going to shoot me. You said you've got farms and food up where you are. Take us with you?"

Avery thought for a moment, then he looked to the rest of his guards. Wei shook his head. Amy and Summer both nodded. Lionel shrugged. Avery looked back.

"Get everyone out here, in their cold weather gear. Women, kids, any of the men who somehow slept through machine gun fire, everyone."

It took more than a few minutes, but eventually everyone stood in a rough semi-circle around Van Der Beer's body. Avery field-stripped the machine gun and pulled its bolt. He held it in his hand for a moment, as if weighing it, and then threw the little black hunk of metal into the forest.

"One time offer," he began. "We're heading home. You can join us, but there are a few conditions. Daniel, here, was bartering women around like they were property, to be traded and sold. *Fucking unacceptable*, people. Men, if the woman—or women—in your house were sold, kidnapped, or in any way forced to be there, *I will find out*. They'll never find your body. If that's you... walk away. For that matter, try to coerce 'your' woman to leave with you and you'll join Mister Van Der Beer in hell right now. Does anyone doubt me on that?"

No one moved.

"Good. There are wagons just down the road. Follow the tracks, you can't miss 'em. If there's room aboard, hop on, ladies first. We leave in ten minutes."

It was with some relief that most of the women present broke from the crowd immediately. Avery counted nineteen, including some who were clearly in their early teens, which twisted at his guts, while also reassuring him that he was doing the right thing.

Dylan was the only male to cross the barricade. Amy and Summer went to the only two women who'd remained and spoke to them quietly. One of them was Josée.

The woman in the cardboard boots looked long and hard at Marcel, in his orange hunting toque, before she unleashed a torrent of hate *en francais*. The words meant nothing to Avery, but the meaning was clear. Marcel had the decency to look ashamed. Lionel's eyebrows rose, impressed by the rant. Then she ran down the off ramp to join the others.

As Avery and his team made their way down to follow them, Wei spoke. "You know they're going to be a problem. They're armed, their bossman is dead, and you've just stolen 'their' women away? They're gonna hate you something fierce."

"Of course," Avery said. "But one thing at a time. We'll get our new people home, get them established. We'll have to increase our own guard rotation, just in case, and wait for the snows to melt."

"And then?" Amy asked.

"And then... The innocents are safe, and we do unto others before they do unto us. Roll out."

About the author:

Jamie Ibson is from the frozen wastelands of Canuckistan, where moose, bears, and geese battle for domination among the hockey rinks, igloos, and Tim Hortons. After joining the Canadian army reserves in high school, he spent half of 2001 in Bosnia as a peacekeeper and came home shortly after 9/11 with a deep sense of foreboding. After graduating college, he landed a job in law enforcement and was posted to the left coast from 2007 to 2021. He retired from law enforcement in early 2021 and moved clear across the country to write full time in the Maritimes.

Jamie's website can be found at https://ibsonwrites.ca, where he has free short stories available for download. He is also on Facebook and runs The Frozen Hoser's Winter Wasteland on Discord.

He is married to the lovely Michelle, and they have cats.

Green Leaf: Civil War

H David Blalock

Foreword

It had been four years since the Chinese tried and failed to invade Panama in an effort to control the Canal. In retaliation, hundreds of Sino-Panamanian citizens and businesses were seized by the government, many naturalized Chinese-born Panamanians and their families were executed, and a general tacit understanding set in that the Panama Defense Force could persecute Asians in general.

Meanwhile, the country slowly reverted to what it had been before the Americans pushed Columbia back to its present border and helped create the independent Republic: an agricultural state run by the wealthiest farmers.

The Collapse destroyed more than the global economy. It killed hope for a better life for many. Life, in many ways, had become simpler, but with that simplicity had come challenges previously thought long defeated. Foremost of those challenges was feeding and controlling a population of millions, most of whom had no survival skills at all. There had already been food riots in the larger cities and towns. Famine and disease were familiar companions now, the death toll growing every day. The military guarded what farms and grocery supplies weathered the unrest. An outbreak of cholera decimated large portions of Panama City, Colón, and other major towns. In spite of that, people still fled in droves to major population hubs looking for refuge from sickness, hunger, and bandits.

The cities fell into decay even as people swarmed to them for help. Panama had never been what was termed a "first-world country." It had to import most of its oil and foodstuffs from overseas. Motor vehicles became reserved for the military and VIPs, with the rest of the population having to settle for horseback. Some enterprising souls sent divers into Panama City bay to strip the sunken Chinese fleet of whatever could be found. Most of that was confiscated by the military as soon as the salvage crews were discovered by city patrols. The new government set up its own printing press to issue native currency, as the US had previously printed the Balboa. The government also set up programs to clear the debris from Panama Bay and dredge the remains of the Centennial Bridge from the Canal. The purpose, the government told the populace, was to enable the reopening of trade and to bring in more goods. The real purpose was to keep the people busy, since everyone in the government understood the Collapse had all but wiped out international travel and trade.

But the residual effect of the Chinese invasion itself had not yet faded.

- 1 -

December 15, 2039
Cementerio Iglesia Christiana Evangelista
Las Cañas, Bocas del Toro Province, Panama

"Your uncle was a good friend and a great man."

Colonel Luis Maribo, second in command to General Ricardo Gomez of the 3rd Infantry, nicknamed the *Diablos Rojos*, replaced his uniform cap as he walked. His attaché, an attractive brunette named Captain Maria Barona, strode beside him on his right while Javier Aparicio, dressed in typical funeral white and to whom he addressed his comment, paced his left.

"*Gracias, Coronel*," Aparicio said. He had to lengthen his own stride a little to stay abreast of Maribo because of the nearly one foot difference in their height. "*Tio* spoke very highly of you as well."

They stopped as they reached Maribo's car.

"We owe him much, Javier. Without his help capturing the Centennial Bridge, Panama would have been lost to the Chinese invaders," he said.

Barona opened the car door as Maribo gazed out over the little cemetery. What had only a few years ago been virgin forest was cleared to accommodate the result of years of starvation and disease brought on by the Collapse and the aftermath of the Chinese invasion. With the Canal blocked, what little trade and import had survived the global disaster dried up. The interior villages were reverting to self-sufficiency, but it was hard and the jungle was unforgiving.

"A shame we could not send him back to America for burial," he said.

Aparicio turned to look as well. "He often came here after *Tia* died. I think he will rest well beside her."

Maribo nodded, sighing. "We have lost too many friends these last two years."

"*Si*," Aparicio replied. "I heard of *General* Morena's passing last month. A great national hero."

"So he was," Maribo agreed. "A good man who did his duty though well-advanced in years."

"I would have liked to have met him."

Maribo smiled. "He would have liked you, I am sure." He shook Aparicio's hand. "*Adios*. Stay well and say hello to everyone in Punta Róbalo for me."

"*Lo hare, Coronel. Dios le bendiga.*"

As they drove away, Barona handed him the dispatch he'd refused to read before the funeral. He had a feeling he knew what was in it and wanted to put off knowing for sure as long as possible, as if that might change its content. He stared at it without reading, stretching the moment as long as he could.

"Luis?" Barona said.

"Yes, yes, I know." He focused on the message. "It is as I feared. Gomez has been promoted to *General de Fuerzas*." He tossed the dispatch into the floorboard with a curse. His service with Gomez during the Chinese invasion had convinced him the man had ambitions far beyond that of mere military power. "President Menendez is a fool."

"In his defense, he had little choice," Barona said.

Maribo grunted. "Politicians," he said.

"What else could he do?" Barona went on as the car swung onto *Ruta Rambála*, the main highway.

"I know. But all he has done is bought a little time."

She grimaced. "I understand. I was at Chilibre, too. I remember."

Chilibre. Maribo grimaced at the memory of the near debacle against the Chinese remnants who had tried to wage unconventional war against the new Panamanian government after the failure of the initial invasion. Gomez had sent him with a tiny force against an unknown number of Chinese in the very headquarters of the enemy. If not for the intervention of General Morena, he and his entire group would undoubtedly have been obliterated.

They rode on in silence for a while. The landscape around them had never been developed beyond the occasional farm and now even some of those were reverting to nature as the farmers, driven by the death of foreign markets, fled to the cities looking for work. They passed an ox-drawn cart heading in the opposite direction. The driver ignored them, nodding in his seat. Time was no longer the master of humanity; clocks had lost their hold. Now it was simple survival that held the main concern.

"Do you think you are a target?" Barona asked at last.

Maribo thought about that. "Gomez has a long memory and he has *Los Matadores* behind him. Four years of recruiting has made them that much more formidable."

"I do not think he likes that name for his men," Barona said.

He didn't answer. He was remembering Gomez and his Red Devil detachment's push to recapture Panama City from the Chinese. How many innocent countrymen had been caught in the crossfire of that rush from Penonomé after the invaders' defeat there in the west? It was then the unit had earned its name of *Matadores Rojos*, Red Killers. Town after town along the way had fallen to the merciless advance. In its wake, the people of La Chorrerra, Arraijan, and countless tiny settlements and farms had not dared leave their homes for hours or even days after the Red Devils' assault. Back then, the Devils had numbered only a few hundred. Now, it topped 2,000. President Menendez was right to be worried.

He had to do something, anything, just in case his worst fears should come to pass. One thing he had learned, it was better to be prepared than surprised.

They stopped at the checkpoint outside the remains of the gas station at the corner of *Ruta Rambála* and Highway 10. The two Panama Defense Force guards saluted as he exited the car.

"I need to talk to the 5th Headquarters in Colón," he told them.

"Right away, *Coronel.*"

Barona came up beside him. "Faron?"

Maribo nodded. "He answered the call to Chilibre from Morena. We should find out how he feels about Gomez."

"And whether he might defend the president against a possible coup?"

"Maria," he said with a smile, "you must be psychic."

El Luvital village
Darien Province
60 miles east of Panama City

"They took my store and killed my son!" Cho Fu Lee paced, angry, from one wall of the little hut to the other. "They will pay!"

The others in the hut, four men and a woman, watched him in silence. Two were Chinese immigrants and the other three looked Latin but had Chinese parents.

"It has been four years, Cho," said the oldest of the five, a grey-haired Latino named Tonio Chan. "The Chinese are long gone. The PDF grow stronger by the day."

"I say we go to Columbia," said another of the Latinos, Georgio Sung. "If we stay here, we will be arrested, maybe killed. The PDF has not secured the Darien yet."

"No," Cho snapped. "I came here fifteen years ago with nothing but the clothes on my back to escape China and make a new life. I have to defend what I have built here." He paused, glaring at the others. "Have you not lost enough already?"

"The wise man knows his own limits," pointed out the middle-aged Chinese named Lei Gong. A livid scar ran along his right forearm. "You saw how the *Matadores*…"

"*Hunzhang!*" Cho barked. "I have not forgotten, nor should you!"

"We have not," said Lee Ming, the Chinese woman beside him. "But what chance have we?"

Cho began pacing again. "There must be a way," he mumbled.

Silence settled over the room, broken only by the click of Cho's heels against the floor.

"The Chinese commander at Chilibre seemed to think he could weaken the PDF with raids and sabotage," Chan observed.

"But he had regular troops to back him up," Gong argued,

shaking his head. "We have no such advantage."

"And he failed, even so," Sung added.

Cho stopped. He looked at Chan and smiled. "He failed, yes. But why?"

They glanced at each other but no one answered.

"Because he concentrated his forces in one place," Cho said. "He depended too much on his Chinese troops."

"So?" Lei Gong asked.

"If he had decentralized his force, made it a true guerrilla effort..."

"Then the PDF could not have beaten him? Is that what you mean?"

"Exactly!" Cho now began pacing, excited and animated as he spoke. "If we want to take back our own, we have to act now. The longer we wait, the harder it will be."

"We are only six against an army," Chan complained.

"So we must find more," Cho said.

"How?" Lei Ming asked.

"We pick a target, one we know we can take, and use that victory to recruit others. We have weapons left behind by the invaders hidden at Sung's farm."

The others looked doubtful.

"Exactly what target do you intend to strike?" Sung asked.

Cho grinned. "I have an idea."

PDF Military Checkpoint
Ruta Rambála and Highway 10

"This is *Coronel* Faron."

"*Coronel*, I think you have heard of *General* Gomez's promotion," Maribo said.

"I have."

"What is your opinion of *General* Gomez?"

There was silence on the other end of the line. Maribo frowned. Had he made a mistake? José Faron was commander of the Colón regiment, located on the other end of the Canal from Panama City, after all. He might not even consider the affairs in the capitol relevant now that the Collapse and invasion had changed thing so drastically.

"Why do you ask?" Faron said.

Maribo steeled himself. He realized the next few words could seal his fate.

"I served under Gomez," he began. "I saw how he commanded the 3rd in its drive from Penonomé. I saw his disregard for his troops. He was so focused on reaching the capitol, I'm convinced he would have sacrificed every man." He took a breath, then made the statement that would drive it home. "I do not believe he holds the country's interests over his own."

It was done. Now it was up to Faron. Maribo licked his lips and stifled a nervous cough. He throat, suddenly dry, felt hollow.

"I see," Faron said slowly. A few seconds ticked by. Maribo felt the beginnings of dread. If Faron threw in with Gomez…

"I am concerned Gomez may have certain ambitions," Maribo added. "Ambitions that may further destabilize the new government."

"I understand the concern, *Coronel*," Faron said. "I wondered about his orders to send such a small force against the Chinese in Chilibre."

Hope rose in Maribo. He refrained from interrupting the other man's train of thought. It seemed to be headed in the right direction. A wrong word could derail it.

"What exactly do you propose?" Faron asked. "You should know, I am a patriot. I will not deny legitimate orders."

"Nor am I asking you to," Maribo said. "I merely ask that you watch his actions carefully and consider whether they serve Panama best."

"Of course. My country can always depend on me."

"Then I believe we are in agreement."

"We are, *Coronel*."

"I will be in touch," Maribo said.

"I look forward to your call, *amigo*."

Maribo hung up the phone with a sigh of relief. He looked at Barona. "I believe Faron is with us."

She smiled. "Good news."

He nodded. "It is a beginning."

December 19
8:00 AM
Panama City, Panama

The promotion ceremony for Gomez began with a parade of Red Devils through the streets of Panama City. Gomez, uniform covered in bright medals and ribbons he'd won in previous engagements against the Americans and Chinese, strode with head high at the forefront of the troops. His 3rd Infantry, nicknamed *Los Diablos Rojos* by the military and *Los Matadores Rojos* by the people, strutted in ranks, eyes ahead and weapons carried ready. Curious onlookers lined Avenida Balboa as the procession made its way to the newly rebuilt Presidential Palace. A grandstand had been erected in front of the building. President Menendez, his cabinet, advisors, and military commanders stood as Gomez and his men marched to stop before them.

The strains of *Himno Istmeño*, the Panamanian national anthem, blasted from loudspeakers. Gomez scanned the dignitaries, gauging their worthiness. Panama needed strong leadership, men of action and decision. The time for diplomacies and compromise was past. With The Collapse, it was every country for itself. The hell with deals. Panama would dominate the weak socialist governments of its neighbors, governments that crumbled of their own corruption within two years of the failed Chinese invasion.

And at the helm of the newly expanded Panama would be one General Ricardo Gomez Enterrez, savior of Central America.

Perhaps even further...

Maribo watched Gomez glare at the assembly and every doubt he might have entertained evaporated. He wondered if Menendez caught the way the man stood, the steel and ambition in his demeanor. It was obvious to Maribo that Gomez had plans over and above this promotion, but could anyone else, anyone who had not seen him in combat, perceive that single-mindedness Gomez exuded?

The ceremony continued but Maribo barely heard the speeches and presentation. The memories of the screams of the wounded and dying, the thunder of the Red Devil guns, the sight of the bodies crushed under Gomez's advance, blocked out most of the farcical celebration. The only clear image he caught from the ceremony was Gomez turning to the crowd, now as supreme commander of the Panama Defense Forces, his face a mix of pride with more than a glint of greed.

7:30 PM

"I asked you to meet me here because I cannot be sure the office is not bugged," Maribo said.

"I understand, Luis," Barona replied.

They sat on the seawall facing Panama Bay in the Capitol. As a boy, Maribo watched ships out there as they waited to transit the Canal on their way to mysterious destinations in the Caribbean or even further away. Often, he had fantasized being on one of those ships traveling to exotic places: the islands dotting the Atlantic, the coasts of America, even Africa and Europe. He smiled sadly at the memories. As things were, they could be no more than dreams now.

"Luis?"

Maribo shook himself and looked at her. "Sorry, I was just thinking."

She nodded. They had become close as the years went by. Assigned as his attaché shortly after the Chinese defeat, Captain Barona was more than just that now. She was his confidant, his right arm, his friend. He trusted her... and maybe felt more than trust.

"What did you want to talk about?" she asked.

He gazed back out to sea. The remains of the sunken Chinese fleet still broke the oily surface of the Bay. Seawater was beginning to eat away at the visible superstructures. Bodies, or parts of them, still sometimes washed ashore. He tried not to think about that and turned his attention to the matter at hand.

"We need to prepare for what Gomez is planning," he said. "Whatever that may be."

"*Si*," she said. "What do you want me to do?"

"Gomez's Red Devil battalion forms the heart of his forces," Maribo went on. "But only those who fought alongside him against the Chinese are loyal to him personally. We need to measure the loyalty of the rest of the 3rd. We must do this carefully, without raising suspicion."

"I can access the records of the new recruits," she suggested.

"That would be a start. I know most came to the city to escape the chaos of the interior and have very little military training."

"Have you heard anything from Faron?"

Maribo shook his head. "I think it best not to pressure

him too much. Colón has its own problems right now."

"*Bien, pues.*"

"Before I approach him again, I want to have some solid evidence against Gomez."

"*Claro.* Until we know his plan, we have only suspicions."

"Which is not enough," he said.

She stood. "I will get started right away."

He took her hand as she turned. "*Espere*, Maria."

She tilted her head at him. The sea breeze rustled her hair across her face and back. He felt his heart flutter and wondered at that. He'd never considered himself a romantic. Had the hardships of the last few years softened him? Perhaps. All he knew was there was something he wanted more than anything right then.

"Sit with me for a while longer?" he asked.

She smiled. "Of course, Luis."

December 21
3:32 PM
PDF Military Checkpoint
Torti, Panama Province
Intersection of Pan-American Highway and
Corredor Sur, Autopista Panama-La Chorrera
48 miles east of Panama City

Explosions shook the buildings around the checkpoint, sending glass and concrete high into the air. The two PDF guards died instantly. People scattered for cover as Cho and his group fired at the PDF detail emerging from their ready area station, most of them struggling to discern the enemy from the fleeing civilians. The attackers cut them down before they could get off a single shot.

Like most skirmishes, it was all over in minutes. Cho personally delivered the *coup de grace* to any wounded survivors.

"*Shènglì!*" He grinned. "And this is just the beginning!"

"We should go," Chan said, casting his eyes around for more enemy. "If any of them radioed the alarm…"

Cho laughed. "I hope they did."

Chan shook his head. Sung drew up beside him. "What now?"

"Strip the bodies and take their weapons," Cho ordered. "Look for more in the station. Take whatever you can carry."

"Why strip the bodies?" Chan asked.

"The uniforms," Cho answered. "We'll be more successful creating confusion in the PDF ranks if they think their own are rebelling."

People began peering at them from cover now that the shooting had ceased. Cho waved at them.

"The army took your lives from you," he shouted. "They didn't care who they killed or what they destroyed. We are going to take back what is ours! Join us now, for the sake of your children, your women, before they take more!"

Several young men stepped forward, many showing signs of recent mistreatment and new scars.

Cho smiled.

December 22
11:00 AM
Panama Defense Force Central Command
Panama City, Panama
Main Conference Room

The atmosphere in the room was tense and thick with dark promise. The government's highest officers sat around the great conference table, watching nervously as the two most powerful men in Panama squared off. President Menendez, bespectacled and balding, looked small standing against the barrel-chested, salt and pepper gray-maned and battle scarred General Gomez.

"You overstepped your authority, *General*. Only the government can approve martial law."

Gomez smirked. "You gave me authority for the disposition of troops when you promoted me."

"You are still answerable to me," the president said.

"Of course," Gomez replied with a slight bow.

"And I order you to stand down your troops in the city immediately!"

Gomez crossed his arms. "The security of the nation is critical," he said. "There are still insurgents to deal with."

"They will be, but on *my* order, not *yours*!"

The general looked around at the assembled company. "*Caballeros*, who among you doubts my patriotism? It was my men who recaptured Panama City from the rebels after the Chinese fled. It was my men who pacified the country, saved it from chaos." He looked back at Menendez. "Isn't that why I was put in command?"

The president lapsed into glum silence.

"I love this country," Gomez continued. "Too long have we ignored the needs of our people and allowed foreigners to bleed our beloved nation dry. First it was the Americans until Torrijos forced them to return our Canal. But they invaded again, claiming it was because of Noriega, but it was really to weaken our defenses. If not for their commitment in the Middle East, they would have come back to reclaim the Canal and again put us under their boot."

"They *did* help us against the Chinese," Maribo put in.

Gomez glowered at him. "You were there, *Coronel*. You saw what their bombers did to the city."

"They destroyed the Chinese fleet," Maribo countered.

"And made the Bay impassable!" Gomez snapped. "Most of our fishing fleet was sunk and the city made ruin!"

Maribo settled back in his seat and crossed his arms.

Gomez rounded on the others. "America is not our friend. China is not our friend. Panama is on her own," he said.

"Costa Rica..." Menendez began.

"...must see to itself, as must we," Gomez interrupted. He leaned forward on the conference table. "*Caballeros*, I appeal to your sense of duty. Panama must come first!"

There was a general murmur of agreement.

Gomez straightened. "I ask for emergency powers to pacify any insurgency to insure the safety and well-being of our people."

Menendez shot up. "Your request is refused!" he barked.

Gomez looked at him, one eyebrow raised. "With respect, *Señor Presidente*, this is still a democracy." He turned to face the table. "I call for a vote."

3:47 PM
Panama Defense Force Central Command
Office of General de Fuerzas

"Reports are coming in of attacks on checkpoints between Tocumen and the Darien, *señor*."

General Gomez bolted up from behind his desk, sending the other men in the room back a step.

"*¡Malditos Chinos!*" Gomez growled. "They think they can

beat my men? Order all Chinese arrested. I want five Chinese executed for every Panamanian killed by these cursed insurgents. This *mierda* will stop if we have to wipe out every Asian in this country!"

Martinez saluted and scurried out to relay the order.

"*Señor*," Abilio Duarte, military advisor for Darien Province, began, "that seems a bit counterproductive."

Gomez glowered at him. "Are you questioning my orders?"

Duarte swallowed. "No, *señor*, but might it drive more to the insurgents for protection?"

"There can be no protection from our patriots and loyal countrymen," Gomez countered. "Post a bounty of 500 Balboas for information leading to the arrest and capture of any Chinese." He set his jaw. "The invaders were wiped out. Their collaborators will meet the same fate."

4:35 PM
Panama Defense Force Central Command
Office of the Commander, 1st Regiment

Maribo walked into his office to find several PDF sporting the Red Devil insignia waiting for him. Barona stood by them, face carefully neutral.

The ranking officer approached. "You will come with us, *Coronel*," the man said. "*General* Gomez wants to see you."

A chill went through him. The soldier motioned with his weapon he should start walking. Maribo held up a hand and preceded the guards to Gomez's office.

The room had been returned to the opulence Gomez entertained before his exile to the western city of David's *Commandancia Oeste* after Colonel Morena's promotion to *General de Fuerzas*. There had never been much love between Gomez and Morena even during the Chinese invasion. The old man's promotion had been a ploy by Menendez to isolate Gomez from national office, but Morena's passing left the president no choice but to raise Gomez, the next highest ranking officer, to the post.

Maribo knew Gomez was the type who thirsted for power and held grudges, nurturing them as a doting mother would a child. He suspected Gomez disliked him personally, but Maribo had never given the man reason for grudge. At least, not that he knew of.

Gomez looked him up and down from behind the massive desk dominating the room. Maribo saluted.

"*Coronel* Maribo, reporting as requested, *señor*."

Gomez acknowledged the salute and waved the guards out. He peered at Maribo for a moment as they left.

"Take a seat," Gomez said.

Maribo sat in one of the three chairs facing the desk, back straight.

"Relax, Maribo," the general said. "I just want to talk."

He settled back into the chair slowly. Gomez grinned at his discomfort.

"You had some interesting thoughts in the meeting with the president earlier," Gomez began. "I would like to know what objections, if any, you might have to a campaign to unite our forces against foreign aggression."

Maribo frowned. "Foreign aggression?"

The general leaned forward. "There are reports of Chinese insurgents attacking military targets. Have you received any such information?"

"No, *General*."

Gomez eyed him carefully. Maribo stared back. He didn't know what Gomez was expecting him to say. Did he want a vow of loyalty? A pronouncement of fealty to the nation's defense? Or was he probing for something else?

At last, Gomez leaned back, scowling. "I see." He picked up an envelope from a pile of similar correspondence and tossed it to Maribo. "Your orders. You are to take over *Commandancia Oeste*. Pacify all insurgency by any means necessary. Report any and all progress directly to me. *¿Entendido?*"

"*Sí, señor.*"

"Dismissed."

Maribo stood, tucked the orders under his arm, saluted, and left. He could feel Gomez's eyes on him with every step.

Barona nearly hugged him as he walked back into his office.

"Thank God," she said. "I feared the worst when the Red Devils showed up."

Maribo slammed the envelope on his desk. "It's almost that bad," he said. "I've been ordered to take over at David."

She blinked. "The *Commandancia*?"

He nodded.

"Well," she said slowly, "it *is* a kind of promotion."

Maribo walked to the window looking out over the Bay. "More like an exile," he said. "I won't be able to stay abreast of Gomez's plans. Here, I could be the one dissenting voice at the table, and he will need unanimous agreement for whatever he is planning, I am sure."

She picked up the envelope and opened it to scan the document. "He *has* given you free reign of the west."

He turned to look at her. "The western forces are green, untested in combat. All the veterans are here or in Colón. I am being neutralized as a threat."

"Perhaps," she agreed. "But there is Faron and the 5th."

He grimaced. "Yes, and I am sure Gomez is taking steps to counter that possibility as well."

She went silent as Maribo sank into his desk chair.

"Gomez is no fool," he said. "He probably spent the last four years plotting." He clenched his fist. "The man must be stopped."

December 23
9:02 AM
Commandancia Oeste Headquarters
San Jose de David, Chiriqui Province
275 miles west of Panama City

Maribo and Barona arrived to find the headquarters quiet. Only a few soldiers manned the base, all obviously post-invasion recruits in ill-fitting uniforms. They returned the hesitant salutes thrown toward them and made their way to the commander's office. A man wearing captain's rank stood behind the desk in the back of the room as they entered.

"*Capitan Fernando Rivera a sus ordenes*, General Maribo," he said, saluting.

"As you were, Rivera. And it is still *Coronel* Maribo."

"*Lo siento, señor*," the captain said, stepping around the desk to allow Maribo his seat. "We were told to expect a general."

Maribo grinned. "Disappointed?"

"I... Of course not, *señor*."

Maribo shuffled the paperwork covering the desk. "What is all this?"

"Recruitment reports, logistics requests, manning figures..."

"Are there no other staff here?" Barona asked.

"No, *Capitan*. *El General* Gomez took his staff with him to Panama City."

"Of course he did," Maribo mumbled. "Have all headquarters personnel meet in the main room in two hours."

Rivera saluted and left. Barona watched him go, then looked at Maribo.

"Well," she said. "It looks like we have our work cut out for us."

Maribo nodded. "*Oeste* must be built back from the scraps Gomez has left us."

"There is one good thing about this," she said.

"That is?"

"We need not worry Gomez left any of his own behind. We have a clean slate."

- 2 -

The Darien Province was still mostly rainforest, a wild buffer between the eastern settlements of Panama and the Columbian border. Before The Collapse, it had been safe haven for Columbian rebels and drug runners. Afterward, it reverted to its primeval state, full of wildlife and those native tribes that survived the encroaching developments from the west.

Cho and his growing movement found protection in its depths. The thick undergrowth and network of rivers and streams served them well to hide from PDF pursuers. Cho began setting up camps in its shelter, starting at Yaviza, hardening his acquisitions with new recruits and disrupting supply lines to the northeastern Emberá Province. Within just a few weeks, Cho controlled most of Darien Province as well. The PDF abandoned the province and fell back to Tocumen in Panama Province to form a defensive line against his advance.

General Gomez took the news badly.

January 10, 2040
10:54 AM
Panama Defense Force Central Command
Main Conference Room

"Impossible!" Gomez shouted at the room full of commanders. "A bunch of *maricon* shopkeepers and their *bastardos* taking our land?" He pointed at the men seated before him. "*Cobardes*! Do what must be done! Kill them all! Men, women, children! *¡Todos! ¿Entienden?* Use whatever resources you need, just put down that rebellion!"

The commanders looked at each other nervously.

Finally, Duarte spoke. "*General*, they always run into the *selva* in Darien..."

"So?" Gomez barked.

"Our tanks and vehicles cannot penetrate the heavy brush far enough, *señor*, and it is impossible to spot them from the air under the forest canopy."

"*¡Idiota!* Burn them out!"

"But..."

"I do not care if you have to burn it all the way to Columbia! Burn them out!"

"*Señor...*"

"*¡Vete! ¡Ahora!*"

The commanders scrambled for the door. Gomez cursed them under his breath and turned to Martinez.

"Contact Faron. I want the 5th to push east from Colón. The Chinese *pendejos* should get no refuge to the north. Tell him to execute all Orientals he finds. There will be no escape for any Chinese." He stopped the aide as Martinez turned to leave. "And get Maribo at *Oeste* to outfit a group to Bocas del Toro, just in case the rebels flee to sea and try to land there."

"*Si, señor.*"

Gomez leaned against the conference table. "*Nadie*, nobody will defeat our patriotic forces," he swore. "Panama is for Panamanians or for no one. *Lo juro.*"

3:54 PM
Commandancia Oeste

"*Coronel* Faron for you, *señor*."

Maribo took the phone from Barona. "*¿Si?*"

"*Coronel* Maribo," came the 5th Infantry commander's voice, tense. "I have received orders from command to take my men east into Kuna Yala Province and put down any resistance."

"I have similar orders to Bocas," Maribo replied.

"My orders further state to eliminate any Chinese I find.

No exceptions."

"*What?*"

"It appears *General* Gomez has decided on a pogrom," Faron said. "My orders do not specify exemptions of Panamanian nationals."

"Are you saying anyone who even *looks* Chinese is to be eliminated?" Maribo asked.

"Confirmed. I asked for clarification and was told to execute any and all Asians in appearance to ensure compliance with the order."

"Any...? But many Panamanians now have Chinese or Oriental ancestry. Surely..."

"I was given no authority to differentiate."

Maribo was speechless. Silence settled over the office. Barona, unable to hear Faron's side of the conversation, but disturbed by Maribo's reaction, frowned at him.

"It is my considered opinion, *Coronel*, that *General* Gomez is unfit for command," Faron said.

Maribo's heart skipped a beat.

Faron went on. "I believe we should meet in person and discuss the matter further."

"Agreed," Maribo said when he was able to find his voice. "Where and when?"

January 11

After the failure of the Chinese invasion, Sino-Panamanians and their families found themselves victims of retaliation for the PLA's violence. They were forced to gather into segregated areas in the cities and towns "for their safety and support." Armed defense units guarded their perimeters, clashing with locals until an uneasy truce fell into place. The result was a number of ghettos, camps that became targets for Gomez's pogrom.

In Panama City, the main camp was set up in the old section of Casco Viejo and contained more than 2,000 people. Situated on a peninsula surrounded on three sides by Panama Bay and mostly ruined by the American bombing, living conditions were difficult at best. The inhabitants built shelters from whatever they could find, sometimes merely scrap wood and cardboard. Gomez decided the rebels needed to know how dedicated he was to putting down their insurgency and ordered the camp destroyed. The peninsula was cordoned off with troops and mortars fired into the buildings, starting fires that raged for days. Some of the people in the camp tried to swim off the peninsula to reach what remained of the Cinta Costera Bridge in the Bay, but the seawater's deceptive cold temperature and PDF patrol boats soon stopped that. It was later estimated that within 12 hours, every inhabitant of the camp had been killed.

Gomez went on national television and radio to announce that Chinese collaborators in the city had been put down and that efforts were underway to purge the last vestiges of the Chinese threat.

The public in Panama City loudly applauded the news.

5:55 PM
Penonomé, Coclé Province
95 miles west of Panama City
Radio Hogar building

Maribo watched the broadcast from his meeting with Faron. They sat in the local radio station, a map of Panama spread out on a table before them.

"The man has gone mad," Maribo said. "Some of those people were second and third generation nationals. Panamanians! He murdered our own!"

Faron shook his head and grunted in agreement. "*Increíble*, but he knows how to play on the fears of those who went through the Chinese occupation. How do we deal with that?"

Maribo sighed. How, indeed? Faron had put his finger on the crux of the problem. The population of the capitol had become loyal to Gomez. They bought his propaganda and, just as people living in fear anywhere, were willing to follow a strong and decisive leader. He promised them security from the chaos gripping the rest of the world. It was going to be difficult to convince them that Gomez was not the man they thought him to be: their savior. Drastic action might be their only chance, and that meant taking a significant risk Faron might not like.

"What can we do?" Faron asked. "Our forces are half his number and far less better equipped. He controls the national treasury, the capitol, and most of the eastern side of the Canal."

"Yes," Maribo admitted, "but there are increasing reports of Chinese insurgency there."

"What are you saying?"

"My sources tell me the insurgents are led by Chinese immigrants," Maribo told him. "Now, the last of the invading force surrendered at Chilibre years ago. This new movement is made up of naturalized and native-born Panamanians."

"Go on," Faron said.

"If we can convince the insurgency to work with us against Gomez..."

"...it would negate his advantage in numbers and open a new front?" Faron shook his head. "Risky. We do not know the insurgents are strong enough to be that much of a threat."

"Nor does Gomez," Maribo reminded. "With a little help from us, the insurgency could look it, though."

Faron gazed at nothing for a bit. Maribo let the man think, consider the implications and permutations. He knew from experience that Faron was a careful man, but he had little combat experience. The Chinese invaders had been in retreat by the time his troops reached Gamboa all those years ago, so what he had done was little more than mopping-up and pacifying a routed enemy. Maribo was asking him to face the real possibility of pitched battle, and that against his own countrymen.

"What if the insurgents refuse to cooperate?" Faron asked at last.

Maribo shrugged. "Nothing changes. We would just have to find another way to weaken Gomez."

Faron slowly nodded. "Very well, how do you propose to contact them?"

"Through the naturalized Chinese in the *Oeste* ranks. I can give several of them messages for the insurgents and send them east. With luck, at least one will be able to get through and connect. Meanwhile..." He stood and brushed his pants straight. "I have a broadcast of my own to make."

"You realize, once you do, there is no turning back whether the insurgency agrees or not," Faron said.

"Yes, and if you want to distance yourself from this, I understand."

The 5th Commander stood and grinned. "*Coronel*, I think my simply being here with you has already condemned me in the eyes of Gomez's spies."

Maribo shook his hand. "Thank you."

"Do not thank me yet, *Coronel*. We may be cursing each other before this is over."

Maribo had carefully avoided carrying out Gomez's orders to eliminate any Asians from the provinces under his command through simply failing to relay the orders to his subordinates. After Gomez's national broadcast of the executions in Panama City, he was swamped by inquiries about his intentions. That was his reason for being in the radio station.

The first "shot" fired in what became known as the Civil War was his radio broadcast from *Radio Hogar* as commander of the *Oeste* forces to ignore General Gomez's order for ethnic cleansing as "unconstitutional, barbaric, and unthinkable to civilized men." The speech and its message of resistance quickly spread through the country. Immediately thereafter, Gomez stripped Maribo of his PDF rank *in absentia* and ordered his entire staff arrested for treason.

January 13
6:22 PM
Panama Libre Headquarters
Escuela Gerardo Bacorizo building
Carrizal, Darien Province
65 miles east of Panama City

"There is a message from the rebel Maribo," Sung said.

Cho eyed his friend. "What does it say?"

"They want to talk."

"Talk? Did they say what about?"

"I believe they want to join forces."

Cho frowned. He had heard Gomez's broadcast with horror, then Maribo's broadcast in confusion. Now, this message from Maribo himself, asking for help against Gomez?

What, in the name of all that was holy, was going on?

"We should strike now," Sung said. "The PDF is coming apart. We may never get another chance like this."

"I agree," Cho said, "but what if this Maribo is sincere?" He shook his head. "No, tell them we will meet."

"But..."

Cho stopped the retort. "Do not worry. I will not go. Send

Lei and Lee. If this Maribo is following Gomez's orders and this is some kind of trick, we need to know that as well."

"If Maribo is working with Gomez, they might not return," Sung said. "Should we not just…"

Cho shook his head. "This is no time for rash action, not after so many successful raids. Our strength grows, but we still would not stand a chance in a regular attack."

Sung snorted. "Caution? From you? That's different. What happened to your passion?"

Cho glared at him. "It has become tempered by time and experience," he snapped. "Too many civilians have been caught in the middle, including those two thousand in Panama City. Or have you forgotten them?"

Sung went quiet and looked away.

Cho relented, placing a hand on his friend's chest. "This *is* time for caution," he said. "We need to wait and watch, to see if this really is a break in the ranks or just a ruse." He squeezed the man's shoulder. "Carry on with the raids as planned. Keep up the pressure, but keep your eyes and ears open, too."

"*Wǒ fúcóng, zhǐhuī guān.*"

As Sung left, Cho considered the turn of events. If the rebels were sincere, there was a real chance for victory. Not a quick one, surely, but even a chance to force concessions from Gomez would benefit the cause immensely.

It came down to this one meeting and a show of trust between Maribo and himself. They might have differing reasons for resisting Gomez but perhaps their goals did coincide.

He found himself entertaining hope that Maribo really was sincere. If the Panamanian's rebels were as strong as rumored, it might be worth taking the chance, after all.

7:00 PM
Panama Defense Force Central Command
Main Conference Room

"We sent a detail to David to arrest Maribo, but he has escaped," Martinez reported to the assembled advisors.

General Gomez's face reddened with rage. He pounded his fist on the conference table. "Maribo and his officers must be captured and brought to trial! No excuses! He is a traitor to his country, a renegade!"

He stood and began pacing, mumbling under his breath. The others in the room remained quietly watching him as he seemed to be talking to himself. Several looked at each other with raised eyebrows, exchanging silent feeling.

Finally Gomez paused and leaned against the table on his fists. "*Coronel* Almeda," he said.

Halfway down the table, a man in his late thirties sporting a prematurely grey and balding scalp stood. "*Si, mi General.*"

"You will take two platoons to Chiriqui and pacify the province. I want *Commandancia Oeste* back under legitimate PDF control."

"*A sus ordenes, señor.*"

Gomez looked to the other side of the table. "*Coronel* Verdura."

A younger man stood, a scar running across his left cheek that began under the patch over his left eye.

"Take a force to Colón. Intelligence has informed me that Faron has thrown in with Maribo. Arrest him and take over there."

"*Si, señor.*"

"The rest of you," Gomez went on, pointing at them, "I expect the curfews and arrests to continue. Any resistance is to be met with lethal force. *¿Entienden?*"

A chorus of affirmatives sounded.

"I will have order!" Gomez shouted. "Now, go!"

January 15
10:22 AM
Commandancia Oeste

Almeda was not surprised to find Maribo missing from *Oeste*. He was surprised, however, to find the post almost completely abandoned. It had taken him some time to pull together a force he felt confident would effectively defeat any resistance from Maribo should the man not listen to his proposition. Now, as his column ground to a halt, not even the guard at the front door of the Commander's office challenged him.

"Where is everyone?" he demanded.

"They have all gone, *señor*," the guard replied.

"I can see that, *idiota*! Where did they go?"

The man shrugged. "I do not know, *señor*. I was ordered to stand guard. That is all I know."

Almeda stopped the urge to slap the man and instead turned to his sergeant. "Spread out. Find the missing men and set up a perimeter. I'm going in to see if Maribo left anything behind."

The sergeant saluted and went off to comply as Almeda brushed past the guard into the office. Once inside, he sank into the desk chair and cursed. He should have known Maribo wouldn't leave his men behind when abandoning the site. Still, he had hoped someone had been left he could talk to.

It had been a stroke of luck that Gomez assigned him to *Oeste*. He had already been wondering how to separate himself from the capitol without falling afoul of the general. Watching Gomez become increasingly unbalanced had convinced him the man's ambitions were overtaking his sense of national pride. With the Canal blocked, medicine scarce in the city after the cholera outbreak, and a population more and more dependent on the military to stop the rising violent crime, Panama City had become someplace he would rather not be. Maribo and his rebels might not be able to improve living conditions in the city, but it was unlikely Gomez was interested in doing anything to solve the nation's problems unless it benefited him personally. Then, when Gomez had ordered the execution of the 2,000, his fears were confirmed.

He passed a hand over his face and sighed. He needed desperately to get in touch with the man. There was so little time to get things done without Gomez getting wise. Well, if Maribo and Faron were working together, perhaps he could message the headquarters in Colón.

If Verdura hadn't already taken it.

It was worth a try. He picked up the phone, but when no one answered the switchboard, he slammed the receiver down. Reaching into his pocket, he retrieved his cellphone. The signals were not very reliable any more, but he figured he'd chance it. He dialed.

"5th Infantry Headquarters. *Corporal* Perez speaking."

"*Corporal*, this is *Coronel* Almeda at *Oeste*. I need to speak to *Coronel* Faron immediately."

"*Lo siento, Coronel*, but *Coronel* Faron is not here."

"Where is he?"

"I do not know, *señor*. He left several days ago."

"Who is in command there now?"

"*Capitan* Serrano, *señor*."

"Let me speak to him."

"*Si, señor.* One moment."

After what seemed to be an interminable pause, "*Capitan* Serrano."

"Serrano, listen closely. *Coronel* Verdura has orders from *General* Gomez to take command there."

"Very good, sir."

"No, it is not," Almeda snapped. "The order is a fraud. How many men do you have there?"

There was a slight pause. Almeda frowned.

"Only about twenty, *señor*. *Coronel* Faron took the bulk of our troops on maneuvers," Serrano said at last.

Almeda thought for a moment. Serrano's hesitation might have been a signal he was wondering whether Almeda was telling the truth. Time to take another tack. "Round up your men at once and follow him with anything you can carry. I have reason to believe Verdura plans to break off from Gomez and set up his own camp."

Serrano's response was immediate. "*Bien*. We will be gone within the hour."

"Good man. Advise *Coronel* Faron about this when you rendezvous."

Almeda cut the connection and leaned back in the seat, closing his eyes. Once Serrano told Faron about the call, he would have his connection.

If Serrano got out before Verdura's troops arrived, that is.

January 16
10:00 AM
Puerto Pilon, Colón Province
Iglesia Cristo Victoria
12 miles east of Colón

The meeting place selected was a little Assembly of God church. The minister had agreed to allow it with the proviso that none of his flock would be required to attend, though Maribo had never intended to make such a demand. Apparently, news of his break from Gomez had reached even the small village. The locals were nervous at the presence of so many military, especially rebel military. As the time for the meeting approached, the streets emptied and everything came to a halt. Outside the church, Barona stood by Maribo's car while an APC with a full complement of men guarded the church entrance.

A small sedan rolled down the abandoned streets to stop short of the APC. Four people got out, three men and a woman. Two of the men were armed and immediately stepped between the others and Maribo's men.

Barona approached the group. "*Descanse soldado*," she ordered. Maribo's guard lowered their weapons. She turned to the visitors. "If you will follow me, please."

Maribo rose from his seat to watch as Barona escorted the Chinese into the room. His own bodyguard snapped to attention, alert for any threatening movement. The Chinese representatives walked between their own guard, who eyed everyone in the room warily. The sight of the woman reminded Maribo that Barona had volunteered to come with him over his objections. He felt a twinge at the thought, then pushed it away.

He motioned the delegates to the seats beside him. They bowed and sat without a word. He looked around.

"*Calma*, gentlemen," he ordered the guard. "We are only here to talk."

Slowly, the Panamanian and Chinese soldiers relaxed.

Maribo settled into his own seat. "I am *Coronel* Luis Maribo," he told the delegates. "Thank you for coming."

"Thank you for the invitation," the man said with a soft Chinese accent. "Unfortunately, our commanding officer cannot attend."

Maribo noted the man neglected to introduce himself. *Understandable*, he thought. *Trust must be earned.* He nodded. "I hope he is in good health?"

"There are many demands on his time, but he is well, thank you."

The woman leaned close to the man's ear and whispered something Maribo thought might be in Chinese. The man nodded and waved her away.

"We were surprised to receive your message," the man said. "If it had not come by way of a Chinese, we would have ignored it completely."

"There are many Chinese immigrants and families under my care now," Maribo said. "They are my countrymen. They deserve to be protected."

The man blinked and hummed an affirmative. "Your message indicated you wanted to talk. May I inquire as to your intentions?"

"Yes, of course." Maribo leaned forward, causing the woman to shift slightly in her seat. He saw the reaction and straightened, raising his hand. "Forgive me. I know this must be frightening for you, coming here nearly alone, but please know I mean you no harm. I am sincere in my wish to come to agreement with you about the safety and well-being not only of your families, but of my country."

The man patted her knee and mumbled a couple of words. Maribo knew that these two weren't just a couple of representatives sent into the lion's den, as it were. They had to be part of the insurgency inner circle, and their presence was going to be more than just to talk. They were present to make an agreement or kill any chance of alliance.

"We are all Panamanians," Maribo continued, firmly determined to make it clear he wanted the truth known as to his intent. "*General* Gomez has forgotten that. He is only interested in one thing: his own position and power over the country…"

"But did you not serve under *General* Gomez?" the man cut in.

Maribo grimaced and nodded. "Yes, I did. I was his second when the Red Devils pushed from Penonomé to Panama City."

"The bloodiest part of the entire campaign, as I understand it," the man said, his face inscrutable. "Many civilians were killed."

Maribo sighed. How to explain his part in that? It wouldn't be sufficient to simply claim he was following orders.

"It is something I intensely regret," he admitted. "I can offer no excuse, make no explanation to rationalize what was done. But serving under Gomez was how I came to understand the man and his ambitions. It is how I know my country is in danger of losing the many freedoms we had before the invasion."

The man seemed to consider his words for a moment. Finally, he glanced at the woman, who nodded.

"We are not sure how much help we can be in your effort," he said. "We are a raiding force, not a serious military threat."

That the delegate was hinting at negotiation heartened Maribo.

"I understand," he said. "But we can provide you with captured weapons from the invasion, intelligence gathered about Gomez's forces, supplies, and medicines."

The woman leaned in again and whispered into the man's ear. He nodded and mumbled something back to her.

She looked at Maribo. "*Coronel*," she said, "do you have children?"

Maribo couldn't help but glance at Barona, who was standing a little away from them. She grinned at him.

"No," he answered.

"Then perhaps you would like to visit our compound and see the children there who have run to us for protection from the Panamanian army?" she said, an edge on her voice.

Maribo took a deep breath. Personally going to the insurgents' camp was a big risk, but how could he refuse? If he was to build the trust they needed to succeed, there seemed to be little option.

"I would be honored," he managed to say. He hurried on as Barona started forward. "I will come alone and without guards. Will that be all right?"

The man looked nonplussed. The woman smiled and nodded. "Of course," she said.

"Then shall we go?" Maribo said, rising. He shook his head at Barona as she began to object. "There is much to do and little time."

5:22 PM
Portobelo, Colón Province
Fuerte de San Jerónimo
30 miles east of Colón

Faron received the news from Serrano of Verdura's occupation of Colón with a sense of resignation. He had to admit, it was inevitable that Gomez would move to strengthen his hold on the Canal. When and if it was repaired enough to start working again, any trade would bolster his popular support and further entrench him into power.

The fact Almeda had warned of Verdura's advance was interesting. He wasn't exactly sure what to make of it, but shoved aside that concern for later. He was less comfortable to hear of Maribo's intended visit to the insurgents' camp. If that went badly, and he lost Maribo, would the man's forces stay loyal to the cause?

He stood on the wall of the old Spanish fortification facing the Caribbean, leaning against one of the antique cannons lined up to protect the coast, watching the ocean turn gray as a storm front gathered. He hoped that wasn't a bad omen.

"*Senor*, there is someone in the headquarters to see you."

Faron tore himself from the view to look at his aide. "Who is it?"

"Provincial Governor Duarte."

Faron raised an eyebrow. "What would the Darien governor want with me?" he asked himself.

"I came to offer you an insight into what is happening in the capitol," a voice said from beyond the cannons to his right. "And perhaps a little more, if you will trust me."

Faron nodded at Duarte. "Let us talk."

- 3 -

January 17
5:30 AM
Tocumen International Airport
Tocumen, Panama Province
Suburb of Panama City

The grey of false dawn was just beginning to push back the night. The airport's night shift employees puttered through the last of their chores, cleaning and polishing. A few early shopkeepers, still optimistic that business would soon pick up in spite of everything, worried over their inventories and books. The PDF guard lounged, nodded, and smoked in the quiet of the early morning activities. Tocumen was no longer the international airport it had been when it hosted commercial and private traffic from every nation in the Americas and the Caribbean. It now handled little more than national military traffic patrols and the occasional private transport.

Cho's *Panama Libre* forces, supplemented by a platoon from Maribo's *Corsarios*, sprang on the sleeping defenders along the main highway from the northwest and from across the fields on the southeast. In the half-light of the rising sun, the bleary-eyed PDF detail had trouble determining which side was at greater threat. Alarms cut through the morning air with a teeth-shattering noise that echoed off the hangars and main terminal, sending the employees scurrying for shelter.

Men ran from the PDF barracks, built from half the covered parking lot across from the terminal, to attempt a formation and some kind of order, but Cho's troops swarmed the area, capturing the barracks and gunning down the resistance as they came.

On the other side of the airport, the *Corsarios* crossed the runways where heavy vehicles blocked the possibility of aircraft traffic while the lighter vehicles rushed to capture seven helicopters sitting on the apron outside the terminal. The helicopters had been recovered from the Chinese after the invasion but never used. Maribo intended to see to it that his new Chinese friends were given the opportunity to cooperate with their refit from Chinese language to Spanish language controls. There was some contest from a squad of PDF left to guard them, but after three went down from a well-placed *Corsairo* grenade, they dropped their weapons and gave up.

Tocumen airport fell to the rebel forces in less than twenty minutes.

6:47 AM
Panama Defense Force Central Command
Office of General de Fuerzas

"*General*, the rebels have taken Tocumen airport. They are nearly inside the city."

"*Do you think I am blind?*" Gomez thundered at Martinez. "I have seen the reports." He ground his teeth. "Almeda refuses to move from *Oeste*. He *claims* he is having trouble with Maribo's *Corsarios*, and yet intelligence says the *Corsarios* were part of the attack on Tocumen!" He stood and began pacing, waving his arms as he ranted. "Faron has disappeared with the entire 5th Infantry. The *maldito Chinos* continue to grow in strength. My commanders are incompetent cowards!"

A courier entered and saluted. "*Perdoneme, General.* I have a dispatch from Verdura."

He offered a package to Gomez. Gomez waved to Martinez, who accepted the package and opened it while the general continued to pace, foully mumbling to himself.

"Verdura reports sightings of the 5th about twenty-five kilometers east of Colón," Martinez relayed. "He is requesting orders."

Gomez tossed his head back in frustration. "Must I do everything? Tell him to move against the 5th, capture Faron, and send him here for trial."

"I will draw up the papers imm..."

"*Al diablo con los papeles!* You, messenger. *Name!*" Gomez barked.

Clearly startled, the soldier gulped audibly. "Enrique, *señor*."

"Well, Enrique, you heard my orders. Go. Tell Verdura."

The courier saluted. "*Si, señor. A la orden.*"

"Martinez," the general began, pausing in his pacing as the courier nearly ran out of the room, "it is time we started using the Red Devils to put an end to this. Muster the entire force. We are going to take Tocumen first, then drive the insurgents back to Columbia. Once that is done and the insurgency is put down, we will deal with Maribo and Faron." He grinned. "I will personally oversee their trials."

Even Martinez shuddered at the sight of that grin. He was glad not to be Maribo or Faron. He had been the general's right hand for years, but Gomez was changing, and that change frightened him.

9:04 AM
Portobelo Police Substation

"Our spies report troop movement from Colón along Highway 3," his radio operator told Faron.

"We have sixty men in Puerto Pilon, *señor*, but they are only lightly armed," his lieutenant reported.

Faron considered the map spread on the table in the little substation ready room. "How large is the enemy force?"

"Difficult to tell, but at least two companies, perhaps more. Several troop trucks and a couple of APCs."

Faron grunted. "Not good odds." He frowned as he thought. "We might be able to use the Pilon garrison as a covering force. Have them pull back to..." He ran a finger along the road on the map to the east of Puerto Pilon. "This fork here. Picaflor. Have them set up an ambush. The enemy column will have to slow on the curve. We will break them up there. I will take our company here in Portobelo to meet them. We should arrive at about the same time."

The radio operator began relaying the orders as the lieutenant left to gather the 5th for battle. Faron leaned over the map and frowned. Two companies from Colón? They had to be Gomez's men. Who was in command? As far as he knew, only Maribo, Gomez, and himself had recent combat experience.

"*Señor*," the radio operator said. "I have a message coming in." He turned a surprised look at Faron. "It is from *Oeste*, *señor*. *Coronel* Almeda."

"Almeda?" The name was familiar. An older man, as he recalled. More of a politician than a soldier. That might be a good sign. Faron took the receiver. "Yes, *Coronel*?"

"I just received orders from *General* Gomez to proceed to the *Puente Atlantico*, effect repairs, and secure Colón. Apparently, *Coronel* Verdura was sent to replace you and, finding you gone, has committed all his forces against you."

The *Puente Atlantico*, completed in 2019, crossed the Canal on its Atlantic end and had partially collapsed during an earthquake in 2026. The span itself still stood but much of the bridge deck had fallen into the Canal. Dredging had quickly cleared the waterway, but repairs had only been partially complete by the time of the global Collapse.

Faron was pleasantly surprised at Almeda's forthrightness. "Do you know Verdura's strength?" he asked, hoping he wasn't pressing his luck.

Almeda laughed. "Trusting me now, *Coronel*?"

"Should I not?"

"I am glad you do. Gomez will be a formidable enemy."

"Of that, I am sure."

"Last I was advised, Verdura had three companies of one hundred men, four M224 mortars, and two Type 92 APCs captured from the Chinese invaders. His men are mostly conscripts, with only a few veterans serving as officers. Does that help?"

"Very much. Thank you, *Coronel*."

"*De nada*. I hope to meet you soon, Faron. We have much to discuss."

"I look forward to it."

11:15 AM
Interchange
Pan-American Highway Corredor Sur and Calle Pluton
East Panama City

The sound brought the PDF guards at the interchange station out to shade their eyes against the midday glare and try to locate the helicopters. Almost immediately, gunfire erupted from the woods south of their position, sending them back to the shelter of the station situated in the center of the complex switchback ramp. Their retreat gave them respite from the attack but made them unable to stop the trucks that thundered past the toll plaza on the overpass above them.

The station commander scrambled for the radio. "We are taking fire," he reported.

"Hold your position," came the reply from Command. "*General* Gomez is on his way with the Red Devils. They should arrive within a few minutes."

In the lead truck, Maribo reached for his own radio. "We are through, *Libre*. Thanks." he said. "Any sign of troops on the road, *Aguila*?"

"No, *señor*," came the response from the helicopter. "All clear... *Espere*."

Maribo waited impatiently as the seconds dragged by until the pilot came back on.

"There is a large force headed your way, *señor*," the pilot said. "Estimate about thirty trucks, two tanks. Say... three hundred to four hundred men. Five minutes, give or take, to your position."

Maribo cursed. "Understood, *Aguila*. Do not engage. Remain clear. Use the buildings for cover. Wait for my signal."

"*A la orden, Coronel*."

Maribo turned to the driver. "Turn off into that residential area ahead." He twisted the channel on his radio. "This is Maribo. Follow and prepare to dismount. Second unit, deploy as planned. *Libre*, are you on?"

"Headed your way now. ETA ten minutes," was Cho's response.

"Acknowledged."

The *Corsarios* swung down the embankment to the south of the highway and into an area thick with houses that could have all been made from the same design. Uniformly white and unassuming, arrayed in ranks, they faced a large school as if formed up for an extracurricular event. Maribo's trucks rattled across the packed earth area around the two-storey school and continued south along a little lane that left the residential area. They continued for a few hundred meters to stop in front of a lone building announcing itself to be a driver's license bureau. People gathered at its windows to stare in confusion as the trucks spread out in the parking lot and into a large clearing across the road.

Maribo ordered the dismount and sent two squads through the woods west of their position to clear a path back to the main road. The rest he ordered to create a defensive line. Men pushed cars from the parking lot into an ersatz barricade.

"Hold here," he said. "Let them come to us."

"*Señor*," a sergeant nearby shouted, "what about the civilians?"

"Take two men and get them out of there," Maribo said.

A rumbling brought his attention back to the road. The sight of the T99 tank told him all he needed to know about Gomez's intentions.

11:22 AM
Picaflor, Colón Province
19 miles east of Colón

The road takes nearly a right-angle left turn at Picaflor just after the fork. It is only a two lane and the APCs in the lead took up most of that. People stood outside the cantina just off the right-hand fork, watching Verdura's column go by.

As the APCs passed a group of buildings in the area between the fork, explosions shook the air and the civilians ran for cover. One of the APCs shuddered to a halt and began smoking heavily. Its rear door popped open and men spilled out to scurry for cover. The other lumbered around, trying to bring its 12.7mm machine gun to bear against the enemy.

The column stopped and troop trucks emptied in a hurry while gunfire crackled from both sides of the street. Men tumbled from the trucks, most unhurt but some falling dead before their feet hit the ground.

Two trucks burst into flame as grenades blew up in their beds. Black smoke billowed out of them, then the ammo boxes they carried began cooking off, sending rounds in every direction. Troops on both sides kept their heads down as best they could until the fusillade ended. There was a brief few seconds of silence before the combatants resumed firing.

The sound of jets overhead brought everyone's eyes up. Two JH-7 fighter-bombers swept by, turned, and headed for Verdura's column. Their 23mm guns burped, sending bits of the road into the air and tearing into the troops who frantically dashed for shelter in the wood. The jets roared by, turned, and strafed again before disappearing.

No one left cover, anxiously watching the sky. In the sudden quiet, a new rumbling began.

The advance vehicles of the 5th Infantry rounded the curve.

"First unit, attack the APCs!"

Faron's orders, barked through the radio, brought a flurry of activity. Three men with RPGs hopped off their trucks and set up. In less than a minute, the hiss of rockets cut through the air, followed almost at once by a thunderous boom as the rounds impacted the APCs. Both flared into huge clouds of fire and smoke, sending shrapnel everywhere. Men dove for cover but many of Verdura's forces were caught in the shower of metal.

"Second unit, move in!"

Stunned and demoralized by the ambush, the strafing, and the loss of the APCs, many of Verdura's men threw down their weapons and fled. A few put up a half-hearted resistance, but for all intents and purposes, the battle was over.

East Panama City
near Esmeralda Driver's License Bureau

Maribo peered through his binocs at the Jeep running ahead of the tank.

"Of course," he said to himself.

"What is it, *señor*?" his driver asked.

"Gomez." Maribo lowered the glasses. "It is Gomez. I am surprised it took him this long to take personal command. Those will be Red Devils, his elite."

The oncoming column halted and a tense silence settled over the scene as the opposing forces left their trucks to deploy.

"Maribo!" came Gomez's voice over a loudspeaker mounted on the tank. "Surrender and your men will be allowed to go free."

Maribo ignored the threat and turned to his lieutenant.

"Check our west flank," he said. "The woods are good cover for the men on both sides. Gomez will try to encircle us."

"*Si, señor.*" The lieutenant ran to comply.

"You have one minute, Maribo! One minute!" Gomez announced.

Maribo fitted his radio headset. "Second unit, sitrep."

"In position," Barona reported.

"Acknowledged."

"*Corsario*, this is *Libre*. We have enemy in sight. Two minutes to position."

"Acknowledged, *Libre*."

Seconds ticked by as Maribo checked his own sidearm and waved to the sergeant returning from evacuating the civilians from the license bureau building. The man ran up to him.

"Take a squad onto the roof of the building and put down covering fire as needed," Maribo told him.

The sergeant saluted and summoned three men nearby to follow him.

"Thirty seconds!" the loudspeaker barked.

Maribo took a deep breath. He looked around at his men, noted their grim faces. Too many youngsters, too many. How many would never see another sunrise?

A breeze freshened the air for a moment and he caught the scent of the sea. It was hard to believe the Bay was less than a quarter mile south of their position. The Rio Juan Diaz guarded their left flank, the Bay their rear. Cho's *Panama Libre* group would be approaching from their right and Barona's Second Unit was set up as snipers on the rooftops of the houses to their northeast.

Things were going more or less according to plan. They had wanted to get further into the city before confronting the defenders, but this would have to do. Now came the real test.

"*No plan survives first contact with the enemy.*"

Why did he just think of that?

The tank announced time was up.

The round struck the license bureau building about midway up the north wall. The edifice shook and the wall crumbled.

"Open fire!" Maribo shouted.

His units volleyed toward the enemy, initially doing little damage. Maribo hadn't expected it to. He wanted Gomez to know he wasn't planning on giving up without a fight. He knew the general wanted that fight and maybe the man would do what he had always done: plunge headlong into the fray.

Just as he thought, Gomez's Jeep shot ahead of the tank, the general yelling encouragement to his men as they ran at Maribo's line. The tank ground the lane's asphalt under as it rolled forward, turret turning to fire at the car barricade. Its report rattled the windows left in the building as five of the cars and seventeen men were blown into the air.

Maribo squeezed the trigger of his FN P90 until the mag emptied, but only managed to hit one of the Jeep's tires, sending it reeling to the left and onto the shoulder. Gomez and his driver leapt from the crippled vehicle and continued their advance, firing as they came.

Maribo could feel the wind of the bullets by his head. Something struck him on the left side but he barely felt it. He slammed another mag home and leveled it at Gomez. He could almost picture the ferocious grin on the man's face as the general's weapon came to bear.

"Second unit! Fire!" Maribo barked. He steadied his aim. There would be one chance.

Gomez's driver went down, headless. Behind the general, men Maribo hadn't noticed in the excitement began to fall as well. Gomez twisted hard to his right, hit in his shoulder, but kept coming. Maribo fired just as it happened, missing Gomez. He cursed.

Shots from the building rooftop took out several Red Devils swarming the barricade. Men who survived the barricade's destruction fell into hand-to-hand with those who made it through.

All at once, someone was beside him, firing at the oncoming troops, shouting in Chinese.

"Wŏmen de jiārén! Wŏ shā nǐ!"

Gomez was suddenly in front of him.

Maribo pulled the trigger.

Nothing happened.

For a second, it didn't register. Then he realized what had happened.

The damned thing jammed.

Gomez grinned wolfishly. He raised his 1911 and pointed it at Maribo's head. "*Adios*, traitor."

The shot was deafening.

Gomez's eyes went wide. He stumbled backward, blood

spreading across the front of his uniform. Maribo blinked, ears ringing, the sounds around him muted behind that tone.

"*Hùndàn!*" he heard Cho yell as he fired again. The bullet hit Gomez in his throat. "*Gòu zaī zi!*" The shot hit Gomez in his stomach. "*Wáng bā dàn!*" Another shot.

Gomez's head jerked back and he collapsed. Cho stood over the corpse and emptied the rest of his magazine into it.

The roar of jets overhead went nearly unheard as Maribo suddenly realized his shoulder was killing him. He looked dumbly at it, noted with dispassionate interest the blood flowing down his uniform.

He fell to his knees. Blackness closed down on his vision as the sounds of the battle faded completely.

He passed out.

Epilogue

Voices, some familiar, most not. Explosions, shouts, firing, more explosions...

Maribo opened his eyes slowly, trying to ignore the pain in his shoulder. It wasn't as bad as he remembered. There was a kind of fuzzy edge to it.

He found himself looking at a fluorescent light. Turning his head, he realized he lay in a hospital bed, an IV hanging to his left. Barona slept in a chair next to him, covered in a blanket with the label "Propiedad de Hospital Gorgas."

The door opened and a man in a white coat entered, followed by Cho and Faron. Barona startled awake.

"He is quite weak," the doctor observed. "He needs his rest."

"We understand," Faron said. "Give us some privacy."

The doctor grimaced and reluctantly left. The men nodded at Barona, who stood, folding the blanket.

"*Capitan*," Cho said. "Good to see you."

"And you, *señor*," she replied, placing the blanket on the chair. She looked at Faron. "*Coronel.*"

Faron acknowledged her greeting without a word and stepped to Maribo's bedside. "How are you feeling?" he asked.

At first, all Maribo could manage was a croak. Barona handed him a plastic cup of water.

"I have felt better," he said with an effort. Just speaking

was exhausting, as if his lungs were tired. That fuzzy feeling seemed to cover his words as well.

"We thought you might like to know what has happened," Faron went on. "The Red Devils have been disbanded. Gomez's advisers have all resigned except for Duarte. He is vice-president now. Cho's *Libre* unit has been assigned to the regular PDF as 10th Infantry."

"Menendez?" Maribo asked.

Faron smiled. "He is well. Gomez may have taken power, but he knew that eliminating Menendez might be unpopular. The man was cunning when it came to politics, if nothing else."

Another man in uniform peered through the doorway. "May I come in?"

Faron beckoned him. "*General* Maribo, this is *Coronel* Almeda. He sent the jets to support us at Picaflor and you against the Red Devils."

"Nice to finally meet the great leader of the rebellion," Almeda said with a wry grin.

Maribo wanted to chuckle, but a sudden pain stopped it.

Barona grabbed his hand. "Easy, Luis," she said softly.

He squeezed her hand. "I am okay," he assured her. It dawned on him what Faron had said. "*General?*"

"Oh, yes," Faron said. "Menendez has promoted you to *General de Fuerzas*. The ceremony will take place as soon as you are able."

Maribo groaned theatrically. Barona and the rest laughed.

The doctor reappeared at the door. "I really must insist you allow the *general* to rest now."

Everyone started to leave, but Maribo held on to Barona's hand.

"Stay."

She smiled and sat on the bed beside him.

"There is something I need to ask you," he said.

"I know," she said, her smile growing wider. "And the answer is yes."

The Sussex Job

Tim C. Taylor

2075
Birmingham, England

The old man could smell the Orthodoxies before their procession even entered the Great Hall.

Woody resins, exotic herbs and spices, sweetness too. Was that honey? He didn't have the words to describe such aromas, but the Orthodoxies would always strive to outdo the Catholics, and the result excited even his dulled senses.

Not much did these days.

Some of the younger servants standing with him at the back of the hall glanced his way, their eyes flecked with anxiety. The prettier women were the most nervous, and with good reason. The Orthodoxies were the last of the Quinta leadership to arrive, and when they had taken their place in the hall, the servants would soon be called to perform their duties.

With each passing year, the five factions of the Quinta worked harder to outdo each other in callous abuse of their servants. The lower they were degraded, the higher their betters were elevated. That's how those at the top appeared to see it, but the old man regarded the performative abuse as a sign of weakness.

It wasn't just slaps, kicks, and yelling. Rough fondling between the legs was almost as common for the male servants these days as it always had been for the women. Not because most of the Quinta membership got a kick out of it. They just wanted to show they could.

His anticipation of the horrors to come was interrupted by a servant woman giving him a steady look from her piercing blue eyes. She was trying to make a connection to him.

He frowned, but she didn't look away. Her only concern, it seemed, was that he should notice her.

Blonde hair tied back into a bun emphasized the roundness of her pretty face. In the secrecy of his head, he decided she was probably Polish or Russian, but it was so difficult to tell these days. England was a confusing place. Perhaps she saw his seniority and had convinced herself that he had the power to shield her.

All he could offer her was a weak smile before he looked away.

He could protect no one.

The Orthodox procession arrived, a visual feast for eyes accustomed to the drab, dull, and damaged in the decades after the Fall. The priests wore pristine white robes with gilt hems and collars. The Patriarch himself was clad in gleaming gold threads and wore a domed hat of the same opulent material. There was a cross bearer too, and a priest swinging a censer smoking with incense.

The Orthodox Church drew on two thousand years of experience to launch a multi-sensory assault on the onlookers. For the old man, though, their chanting was only a dull rumble in his ears.

He had lived long enough to remember a time of doctors and pharmacies. The National Health Service. A few drops of olive oil every day and his hearing would probably be restored, the crippling ear pain ended.

When had olive oil disappeared from everyday life? It had been so long ago that it was impossible to piece together the sequence of decay.

The Patriarch's party slowly processed to its allocated space among the Quinta leadership.

As cohosts for this court council being held in Birmingham, the Sikhs and Hindus looked upon the Orthodoxies with benevolent welcome. By contrast, the Muslims and Catholics showered them with unguarded contempt.

The old man shook his head. It had been almost a decade since the Quinta had established itself as the successor state in what had been the Midlands and South Yorkshire. Initially, he'd assumed the mutual loathing and suspicion would soon tear it apart.

Now he realized they were the perfect attributes to bind the disparate groups together in the face of the other powers and perils in fallen Britain. The Quinta would not last forever, but it would outlive him.

An elbow dug into his ribs, and he took a sharp intake of breath laced with sudden panic.

His mind had drifted again.

If anyone important had seen his attention wane and decided it was insolence, his head would be on one of the spikes above the entrance to the Midland Palace.

He mouthed his thanks to the woman who'd poked him. The pretty one who had given him the eye earlier.

What was her name? She looked distinctive but he couldn't remember anything about her. Brain like a sieve these days.

"Keep it together, Prof."

She spoke with authority. Servants did not speak that way.

And that wasn't what he was called.

"My name is Will," he whispered.

She narrowed her eyes. "You *are* Professor Wilson Jarra? Yeah?"

His mouth dropped open. "Once. An age ago, but no more. Who the fuck are you?"

"Danuta. People call me a salvager, but I prefer the term collector, because I collect precious relics from the past. Ain't never been paid to retrieve a living relic before."

"I'm just an old man. Leave me be."

"Don't mistake this caper for a rescue." She reached inside her clothing. "This is a collection."

She drew out a small handheld device, like the keys he remembered from a lifetime ago. People had used them to unlock cars. When she pressed its button, an explosion puffed out of the end wall. The banner mounted there was falling. Screams and shouts were filling the hall. Weapons were being drawn. What was happening?

Then this Danuta turned him around and pushed him toward the service door.

It was all he could do to keep his feet.

Danuta made for the cellars.

The team's eager new boy, Raffy, was turning out to be a research genius. He'd uncovered that the Midland Palace had once been the Midland Hotel and had allegedly boasted the largest selection of beers in the country. That meant a cellar. And a cellar would have a hatch for the draymen to deliver their barrels of beer. That was how she intended to get out.

She found what she was looking for in a whitewashed room with cracked plastic tubes still feeding up through the ceiling. After checking that the professor was too dazed to run off, she pushed open the double cellar doors, letting in the cool air of the former hotel's yard.

Standing on tiptoe, she placed her hands onto the metal of the surround and hauled herself up, only to be greeted by the grinning face of a waiting Quinta guard.

Arabic script was stitched into his jacket, marking his allegiance to the Muslim faction, though his freckled pale skin and ginger beard looked neither Arabic nor Pakistani.

"Up you come." The guard slapped his baton on his open palm. His pistol remained in its hip holster.

Danuta trembled as she pulled herself up to the level of the yard, hoping her show of fear would keep his firearm where it was.

When she emerged onto the cold stone cobbles of the yard, she shivered anyway. The Great Hall had been ostentatiously heated, but outside, the late morning sun couldn't penetrate the chill air to warm her through her flimsy white blouse.

"My. My." The guard's gaze settled on her blouse. "A runaway slave, and a pretty one at that. This is my lucky day. But it ain't yours, darlin'." He interrupted his leering to peer down into the cellar. "How many more of you are down there?"

Danuta bowed her head and edged closer.

"Hey! I asked you a fookin' question."

The Prof's voice rose from the depths. "It's just me, sir."

Head still down, Danuta rubbed her wrist over the mark on her neck that pronounced her lowly status as a so-called servant. Hers was fake. The Prof's had been applied with a branding iron.

"Thank you," she told the guard.

"Excuse me? Are you taking the fookin' piss?"

"No. I'm thanking you for your honesty. You're the first person since I got here who hasn't called me a servant."

The guard frowned, but he was watching the old man who was standing on an upturned crate and struggling to get out the cellar. "I don't like your tone, slave bitch."

"I'm not a slave. And if I'm a servant, I have only one master. Wealth and... adventure. Adventure and wealth. Two masters..." She edged closer under cover of an ancient joke Baz had once tried explaining. "Wealth, adventure, and..."

The guard hesitated. Then panic jolted through him, and he was frantically reaching for his pistol.

Too late. Danuta flicked out the knife she'd been hiding in her palm and slashed his throat.

He stared at her through eyes wide with denial.

Blood pulsed in cascades down his neck, staining his beard and clothing.

Shaking with fear, he angled his neck down to lower his gaze, clearly terrified by the prospect of what he would see. By then, Danuta had already relieved him of his pistol.

She momentarily searched for some dramatic parting words—these details were important to maintaining one's reputation in this business—but she heard running footsteps coming their way. She racked the pistol's slide and assumed a shooting stance.

It was only Baz.

With a single glance, the boss took in the situation in the yard before giving Danuta a brief nod and helping out the professor. "Job's done. Let's move out."

They hurried through enormous mounds of cleared rubble and descended through thick undergrowth to what had once been an important railroad hub.

There were carcasses of a dozen lines here, the metal rails long since salvaged, leaving the cracked concrete sleepers behind. Birmingham had been a vibrant living city once. The number of people who must have passed through here each day boggled Danuta's mind.

On the way, Baz filled her in on his side of the escapade. In his disguise as a guard, he'd managed to knock off hats and turbans, hurl unforgivable insults at each of the Quinta groups and fire dozens of pistol rounds inside the hotel.

Even from the tracks, they could hear pandemonium and gunfire inside the palace.

The Quinta's under attack!

The backstabbing Catholics are taking over!

The Neo-Comms are back!

Danuta could easily imagine the rumors and accusations swirling around the place like a hot summer wind. No one would guess that all this palaver had been to steal away one worthless old man.

Baz wasn't boasting when he pointed out how well their plan had gone so far. He was quietly reminding her why he led the group.

But the caper wasn't over until they'd all gotten paid.

They made for a brick hut that had been built at the end of a platform. They'd stashed their equipment and change of clothing there. Once clad in thick woolen overcoats and with an orange knitted hat pulled over the professor's tight white hair, they set off again, making for Canal Wharf half a mile away.

Danuta could detect no signs of pursuit.

But she felt sure it was coming.

Krystyn had spent weeks mentally preparing for this moment, praying it would never actually come to pass.

From her post on the roof of the tallest undamaged building on Hill Street, she tracked the three turbaned gunmen as they stepped across the tracks and deeper into her firing arc. One tapped the shoulders of his companions and then pointed at Baz.

She had already gathered her breathing into a gentle rhythm. She decided to count three more breaths, holding her fire in case more targets came into view.

Baz had worked on her, persuading her of the need for the sacrifice she was about to make. The boss looked and spoke in a quietly understated fashion, and yet somehow he could charm the hind legs off a donkey. He'd had no trouble charming away something just as valuable to her.

After two more breaths, the gunman in the middle raised his AK-47 and Krystyn could wait no longer.

Through the ACOG scope, the man's mouth opened in glee. The image was so sharp, she could see half-dried gravy in his beard. Filthy man.

She squeezed off a shot.

The L129A1 was a glorious weapon, if a little heavy. Its bipod rocked against the roof's lip, throwing a sharp punch against her shoulder, but she controlled it, never losing the sight picture of the three gunmen.

The other two targets were in the process of bringing their

rifles to their shoulders, not yet processing the fact that their comrade had taken a 7.62 round through his head.

This was why she loved her L129 so much. The follow-up.

She took the other two down, the last managing a wild shot at Danuta and Baz's group before she dropped him.

Then she delivered another headshot to all three and assured herself through the scope that she had eliminated this threat. She eased back the zoom and panned right to see Baz, Danuta, and the merchandize had gone to ground, hugging the gravel behind the slight rise of a line of sleepers. Baz got to his feet and gave a thumbs-up in her general direction.

She watched over them until they cleared the tracks. This was the moment when her orders were to get out and head with all speed to the extraction point.

But she couldn't leave her L129 so easily.

She took a last look through its scope and was struck by a thrill of satisfaction when she spotted movement on the roof of the old New Street rail terminus. Treading carefully to avoid falling through the fragile roof were a sharpshooter with a scoped rifle and a spotter armed with binoculars.

"I'll miss you," she told her 129, once she'd shot first the sharpshooter and then the spotter.

A lump came to her throat. Danuta sometimes told her that she had a cold heart, that she would only know cold men until she learned to thaw. But Danuta was a romantic, as soft-headed as an overboiled cabbage. Krystyn wasn't cold. She was different. And she'd been through a lot with her L129. But it was too heavy to carry, and they wouldn't be able to shoot their way out of Quinta territory on this mission.

The client had promised a replacement, but it wouldn't be *her* L129. The others laughed, but she would be able to tell the difference.

She abandoned her rifle and ran to the fire escape unarmed.

At this point in the operation, bearing arms was a liability. It was time to melt away.

Krystyn was last back.

He hoped the others were buying his cool as a cucumber act, but it wasn't until every member of his team was safely back in his sight that Baz's heart rate eased back from the red zone.

"Cast off, Danuta," he ordered.

"Where are we going?" asked the professor. They were the first words he'd heard from him.

"Answers later." Baz's gaze didn't leave the banks of Canal Wharf. "Get below, Professor. Keep out of sight."

As soon as Krystyn stepped aboard, Raffy opened the throttle and the boat sped away along the Worcester and Birmingham Canal. Which in the case of their coal-powered barge, laden with grain sacks, meant they were soon up to a brisk walking pace.

It gave Baz plenty of time to worry.

First he'd recruited the two girls and now young Raffy too. He detested the responsibility of putting others in danger, but he needed a team around him to bring in the big contracts. And they were being paid serious money to collect the ancient professor. Far more than made sense.

The way Baz saw it, either the high payout meant their client was going to double cross them, or the prof was a test, a step towards an even bigger payday.

He was gambling all their lives on it being the latter.

A mile farther on and Baz judged it was time to ditch the remaining weapons at the bottom of the canal and to give their collectible a reason for being snatched from the Quinta. It was the least Baz could do, considering what they were about to inflict on the old man.

"The client is based in Bristol," Baz told him as he picked up the teapot and poured a cup for the professor. "Do you remember working on a project there before the Fall?"

The old man scratched his head. He seemed genuinely puzzled. "You mean the tidal barrage in the Bristol Channel?"

"Yeah. The contraption that makes electricity."

"Preposterous."

Baz enjoyed the man's rich accent, a distant echo of Jamaica. You didn't hear it much in the Midlands these days.

"It was only ever a proof of concept we developed for the University of St Andrews. Everything collapsed around us, of course, but St Andrews was still developing the technology up in Scotland." His eyes glazed for a moment. "No! Even if we could get it working, generating the current is only the start.

You need the infrastructure to go with it. Cables, transformers, battery storage, lagoon maintenance..." His mouth froze open, his eyes suddenly wild with fear.

"Yeah," said Baz. "In future, I'd keep quiet about the it-won't-work part. Don't worry, our job is to bring you in. What happens next is none of our business."

"What if I don't want to do this?" he whispered.

Baz gave him a cold stare. "We're getting paid to deliver you alive. Didn't say nothing about bringing you back willingly."

The old man raised his hands in surrender. He might have been an academic once, but they were hard and cracked with use now. "There's no need to fight. I'm only thinking aloud."

"Good, but learn to think in your head. And do so quickly, because we're not out of the woods yet, Professor. Finish your tea, then go find Danuta and tell her it's time to give you your disguise."

Grinning, Baz brought out the Patriarch's golden hat from underneath his shirt. "Meanwhile, I need to stash this little memento of our escapade."

Eight miles from the Midland Palace, a chain blocked the canal on the approach to the Wast Hills Tunnel.

Mounted riflemen on both towpaths had met the barge a few hundred yards out and told them to moor at the chain for inspection.

"All right, let's be 'aving you," said a burly man with an extravagant black moustache. He beckoned them onto the towpath. "You're being searched, and we're boarding your barge."

"What's going on?" Baz asked him.

"We are the ones with the guns, mate. That means we ask the questions, and you keep your fookin' trap shut." He shrugged. "It's just 'ow it works, innit? You can keep yer skimpies on. Everything else comes off, and I'll warn you. We're not in a mood to piss about."

Baz's people were assembled on the tow path and strip-searched.

One of the soldiers grew tired of the professor's cringing and mewling. Slapping the old man didn't help. "What's up with this one?"

"Accident at the gunpowder factory," Baz explained. "I took him on as a favor. Regretting it now."

The Prof's act was convincing. Danuta had smeared acid over his neck and lower face. It had burned off the slave brand. A lot of his face with it. At least no one would recognize him now.

Aboard the barge, the soldiers were turning everything upside down in search of contraband or weapons. When they found nothing, they moved on to the boat's cargo of barley. Baz winced as they slid knives through the grain bags.

His original plan had been to hide the professor in one of those sacks. It had been Raffy's idea to burn his skin instead and leave him in plain sight. Things looked dicey enough as it was, because inside one of those grain sacks was a shiny patriarch's hat.

He really should have ditched it too, but old habits didn't surrender easily to common sense.

He got away with it. This time. The searches turned up nothing.

"Okay," said the man with the moustache. "Put your clothes back on and go." He adopted a marginally guilty expression and nodded at Baz. "Soz about the boat. Just doing me job, innit? Now fook off before I decide to steal your cargo."

Baz acted annoyed but too cowed to express it. People often told him he could have been an actor before the Fall, and Baz thought they were probably right.

In truth, he was overjoyed. They'd all made it out alive with the collectible and his golden memento. And Raffy the new boy had proved himself good and proper.

Lovely jubbly.

Leigh Woods, Greater Bristol

Where the woodland trails crossed, the rider brought his horse to a halt, staring along the straight path lined with leaf litter.

Despite the shade of the tree canopy, broad sunglasses obscured his eyes. The ear flaps of his leather riding helmet were tied under his bearded chin, and the combined effect meant his face was difficult to identify.

Baz didn't have to. He recognized the man's horse. Its skewbald chestnut-and-white coat was distinctive, as was its habit of tilting its head as it looked at you, as if asking a question.

Satisfied this was Grayson, the fixer for the boss of Greater Bristol, Baz emerged from the trees. As he left cover, a nasty thought smacked into him. What if he was *meant* to recognize the horse, so he wouldn't look too carefully at the rider...?

His eyes flashed to the horseman's sword and the carbine on his saddle.

But Grayson lowered his shades and offered Baz a cold smile. "Professor Jarra checks out. Congratulations on a job well done."

He drew a large pouch from his saddlebag and threw it to Baz. It was heavy with silver pennies.

Baz decided it was best not to count the coins and assess their quality in front of this man. But he would do so, later.

"The other items to cover your fees and expenses will be delivered to your room in the tavern tonight."

"Thank you," Baz said. "And if you require any further items to be found—"

"The boss wants to meet you."

"Just like that?"

"The professor was a test run." Grayson looked for a reaction.

"No!" Baz gasped with shock. Fake, of course. "I thought it was vital for the interests of Greater Bristol that you generate electricity out of a rotting machine. The one the professor claims could power literally hundreds of electric lamps, so long as they were kept very close to the shoreline. And the tide was flowing in the right direction."

"You could have just said yes without all the sarcasm."

"Where would be the fun in that?" Baz took a deep breath. "Lay it on, Grayson. Who do you need collecting?"

"You will be informed at the Clifton Observatory tomorrow. At dawn. Don't screw this up, Baz. This job is bigger than you and your tiny band of rogues. It's vital to everyone in the entire country that you deliver."

Grayson rode off, leaving Baz scratching his head. Who the hell could he be talking about? And why had he talked about it being so important for the country? There weren't any countries. Not any more. Not even Russia.

But if there was one thing he'd learned about the man, it was that every word Grayson uttered was carefully considered to serve his purpose.

"Impressive, don't you think?"

Baz wasn't clear whether Councilman Topaz meant the circular view of the Clifton Suspension Bridge, or the way it had been projected onto the table in the darkened room. Something Topaz had called a camera obscura. He covered both bases with a crisp, "Yes, sir."

"The early Victorians thought so when Brunel's design was constructed over two hundred years ago."

Ahh. So it was about the bridge.

"People believed in progress in that era, Mr. Din."

"Please, call me Baz."

"Don't interrupt, Mr. Din. When this bridge first spanned the Avon, disease was rife, and working conditions for most people would seem appalling, even to us today. Life expectancy had been declining, though not as precipitously as we experienced after the Fall. To the wretched poor of that long-ago time, this great wrought-iron bridge was a symbol of progress. Their lives were brutish and short, but this bridge was more than a route from one bank of the Avon to the other; it led to an awe-inspiring future. And it was a *British* future. Britain ruled the waves in that era, and that was no idle boast. People could feel pride in such a virile nation. Do you think the citizens clinging to the ruins of the city feel the same pride for Greater Bristol?"

Baz hated it when clients invited him to talk politics. The best approach he'd learned was to be informed and act ignorant. "I don't know, sir. I'm impressed that you keep the bridge well maintained, and the people of Bristol seem calmer than most folk I encounter around these islands. However, they still lock and bar all doors and windows at night, same as everyone else."

"Yes. We've kept Bristol itself relatively safe in recent years. That has encouraged neighboring communities to join us. Today, Greater Bristol includes all of southwest England and most of South Wales and yet my official title is Chair of the External Affairs Committee for Bristol City Council. We are led in theory by the Mayor of Bristol, though it is no secret that he belongs to me. His title is scarcely more rousing than mine."

Councilman Topaz paused and looked at Baz expectantly. Apparently, this was a conversation, no longer a rambling monologue.

Baz obliged. "After the Fall, with the old certainties collapsing over their heads, I expect people took comfort from being told what to do by Bristol City Council precisely *because* it sounded so ordinary. Especially compared to the extraordinary events taking place across the rest of the islands."

"Indeed." Topaz seemed pleased. "Time marches inexorably on, Mr. Din. We were raised in a period of chaos and invasions, you and I. *Ordinary* worked well in a world going insane. We are no longer young men, and I must look to future generations. I cannot expect them to fight and die in the uninspiring name of Bristol City Council. They will not flock to the banner of a mayor. I need a more inspiring figurehead. A new name for the state I am building here. And I want to build it upon deep foundations. Deep with history. Wessex shall arise reborn."

Baz pursed his lips, his confusion now genuine. Wessex, Sussex, Essex, Middlesex: the people of olden days must have had only one thing on their minds. It was a worldview Baz could get behind, but all these sex names were fucking confusing. "I'm sorry, sir. I don't understand."

"It was the darkest days of the Viking invasions."

Baz shook his head. There had been the Russians, the Euros, the Scots, and the Neo-Comms, of course. He didn't remember a *Viking* invasion.

"Over a thousand years ago," said Topaz, "at a place not far from here, King Alfred of Wessex rallied the survivors of his shattered world and fought back against invasion and chaos. He won a stunning victory against the Vikings and established peace and prosperity. The story still resonates, and it makes far more sense to the people of today than talk of Spitfires, battleships, and cyber war. If I can reconnect with that story, I can wield its power to bring my people a symbol of renewal. Of strength and stability. But Alfred was a king. For my dream of Wessex to become reality, I require more than a mere mayor to be its figurehead. I need the last royal in Britain. And you, Mr. Din, will collect him for me."

Colchester, Anglia

Baz tapped Raffy on the shoulder. "I'm gonna patrol. When I get back, let's run through what we've learned about the castle."

"Okay, boss."

They had set up an observation post on the roof of All Saints church tower. The medieval flint-built edifice had survived even the perils of the 21st century, although the south- and north-facing crenellations had been badly damaged. Under cover of night, they had rearranged the rubble to leave observation holes. For the west and east sides of the tower, they used periscopes shielded by netting.

The view over the castle and the surrounding area of Colchester town was excellent. In fact, it was too good. With the castle literally on the other side of the road, Baz's biggest fear was that someone in the castle would observe *them*.

The only other candidate observation post was the huge Roman-style brick water tower named Jumbo, which was slightly higher than the castle. But that was heavily guarded by the Eslingas Militia, the Eslingas being the ruling political movement, and its militia a home for former fighters of the Red Front after the collapse of the Neo-Comms.

He left Raffy keeping watch on the castle to the north and crawled under cover of the battlements to check what was going on around them.

The area to the east and south was mostly rubble and rats. Disease and decay too, according to the stench in his nose. He could see no one moving, though the rubble offered many opportunities for concealment if anyone wanted to sneak up on them.

To the west, Colchester had suffered less from the shelling, and he could see townsfolk going about their business. Streets had been cleared and the occasional multi-story building still stood.

Most showed brutalist Neo-Comm propaganda plastered onto the walls, emerging through the Eslingas slogans and symbols that had been painted over but quickly faded.

Baz was not a philosophical man, but even he was struck with the symbolism. The leaders of fractious Britain since the Fall, along with their philosophies and slogans, had become so increasingly flimsy that older histories of this ancient land were showing through.

The people of Baz's generation were nothing more than fleeting squatters in these islands, to be quickly forgotten by the future because they would leave nothing of note behind.

Shit! That was a depressing thought. But it also made Baz

think there was something substantial to Councilman Topaz's plan.

He'd asked around and had been surprised how many people still knew something of the story of King Alfred's victory against the Vikings. Even after more than a thousand years. That story had power. If Baz's team could steal away the fat royal fool kept secure inside the castle, then Topaz could harness him to those stories of Dark Age Wessex and drag its power into these new dark ages.

If there were historians of the future, they would learn nothing of Baz or his team. But if they succeeded in this venture, a successful rebirth of Wessex *would* be written about.

What they did here in Colchester might be important. Baz had never considered that he would do anything that actually mattered.

He found he liked the notion and was smiling to himself when he returned to Raffy and asked the kid to kick off his report.

"It's the largest Norman keep in Europe, built by William the Conqueror in the 1070s to secure this region of occupied England. Its weirdly pink stone is because it's mostly constructed from scavenged building material from Roman Colchester. In fact, the castle uses the largest Roman temple in Britain as its foundation, a temple burned down around 60AD by the Celtic rebel Boudica."

"How can you possibly know all this shit that happened centuries ago?"

Raffy frowned, but he didn't break away from his observation of the castle. "This church was deconsecrated and turned in a museum long before the Fall. Didn't you read the material downstairs?"

That hadn't occurred to Baz. "Skip a few centuries, Raffy. Then carry on."

"The walls are one hundred feet high. The top half is long gone, demolished in the 1600s to sell as building material. In the 1700s, the remainder was restored. Windows were put in and the south-facing walls and towers roofed with those fancy red tiles in the Italian style of the period. A domed observatory was added—"

"Raffy?"

"Yeah, boss."

"This town is thousands of years old. A lot has happened

in that time. I get that. Maybe one day when the world is soft and peachy, I'll come back for a fucking vacation. Then I might actually care. On this trip, I want to know how we get into that castle, and just as important—"

"Ways of getting out."

"Better." He considered the lad. Had he been too harsh? No. Raffy could take his chiding all day long and nothing would kill his puppy dog eagerness to prove himself. "Take a deep breath, Raffy boy, and remind yourself that you aren't a historian. Then try again."

"Yeah, boss." He did. Raffy literally took a deep breath, held it for a few seconds, and then let out a stream of details. "Water supply and sewage systems were screwed during the shelling. I mean totally obliterated. So there are no convenient pipes for us to get in or out."

"What's their water supply?"

"There's a castle well but its water isn't safe to drink. They're trying to fix that, but meanwhile they take water carted each day from the river and boil some for drinking. They've also stockpiled enough bottled water to survive a short siege."

Baz already knew all this. What he really wanted was to hear it rearranged in a way that sparked fresh ideas. "What else?"

"I estimate thirty militiamen guard the castle. If the general secretary is there, she'll add at least another twenty of her personal guard. Lord Sussex spends most of his time in that dome on the tower to the left. It's called the cupola. When he leaves the castle, there's always at least a dozen guards with him. The way they're positioned suggests they're not only protecting him from harm but from him escaping, too. He's a prisoner."

"He's a valuable asset. That's why we're here, Raffy."

"So what's the plan?"

"Patience. We find an in."

"What if we don't?"

"Then we will need plenty of rope. Let's hope it doesn't come to scaling the walls. Who else comes and goes into that castle?"

"Maids and cleaners. Suppliers of food and beverages. The dung collector. Carpenters. Prostitutes and other entertainers. Eslingas party officials."

"Dung collector. Hmmm. Tell me more..."

The militiaman waiting at the bar tapped his friend on the shoulder and sniffed the air theatrically, wrinkling his nose with disgust. "Hey, Tom," he shouted across the bar at the man filling three tankards from a barrel. "Your pub's got an odor problem; we could smell it halfway down Mersea Road."

"The hell you say." The barman settled the beers down on the bar and took in the situation with a glance. "Have a heart," he muttered as he scooped up the silver bits in payment.

All three militiamen laughed at that. Here at the Odd One Out pub, they were off duty, without the usual crossed webbing belts and weapons. They still wore their paratrooper berets with the feathers dyed red over white.

In Colchester, if you wore the burgundy beret of the Eslingas Militia, you could more or less do whatever you wanted.

One of them spun around with an outstretched finger like a fleshy weathervane. "Don't you worry yourself, Tom. I've found your problem."

He pointed out a man sitting alone, oblivious to the attention, his world shrunk to the mug of beer on the table before him.

The militiamen fanned out around the fellow until finally he looked up and saw his doom.

"You stink worse than a leper's arse," accused one of the Eslingas men.

"Worse than your whore mother's pus-stained drawers," said another.

There came a pause as they waited for the third militiaman to top the insult. But his face was blank. All three broke into laughter.

"My mum died a long time ago," said the victim. "And if I smell, it's my job. I swear I washed thoroughly before I came out. I can't wash any more than I already have."

"We know who you are, Dmitri. We see you slink into the castle when decent folk are abed. And we know what you do. You're a professional shit shoveler. A gong farmer."

"Yeah, a professional odor, too." The militiamen guffawed. "A perpetual offense to this town. But we're bighearted fellows in the militia. Let us help you."

The man who had first pointed him out lifted Dimitri's

beer and slowly poured it over the dung collector's head. All three then poured their own ales over the man, drenching him from his mop of black hair to his trousers that dripped into a foaming puddle on the floorboards.

"No need to thank us," the ringleader said. "That will be three silver pennies to replace our beers."

"But... But they cost a fraction of that!"

The militiaman's face glowed with evil glee. "You're forgetting the service charge." His features switched into a snarl that made Dimitri jump. He grabbed his victim by the collar and lifted him half out of his seat. "We take debtors to the castle dungeon. Do you know what we do there to people we don't like?"

Dmitri was a big man himself, but he trembled like a sapling in a stiff breeze, handing over a purse of coins. "Please. It's all I have."

One of the men made a show of pinching his nose while he tipped over the pouch and showered coins onto the table. It didn't quite come to three silver pennies, but it was close.

"We'll let you off this time," said the man still gripping his collar. "Take your odor downwind."

Dimitri didn't need telling twice. He hurried for the front door, his feet squelching in his clogs, but was intercepted by a leg stretched across his way.

"Stay there," said a voice. "Let me get you a pint."

"I don't want to hang around."

"I insist. However, I can see you're having a bad day, so let me get you as many beers as you can take. We can drink outside, if you like."

Dmitri frowned, confused, but beer was his only solace. He nodded.

"Good. My name is Baz. How would you like to put one over on those Eslingas arseholes? You can make them look bad *and* get paid for it."

Dimitri's eyes hooded with suspicion. "I ain't joining the Neo-Comms, if that's who you are."

Baz spat on the floor. "All ideologies can go fuck themselves. Look where they got the world. No, Dimitri, I'm only interested in a little light larceny. And seeing those bullies put in the town stocks where they belong."

"What's the catch?"

"None. Not for you, anyway. In fact, quite the reverse." Baz slapped a comradely arm over the man's shoulder. "Business must be booming, Dmitri, me ol' mate. You've just taken on some apprentices."

At the end of the wooden bridge across the dry moat, Baz and Raffy groaned with relief as they temporarily set down the heavy dong cart they'd dragged through Colchester.

In the yellow light of the kerosene lamps hung over the castle door, the dung steamed into the night.

At Dmitri's urging, they had acclimatized themselves to the stink over the last few days at his gong farm on the town's outskirts. Baz barely noticed the reek that had to be coming from the foul ordure. The stains worked into his smock were another matter. He shuddered at the thought of wearing such revolting garments next to the skin, getting the disgust out of his system before the guards saw him.

As the master of this gong crew, Dmitri hadn't troubled himself with pulling the heavy cart, leaving Baz and Raffy to haul on the shafts. Now he proceeded alone to the heavy castle door set with metal studs. He had his fist raised, ready to rap on the portal, when the viewport slid open and a voice called out, "Oi! Keep your filthy mitts off my door!"

Dimitri stepped back. The sounds of bolts and bars being moved came through the door. It creaked open. After three weeks of surveillance and plotting, they were finally about to enter the castle.

Two militiamen guarded the gateway, assault rifles slung over their shoulders. They seemed pleased to have something to relieve the monotony of the long night watch.

"You're supposed to take the bloody stuff away," one admonished Dimitri good-naturedly. "Not bring it with you, you daft pillock."

"What?" Dimitri acted offended. "You think only people in your precious castle need to shit? It's a growth industry, my friend. You ever get bored of opening and closing this door for a living, you look me up and we'll see if I can't find you a job."

"Just as well my nose is blocked with this sodding cold. Go on. Get yourselves inside and go about your business."

Baz and Raffy picked up their shafts once more and dragged the dung cart after Dimitri, following him to the ground floor latrines.

The interior wasn't what Baz had expected. He'd seen inside the inner courtyards of a few reoccupied castles, but this place had been fully roofed for centuries and had been a museum before the Fall. Most of the interior was rough stonework from a thousand years ago, but some of the walls were hung with threadbare tapestries and ancient mosaics with missing tiles. There was an upper floor that was a series of stone columns and ornamental archways, accessed by a gently sloping wheelchair ramp. At the center of the ground floor was a glass elevator that still seemed to be in regular use, though now moved by ropes and ratchets.

"Halt!"

The sergeant of the guard had emerged from the gatehouse and was giving Dimitri's new apprentices a suspicious glare. "Search them."

The two other guards radiated displeasure but did as they were told, patting down all three gong men before taking long spears off the wall display marked REPLICA LATE-ROMAN ARMY EQUIPMENT. They thrust the spears deep into the dung.

For some reason, while the cart was being checked for anything untoward, the sergeant singled out Baz for the evil eye. Baz forced himself to keep calm and not worry about the man's thoroughness.

Hidden inside the dung were weapons, rope, a change of clothing, a breathing tube, and other small items of equipment, all kept clean inside waxed bags.

On the way out, the plan was to hide Raffy in there, his place at the cart's shaft to be taken by Lord Sussex wearing clogs and shit stains.

Baz suspected that real Roman legionaries wouldn't be impressed by these replica spears, but it would be a bad day for Raffy if one of those spear heads pierced his intestines on the way out. A bad day for all of them.

That prospect still lay ahead, because the guards declared the dung cart clear of contraband or hidden armies. Their sergeant waved Baz's team on their way.

Baz put his lock pick away. Sussex's door wasn't locked.

He glanced at the guard Raffy was gagging and binding. Had the man been there to keep intruders out or the royal person in?

His presence could be more evidence that there was more to Councilor Topaz's lie than Baz had first suspected. They would soon find out.

He considered the guard again. The duke was housed in the cupola, a circular room built onto the remnants of the southwest tower. Access was via a spiral stone staircase from the main gate, or as they had come, via the roof. If they needed to get down the stairs in a hurry, that guard was going to be in the way.

In his youth, Baz would have simply slit the man's throat. In recent years, though, his conscience troubled him enough to wake him at night. He didn't want Raffy to suffer the same fate.

"Truss him real good," he told the boy. "Then watch the roof."

"Roger that, boss."

Baz took two deep breaths. Then he pushed his way in.

Inside was a dome of opulence. Wall hangings, a four-poster bed, plush tables and seats. A guard was half asleep in a wingback sofa chair.

Before he came fully alert, Baz had a pistol against the man's forehead.

The curtain drew back across the bed and a pale face thrust out. "Who the devil are you?"

"I mean you no harm, my lord." Baz turned the guard to face the wall and pushed the pistol into his back. "Nor him if he wants to see the dawn."

The duke's face pinched. For a moment, Baz thought he saw the ruthlessness of a cruel predator in those narrowed eyes. Then they widened and Sussex clapped his hands with delight. Like a spoiled little girl.

"I declare, I recognize you. Several times in recent weeks, as I traveled the streets of this town, there you were in the throng, giving me the strangest look, as if attempting to make a communication with your superior. Yet whenever I sent my men to retrieve you, you were never to be found."

"That was an alternate strategy, my lord. It's not easy achieving an audience without attracting attention. Hence tonight's unsubtle approach. I have a message to convey. Shall you hear it?"

Sussex threw back the heavy sheets and got out of bed, clad in striped pajamas and a night cap. The two men sized each other up.

Baz was unimpressed.

Lord Sussex was well fed. Not fat exactly, but here was a man who'd never gone hungry in his life. Despite the Fall, a little royal blood still meant a life of ultimate privilege. Even the way the man studied him had a simpering quality, as if he were playing a jolly game with rules he hadn't quite figured out.

It was enough to make Baz want to join the Neo-Comms... for about a heartbeat, until his brain supplied memories of flyblown corpses choking the streets.

"I will hear this message." Sussex gestured toward the rear of the chamber. "Benton, please refrain from raising the general alarm for the time being."

"Yes, my lord," came a hidden voice, perhaps behind one of the wall hangings. The voice sounded familiar.

When Baz didn't immediately speak, Sussex pouted. "Have you forgotten your tongue, man?"

"My message is sensitive."

Sussex laughed. "Benton has enough dirt on me to bury the entire castle and the land as far as the eye can see."

He moved closer to Baz and regarded the guard coolly. "Not so Mr. Franzen, the poor fellow you are inconveniencing with your pistol. He's not been in my household long. Give Franzen your weapons. Then he and they shall wait quietly outside the door, without alerting the guards down at the gatehouse, while you deliver your... sensitivities."

Baz didn't hesitate. He'd always decided that the only practical way to get Sussex out was if he came willingly. He handed over his pistol and the knife sheathed at his calf. When Franzen left and the heavy wooden door pulled tight behind him in its frame, Sussex sighed with relief and pulled a green velvet chair from a writing desk set against the wall.

After an embarrassing moment when Baz stepped forward, thinking to rest his butt on the seat, the royal duke sat down himself. He waved at Baz without bothering to look at him. "Proceed."

"I bear you an offer. You exchange your imminent death for a new life and a new role. An elevated one."

"Your offer bores me already, and so do you. I find this life comfortable. And suffocated with guards as I am, I scarcely find you threatening. Other than your odor, perhaps. Have you been rolling in manure?"

"Never mind me. Weren't you born to be more than this, my lord? Here you are nothing but a pampered figurehead, kept prisoner in Colchester Castle by the general secretary and aired at public appearances for her convenience."

"Have a care! I have had men's tongues cut out for less." Sussex sniffed haughtily and looked away. The anger seemed real, but Baz thought the man was using it to shield his excitement from view. He was highly intrigued. Flattered, too.

The last royal in the land made a flouncing performance of mastering his indignation before graciously deigning to look upon the uncouth fellow who had uttered these calumnies.

To Baz's surprise, the haughty aura cast by Sussex evaporated. He slumped in his plush chair and for the first time the man appeared as he truly was. A pampered pet, terrified of the day his owner would tire of him.

"Despite your rudeness," Sussex said in a quiet voice, "nonetheless, you speak an inconvenient truth. My position here, these *spacious* apartments..." He gestured at the fancily equipped room that was nonetheless far from spacious. He scowled at the wooden door. "And many of those who guard it do so at the pleasure of the General Secretary of Eslingas, the ruler of Anglia. What of it, sir?"

"Your problem, my lord, is that the general secretary is about to shift from seeing you as a convenience to an inconvenience. Instead of someone who represents a connection to a past she condemns as problematic, it would be far better for the people of Anglia to look up to someone who represents the future. A progressive future. Who better than the general secretary herself, now that she considers her position to be secure?"

Sussex's face hardened.

As the last survivor of the main British royal line, Lord Sussex had been a pawn more than once in the attempts by a kaleidoscope of successor states to give them veneers of legitimacy.

Baz had made a lazy assumption that this man was nothing better than a fattened fool, but he sensed that Sussex had known this day would eventually come.

"Whence come you by this information?"

"Councilman Topaz of—"

"Ahh. Now the curtain is pulled back and reveals the eminence grise of Greater Bristol."

"Or," Baz suggested, "of Wessex."

Baz had no fucking idea what an eminence grise was, but he knew he'd hit the bullseye as soon as he dropped the word Wessex.

Hook, line, and sinker.

Was the general secretary really planning on retiring her royal asset? He had no idea. But the target bought it.

Eyes sparkling, Sussex flicked out his hand at the wrist, as if waving to a fawning crowd from a royal coach. "I assume the Mayor of Bristol is no longer an adequate outlet for Topaz's ambitions. What role does he envision for me?"

"Prince of Wessex. At least for now. You would be the head of a royal dynasty. The New House of Wessex."

Baz allowed his target a few moments to steep in his royal fantasy. Then he regretted the delay when a hue and cry erupted through the castle.

Raffy pushed open the door and handed back Baz's pistol and knife. "We've been rumbled, boss."

"What of the man you took this pistol from?" Sussex demanded of Raffy.

"Dead, my lord."

The boy hadn't hesitated. Baz had high hopes for him.

Sussex beamed with delight. "Excellent. That saves me the bother of doing it myself. What? Oh, don't look so shocked. Franzen was the general secretary's man and didn't even have the manners to pretend otherwise. Now leave my chambers and Godspeed. Benton, the alarm, if you please."

A siren began blaring from the guardhouse at the base of the tower.

Baz and Raffy ran for it.

Pistols drawn, and with rope still coiled over their shoulders, the two collectors descended the tower's spiral. The sound of heavy boots ascending the same ancient steps sent them retreating back up, Baz intending to lead them out onto the roof.

As he climbed the last upward turn of the tower, he glimpsed a figure dart out of the cupola and through the door to the roof. It didn't look like Sussex. It had to be Benton.

They followed him out onto the roof, and when Baz shut

the door, his heart skipped a beat. There was a key in the lock. He turned it. That hadn't been there before.

The escape plan was to climb down the northwest tower, Raffy having selected it as the one with the most intact crenellations to tie their rope to. They just had to hope that one would be strong enough to bear their weight.

Across the unsafe roofing between them and the northwest tower was a steel walkway burnished a coppery sheen in the glow of the kerosene lamps. A hooded figure stood halfway across. Benton—presumably—turned to them. Baz squinted but his eyes couldn't penetrate the deep shadow of the man's hood.

"The locked door won't stop them for long," Benton warned. "They'll come up from the northeast tower. Climb down the sloping roof below the cupola. There's rope already tied there for you."

Benton was applying a false growl to his voice, but Baz knew it from somewhere.

Somebody was being set up, and Baz had a feeling it was him. Yet his instincts told him to trust this warning, and he'd learned not to waste time questioning his gut when weapons were about to get shooty.

"Err, boss?"

"Follow me, lad!"

Baz climbed onto the metal handhold that ran alongside the walkway and jumped onto the sloping red tiles that overhung the tower below the cupola. They looked totally out of place on a castle, but he had no difficulty clambering down them on his butt. Good job it wasn't raining. Or icy.

His flashlight revealed a hook driven into the stone where the tower butted against the west wall. From this hook, a rope dangled into the darkness. Hopefully as far as the ground, almost a hundred feet below.

"We brought our own ropes," Raffy complained from the top of the wall. "I can tie ours to the handrail."

Baz laughed. The boy was annoyed because he'd acquired the rope and they'd snuck it into the castle and carried it with them all this way.

"Benton knows this castle better than we do, Raffy. I'll go first. If I fall and die, then you try it your way."

Baz jumped for Benton's rope. He imagined Raffy's heart leaping up his throat to watch the high stakes maneuver, but it was easier than it looked. The positioning of the rope was carefully designed for this purpose, although how the hook had been placed there he'd love to know. In the map of the castle he'd built in his head from weeks of observation, he knew the rope dropped through a blind spot, avoiding all windows and walkways.

When the rope neither snapped under his weight nor unraveled, he descended with practiced speed.

"What're you waiting for?" he called up. "Climb on."

He felt the rope tense under Raffy's extra weight. It held fast. Baz abseiled down, keeping an eye on the darkness below and an ear on the guards he could hear running around the far side of the roof.

He was intent on watching the ground for signs of militiamen when his hand grabbed thin air and he juddered to a stop, his weight carried by one hand and an arm that connected to a shoulder joint that was threatening to pop.

As if that weren't enough, his hand was slipping.

Baz swung his free hand up to grab the end of the rope.

His grip was secure for the moment, but no matter how hard he stared into the dark below him, he couldn't see the ground.

Raffy whispered, "Jump!"

"Easy for you to say."

"You've old man's eyes, boss. I can see the ground. It's just below you. Trust me."

Baz let go and dropped.

And kept on falling.

Fear spiked through him because the ground wasn't there!

The moment of panic must have lasted no more than a fraction of a second, but he was consumed by it.

Then the ground hit hard, and he was rolling, trying to absorb the impact.

He came to rest on his back in the damp grass looking up at Raffy dangling from the end of the rope. He was only ten feet above the ground. Only ten! The lad let go and landed in a crouch with barely a grunt.

Damn! Baz had to admit that his body didn't bounce as well as it once had.

Raffy hauled him up by his right hand. His left was sprained or broken. His knees weren't much happier, and his bruised ribs were protesting, but he had to get away.

Ignoring his injuries, they pushed north through the manicured lawn of the castle grounds, heading for the boating lake, where the girls would be waiting with med kits and rifles.

"There they are!" screamed a voice from the castle wall.

Baz picked up the pace.

Rifle bullets thudded into the grass.

"Make for the trees," Raffy shouted.

The line of trees was only thirty yards away. Beyond that, the ground sloped down sharply and would shield them from the castle wall. If they made it past the trees, they would be okay.

He momentarily thought of Dimitri, stuck inside the castle. The gong farmer had been paid handsomely in silver. He was no longer Baz's problem.

They crossed a path, rounds pinging off its surface only inches away. The sharpshooters on the castle wall must have night vision scopes. He hadn't accounted for that. "Fuck! I thought this was going to be easy."

"Yeah, so did Dimitri. Now can we try my idea?" Raffy was running for his life, but his words were filled with excitement. "Now the royal nob's on board, we just have to get him out. My plan's the best way. You know it is."

The lad had a point, but Baz wasn't ready to concede just yet. Besides, he hadn't spare breath in his lungs to reply.

He lunged for the cover of the trees. He tripped. Tumbled. Rolled down the steep bank on the far side, but he was laughing because the fall dropped him into the soft caress of a ditch filled with ferns.

Raffy fell, too, crying out in pain or shock.

Baz turned back, but he couldn't see the castle through the trees. They'd made it!

The lad was panting. For a moment, Baz was pleased he had endurance that the kid hadn't yet developed. Then he realized he was hearing the staccato breaths from a stabbing pain. Raffy must have fallen badly. "Raffy, can you make it to the exfil point?"

"Not over the wall."

The clouds had lifted, and Baz could see a little of the route ahead in the moonlight. A low Roman wall ran across their path. They had meant to leap over it, but he remembered there was a gap to their right where there had once been a gate.

"We'll bear right. Let's get to the far side of the wall. It'll be hard cover and I can signal the girls to come help from there."

"Boss, I've been shot."

"Bugger!"

"Steady on, boss. I'm not dead. Flesh wound. Stings like hell, but I'll make it. Let's get to the far side of the bandstand. You can signal from there."

With Raffy leaning heavily on his shoulder, Baz carried him out of the ditch and over to the bandstand, laying him on the concrete on the far side of its stone dais from the castle. Baz risked using his flashlight to inspect the wound.

A hole had been blasted through the top of Raffy's chest and the lad was losing a lot of blood. But he wasn't gone yet, and Baz wasn't abandoning him. Krystyn and Danuta were waiting for them at the boating lake. It was only a few hundred yards farther on, but the slope down was precipitous. If he tried to reach them with Raffy in the darkness, they would probably both tumble arse over tit.

Coming to a decision, Baz took off his shirt, folded it up, and used his knee to press it hard against the boy's wound. He directed his flashlight at the boating lake and flicked it on and off in the prearranged signal to tell the girls to come rescue their arses.

"Raffy? Raffy? Rafiq! Talk to me, boy."

But Raffy's only reply was his wheezing chest beneath Baz's knee.

He stared into the dark, trying desperately to see the girls, to draw hope from them. He didn't spot them until they were only a few feet away. When they didn't want to be seen, they were silent and invisible.

One had an assault rifle at the ready, the other a med kit.

Krystyn pushed his knee away and replaced it with a hand. Her other hand held clean sterile linen padding; a flashlight gripped in her teeth illuminated Raffy's wound.

She didn't apply the pad.

Instead, she withdrew Baz's blood-soaked shirt. Raffy's blood had stopped flowing out of the wound.

It was many seconds before anyone spoke.

"I'm not leaving him," said Baz.

Danuta sucked in a breath. "He's dead."

"I know. And we're not leaving him."

He could sense disapproval from the two women, but they

didn't fight him on this. "Very well," Krystyn said. "We leave together."

They buried him a mile to the north, on a hillside overlooking Colchester. Below them, the castle and the huge fake-Roman water tower were silhouetted against the dawn. Raffy had spent weeks watching the town. Now he would do so for eternity.

After they'd stood in silence for several minutes, Baz drew things to a close. "Wherever you're headed, Rafiq Kirk, may you find peace there."

"And excitement," Krystyn said.

"Girls, too." Danuta laughed. "Not cynical old nanny goats like us. Young, soft, and stupid. Just the way you liked them, Raffy."

"Oh," said Krystyn. "And those hot samosas he kept making us try."

"Those, too," Baz agreed. "So long, kid."

He felt the others turn to him, looking for his lead.

Baz kept his gaze on the castle. "We follow Raffy's plan."

"No," said Danuta. "I'm cut up about poor Raffy, but I'm not following his stupid plan just because I'm sad."

"We *are* doing it for Raffy," Baz said, "but we're also doing it for us. Have you a better plan?" He rounded on her. "Do you still want that payout?"

"I do."

"If you won't do it, Krystyn can take your place." He checked with Krystyn, who nodded her consent.

Danuta shook her head. "No, I'll do it. This is more my kind of operation." She crouched down and placed her palm over the freshly tilled soil. "I hope you're enjoying this, Rafiq. I warn you, though. If your plan doesn't work, I'm going to come down to hell and make your afterlife a misery."

Lord Sussex leaned through the north window of his cupola and stared at the red tiles below, willing someone to come rescue him. He was fed up to the back teeth with pretending to be a real-life prince locked in a tower, straight out of one of those garbage Disney movies he'd watched as a kid.

Ironically, after the abortive extraction by the emissaries of

Councilman Topaz, his spies told him that the general secretary really was preparing the way for her tame royal to have an unfortunate accident.

The act he'd sold to Din was becoming reality.

The general secretary was a ditherer, but Sussex couldn't count on her vacillation much longer. Barry Din remained his preferred option. His sources insisted that the man was the best in the country for smuggling items from beneath the noses of the powerful.

But if Din didn't deliver in the next few days, there would be nothing for it but to flee to Bristol using his own resources. He might not live through that experience. Even if he did, the next phase would be infinitely more dangerous if Topaz's people hadn't been the ones to rescue the poor prince in the tower.

There was a knock on the door and the maid appeared, pushing a trolley of cleaning things.

No.

This woman wore the same attire, but she wasn't his Sarah.

His heart thumping, he beamed at his guard. "Federov, my good man, why don't you take a well-deserved break from your onerous duties?"

The fellow was hesitant, but when Sussex added a wink, Federov returned a comradely leer. "Very good, my lord."

When Federov had gone, the maid gave Sussex a coquettish smile. "You're very presumptuous, my lord."

The new maid wore an oversized white linen apron over a gray blouse and skirt. Oval face, brown eyes, cheeks like hillocks, mid-thirties. She would be beautiful if she let her hair down, but Sussex wasn't checking her out for her looks. He wanted to know if he'd seen her before, perhaps one of the general secretary's people sent to kill him.

He was sure he didn't know her. He decided she must work for Din.

"Cut the banter," he told her. "Let's get to business."

The woman raised a playful eyebrow. Then she shrugged off her apron and began unbuttoning her blouse.

Sussex's jaw dropped, caught between disappointment that this wasn't a rescue plot, but excited at the sight of a beautiful woman disrobing for his pleasure.

He stuck out a warning finger. "Wait a second, if you

please."

The moment when a desirable woman's breasts spilled into view for the first time was a wonder he might never experience again. He went to his dresser to pick up his spectacles to appreciate her properly.

But the woman disobeyed him. She took off her blouse and handed her garment to him!

"Oh." Glasses forgotten, he watched her unzip her skirt.

She'd been wearing two identical blouses. Underneath her skirt, another apron was wrapped about her hips over another skirt.

"Let's get this straight," he said. "Your plan is for me to escape dressed up as a servant girl. Who do you think I am? Bonnie Prince Charlie?"

She frowned, tracing her finger in the air. "No, that was your grandfather. And it isn't my plan. It's Raffy's."

The woman was unhinged. "Never mind. Let's get this over with."

She stood right in front of him and stared at his face. Bold as brass! He'd never encountered such an insolent wench.

"It's not just the clothes, my lord. You'll need a ton of foundation. Another shave, too, and then nude lipstick and a little eyeliner. I've some pretty sandals in my trolley."

"Is all that really necessary?"

"Yes. Strip! We don't have much time."

"What's your name?"

Danuta sucked in her lower lip and watched the exchange between the fat guard in the paratrooper beret and the would-be Prince of Wessex in lipstick and a modest heel. She hadn't planned for him to attract this sort of attention. Men continuously managed to disappoint her.

Lord Sussex replied in a shy whisper. "I'm Anna."

Danuta gave the other militiaman guarding the castle gate a wink and then put a hand on an outthrust hip to address his friend hitting on Lord Sussex. "You've set your sights a little low, haven't you, soldier?"

"I'm not a soldier," he protested. "I'm a security consultant."

"Does it pay well?"

"Very."

"Ain't no damned justice," the other guard growled under his breath.

"Forget Anna," Danuta hurriedly told the fat security consultant. "Why don't you share some of your pay with me?"

He licked his lips as if he thought that was sexy. Meanwhile, he mentally stripped Danuta, caressing her body with his gaze. "Maybe I will."

"I live close by. In the Dutch Quarter. It's the house standing alone in Stockwell Street with the yellow walls. Ask for Jennifer."

"I'll do that. But I'd rather enjoy you both together."

The regular guard waved them on their way. "Get out of here before he shows off the size of his money pouch."

Before they cleared the gateway, the saucy guard lunged forward and landed a meaty slap on Lord Sussex's royal rump. The poor man nearly jumped out of his skin, which made both guards laugh their heads off.

When they'd reached the far end of the moat, Danuta turned and gave both guards the finger. "Beasts!"

That only made them laugh harder.

Collectible in tow, Danuta headed for the town center, but as soon as they were out of sight of the castle, they switched direction and hurried to the Hythe Docks where their ship was waiting to sail on the tide.

Queen's Square, Bristol

"You could retire," said Krystyn. "We could *all* retire."

"Don't spoil his day of triumph," Danuta said.

"Whose? Baz or the prince?"

"Ahh, the prince to be..." Danuta's dreamy voice was winding Baz up. "I remember when he was just Anna the simple serving wench with a peachy bum."

Baz ignored them and allowed himself to be swept up in the crowd's excitement, waving his hat in the air.

The coronation procession had wound its way through the streets of Old Bristol, temporarily swept clear of garbage, dung, vermin, and poverty. Today the route was adorned with flags. He'd never seen so many banners in one place. They were different sizes and subtle variations in design and color, but all displayed a golden dragon on a red background.

The flag of Wessex.

Trimmed and weeded, the ornate lawns of Queen's Square served as the site of coronation itself, and Baz's team had an excellent view of the platform erected at its center.

"Here comes the big moment," said Krystyn.

A hush came over the crowd, all eyes on the platform.

Lord Sussex knelt before former Councilman Topaz, now the first High Councilor of Wessex. Sussex bowed his head slightly and Topaz placed the crown of Wessex on his head.

Eyes closed, the last royal continued to kneel for almost a minute while he mouthed a silent prayer.

The man had knelt before the crowd as Lord Sussex. Now he arose as Prince of Wessex.

The cheer from the people was so hearty it astonished Baz. He'd never seen so many happy people. And the drinking hadn't even properly begun.

Topaz lifted his hands and declared, "Long live the prince!"

"Job done," Danuta said when the chanting subsided.

"No." Baz shook his head. "I have a feeling we're only just beginning."

"Come."

Such a simple word, but the prince layered it with meaning.

It had been three weeks since the coronation, and Baz had been invited by the new prince to join a stag hunt on Exmoor.

Mist clung to the moors, relentlessly soaking Baz's clothing. The prince himself was mounted on a white steed, but Baz and his entourage followed on mountain bikes, hunting rifles slung over their backs. At least the exercise kept the cold at bay.

The shooting party had descended into a river valley, intending to cross the River Barle at a primitive bridge made of huge stone slabs.

Or so Baz had thought.

The prince had dismounted and handed his reins to a lackey, striding across the damp stones alone and on foot.

Baz followed.

Halfway across, the prince stopped, and Baz looked back. The horse and the entourage had disappeared into the trees lining the river.

At least Baz's bike was still there.

"We're not here to hunt stags are we, my lord?"

"Good heavens, no. To clarify, I shall indeed enjoy the day's hunting. You shall endure it with a smile on your face. Neither has anything to do with why you are here."

A whistle blew from the trees behind them.

Baz reached for the rifle over his back. "Should I be concerned for your safety?"

"Don't be ridiculous. This is the first chance I've had to speak to you without listening devices or spies. Of course I'm not in danger."

A hooded man approached from the far bank, mounted on a chestnut horse.

The rider bowed his head when he met them on the bridge. "My lord."

"Benton," the prince acknowledged.

The rider drew back his hood.

Baz's eyes popped. A score of questions bubbled up, but he answered every one before they reached his lips. "Well played," he said. "Grayson."

"My name is Benton Grayson, and you need to tell me whether you are still in business as a collector."

"I am. *We* are."

"Delighted to hear it," the prince said. "I am now Prince of Wessex but what is this political confection other than an old name? Beneath the flag waving, it's a sham that won't outlast Topaz. In the days of Alfred, this was a kingdom, and he was a king. To thrive, Wessex must be a kingdom once more, don't you agree?"

"The prince has a task for you," Benton Grayson said before Baz felt compelled to answer. "Topaz has outlived his usefulness. Before he realizes this, the prince wishes you to collect evidence of corruption and abuse among the powerful. You will find plenty, but you will also make deliveries, planting evidence of wrongdoing to either blackmail or discredit as the prince sees fit."

Wessex was staring at Baz. Studying his reaction. Calculating. His eyes held a cool intelligence, and to think Baz had once considered him a fattened fool. He'd never been that.

"If there's one useful thing my parents instilled in me," the prince said, "it's the importance of dynasty. Every lie, every betrayal, every murder can be justified if it means my royal line survives and prospers. The success of my dynasty and of

Wessex are intimately bound to one another. What do you say, man?"

Outmaneuvered, tempted by glittering riches and the prospect of adventure, Baz had only one possible reply.

"Long live the king!"

THE RISING SUN

Mark Stallings

April 29, 1995
Misaki Park

"Do you know what today is, Mister Hansen?" At the silence, Gichin turned to regard the American. "It is Showa No Hi. Originally, it was the emperor's birthday. Emperor Showa. You knew him as Hirohito, our emperor during World War II. Now, it is a day of reflection of our country's turbulent past and a time for us to think about the future. Appropriate, don't you think?"

Hansen shifted uncomfortably. "Minister, why are we meeting out here?" The park was situated on the eastern edge of Japan and gave a commanding view of the Pacific ocean. As it was the middle of the day, there weren't many visitors. Just a few older people looking for their own answers in the peaceful park.

"I wanted you to see where it will begin." Gichin pointed to the harbor directly west of where they stood. "The ship I have arranged is due to dock here within the hour. Do you have the software for the pods?"

Hansen extended a flash drive. "It has the latest design schematics from Doctor Shankur. You will also find the stl files to fabricate the circuit boards. The code for the eProms is also on the drive."

Gichin took it from him and tucked it inside his suit jacket. "You have done my country a great service, Hansen-san. Please convey my gratitude to Siree-sama." Gichin bowed slightly.

That seemed to startle Hansen, as his bow was awkward. Gichin smiled.

"I was told to ask about the next communications satellite?" Hansen asked.

"The modifications agreed upon have been inserted at the base code level. It will be launched and operational long before it is needed. You can convey that to your superiors?" Gishin wondered that the Americans had been able to do anything in secret, wanting to micromanage every aspect of the initiative, even here in Japan.

A fit man in a dark suit stepped up to the pair. "It seems our time together is over." Gishin inclined his head. "Safe journeys, Mister Hansen." He watched the two men head to the waiting sedan and returned to watching as the ship carrying his country's future navigated the harbor.

The crunch of gravel announced the return of his assistant. Gishin held out the flash drive. "Make sure this is copied before you give it to those corporate jackals." The aide nodded. "And tell that drunkard Norio that his Yakuza need to be discreet moving those pods. I don't want the inspectors sniffing around. I have enough problems with the Defense Force asking why I am draining their experienced soldiers."

"Hai!" The aide bowed and left swiftly. Gichin strolled around the park, reflecting on what was to come. He had just ensured that his country and his emperor would survive whatever was to come.

Fifty-three years after The Collapse
Ichi Base

A keening electronic wail sliced through Yuichi's consciousness. Thumping. *Ugh, is it time for school?* He tried to say his usual "Five more minutes." But all that came out was a croak. *That's weird.* Yuichi tried to open his eyes, but they were crusted shut. He heard voices exclaim loudly as he stirred. Finally able to get his eyes working, he looked around the dim area. Everything was blurry and distorted. "Nani?" he croaked.

With a hiss, the lid to his CHILSS (Cryogenic Human Life Support Structures) lifted. The world cleared instantly as the plexiglass slid away.

"Drink this." A drink packet was pushed into his hands. He greedily slurped the liquid. The Go Juice he used to get in Roppongi had nothing on this. He could feel energy and clarity coursing through his body, instantly making the world three shades sharper. The rush of voices transformed from noise to distinct conversations.

"Daijobu?" someone asked. Yuichi looked up and saw a young man, only slightly older than himself, wearing a dark blue uniform. The Kanji for One on the shoulder.

"Yes, I am all right." Yuichi tried to get out of the pod.

"Let me help you. I am Lieutenant Watanabe. Toshiro." He pulled Yuichi out of the pod and helped him stand on legs that were little more than wet udon noodles.

He was in a room with nine other pods. Water was pouring down the wall furthest from the only door, which was shut. Four people were trying to pry the door open with improvised tools. Only six people? "The other pods?" he asked.

Toshiro shrugged and pointed. "One empty, three look smashed. The people in them are dead."

Horror spread over Yuichi. "Dead?" Toshiro nodded. It seemed minutes ago Yuichi was taking a sleeping pill and his uncle was laughing. Keiko was next to him. "Keiko?" Yuichi blurted. Toshiro shook his head.

"Not in this room. Maybe one of the others."

The sounds of running water became apparent as the conversations died. "What's going on? Why the water?" Yuichi asked.

"The room is flooding"—he pointed at the ankle-deep water below their platform—"and it is rising fast." Toshiro pointed at the door. "It won't open, and the keypad was smashed."

"Any other way out? Vents?" Yuichi scanned the ceiling.

"Too small."

His brain was going into overdrive working the problem. He loved watching the spy movies. *Mission Impossible*. The best that Hollywood had put out. "Let's go to the door." Toshiro helped him down the stairs, and the water was cold as he splashed through it.

The panel next to the door was broken, the keypad cracked in half. He looked at the panel. Something about it sparked a memory. What was it? Yuichi looked around. He shaded his eyes from the... lights!

"The lights are still on," Yuichi declared. The others just stared at him. "If there are lights, there is power." He pointed at the door. "The latch requires power." They didn't understand where he was going. He stepped up to the keypad and pulled it off its mount. He talked as he went. "If the latch requires power, and the power is still on, then if the latch loses power, it will open. Standard safety mechanism." Heads were nodding. He reached in and pulled the wires out of the keypad. People installing any sort of electronics always stuffed the excess back into the wall. You never knew if you might have to splice some later.

"Wait!" one of the others called. His name tag read Sato. "If you touch the wires to the water, won't we get electrocuted?"

Yuichi hadn't thought of that. He nodded and looked around. "Get on the pods." He pointed. "I'll set this up." He pushed the wires back into the hole so they were just a few centimeters above the water. Yuichi chased them to the pods. Sato helped him up the stairs and onto the pod and out of the water. They waited.

"What if it does nothing?" the other asked.

"Just wait for it," Toshiro said with confidence.

It took fifteen minutes for the water to rise high enough to reach the wires. There was a white-blue arc, then the room went dark as the lights went out.

"I hope that was the breaker," Yuichi said.

The silence was only broken with the trickle of water, then a loud chunk and the door latch let loose.

"That's it, let's go!" Yuichi said. The men helped each other off the pods and into the water to the door. Yuichi grabbed the handle and pulled. Nothing happened. He tried again. Nothing.

"It's not opening," he said.

"It's the water. The weight is holding the door closed," Sato said. "Everyone get a hold of the handle or the waist of someone and, on the count of three, pull." They sloshed through the thigh-deep water now as they moved into position. "Ich, Ni, SAN!"

They all pulled. Nothing happened. Then, imperceptibly, the door moved a millimeter.

"Keep pulling! It's moving!" Yuichi yelled. "Gambate!" They all pulled and with a sucking sound, the door pulled open and water began rushing through. In moments, the level was enough for them to pull the door the rest of the way open.

Alarmed shouts from down the corridor preceded boots splashing in the water.

June 19, 2076
Ichi Base

Yuichi was brought into what looked like a command center. They gave him a towel and a bottle of water.

"The commander will be with you shortly," his escort told him and stepped out of the room. Yuichi glanced around the room. It looked like any other high-tech briefing room he had been in. It had flat-panel monitors mounted on the walls and the far wall was an opaque glass. He guessed that the switch on the side made it clear.

An older military man and his aides bustled into the room. He took a seat across from Yuichi and placed a computer tablet and a tall mug on the table before him. He wore a uniform similar to the Japanese Defense Force, but with a mix of both modern components and a traditional styling. He regarded Yuichi with curious eyes. Yuichi sat quietly and waited for him to speak.

After a few minutes, the man grunted and nodded. A slight smile on his face showed Yuichi that his decision to wait quietly was the correct one. "I am Commander Aruga Kosaku. I was appointed by your uncle to lead Iron Blossom." At Yuichi's confused look, Kosaku leaned forward slightly. "How much were you briefed before you went into cryo-stasis?"

Yuichi opened the bottle of water and took a drink. "Not much. My uncle said it was necessary. It was quick. I went to a room. Changed into yukata and they gave me a pill to take and took my blood pressure. They explained we were going someplace safe in case of attack." A thought snapped him into focus. "Keiko? Where is Keiko? She is supposed to be here with me."

The commander turned to his aide. "Find out." He looked back at Yuichi. "I know this is a lot to take in, but there is more you need to know."

"Are the attacks over?" Yuichi blurted.

Kosaku tilted his head. "In a manner of speaking, yes." His expression was enigmatic. He slid the computer tablet across the table to Yuichi. "This message will explain better than I can."

Curiosity overcame his anxiety, and he pushed the power button on the device. His uncle's face appeared in a video. He looked haggard despite wearing a freshly pressed shirt and suit coat.

"Yuichi, I hope you receive this in good health. I know your departure for the bunker at Ichi Base was abrupt. Once we got word of thermonuclear weapons detonating in the United States, Iron Blossom was set in motion. To ensure succession, the imperial line was housed in separate locations." He paused and mumbled to someone off camera. An aide handed a glass of water to Kosaku. He drank, then continued. "While you were asleep, things in America unraveled quickly, pushed by treachery from both China and North Korea. The politicians pushed for an isolationist policy as they prohibited our forces from interfering." His uncle stared down at his hands for a long moment. His head snapped up, and he stared into the camera with burning eyes. "Right until the North Koreans detonated a tactical nuclear weapon in the Tokyo Imperial Palace. I'm sorry, Yuichi, but the imperial family is all dead. Somehow they knew of Iron Blossom and waited until the worst possible moment to decapitate the Chrysanthemum Throne."

Yuchi paused the video and looked up at the commander. "You have seen this?" he asked. Kosaku nodded. "The entire family is dead?"

"Except you, your uncle, and a cousin." Kosaku pointed at the tablet. "There's more you need to see."

Yuichi took a deep breath and let it out. His hand shook as he pressed play.

"It could only have happened by betrayal from within. Masato of the Imperial Guard thinks it was a North Korean spy." He leaned forward. "Be careful, Yuichi. We don't know who did it or how many there may be." His uncle took another drink of water. "There's more, I am afraid. At the same time they killed the emperor, a series of electromagnetic pulse or EMP weapons were set off in every major city of Japan. There was a complete breakdown in communications' infrastructure. NTT is still trying to get cellular working, but the EMP seems to have fried most of the cell towers." He dropped into a soft, almost conspiratorial tone. "Yuichi, they had planned this for a long time. The weapons, the planning, and... rice crop failures." He paused for a moment, responding to someone off camera. "The professors at Todai found a genetically engineered blight that spliced the most dangerous characteristics of the worst of the rice blights we've ever seen. I mention this, Yuichi, because this took time to engineer. And a longer time to grow, then be weaponized and deployed to the rice fields around Japan. They engineered the perfect tsunami of chaos and destruction." The video cut off to a black screen.

Yuichi looked up.

The commander held up a hand. "Keep watching, it continues," he told the distraught young man.

Yuichi reached out a finger and advanced the video. He didn't have to go far before his uncle came back on. This time, he was in a different room and in a different suit, and without a tie. If he was haggard before, now he was beleaguered, with dark bags under his eyes and a haunted expression.

"Yuichi, I am about to head to the other installation for Iron Blossom, Ni Base. Russia has invaded Europe. The Russian forces in Vladivostok have invaded Hokkaido. And the North Koreans have invaded Honshu near Niigata. Our communications are terrible and I have to be moved for safety. We've been constantly moving and somehow they keep finding us." The lights dimmed in the room for a long second, then the emergency lights came on. "We should be woken up at the same time. The sites are linked somehow. You must meet up with me. Listen to your advisors, Yuichi, until we reunite." The screen went black. This time, it was the end of the video.

He sighed. *Uncle will make things right*, Yuichi thought. "Is there another video?"

"There is not."

"Have you heard from Ni Base?"

Kosaku shook his head. "We are still bringing our systems on line and have been unable to reach anyone."

Yuichi's mind was racing. He couldn't believe the world went crazy, and he didn't know what to do.

The commander coughed politely. Yuichi looked up.

"There is one more thing you need to know." The way he said it made the hairs on the back of his neck stand up.

Hesitantly, he asked, "Yes?"

"What year was it when you went into stasis?" Kosaku asked softly.

Yuichi's heart raced with fear. "It is 2023."

"It *was* 2023." Kosaku smiled grimly. "That was fifty-three years ago."

Yuichi gaped at him. "It's..." Yuichi struggled with the math, his mind reeling.

"2076," the commander confirmed.

Yuichi's head swam, and the commander receded down a

long, dark tunnel. Water hit him in the face, shocking him back to his senses.

"Stay with me, Yuichi. We need you here with us." Kosaku stood with an empty glass in his hand.

Yuichi grabbed the towel next to him to wipe his face and stood up. As he paced around the room, Kosaku and his two aides watched him with wary concern.

Yuichi stopped suddenly. "What has happened to Japan in the last fifty years?"

Kosaku shrugged. "We need more intel, so we are going to send a patrol out into the surrounding area."

That sparked another thought in Yuichi. "Where are we?"

"We are in an underground facility near the Fukushima reactor complex." The commander waved to one of the aides. "Bring in the others." At Yuichi's questioning glance, he said, "The advisors your uncle mentioned in the video." He glanced at the door, then leaned forward. "There was an interesting selection of people that were put into cyro. Some politicos from the emperor's court. A couple MPs. A number of cronies from the corporations, some military staff and support personnel, along with a thousand soldiers from the JDF with an emphasis on combat experience." He took another glance at the door. "Your advisors will be in shortly. They are made up of me, the military leader; two members of the American military sent for liaison; the heads of the two corporations that made this bunker and the CHILSS possible—they are full of themselves; a Buddhist priest who happens to be my brother; and four traditional martial arts masters." He shrugged. "Your uncle wanted to make sure we stayed grounded in tradition."

"You and my uncle keep saying 'my advisors.' What does that mean?" Yuichi asked.

"Until we connect with the other base, or if something happened, then you, as the resident member of the Imperial family, are our leader." Kosaku bowed in his seat.

Yuichi just stared at him. "The emperor is a figurehead, and I'm *distantly* related." His mind reeled at the thought of leading anything other than a trip to the movie theater.

The door opened and Kosaku stood up, meeting Yuichi's eyes. "The emperor chose you," he said softly.

Yuichi also rose. "My uncle will solve this when we get to him."

The advisers filed in and stood behind seats around the

table.

Kosaku clapped his hands once. Everyone bowed to Yuichi. Stunned, he returned the bow.

"Please be seated. We have a lot to cover." Kosaku smiled at Yuichi as he took his seat.

June 20
Fukushima Reactor Complex

The team exited the elevator into the black of the room. It was bare, specifically cleared out and hidden in the back of one of the buildings. One of the men stepped up to a heavy steel door and flipped a light switch, then peeked into the room through a peephole that lined up precisely with his NVGs. The switch activated IR lights visible only to someone with NVGs. He whispered, "The room is clear."

They ratcheted open the door, removing the two steel bars across the frame. The door whispered open. The team leader used hand signals to motion for the group to stack up on the door. "Go." The team pushed the door open, weapons ready, and filed into the main area of the abandoned building. Nothing stirred at 4 AM.

Their mission was to scout the area and find locals that could give them an idea of what was happening outside: the political landscape and basically what had been going on over the last fifty years. The team leader motioned for the group to break into two squads and separate. Alpha Team was going to head northwest. Beta Team was going to head directly west, then push south. Since Fukushima was located on the east coast of Japan, both teams had a lot of area to cover.

Over the next two hours, Alpha Team pushed six kilometers to the nearest village, their objective as the sun rose behind them. That helped screen the team as they set up an observation position on the local village.

Captain Nishizaki crouched down next to Sergeant Yoshi 'Kuma' Matsumoto. Because he carried all the commo gear as well as his kit, his teammates called him Kuma—the Bear. While in their OP, Kuma's role was to monitor radio transmissions. He was slowly moving through the spectrum when the team leader crouched down next to him.

"Kuma, are you getting anything?"

"No, sir." He tapped a chart of known frequencies. "Those

are dead air, all across the spectrum. I'm almost through FM. About to scan the AM bands, then I'll shift over to UHF and VHF."

"Sir, there's a truck on the road headed to the village. It's about four klicks out," the soldier nearest the village announced.

Nishizaki pointed at two men. "Get the UAV up." They had two unmanned aerial vehicles with them. One was for reconnaissance, the other was an attack drone. The men started unpacking the UAV. Nishizaki turned to Kuma. "Report it."

June 20
Ichi Base—Tactical Operations Command

"Officer of the watch," the communications tech said suddenly, breaking into the quiet room like a thunderclap.

Boots pounded across the steel decking. "What is it?" Captain Matsumoto asked, leaning in to look at the sergeant's screen.

Katakana and Hiragana scrolled past as the systems transcribed the communications in real time.

"Alpha Team has reported a vehicle moving near their target village. They have launched a UAV. Images should be coming in"—he pointed to a console on his left—"now." The dark monitor lit up with their first view of outside in more than fifty years.

"The UAV is coming around into its orbit." He typed keys and the optics on the UAV oriented in on the vehicle moving down the road.

"Can we identify that vehicle?" the captain asked.

The commo tech flipped a switch, and a speaker came to life next to him. "Base, this is Alpha-four. Identification on the vehicle is Russian BMP-1."

Matsumoto flushed; he had not thought the forward team could hear him. The sergeant sat watching with a straight face.

The captain nodded. Russians this far across Honshu was not a positive sign. He leaned forward and spoke into the mic the sergeant pointed at. "Alpha-four, this is Base. Can you identify unit markings?" He looked at the UAV video. It had a great video quality. "Can you zoom in on the BMP?" he asked the tech.

The video snapped in close. They could see the vehicle had seen better days. A sun fly had been stretched over where the turret had been and if it had been painted, it wasn't in the last decade.

"Can you verify there is only the one vehicle?" Matsumoto asked.

The view on the UAV snapped out as it looked at a wider angle. No other vehicles moved on the road, but they saw movement in the village. "What do you think they are doing?"

"Not sure, sir." The sergeant began zooming in on the villagers.

"Base, Alpha-four. We hear small arms fire from the village. It seems directed at the BMP. How do you advise, over?"

Captain Matsumoto walked to his console and picked up a phone. "Sir, we have a situation. Russian BMP is attacking the village outside." The tech watched the captain. "No, sir, our men are not in danger at the moment." The captain looked at the feed. The BMP had stopped at the edge of the village and it appeared a crew-served weapon was engaging the villagers. "Yes, sir." The captain hung up the phone and moved to the mic. "Alpha-four, Base. You are to engage BMP with Switchblade. Support the village and report back intel. Over."

He could hear the excitement in the solder's voice. "Roger, base. Wilco. Out."

The captain pulled a chair over so they could watch the UAV feed. The Switchblade was a man-portable drone designed to attack armor and vehicles. It was basically a kamikaze drone that expended itself to destroy the target. He was sure the American designers were inspired by Matsumoto's ancestors. The thought made him smile.

They didn't have long to wait. The UAV's high-resolution video showed the streak of the Switchblade as it struck the vehicle. A large flash and billowing fireball marked the death of the vehicle.

The radio crackled. "Base, this is Alpha-four. That is a kill on the target. Alpha-Six is moving down to the village. Will report findings. Over."

"Alpha-four, Base, Good work," he said, then added quietly, "Gambate."

The techs had already pulled the feed and were watching the kill in slow motion on another screen when Matsumoto's phone rang.

June 21, 1345 hours
Ichi Base—Briefing Room

Akito Ishikawa, head of Ramune Corporation, slammed his hand down on the table. "If the Russians are running wild across Honshu, we need to stay safe in our fortress and wait for the others to come to our assistance!" He was red in the face from shouting.

Commander Kosaku watched Ishikawa bluster impassively. Yuichi admired his calm. Ever since they had heard about the Russian raiders that attacked the village on an annual tribute collection, and the news that both the Chinese and North Koreans had established raiding camps on the mainland, the head of Ramune had shouted down any idea of going out to meet the enemy.

"Are you done?" Kosaku asked him when it seemed he had finally wound down. "I'm going to have to remind you that you are a guest here, Mister Ishikawa, and you will treat your fellow guests with respect—"

Ishikawa shot to his feet and opened his mouth to start another tirade when the door to the room slammed open and four very large soldiers entered with batons.

"—or I will have you beaten and thrown out of this facility," Kosaku continued in a calm, clear voice. He locked eyes with Akito Ishikawa, daring him to cross the line.

Ishikawa broke eye contact first, conceding. His gaze shifted to the other corporate head present. "Hiroshi?" he almost pleaded.

Hiroshi Suzuki led the Osaka Keiretsu that had won the military contracts for the CHILSS and associated computer and hardware technology that ran through the complex. "We need to re-establish the dominance of Japan, Akito. It is why we participated in this program. The world was in trouble." Suzuki folded his arms across his chest. "I don't like being ordered about by the military either, but if there are actually Russians, Chinese, and Koreans here, we need them."

Ishikawa sat in his chair stiffly, back ramrod straight. Yuichi had seen the look before. *This guy is going to be trouble,* Yuichi thought.

Yuichi leaned forward. "We need to get to Ni Base and to my uncle. He will make sense of this mess." He pointed to the map on the table. Since the encounter, the base had launched two Kawasaki-made Global Hawk UAVs. They had a larger flight duration than the Puma the Alpha team had deployed for ISR: intelligence, surveillance, reconnaissance.

Kosaku addressed the two American officers. "Major Hight, Major Brannon, have you been able to contact any of the U.S. forces in Japan?"

Major Hight shook his head. "We aren't sure that after all this time, any of the U.S. assets are still active in the area. As the Global Hawks range out further, we can use them to relay to U.S. frequencies, but so far, nothing."

"Thank you." Kosaku turned to a JDF major. "When will the helicopters be ready?"

The man straightened in his chair. "The maintenance crews are working on Kawasaki Chinooks and the Mitsubishi Blackhawks. Helos are temperamental when they are new and continuously maintained. After fifty years, we must replace the seals and gaskets." He spread his hands. "We have some good news. We have two SB-1 Defiants and four pilots who are checked out on them."

Yuichi had never heard of a Defiant. He knew the other helicopters from Call of Duty. "What's a Defiant?"

The JDF major smiled. "It is the next generation of assault helicopters designed to replace the Black Hawks. It has advanced dual rotors and a top speed over 380 kilometers per hour."

"Is that fast?" Yuichi wasn't sure how that compared to the Black Hawk.

The major nodded. "A hundred kilometers per hour faster and with a lower acoustic footprint. Means they won't hear you coming until it's too late."

Heads nodded around the room.

"Then we should use the Defiants to get to Ni Base as quickly as possible," Yuichi declared.

"Hang on," Ishikawa spoke up. "Those are our only working helicopters. We can't risk them—"

Yuichi had had enough of this guy. "What's the matter with you? Your emperor needs us. Japan needs us to get out there and rebuild. To bring back the world we left." Yuichi found he had risen from his seat with the exchange.

"Oss!" A voice cut through the tension in the room. All eyes turned to the simply robed man at the end of the table.

Steve Hara was a Karate Grandmaster. Still in his forties, he exuded a calm power that radiated from him and settled the tempers in the room.

Kosaku nodded appreciatively. "We will task one of the UAVs over the area where the base is. At the same time, we will prepare two teams to head to Ni Base by helicopter and contact our counterparts there and rejoin with the emperor." He looked at Yuichi expectantly.

It took him a minute to digest what had just happened, then he stood up. The others in the room also stood. People immediately filed out of the room, some like Ishikawa to get away, others to be about their tasks. Yuichi watched them leave.

"It's not easy, is it?" Steve Hara said from behind him.

Yuichi turned and leaned against the table. "How did you get into this, Steve?"

The man shrugged. "I had just gotten divorced and had been training JDF for years. When I was approached, it seemed like an interesting opportunity."

"Opportunity?" Yuichi wasn't sure what kinds of opportunities there might be.

"Sure. How often do you get offered a chance to travel into the future with a mandate to preserve the traditions?" He smiled at Yuichi. "Which reminds me, when you get back from Ni Base, we will schedule time for your training."

"Training? Are you going to teach me Karate?"

"I am. And history. And the surrounding traditions. As are the other three martial masters that are here. We were given a directive from the emperor himself." Steve bowed. "It is my duty to serve."

Yuichi returned the bow. "I'm not sure how good I'll be at it, but it's not like I can go to the mall."

June 22, 1800 hours
Ichi Base—Armory

"I'm going," Yuichi said flatly as he buckled on gear that the sergeant manning the armory handed him. Steve Hara worked to adjust the equipment as Yuichi finished buckling it up.

Commander Kosaku was not amused. "We need you here. What happens if—"

Yuichi stopped him. "Nothing. My uncle is the number one priority. Anything else is secondary. Besides, I'll have Steve with me."

"Nope. I don't get into helicopters." Steve smiled at Yuichi's shocked expression, then pointed behind Yuichi. "He likes helicopters."

Yuichi glanced over his shoulder. Susumu Kodai, Grandmaster of Ninjutsu, stood all decked out in gear, mostly identical to Yuichi's. The big difference was the sword he wore strapped to his back.

He held out two knives in sheaths to Yuichi. "Put these on where you can reach them with either hand." He pointed to his own chest, and the knife handles sticking up at various points. Yuichi quickly strapped the blades into place.

"Have you ever fired a weapon?" the armorer asked Yuichi.

"I completed the mandatory defensive tactics course for the Imperial family. Benefits of being a distant relative." Yuichi grinned. "But I'm Shodai League in Onward." It was the leading first-person shooter VR game before the Long Sleep. Yuichi and his classmates were good enough they had gaming sponsors.

"Do not confuse games with reality." Susumu looked every centimeter the no-nonsense stereotype. Yuichi wasn't sure how old the man was. He sucked at judging age. Besides, anyone over twenty-five was ancient.

The armorer handed Yuichi a H&K MP7. It was specially made for the JDF and was chambered in 4.6mm.

Yuichi's eyes lit up. "I've used this in the game." He quickly dropped the magazine, opened the bolt, making sure there was not a round in the chamber. He racked it several times, pointed it in a safe direction, and pulled the trigger. The hammer fell on the empty chamber with a *click*. He adjusted the stock so it fit him, shortened the slack in the sling, brought the weapon up to firing position from slack a couple of times, and looked up into the stunned eyes of everyone in the room. "I told you, I'm really good at Onward."

The armorer handed him a satchel. "It has eight magazines for the weapon in the carrier." He handed Yuichi a small cleaning kit. "Put that in your backpack. Keep it clean and I'll expect it back in the same condition." He looked Yuichi over. "Questions?"

Yuichi shook his head. "Shall we go, Susumu-sama?" The

pair headed off to the hangar. He tried to hide his nervousness. "Ninjutsu?" he asked Susumu. "Do you know all the stuff, like in the movies?"

Susumu surprised Yuichi with a smile. "I was in some of those movies."

Yuichi was stunned. "Really? Which ones?" he asked.

Before he could respond, they were in the hangar. The crew chief guided them to the first of the two black helicopters. She leaned in to give them instructions. "You will sit in the forward seat in the back compartment." She pointed at the headphones. "Put these on. They are noise-canceling and allow you to talk with the crew."

A squad of soldiers came up to join them.

"I am Captain Nishizaki and this is Team Alpha."

Yuichi gave a slight bow. "Captain, I am in your hands. You lead, I will follow." He could tell he surprised the captain. "I'm too scared to be entitled," he said with a smile.

The captain laughed then turned to his squad. "Everyone onboard." Nishizaki took the seat next to Yuichi and put on a headset. Yuichi did the same. They could hear the pilot.

"Base, this is Yari Leader. We are spinning up," the pilot said in a warm contralto.

The crew chief came on the line. "Thank you for flying Amazon air. Due to the flight time, there will not be a beverage service. If you feel you are going to get airsick, there are bags located under your seat."

Everyone chuckled at that. The turbine roared to life.

"Yari Leader, the doors are open. You are clear for flight."

"Flight time is just about one hour," the pilot announced. "We will be going low, so make sure you are buckled."

Yuichi wasn't sure what all they said as he was too excited for his first helicopter ride and military mission to be paying attention, until the captain nudged him in the ribs.

"Yes?" Yuichi was glad the darkness of the cabin hid his embarrassment.

"We are almost there. Command is getting a feed from the UAV on station." Nishizaki tapped his chest-mounted minicomp. He twisted so Yuichi could see the display. There were a bunch of heat signatures in several buildings.

"Locals?" Yuichi asked. "Our team from Ni Base?"

"No response to our calls. We'll land here and hike in. As quiet as these birds are, I don't want to announce our presence if they aren't friendly." Nishizaki patted his shoulder. "They are probably just squatters. We'll know soon enough."

June 23, 0400
Hillside outside Matsushiro

Yuichi was not cut out for hiking through the mountains with gear. He was the generation that relied on seventeen-year-old invincibility and was otherwise Sony PlayStation fit. He could probably kill anyone with his thumb from so much time on the controller. Or his cell phone. *I really miss my phone,* he thought as he crouched down next to Kuma. The team was arrayed on the hill overlooking the buildings the interlopers were in.

Kuma leaned close. "The ISR doesn't show any movement."

The captain came across on the team channel. Yuichi held a hand up to his ear.

"There are five houses. I want two people on each building. Kuma and the cub will provide overwatch. Questions?"

Yuichi was slightly disappointed but knew now was not the time to learn how to clear a room with a real weapon.

Kuma looked at him. "You clear?" At Yuichi's nod, he clicked the radio. "Kuma and cub on overwatch."

Yuichi pulled down his NVGs to watch the team break up into pairs and set up on the doors.

Kuma leaned in again. "If shooting starts, close your left eye when you pull the trigger. It helps your night sight come back quicker. And for Buddha's sake, if you have to shoot, use single shots."

In anything else, Yuichi would have rankled at being treated like a child. This time he was a sponge, trying to take in all the knowledge that might keep him alive.

"In position," Nishizaki said on the comms. Each team in turn clicked the radio twice. Kuma did it for their pair. Yuichi's heart sped up. He was equal parts thrilled and terrified. He felt Kuma tense next to him. The team briefed a slow thirty count before kicking in doors. He heard the first door kick, then Kuma stiffened.

"ISR movement left," Kuma called over the team net. "Overwatch engaging." He ran four steps to the left before dropping down and pointing his weapon.

Yuichi followed, flopping onto the ground and taking a face full of shrub. "What do I do?" He hated how his voice squeaked.

Kuma glanced at him. "Cover our rear." His head snapped back to the front. Two silenced pops came from his rifle. They were using suppressed weapons and subsonic rounds. The bolt cycling sounded thunderous. Two more pops.

Yuichi tore his eyes away from the man firing his weapon and watched the scrub behind them. He moved his head from side to side like they taught him. As he just experienced the hard way, NVGs destroyed depth perception. *Was that movement?* Yuichi focused on a shrub that seemed to move. His heart hammered in his ears as he brought his MP7 up and thumbed off the safety. The shrub moved again. He heard another set of pops and the mechanical cycling of the bolt. He jumped when he heard a *zip-zip* like bees. *Ah! Someone is shooting at us,* his thoughts screamed in his head. He saw a head poke out of the shrub and a weapon shifted toward Yuichi. Instinctively, Yuichi pulled the trigger: *pop, pop.* He remembered to close his left eye on the second shot. Even suppressed, a little muzzle flash escaped. The figure dropped. *I got him!* He elated quietly, then the world started to get tight. *Breathe, you idiot,* he heard in his thoughts, and took a breath.

More angry bees snapped past him and Kuma continued to double-tap. "Get ready to shift left four steps. Have to shoot and scoot." He shifted his rifle. "Go." *Pop-pop.*

Yuchi leveraged himself up and ran, counting. Then he dropped. "Go," he called to Kuma. The big man sprang up, took four large steps and dropped. His weapon never moved off the left side.

"You okay?" he asked Yuichi.

"Yeah, I shot someone," Yuichi admitted.

"Good. Keep watching." He reached up to his receiver and keyed the net. "Four bandits down outside. How's it going inside?"

As if in answer to his question, the center-most building exploded in a hail of bullets that sounded like a buzzsaw hitting into wet lumber. Bright light erupted from the shattered windows as the *crump* from a grenade followed along lazily.

Kuma pointed. "That will get people's attention. Watch your zone." He pointed to the right with a knife-hand and turned to watch his zone.

The captain called in. "Building one clear, three bandits down. How's the guest list?"

Kuma thumbed his mike. "So far, the parking lot is empty."

"Parking lot?" Yuichi asked. Then it clicked for him. They were talking in code. He scanned the scrub. Nothing moved. He strained to hear something, anything, over the roar of silence and the constant hammering of his heart in his ears. His mouth was incredibly dry.

"Building two clear. Four bandits napping. Moving to support team three."

Yuichi turned to see the two guys exit the building. An angry bee whipped by him. Yuichi snapped his head back to his zone and there stood another figure, aiming a rifle at the figures exiting. Yuichi pulled the trigger. This time he could see his bullets strike the man, causing a pain-riddled scream to rip from his throat. Yuichi took aim at the now kneeling man and squeezed the trigger again. *Pop.* The man jerked to the side and fell over. Nausea rippled through Yuichi. Video games were on this; this was too real. He turned and vomited into the dirt.

Kuma crouched by him. "Are you hit?" He started pulling at Yuichi's vest.

"No, just sick." Yuichi waved the man off and wiped his mouth with his sleeve. The bitter taste of bile lingered in his mouth.

The comms snapped alive. "Building four is clear. Three down. Coming out."

"Building five clear. Boss, you might want to see this."

"Roger," Nishizaki said. "Four, push right. Overwatch, left. Three?"

"This is Two. Three is gone."

"Dammit. Two, cover left. I'm at Five."

After a couple of minutes, Nishizaki called again. "Kuma, come to Five and bring the cub."

The tone in the captain's voice made the pair hurry to the building. Inside, it was set up with an office on one side and a pair of bunk beds in a separate room on the other. The middle area was set up like a kitchen lounge area. There was one body on the floor in the kitchen. Team Five's leader pointed to the office.

The captain stood looking at the back wall. On it hung a detailed map of an underground bunker. Yuichi stepped close and saw it was a Japanese-produced blueprint and he had played enough Korean video games to recognize that Hangul notes had been scribbled on it.

"Is that Ni Base?" A fresh wave of fear washed through Yuichi.

"Yes." The captain tapped a spot only 200 meters from their current position. "And that is the entrance." He looked at Kuma. "Call it in. I'll get everyone ready for the next stage. Come with me, little cub." He smiled wanly at Yuichi and they exited the building.

June 23, 0625 hours
Hillside outside Matsushiro

"Yokoi and Nakayama were surprised, sir. One of them must have been awake as they went in. It looks like it was Yokoi who finished them off with a grenade." There was a moment of silence from everyone on the team.

"Did they know we were coming?" one soldier asked.

"Why didn't ISR pick up the ones in the trees? Thermal should have seen them," another asked.

The captain raised a hand, and the team quieted down. "I don't know the answer to either question. They have a map of Ni Base. We need to make entrance and hope they haven't breached the doors yet." That sobered everyone up. "Kuma called in to the TOC." He looked at Kuma. "Anything?"

Kuma shook his head. "No, sir. We are to proceed on our mission."

"Questions?" The captain looked at each of them, finally settling on Yuichi. "You okay, little cub? You look like crap."

Before he could answer, Kuma clapped the young man on the shoulder. "The cub has teeth. He killed two, one just as he was about to fire on Team Four when they exited." Everyone nodded. Yuichi's face flushed from the attention they directed at him.

"Good job." Nishizaki bowed to him. After a moment, they all did. He returned the bow. His face was hot. These were experienced warriors. He was a PlayStation Commando. "Let's move down to the entrance before our friends here get help."

As they walked, the captain hung back with Yuichi. "How

many rounds did you expend?"

Yuichi stared at him blankly for a moment. "Um, four? Five? I don't remember. It happened so fast." Yuichi castigated himself mentally for not knowing.

"Don't worry about it. Change your magazine with a fresh one. Put the used one in the hardest to reach slot. If you get to it, you have other things on your mind." He patted Yuichi on the shoulder and moved back up.

The sun was beginning to rise, and it gave the woods the appearance of being in two worlds at the same time. *Kind of like us*, Yuichi thought.

They slowed down to scout out the entrance to the complex. It was a bunker that the Imperial government started in World War II. What better place to hide a real bunker than in a tourist spot?

They spread out and the first pair of soldiers went into the tunnel. The rest watched the trees and parking area for what used to be the visitor center, now just the empty shell marking the corpse of a better time.

"Captain, you need to come down here."

Nishizaki and his teammate made their way into the tunnel. After several minutes, he came back out and waved to Yuichi and Kuma. "I need you to see this so you can report it accurately."

Yuichi nodded and followed Kuma. In the tunnel, they could see the other three soldiers looking around with flashlights. Fifty meters into the space, it opened up. The soldier shone his flashlight on a large package that had been torn open to reveal a heavyset steel door. They could make out the corporate markings for the Ramune Corporation.

Yuichi tilted his head, trying to make the connection. He snapped his fingers. "Ramune had the contract to build the bunkers."

The captain smiled grimly, then pointed behind Yuichi.

Yuichi turned and gaped at the enormity of the cavern. It was so large his flashlight couldn't reach the far end. He highlighted a figure coming into view. It was Susumu Kodai, the Ninja master.

He stopped in front of Yuichi and bowed. "I apologize, Yuichi-sama. Outside, I could only stop four of the men who came at you." He touched his sword and smiled grimly. "But you handled yourself well." He addressed the captain. "I knew about the entrance to the complex, as I grew up in Nagano. This was a favorite field trip we would take." He waved his arm to encompass the giant cavern. "They did an amazing job expanding this. You used to have to hunch to get through it. But it was never a base. Not like what we have." He smiled grimly. "Ni Base never was."

Yuichi's heart dropped to his shoes. "No," he whispered. "My uncle."

June 25, 1546 hours
Ichi Base—Tactical Operations Center

Major Hight and Captain Matsumoto sat with Communications Specialist Ida, working through frequencies as Major Hight worked to establish contact with any remaining U.S. forces in Japan.

"Okay." Hight pointed at his tablet. "There were twenty-three U.S. installations in Japan. One has to have survived."

Matsumoto poured a cup of tea from a carafe. He raised the vessel to Hight, who shook his head. "Ida?" he asked the tech.

She waved her hand furiously.

"Are you okay?"

She leaned over and flipped a switch, and the speaker came alive.

"JDF Ichi Base, this is U.S. Seventh Calvary. Come in, over."

The captain dropped the carafe in shock and Major Hight shot to his feet. He stepped close and Ida pointed at a microphone next to the speaker.

"Seventh Calvary, this is Ichi Base. We read you."

The voice on the other end changed. "This is General Norm Fleming, whom am I speaking with? You don't sound Japanese."

"This is Major Nicolas Hight, U.S. Marines, assigned as liaison to Ichi Base. It's good to hear your voice, sir."

"What's the status, Major?"

"Ichi Base is up and active. We have pushed into the countryside. Encountered Russian and Korean forces. We found Ni Base. It is empty. Like it never was."

Hight looked up as Commander Kosaku and the others filed into the TOC.

"Copy that. Ichi base up and active. Ni Base is stillborn. What about San base?"

The room was silent. Another base? Long moments of shock and amazement dragged on.

The speaker squelched and General Fleming came back on. "Come in, Ichi Base. What is the status of San base? Is the emperor alive?"

Thanks for reading! Dingbat Publishing strives to bring you quality entertainment that doesn't take itself too seriously. I mean honestly, with a name like that, our books have to be good or we're going to be laughed at. Or maybe both.

If you enjoyed this book, the best thing you can do is buy a million more copies and give them to all your friends... erm, leave a review on the readers' website of your preference. All authors love feedback and we take reviews from readers like you seriously. And if you believe that, then feel free to buy a million more copies and give them to all your once and future friends. Not to mention the past ones who will never speak to you again.

Oh, and c'mon over to our website:

www.DingbatPublishing.ninja

Who knows what other books you'll find there?

Cheers,

Gunnar Grey,
publisher, author, and Chief Dingbat

δ

Printed in Great Britain
by Amazon